Roxanne.

Roxanne.

MELANIE MARTINS

Melanie Martins

VAN DEN BOSCH SERIES

BOOK ONE

Melanie Martins, LLC
melaniemartins.com

First published in the United States by Melanie Martins, LLC in 2021.

ISBN ebook 979-8-9852380-8-2

ISBN Paperback 979-8-9852380-9-9

Printed and bound in Great Britain by Clays Ltd, Elcograf S.p.A

This is a 1st Edition.

DISCLAIMER

This novel is a work of fiction written in American-English and is intended for mature audiences. Names, characters, places, and incidents are either the product of the author's imagination or used fictitiously. Any resemblance to actual persons, living or dead, is entirely coincidental. This novel contains strong and explicit language, graphic sexuality, and other sensitive content that may be disturbing for some readers.

To all of you, my dear readers.
Thank you.

"The universe has a way of bringing fated lovers together."
— Andries Van Den Bosch

READING ORDER

While you don't need to have read the *Blossom in Winter* series to start this book, we recommend the following order to get the very best reading experience:

Blossom in Winter series (Petra & Alex's story)

1. Blossom in Winter
2. Lured into Love
3. Lured into Lies
4. Defying Eternity
5. Happily Ever After: Part I, Part II, III, IV

Van Den Bosch series

1. Roxanne. (You are here)
2. Andries.
3. Elise.
4. Dan.

PROLOGUE

Amsterdam, January 31, 2022
Andries

I still remember the day she first said her name. Her voice was nothing like I'd ever heard before—velvet, fine-grained, and smooth. There was something magnetic about it. It was terribly inviting and deeply alluring.

Through the window of my bedroom, I can still see the street she used to walk every single day on her way to work. She'd told me she was a librarian, and that she was currently working in an ancient bookshop in a dusty corner of the city. She'd stay there until late to read rare editions of books that can no longer be found anywhere else in the country. I love reading just as much, especially poetry or those classics that romanticize love. Those that feed your heart and soul. A pity my family doesn't share the same opinion. *"Really? That's what you want to be? A poet? In a family of judges, industrialists, and politicians, you want to be the poet?"* The disappointment in my dad's voice when I told him I didn't want to attend business school and that I wanted to become…well, yeah, a *poet* is not something that is easily forgettable.

The repugnance he has for the word *poet* is enough for me to never talk about my passion and dreams ever again under that roof. No one in my family likes poetry. In fact, any book that doesn't teach you about finance, business, or law is not a book that is allowed to be paraded around the Van den Bosch estate.

She, on the other hand, shared the same passion as I. She liked poetry of many forms, from simple to complex, from Rimbaud to Verlaine. We could spend hours talking about our favorite poets and the exciting lives they led. Then, she would lay her head on my chest, and listen to me while I'd read her some of the poems I'd written.

My poems… As if what I write can be worthy of being called *poems*. But she liked them. At least that's what she'd told me on a handful of occasions. But there were so many other things she also told me that just weren't true….

My eyes drift downward to the carmine-colored leather notebook she gifted me for my most recent birthday, my initials carved on its cover. *Write in it,* she had said. *Aren't you a writer? A poet?*

No woman I had ever met before cared about me in this way. They usually cared about the nobility or the status my family name carries, the money and lifestyle that could follow for being in my circle, but never about me—Andries, the introvert, the wannabe poet, the incurable romantic.

Not one, until I met her.

Now I'm nothing but a foolish boy who fell for a woman he should've never met in the first place.

There's a tear streaming down my cheek, but I can't help it. I shake my head remembering what my sister told me: *Heartbroken poets write their best work.*

But despite my heart being shattered into a thousand pieces, I'm not in the mood to write poetry. No, if I have to write, I will write about her in her entirety—as the woman who stole my heart and played with it, the woman who fooled me, the woman I hate and love the most at the same time: Roxanne.

FIVE MONTHS EARLIER...

CHAPTER 1

Amsterdam, August 19, 2021
Roxanne

"If she has to go abroad, then yes, you need to charge the client a travel fee," I explain kindly to Laura, my new booking manager. "Stephanie will need to spend time traveling so this needs to be invoiced."

"Perfect, I'll do that now," she answers from the other side of the line and I can already hear the sound of her keyboard as she starts typing. "Talk later."

"Alright. Bye." After hanging up, I throw the phone in the cup holder of my car and glance at my watch, keeping an eye on the road as I turn right.

Crap. I'm late again. I park quickly in front of the building entrance, my heart already thundering anxiously fast as I turn off the engine.

Well, here we are.

Heaving a long sigh, I take the gifts for my sister and Mama that lie on the empty seat beside me, and, a bit apprehensively, force myself to exit the car.

I hate birthdays. Especially Mama's, but my thoughts are immediately swept away by a strong gust of wind as I stand outside. Goodness, how come it's so windy in August? It's never been like this before.

Alright, let's get this over with....

I lock the car, and, for the sake of precaution, double-check if there's anything left inside that could draw attention. Despite growing up here, in Bijlmer, I don't trust this neighborhood—it's on the outskirts of Amsterdam, and it reminds me too much of my childhood, which is something I'd rather not recall.

Each time I leave the Porsche here, I feel tempted to call the cops so they can keep an attentive eye on it while I'm upstairs. I don't trust the curious strangers approaching me while I walk toward the building entrance, a shopping gift bag in each hand. I give them a small smile for the sake of politeness, but my heart is growing tighter at every click of my heels.

As I pass through the two young men, I hear one of them whistling at me and the other chuckling. Instinctively, I speed up my pace in direction to the double doors without looking back. It's only 5 p.m., but this area is terrifying even in broad daylight.

Why can't Lili move out from here? I ask myself once more as I get inside and read, *Lift out of order.* This sign has been on and off since I was six—since I moved here with my parents. Lili was still in Mama's womb when we landed in the Netherlands for the first time. I can still remember walking down the streets of Amsterdam in awe of how empty it was. Mind you, when you come from Shenzhen, a city with twenty-five million inhabitants—filled with people constantly screaming or chattering—Amsterdam looks like a Chinese village in the mountains of Zhengou.

As I start taking the stairs, I curse under my breath at my lack of endurance. I really should quit smoking once and for all. It's a ritual I tell myself each time I come here, especially as I reach the second floor and need to stop to get my breath back. Standing still, I support myself against the concrete wall and breathe slowly in and out.

Alright, two more floors to go.

Damn it. How can Lili go up and down these every day without problems? And worse, how can she carry her groceries up to the fourth floor without a lift? I rub my face as I finally work up the courage to continue forward. Crossing the third floor's barrier, my shoes start to set my feet on fire. I should've switched my stilettos to a pair of comfortable flats before coming here, but alas, I was already so late.

Reaching the fourth floor, I'm startled by my iPhone's ringing. Recognizing the ringtone, I immediately know it's Karl calling. I wonder if he's calling to cancel our dinner date for 8 p.m. Truthfully, that would be great, I'm already so tired today. I pick the phone and answer him.

"Hi, sweetheart, how are you doing?" His tone is as fake as his relationship with his wife. Or should I say ex-wife? Though I haven't really been following the news about his divorce.

"Hey, so great to hear from you," I tell him, my voice just as sweet and bubbly. "It's Mama's birthday today, so I'm paying her and Lili a visit."

"Are you serious? That area is so dangerous. Please tell me a driver dropped you off there."

A quick chuckle escapes me at his tone. "Um…"

"Your Porsche is done. R.I.P." While Karl sounds truly worried for my car, I can't help but laugh instead.

"I'm only staying here for two hours then I'll head downtown for our dinner. It's at eight, right?"

A gush of air rolls off his lips. "The guys postponed the dinner for tomorrow. They are too jet lagged to go out tonight."

"Oh, no," I feign sadness. "I was looking forward to seeing you again."

"Me too, Roxie. Do you think you can make it tomorrow?"

I don't answer. Silence will make him more vulnerable.

"Like… I know it'll count still if I cancel your service a few hours before the appointment, but I'm okay with paying the five hundred euros fee. I really need you to come tomorrow."

"I have other plans for tomorrow," I say quietly, the shopping bags starting to feel their weight on my hands.

"I know, sweetheart. I'm sure you do. But this is really important for me. I swear, if you can charm them, do you know how big of a deal it would be?"

My lips curve slightly up and I simply mumble a brief, "I know." I consider putting my bags on the floor to alleviate my wrists for a moment, but I fear that someone might snatch them up as they pass by.

"I already called the restaurant and changed the booking for tomorrow. Please Roxie, make it happen. We have been together for fifteen years now. I'm your oldest client."

"And my favorite," I coo. Which is true since Karl is the one who pays me the most. "If I charm them and they sign the contract with your company, I hope you'll keep your promise."

"I will, babe. I've always kept my promises with you, haven't I?"

I pause, considering his words. "I think so."

Abruptly, I hear a squeak and the door in front of me opening. A petite woman emerges out of the darkness in sweatpants and stands still in the doorway.

"Alright, I have to go. Count me in for tomorrow, then. I'll ask Poppy to send you the invoice for the cancelation fee."

"You're the best, sweetheart. Thank you."

"Bye." And I hang-up, my eyes already meeting my sister's intriguing face as she wonders who I was talking to. "How are you?" I ask, putting on a friendly tone, despite her annoyed expression.

I hear nothing but an exasperated breath before she returns back inside. Unfortunately, I can't say it's the first time she's behaved like this. Her annoyance has become regular when I come home. It's almost as if my presence has become a source of distress for her.

Despite her attitude, I follow her into the old, family apartment and close the door behind me.

Standing in the entry way, I watch Lili, as she's already found her place back in the modest dining room, clearing away the remaining dirty plates from the table.

"Are you okay?" My question hangs in the air and Lili pays no mind to it.

Each time I come here, Lili is always either stressed, annoyed, grumpy, or moody. She's younger than me and yet she has the energy of a woman who's tired of life.

"Do you know what time is it?" she asks, finally facing me, two plates in each hand.

I cut eye contact with her for a moment, reminding myself I didn't manage to arrive in time for lunch. "Eh, I'm sorry—"

"Never mind," she grits between her teeth, before storming into the kitchen.

I pace slowly through the barely lit hallway, my eyes traveling across the many frames hanging on the wall with pictures of Lili and I, and others with Mama. The familiar portraits makes me smile but there's one in particular that perks my attention and I stop in front of it. It's the one taken at my graduation at the University of Amsterdam with my English degree in hand. Damn, my hair was long and black then. I can't help shaking my head at the terrible haircut I had. What a big difference with my current short, wavy blonde hair—Marilyn Monroe style, just the way I like it.

Reaching the kitchen, I stand by the doorway and observe Lili scrubbing lightly at the plates before throwing them into the dishwasher. She is wearing a comfortable pair of gray sweatpants and a cheap t-shirt. Her black hair is pushed back into a messy bun, and I can still see the traces of makeup on her jawline that she must have worn during the day for Mama's birthday.

"Do you need help?" It's the only thing that comes to mind to say.

She stops her task, her head turning in my direction and her eyes zoom at my hands, still holding the gifts. A snort escapes her and her attention returns to the plates.

"Fine," I breathe, knowing exactly why she's behaving this way with me. "I'm sorry for the delay, but—"

"But what?" Her loud tone and deep frown nearly startles me. Lili is now facing me again and I notice the dark circles under her eyes. "There's no excuse to have missed her birthday. You know she only agrees to see you when it's a family event and yet you missed it." Her rebuke makes me swallow the lump in my throat just as fast. Her eyes dart down to my hands for a second, before she exhales loudly in return and adds, "Mama doesn't want anything from you."

"I know that," I say, keeping my voice low. Then I take a few steps in her direction and proceed. "Lili, I'm so sorry for my delay, but one of the girls couldn't make it at the very last minute, so I had to go on her behalf and—"

"Argh…" She rolls her eyes, shaking her head in disgust. "When are you gonna stop with this lifestyle?" Her eyes narrow on me, and she frowns instantly. "Don't you have enough money yet?"

"It's my business and it's giving me a nice, steady income," I riposte back. "So no, I don't intend to stop anytime soon."

"Are you still having sex with them though?" Her question is so intrusive that my whole body tense.

"That's private," I refute defensively.

But Lili doesn't seem to mind. "You promised me at thirty you would stop it, that was five years ago!"

"And I have," I lie; I have just stopped accepting new clients.

She raises an eyebrow, unconvinced. "Really?"

"Yes, now I'm just overseeing the other girls and the management of the agency, that's it." Well, not really, there are three clients I'm still seeing on a regular basis since they are my personal favorites—Karl is one of them.

I raise my hands, showing her the gifts. "Tell Mama that it's you who bought them."

She creases her brows, looking at them. "What is it?"

"Open it," I instruct, reveling in her curiosity.

Lili reaches for a dishcloth to dry her hands and then takes the gifts, heading to the dining room again. There, she puts the bags on the wooden table, opens the first one, and pulls the beige box with a bow out, observing it attentively as it lies between her hands.

"This one is for Mama," I say as Lili opens the box, her eyes alighting on a brand new Burberry cashmere trench coat. "And the other one is for you."

Without saying a word, Lili takes the other box and opens it. Her eyes glitter and I can even feel her joy as her fingers start slowly running through the fabric of her brand new coat. In a quick move, she takes it out completely and checks the length and size.

"You know when you said Mama would need a new coat for fall?" I ask while she's already standing tall in front of the wall mirror, pressing the frock against her body in a half-attempt to try it on. "I thought you might need one too."

"This is…" I can see the sparks in my sister's eyes as she observes herself in the mirror holding her new coat, totally smitten. "Well, it must have cost a fortune, no?"

"Don't worry about that." Poor Lili, even when it's a gift she's still worried about the price tag. We never had expensive things growing up. European brands were simply unattainable to us. We'd buy Vogue magazines, knowing perfectly well all we could afford was to dream about those beautiful outfits.

When Dad left us, Mama had to work twice as hard to sustain both of us. Living in Amsterdam with two young kids and only one income—all while barely being able to speak Dutch—is no easy task. And despite the fact that I'm now making enough to take Lili and Mama out of this apartment and move them to a better place for good, Mama has rejected my financial help since the day my sister decided to tell her where the money was coming from.

"Why don't you try it on?" I ask her, since she's still just holding it in front of her.

"Oh, I, eh… I don't know."

Seeing how undecided she is, I walk toward her, take the coat from her hands, and open it wide for her to slide her arms inside. "Go ahead, girl."

Lili does so a bit apprehensively, cleaning her hands on her sweatpants before sliding them through each sleeves.

She checks herself up and down, her fingers creasing the lapel of the coat, her lips in a straight line.

"Do you like it?" I ask, looking at her reflection in the mirror.

"Yeah, but knowing how you got the money to buy this, just—"

"You look great in it," I answer immediately. "That's all that matters."

Lili heaves a long sigh, her gaze dropping to the floor for a moment. "Mama will never accept such a gift."

Her tone is filled with sadness, and I know all too well that Mom will never accept it if she thinks it's coming from me. "Just tell her it's from you."

Lili shakes her head. "She might be old, but she's not stupid. She knows I can't afford this brand."

"Well, then tell her you were given a raise."

"You and your lies…" She takes a deep breath in, her face deeply serious. "Aren't you tired of always lying to everyone around you?"

"Oh Lili, please," I press. "It's a freaking innocent lie."

"Fine," she hisses. "But that's the last time."

I exhale loudly at her attitude. For a sister, she's far from helpful, let alone supportive. A few beats of silence ensue, until I finally ask, "Is she in her bedroom?"

Lili turns around immediately, facing me eye on eye. "You know she doesn't want to see you." She lowered her voice and I do the same.

"I know but it's her birthday…" I let my words trail off, hoping she'll reconsider my request. "Please, try."

Lili takes her time to answer, but she finally gives a quick nod in agreement. She removes her coat, puts it back on the box, and then starts walking toward Mama's bedroom. I follow closely behind, my stomach already in knots.

We leave the dining room, cross the dark hallway, until we stop in front of a closed door. There, Lili gives a few soft knocks on the wooden surface, her expression even more serious than before. Since we don't hear anything from the other side, she twists the handle and pushes the door wide enough to get a good view.

As I take in the walnut furniture of the bedroom, my eyes land on Mama who is sitting in a rocking chair in front of the window. Her short black hair pushed behind her ears, she seems to be engrossed in a book, but before I can step inside, Lili holds me by the arm, halting me. "Wait here," she says, just above a whisper.

I watch Lili slowly pacing in her direction, and then leaning down to talk to her. Mama's face turns slightly in my direction, but she doesn't look at me. She stoically listens to Lili as she speaks, never displaying any feeling or emotion.

She answers something in my sister's ear and Lili just nods at Mama, before returning to me.

"She doesn't want to see you." Lili's voice is barely audible but enough for me to storm pass her and go to talk to my mom once and for all.

"Roxie!" Lili tries to hold me but I push her away, and make my way inside the bedroom.

"Mama," I say as I stand in front of her, my voice steady but not high. "When are you gonna move past your grudge and talk to me? I'm your daughter!"

But my mother just ignores me, like I'm not even there. Her eyes remain fixed on her book and she pays no attention to anything else.

"C'mon, Roxie, let's go," Lili presses on as she holds me by the arm, trying to drag me back outside.

"It's been over twelve years already," I tell Mom, despite her total indifference. "Am I still dead to you?" The anger in my tone is nearly suffocating.

"Enough," Lili snaps as she keeps pushing my arm to remove me from our mother's side.

Despite my questions and louder voice, Mama seems totally unaffected. She serenely turns the page of her book, adjusts her glasses, and continues reading. When Lili told her how I was making my money twelve years ago, Mama said I was dead to her, but I never thought she'd meant it. I thought after a few days it'd pass and she'd just move on. Boy, I couldn't have been more wrong. Twelve years later, and Mama still hasn't said a single word to me. I had to return the keys to the apartment, take everything I owned from it, and I could never come back here without Lili being around. I'm still allowed to attend family gatherings like her birthday party but even when we are at the dining table together, surrounded by other family members, Mama paid no attention to me. It's like I don't even exist.

While I'm being dragged out of her bedroom, my eyes remain pinned on my mom, and her total indifference for her oldest child.

How can she be so unforgiving?

It's a question I might never have an answer to.

CHAPTER 2

V.D.B estate, August 19, 2021
Andries

"I don't care if you like it or not, this is something worth celebrating!" Dad looks at me with a smile I've rarely seen before, then at the acceptance letter coming from the Business School at the University of Amsterdam. It's the smile he usually gives to Joris or to the know-it-all Elise, or any other of my brothers and sisters, but not to me. I sigh in defeat, knowing that soon I'll either have to face letting him down again or suffer through business school. "Elise, Joris, Hanna!" he shouts across the hallway, forgetting he could simply ring in a group call over the intercom. "Come over here!"

I can't help but exhale loudly in annoyance with his yelling. And just a few moments later, I hear a hoard of elephants running down the stairs. Except it's only Elise and Hanna followed by the young Joris and the five-year-old Aleida.

"What is it?" Elise asks, perching over my dad's shoulder to read the letter.

"It's nothing, really, just an acceptance letter for a program." A program my dad wants me to attend, which I couldn't care less about. I also applied to one of my own liking—for English. But alas, I haven't heard from them yet. Which is strange, since it was actually from the same university.

All of a sudden, Dad wraps an arm around me, squeezing me tight. "Don't be so humble. You worked hard and now you deserve to party hard too." Except I don't like to party. I never have. I'd much rather stay in my bedroom and write or read than socialize with a bunch of acquaintances, but apparently he doesn't know that. "We're gonna throw a party like you've never seen before."

Oh, that I don't doubt. Pops is great at bragging to his entourage about how talented we all are and throwing the most glamorous and sumptuous receptions here in the family estate. It's safe to say this place has hosted more parties than any nightclub in Amsterdam. Don't believe me? This estate was built in the eighteen century... so imagine how many parties the Van den Bosch family has hosted here in the 200 years since. "We'll invite everyone before you leave to Amsterdam."

"Everyone?" I repeat, my brows frowning in confusion.

"Yes! Everyone. Your uncles and aunts, your cousins, your grandmothers... But don't worry, we'll just invite them over for dinner and then we'll do something separate for you and your friends," he adds, giving me a cringeworthy wink.

I can't help but shake my head in disapproval. What does he have in mind? Bringing some hookers by once the clock hits midnight? I don't know, but knowing I'd have to be paraded around and shake hands with everyone that walks through the front door is not something I look forward to.

"Any news about my application?" Elise asks our dad, looking slightly worried. "I applied so long ago."

"Not yet, darling, but I'm sure you're going to be approved too."

"Or maybe not," I answer with a smirk.

"If a dumbass like you got accepted, then there's no reason for me not to."

"Elise!" Dad snaps. "What kind of foul language is that?"

"I'm still the oldest," I tell her for the sake of teasing. "The fact I got the letter of acceptance first is just more evidence you can add to your pitiful diary."

"You know very well they lied about our birth dates," she insists further. "I'm the oldest. It's obvious. And one day I'll prove it to you."

I shake my head at her comment. We only have a year of difference, and despite proving her wrong, she's still persuaded she's older than me, and that Mom and Dad are just lying to her about her birth date.

"I swear, Elise dear… if you were the first-born I'd tell you," Dad's tone with Elise is so pathetic. He talks to her like he's a teddy bear. Let's be clear here, my dad's favorite child is Elise no matter where she stands in age. Plain and simple. Anyone who spends one single day around the house would see it clear as daylight. What Elise wants, Elise gets. The only thing she hasn't gotten—yet—is proof that there was a change to her birth certificate, which she claims the doctors themselves signed when she came out of our mother's womb. Seriously. Even with there being pictures that show the date she was born! I wouldn't be surprised if one day in the near future, Dad pays someone to change her birth certificate and make her one year older—just so she can be the oldest child. Truthfully, it'd be a match made in heaven. He could parade her around and introduce her as the first-born and the one who takes over the future business. After all, she is just like him: enjoys hunting, shaking hands with peeps I couldn't care less about, and is the best host ever—charismatic, smiley, confident, the perfect Van den Bosch.

"Somehow I don't believe you," she retorts back with her usual temper, crossing her arms over her chest. I'd have been sent back to my room for talking with such an attitude. Or sent to the kitchen to be the cook for the day, or to be the butler, who knows. But Elise? Of course not. *She's just expressing herself,* Dad would say each time I'd point out how different he treats us. If Elise would bring back a B+ it would be wonderful. Me? A terrible grade that would lead to a good scolding and punishment.

"What do you want me to do, dear Elise? I didn't decide it." I roll my eyes at Dad's answer. "Look, if you don't receive an answer until next week, I'll personally handle the situation."

I huff at the stupidity of the whole thing. Glancing quickly at my watch, I realize Mom should be back home in thirty minutes. Great. If there is one good thing about this family, it's Mom. She's everything I aspire to be. For a start, she only meets people upon appointment. Even us, her kids. When I was younger, I couldn't understand why my friends could see their moms at any time but not me. But now I understand that Mom simply values her time and solitude more than anything else in the world. She's never been into people, which might explain why she never dated anyone but Dad. She's also a loner like me. What a pity Dad can't understand it.

"Claudia," I call, seeing the maid crossing the hallway. "I'm going back to my room. When Mom is here, can you please let me know?"

"Do you have an appointment?" There goes her usual question.

"At six-thirty in her office."

Claudia smiles, giving me a quick nod. "Sure."

With that ticked off my mind, I leave the hallway and everyone behind, and run back upstairs to my room. There, I lock myself inside and heave a long sigh in frustration.

Fuck, fuck, and fuck!

How come I didn't get any news about my application for the English program? I submitted it long time ago… I grab my phone from the back pocket of my jeans and call the Admissions office at the University of Amsterdam.

As soon as they pick the call, I say, "Hi, um, I was wondering if you have any updates about my application for the English program?"

"And your name is?" a woman asks, a drop of annoyance in her tone.

I slap my palm against my forehead at my own stupidity. "Oh, sorry, eh, Andries."

"Andries what?" she hisses.

I hate having to disclose my family name and I realize a take a few extra seconds to mutter, "Van den Bosch."

"One moment, please," the woman answers. I wait patiently on the line, roaming around my bedroom. Since she's taking her time, I slide the glass door open and step outside to the balcony. Despite having lived here all my life, the view of the gardens, the lawns, trees, and lake continue to be just as impressive. I take a deep breath in, inhaling the fresh breeze of the late afternoon.

"Are you there?" the woman asks.

"Yes, I am."

"Sorry, sir, but your application was rejected."

What! My heart takes a reel at her dry answer. "Rejected?" I repeat louder, unable to believe it.

"Yes," she says robotically.

"But why?"

"Let me see…" While she checks, I remain standing still in front of the balustrade, and look downstairs at the gardens and more precisely at the adjacent terrace. My dad is already there, explaining something to the house staff—most likely about the party he's gonna host. "I see you applied to two programs and got accepted in the other one. This means that the English department thought your application was a mistake."

"No, the other one was," I answer right back, trying my best to keep my temper in check. "Is there a way I can get this one approved and switch programs?"

"Let me check," she repeats, her tone tired. I heave a sigh, impatiently waiting again. "Unfortunately we are totally full for this year."

My body freezes at her words, and for a few seconds I forget to even breathe. I'm not going through with business school. Full stop. That was my dad's idea. Not mine! "I'm sure you can squeeze in just one more student."

"We are already at maximum capacity for this year. Maybe the next one?" she asks like it's no big deal.

"Fuck," I curse under my breath. I'm pretty sure Dad's behind that, but I haven't said my last word. "Can I talk to the person responsible for the approvals, please?"

"Mr. Lewis is not available at the moment."

I huff at her answer—how does she know that? She didn't even bother to check.

"I can schedule an appointment with him if you want."

Oh, now that's a good idea. "Yes please, that would be great."

I can hear her typing on her keyboard as she pulls his schedule. "Would next Thursday, half past one work?"

"Yes, that's fine." I run a hand through my hair, hoping I won't meet with that dude for nothing. "Thanks."

"My pleasure. Is there anything else I can assist you with?" she asks in a weirdly bubbly tone. A big contrast from her earlier one.

"No, that's all. Thank you," I answer.

"Have a great weekend, then."

"You too." As I hang up and put my phone back onto my jeans, I hear a few knocks on my door. I glance at my watch, and notice it's already six-forty. It must be Claudia. I walk back inside and head directly to open the door for her.

"Yes?" I say when I see her.

"Your mom is waiting for you. Should I escort you downstairs?"

"Oh, yeah. Thanks."

I leave my bedroom with a frown, carefully locking the door behind me—a must when Elise is around—and follow Claudia as we cross the hallway, and go down the marble stairs.

Reaching the first floor, we take the right aisle and after a few more steps we finally reach a new closed door. I give her a nod in appreciation and she returns it, before walking away.

I clear my throat, then knock on the door three times out of politeness. Since I fail to hear anything, I open the door wide, my eyes alighting on Mom sitting at her desk. "May I?"

"You are ten minutes late," she points out, her gaze focused on what she's writing.

I guess that's a way to say hello.

Mom hates tardiness so it doesn't surprise me that she doesn't even glance at me. I close the door behind me, and make my way toward her.

"Um, sorry. I was helping Elise with something." That's the only valid excuse I can think of since Elise is always a forgivable reason. "An urgent case?" I ask, aiming to change the subject.

"Mh-mm… I'm just reviewing my conclusions to an appeal," she replies, her eyes never leaving her stack of papers. "How have you been?"

I pace toward the big window at the end of her office, immediately attracted to the natural light and the view it offers to the gardens. There, I stand still, pondering her question. "Well, I got admitted to business school," I tell her pensively as I observe the green lawn and the perfect trees stretching all the way to the lake.

"Oh, that's such a great news," I hear her saying from behind me. I turn around and find Mom standing up and walking in my direction. "Congratulations," she says politely, without sharing the same overbearing level of enthusiasm as Dad.

"Thanks, but—"

"It's not what you wanted, I know," she interposes before I can even finish. That would explain her lack of enthusiasm. At least she isn't faking it.

"I really don't want to go though," I tell her, containing the anger I have against my dad for what he did. "I applied for an English degree."

Mom just exhales loudly in return, her gaze drifting away for a second. "Andries, we already spoke about this."

"I know but—"

"Look, it's just for three years," Mom says, cutting me off again. "Don't you recall our agreement? You take a year off, travel the world, and then come back and go to college?"

"And *I am* going to college," I point out. "But I thought it was gonna be for the degree I wanted."

"Give business school a try," she insists, her hands now on my shoulders as she tries to find my gaze. "I'm sure you'll like it."

I resist the urge to shake my head. The last thing I want to do is to disappoint her after having spent an entire year away from home, barely speaking to anyone. I had wanted to leave since I was fifteen and needless to say I wasn't as easy going as Elise was. "Alright," I reply, knowing it's pointless trying to dissuade her. I have to speak to Mr. Lewis first anyways. "Is there a way you can ask Dad to drop the party though?"

"Oh Andries, your dad is on cloud nine. You aren't gonna take away his favorite hobby, are you?"

"You mean parading us around as his trophies or whatever?" *Yeah, what a bad idea that would be.*

"Look," Mom removes her hands from my shoulders, before her brown eyes drift to the garden for a moment. I do the same, and watch the gardeners passing by as they take care of the lawns. "Very soon, you'll be on your own in Amsterdam, and you won't have to deal with your father and his social gatherings anymore."

A gush of air instantly rolls off my lips, disappointed by the fact Mom isn't on my side this time. "There's no way around this, huh?"

"I'm afraid not," she says, her tone deeper than before. I should've known the last thing Mom would do is tell Dad to cancel an event he's eagerly preparing and looking forward to host. "You know I'm not a big fan of such events either."

Yeah, right... She says that, yet she never does anything to stop Dad from organizing them. Now that I think about it though... Mom might be a loner, but she knows deep down that those parties make Dad happy so I guess she just accepts it out of love for him.

Oh well, no matter what, in about two weeks' time, I'm going to be out of here.

***

I must say, I love silence, truly. In a house filled with five other children—including a two-year-old—and prompt to constant chaos, having noise cancelling headphones is a *must* when I'm in my bedroom trying to write or read. One might think the estate is big enough not to hear the screams of a five-year-old, but it feels like Aleida is on a mission to break the Guinness World Record of the loudest screamer. I'm already missing my year of backpacking and the spiritual retreat in Columbia and Tibet. When I finished high school, I packed my bags and was ready to bid goodbye to the Van den Bosch estate once and for all.

Or so I thought.

Except my dad, as always, had other plans, which included business school, followed by an internship at the headquarters of his company. See, the multi-generational firm is involved in agriculture, food processing, international shipping, and finance. Nothing that's of interest to me. I thought I was clear on that when I left with a one-way flight to Medellín, but alas, Dad made sure to guilt-trip me and persuaded me to believe I was the most ungrateful son a father could have, forcing me to make a pact with him: one year away and then I'd come back to get my business degree.

College.

My goodness... The only enjoyable program I could think of was English. But of course Dad couldn't let me pick the one I wanted.

A sudden vibration on my pocket pull me out from my thoughts, and as I take my iPhone out, my screen flashes with the name "Do not answer!" on it. This should be self-explanatory, and yet...

"What do you want?" I snap at my sister as I answer the call.

"Uh-oh," she answers, a trace of sarcasm on her tone. "You spoke to Mommy already?"

I huff instantly at her comment. I knew I shouldn't have answered, hence the name "Do not answer!" I always regret it. "What do you want, Elise?" I ask again.

"Are you upstairs?"

I ponder for a second whether to tell her yes or to just fuck off. "Yeah, why?"

"Can I come in?" Her tone has become more humble which catches me off guard.

At first, I feel like declining, but since I came back from my trip a month ago, Elise and I had barely spoken. I know she applied to the same school as I, and the fact she hasn't gotten an answer yet might be a hard truth for her to digest. Despite not having the best relationship with her, I decide to accept and invite her in.

A few seconds later and Elise is already knocking on my door like she's ready to break it. Was she just standing outside the door waiting, or what?

"Come in," I shout as I'm just too lazy to stand up and go open her the door. Plus, I'm currently re-reading what I just wrote on my notebook.

"What are you doing on the floor?"

My eyes go up to meet my sister's inquiring face before they return to my notebook. I didn't even notice she had already come inside. "I like to sit on the floor when I write," I tell her simply.

I'm expecting her to snap something stupid, but to my surprise, Elise takes a few steps in my direction and sits right beside me on the marble floor. There, she doesn't say a word, but we exchange a quick smile before I start making some edits to the text I wrote.

Suddenly though, I feel like she's peering over my notebook. "What are you writing?"

"Nothing worth reading," I answer, pulling it closer to me.

"C'mon, let me see," she insists, peering even more.

"No!" I move a bit away from her but she brings herself closer.

"Don't be so shy!" Her hand is about to grab my notebook when I manage to slap it away.

"Stop it," I riposte, before I shut the book closed, putting it down beside me on the floor. "Maybe one day." Noticing her annoyance, I decide to change the subject. "So, what brings you here?"

Upon hearing my question, Elise pinches the bridge of her nose between her fingers for a moment. Whatever she's thinking, it doesn't seem very pleasant. "I called the uni to check on my admission and for some strange reason it's still pending. Something isn't right." She heaves a long sigh, letting those words sink into her. "I thought Dad would at least wait for mine to get approved so we could have a celebration for both of us, but nope, he's already preparing a party for you next Friday."

What? Next Friday? My jaw drops at her comment, but I make a conscious effort to let her finish. "Why does he care so damn much about you, huh? You left for one freaking year and didn't even tell him goodbye."

"I've got no idea," I tell her sincerely. Unlike me, I know Elise is really looking forward to attending business school. Seeing how tormented she is, I put on a more friendly tone and say, "Look, there's no reason for your admission not to be accepted." Her lips slowly turn up into a smile and her face starts finally softening. "If I got in, you have to get in too." I pause for a beat as I think something through. "And since you haven't gotten accepted yet, maybe you won't have to be present at that party."

"Yeah, sure," she says with sarcasm. "As if Dad would let me skip your *lovely* celebration."

"Well, he isn't gonna let me skip it either."

She huffs instantly in return. "Kinda makes sense since it's yours, dumbass," she spits out, softly pinching my arm. Afterwards, her gaze starts drifting away and for a moment she seems to be lost in her own thoughts. "Sometimes I think I should've taken a year off like you did."

My eyes widen in surprise at her revelation. "C'mon," I utter, my tone playful. "You were the best in your class. I wasn't."

Despite my answer, she seems to have paid no attention to it. "Was it really that life changing?"

"You mean backpacking for a year?" I ask, making sure she's still talking about my trip.

Elise just nods in return, her big amber eyes fixed on me.

"Of course, it was definitely worth it."

She gives me a side smile, most likely already thinking about her next question. "Did you, um, did you do any drugs there?"

Oh! My brows rise up, slightly taken aback by her boundless curiosity. Of all the questions she could have asked, that's definitely the last one I would have expected. "I can't tell you about it."

"Why not?" She seems genuinely surprised that I'm unwilling to share such private details about my life. "I *promise* I won't say a word to anyone." *Yeah, right...* I shake my head dismissively. "Please, trust me on this."

Jeez, she can be so damn insistent. "Why do you want to know that?"

"Well, you went to Columbia, so..." she lets her words trail off, cocking her head to the side.

As I look intently into her brown eyes, she seems rather genuine about her interest in my trip. "I did some yeah," I fess out.

"Which ones?" She asks right back.

"Elise..."

"C'mon, tell me," she presses on.

"Mostly ayahuasca," I answer, slightly embarrassed to share something so personal with my sister. "It's a psychedelic plant that makes you see things."

Her brows rise up in surprise, and she nods pensively for a few moments. "And what did you see?"

"Very strange things…" I pause, measuring my next set of words. "Taking it allows for a deep uncovering within your soul. It's like some higher spirit is trying to talk to you and show you the way."

"Wow," she mumbles. "And what did this higher spirit tell you?"

"It's private, dammit!"

"I wanna know," she insists.

"Sorry not today," I snap, standing up and ready for her to leave.

But of course, Elise just looks up at me from the floor, totally still. "Why not?" Her tone is even nicer and more polite than before. "Did he tell you something bad?"

"Time to go." I reach out and push her arm, forcing her to stand up.

"Always so damn secretive," she protests, huffing at me. I don't answer, I'm too focused on dragging her out of my bedroom. "Okay, okay, I'm leaving!" she groans as she releases herself from my grip. Fortunately, Elise makes her way out and I don't waste time shutting and locking the door behind her.

Once the door is finally locked, I heave a long sigh in exhaustion, before returning to sit on the floor. The last thing I want is to share with my sister what I saw during those trips. Yes, I did see and hear very strange things, which is why I wrote them down in my notebook. I also wrote the answers to the voice who spoke to me. I know it must sound crazy, but I'm actually trying to reconnect with this spirit via poetry.

But it wasn't a *he* as Elise said.

It was a *she*.

CHAPTER 3

For some people Monday can be a dreadful day. But for me, Monday is always glorious; synonymous with new opportunities, new ways to expand my business and to represent new faces. There's no better country than the Netherlands to do what I do. I can be who I am, make a living without guilt or shame, and my girls are all treated with decency, respect, and protected under the law. It cost me my relationship with Mama, but despite her disowning me and calling me all the labels in the book, I never stopped trying to make our relationship work—I've always attended her birthday parties (at the exception of the last one where I ran late), her celebrations of Chinese New Year, and even helped her find a better treatment for her back pain and rising sciatica. Despite all my efforts, I'm still dead to her. I still want to believe that one day or another, Mama will look at me not for the job that I do but as *me*, a human, a woman, and her daughter. I know that's a long way to go, but hope never dies.

"Good afternoon, Poppy," I say as I walk into our office reception, returning from a lunch date I had with one of my clients, Charlie.

Located in a quiet historic building in downtown, the interior has been totally renovated and transformed into a modern and elegant business center. I have rented the whole building for my agency—on the first and second floor we have apartments, big and small, where the girls go and meet their clients; and on the third floor we have the bookers that take phone calls, interview girls who want to get enlisted with us, and work on our website.

"Good afternoon, Roxie," she answers, already gathering her things and standing up to follow me into my office. Speeding up her heels to reach me, she leans in, and says, "Peter Walzon was on the phone this morning to book Natasha for the trip to Monaco—"

"Great," I utter, tossing my bag on the couch that lies on the sitting area of my office.

"Um, there's just one small problem though." I frown as I take off my jacket, and notice Poppy chewing her bottom lip. She takes a few more steps toward me and once standing close enough she lowers her voice and says, "You know they have been together for like three months now, and he's totally smitten with her, but..." Poppy lets her words trail off, clearly embarrassed.

"But what?" I ask, pressing her to finish her sentence.

Poppy heaves a sigh, most likely in apprehension. "He asked if he could pay two thousand euros extra for anal, but I know Natasha isn't into that." It's true, I recall perfectly well how she said anal for her was a hard limit. "Should I recommend him someone else, or do I just talk to her?"

"It was on her profile that she wasn't okay with that, no?" I ask.

"Yeah, but—"

"Tell him her boundaries are not negotiable," I say, cutting her off. "If Natasha said no, then it's no."

While I'm about to go and sit on my chair, Poppy cocks her head to the side, thinking something through. "Okay, um, do you mind talking to him? 'Cause he's getting really insistent."

Before I can tell her that she's got to learn how to deal with clients, my iPhone starts ringing nonstop. And by the ringtone, I know it's one of them. I take the phone out of my purse and… "Speak of the devil," I comment as I see his name flashing on the screen. "Hi Peter, how are you?"

"Hi Roxie," Peter greets, his voice always so kind and gentle. "I'm doing well, thank you."

"What can I do for you?" I ask, despite already knowing the answer.

"Well, um, it's about Natasha."

"Oh." Poppy and I share a smile. "What about her?"

"Well, I really like her, you know, um, we have been together for three months now, and she's really sweet and classy, and beautiful, and interesting…" I can't help but roll my eyes as I hear him speak. He's the retired CEO of a public company and yet if I didn't know him, I'd think he's just another teenage boy in love. "Can you advise her to be a bit more, eh, open-minded… sexually speaking? You know, to try new things. I'll pay whatever it takes."

Despite his humble and sweet tone, I'm not flexible when it comes to this. We have a zero tolerance policy on pressuring our girls into things they aren't comfortable with and he knows that. "Peter, I have one of the highest ranked escort agencies in Europe because our women have high standards." I heave a sigh, pausing for a beat as I gather my thoughts. "If Natasha said no, then I'm afraid I won't be able to help you on that."

As I expected, Peter isn't as understanding. "You do realize that any other hooker would do anal for a thousand bucks, right?"

"I do, yes," I tell him sincerely, my tone steady but not harsh. "And you're more than welcome to go and contact them, but Natasha Borzecki won't do it." It was always a hard-limit since the day she came in. She is a beautiful, very smart, classy and funny woman and she holds a bachelor's degree in law. I'd be the last one to pressure her doing something she isn't comfortable with. After a minute of silence, I ask, "Is there anything else I can help you with?"

Without much to add, Peter just mutters, "No, that's it. Thank you."

After our phone call, Poppy just smiles in return and mentally ticks this off of her list. "For Gustav's trip to Capri do you want me to send that new girl or not?" *Oh, now we are talking about another client.* This time I manage to make my way toward my desk and finally sit and recline on my armchair.

"Giselle?" I ask immediately, an ounce of worry in my voice. "She's still so inexperienced." I don't like to send my girls abroad when they are still very new to the industry.

Even if I know everything would go fine, the fact she can't really escape the yacht easily if something goes wrong, doesn't appease me. "How about Stephanie and Caroline instead."

"Shouldn't we at least ask Giselle if she would like to go?" Poppy inquires. "She knows Stephanie and Caroline and if they go without her, she might be resentful." I ponder her observation a bit further. "I mean, they'll be sharing the yacht parties and the fancy restaurants they are attending on their social media pages, shouldn't we at least talk to her?"

"Alright, fine," I say. "I'm gonna talk to her."

All of a sudden, I hear three knocks on my door and a tall man sporting a two-piece suit emerges with a big flower bouquet in his hands. "May I?"

"Oh, Karl!" I leap off of my chair immediately, a big smile on my lips as I go to meet him.

"I know I shouldn't come over without an appointment, but Poppy told me you could see me for five minutes."

"Really?" I look at Poppy who's trying hard to contain her guilty smile.

"Well, if you need anything, let me know," she says before passing past us and closing the door behind her.

I keep admiring and smelling the beautiful flowers, while Karl gather his thoughts.

"Is everything okay?" I ask him as I notice he has been quiet for a moment now.

"Roxie," he says to bring my attention back to him. "We not only signed them in this morning, but my boss even called me directly to congratulate me."

"Oh, wow!" My lips curve up, matching with his excitement. The dinner on Saturday was definitely a success, but I never thought he'd get them to sign so soon. "That's impressive."

"Look, um, he's throwing a party for his oldest son Friday night at his estate and invited me in to discuss an eventual promotion," Karl says, his voice laced with enthusiasm. "This is really huge for my career."

"Of course it is! And I'm super proud of you." I give him a quick pat on his arm, before putting the bouquet on my desk.

"I mean, I'd love for you to join me. It's a private gathering, so a plus one is kinda mandatory, you know."

"Friday night?" I ask, already searching for my calendar on my Mac. "That's very… um, short notice."

"I know, I'll pay a last minute fee." My lips twist into a smile at his understanding. While I remain focused on the screen of my computer as I search for what Poppy booked for me for Friday night, Karl keeps insisting. "You have got to join me, please, Roxie. You're going to awe him like you did with those Chinese guys." As I predicted, I see I have an evening with my second favorite client, Isaak, already booked. My eyes keep darting between the screen and Karl standing behind my desk, unsure how to tell him the truth.

"I…"

"Look," Karl interrupts. "I'm giving you fifty percent of my commission as we agreed. Please, the more business we can close together, the more you can make." I ponder his words thoughtfully. Indeed, given the fact he's doing five percent of each deal he closes, Karl is always priority. After all, just with this deal alone, he's paying me twenty-five thousand euros. I'll figure out what to do with Isaak later.

"And how do you intend to introduce me?" I ask.

"Well, like I did with the other guys."

"As your friend?" I can't hide the amusement in my tone.

"Yes, ma'am. As my friend." And I think neither can he. "Or should I introduce you as my girlfriend?"

"Friend is better," I tell him just as fast. After considering his request, I say, "Alright, I'll do it for you, but this is really an exception I'm making." And despite Karl paying all the cancelation, rebooking, and last-minute fees, I can tell he always hopes his charms will do the trick regarding me putting him above my other clients. But it's not because of his charms that makes him my favorite one—it's because he's not only the client who pays the most, but also the one that brings new business all the time.

"Thank you! Thank you!"

Before I can even reply, my desk phone's ringtone breaks through the office, interrupting our talk.

"I'll pick you up at eight p.m., Friday," he says, before walking around the desk to give me a quick kiss on the cheek. "Good luck," he whispers as I take the call.

"Yes?" I say while waving goodbye at Karl, who's now crossing the door. He waves back at me and closes the door behind him.

"Roxie, I've got a woman named Josianne van Aartsen on the line for you," Poppy informs.

"Josie?" I think to myself out loud. Wow. I haven't spoken to her for so long. Maybe three years or more. I wonder what she is up to. "Of course, put me on the line."

After a few seconds, I hear a new female voice, and my lips twist immediately into a smile. "Hey, how have you been? It has been so long. I hope I'm not disturbing."

"Of course not!" I reply, my tone enthusiastic. "I'm doing great. What about you? Still a prof at the uni?"

"Yes, still teaching English linguistics," she answers with a chuckle. A few beats of silence ensue, before she finally tells me the reason for her calling. "Look, um, I really need to talk to you," Josianne says, her words carrying a seriousness I wasn't expecting. "Face-to-face."

"I can do lunch this week," I say as I check my availability on my calendar. "Thursday, does that work?"

"Yes, can we have lunch on campus, if that's okay?" she asks.

"Alright, one-thirty then?"

"Deal."

CHAPTER 4

Amsterdam, August 26, 2021
Roxanne

The last thing I wanted was to come back to this university, to this campus, and to the memories I have here. As I park the car in front of the English department building, images of my time as a student start flashing through my mind. It was right in front of that building that I texted my first client, who'd also become my most loyal one—Karl.

I met him at a bar, and since he paid for my drinks, we exchanged numbers. The next day he texted me, inviting me out. Since I was not into him, I decided to tell him he'd have to pay me to go out with him as a joke. I thought he'd just decline and leave me alone, but instead, and to my greatest surprise, he had asked me how much. I thought he was joking, and playing along I replied a hundred bucks. "Deal" was his next message. And sure enough a note of a hundred euros was given to me once I got into his car. As I come to think of it, a hundred euros is a laughable fee, which might explain why he agreed to it so easily. Now I wouldn't charge less than a thousand euros for a two hour date.

After getting out of the car, I start strolling around the campus, a nostalgic feeling washing over me. Damn. It has been ten years since the last time I'd been here. Time truly flies. Nothing has changed though, except the campus has much fewer people than usual since the academic year hasn't started yet.

"Excuse me?" I hear a male voice saying from behind me. I turn around and my gaze lays on a tall, young man, sporting a slim fit white shirt, collar slightly open, sleeves rolled up and paired with dark jeans. He looks effortless, but his Patek Philippe watch and the signet ring on his finger catch my attention. His intense deep-set eyes are navy, the kind of blue that screams to be noticed. And they are hard not to get lost in it. I also notice his unruly brown hair, barely brushed on the sides, and his locks slightly falling on his brows in a very charming way. He must be a college student, but a ridiculously handsome one at that. He seems visibly lost and truthfully I feel just the same looking at him. As I observe his face more attentively, there's something sweet and innocent in him that makes me smile. Maybe it's the fact he reminds me of myself when I started college. "Do you know where the Admissions Office is? I have an appointment with Mr. Lewis at one-thirty there, but I can't seem to find it." His lips are full and perfectly sculpted, his scents, his timbre, the way his stare remains pinned on mine, my goodness, it's enough to destabilize me. *Jeez, Roxie! Enough!* I force myself to wake up and focus on his question.

"Um, the Admissions Office…" I glance around trying to remember where that place is. The young man remains standing in front of me, but I notice how his gaze follows my every move as I keep turning my head right and left to find the correct direction. "I do remember I went there once at least," I tell him, pondering the best way for him to get there. "I think you have to turn right and then go straight until you pass the restaurant, and then turn left." I'm not even sure of that but I pretend otherwise.

As I look at him again, his lips twist into a devilish seductive smile, as if he's picturing something naughty—or is it just me picturing it?

"Do you mind coming with me?" he asks, pausing for a beat as he observes me attentively. "I don't think I will manage alone." My heart pounds at his offer, prickly heat coats my arm, and I'm sure my blood pressure is steadily rising. It's absolutely insane, but there's something about his energy that makes me feel like a stupid teenager all over again.

"Of course, I, um, I think it's this way." He gestures for me to go first and I clear my throat trying to get a grip over myself as I pass by him. Yet, as I breathe in, his cologne hits my nostril and it takes everything in me to remain unmoved by it. "Nice cologne," I praise, failing miserably in the indifference department.

"Thanks," he says casually, like he's used to the compliment. "Yours too."

"Oh, it's Chanel Number Five," I tell him, quite proud of my choice until I realize he might have said that just for the sake of politeness. "It's a bit cliché, but my mom bought it for me when I graduated high school and I haven't changed it ever since." What? Why did I tell him that in the first place? That's so freaking personal!

"It's cliché, yeah, but I understand." His tone is laced with warm honesty. Something I've never found in the men I know. "Is your mom a Chanel addict or something? I know many women who are."

I can't help but snort at his question. "Mom? A Chanel addict?" I repeat, shaking my head in amusement. "No, she just knew I loved that perfume, I was always stealing samples from Sephora." Fuck! I bite my tongue immediately. What the heck? I look at him, feeling quite embarrassed at myself, but fortunately he just laughs in return.

"Really? Why samples? Why didn't you steal the real thing?"

His question makes me smile, and the fact he found it amusing rather than reprehensible eases me to tell him the rest. "Well, technically samples aren't for sale, so it was not *really* stealing in my eyes, and I knew I wouldn't get in trouble. But if I had stolen a real perfume and Mama had found out…" I let my words trail off, picturing my bottom set on fire with one of those hard spankings. "And yours?" I ask, aiming to change the subject. "What's the brand of your cologne?"

"Oh, no brand attached, a French perfumer made it for me," he answers, finishing with a small smile—almost like he was embarrassed? It's hard to tell. "He's got one of the finest noses in the world." His eyes are on mine again and for a moment, I feel like he's about to add something else given how thoughtful he seems to be, but he cuts eye contact, looking ahead instead. "Should we turn right?"

I blink twice, refocusing on the path we have to go. "Eh, yes, I think so."

In silence, I notice how tall he is as we walk through campus… and also his posture, so straight and elegant… and the way his hands bounce slightly back and forth on each side of his hips. His facial features are young, but the way he carries himself tells another story.

"Are you a student or something?" we ask in total shock at the very same time.

A laugh escapes us at our perfectly synchronized question, although it's more ridiculous than anything else.

"I graduated a long time ago," I tell him, flattered he thought I was still a student. At my age, I could actually be his professor.

"What was your major?" he asks.

"English."

For some reason, he stops in his tracks, his eyes wide and filled with excitement. "That's exactly what I want to do." *Really?* I look at him with a mix of confusion and disbelief. "Did you like it? How were the profs? I wanna know everything."

Wait—he wants a bachelor's degree in English? Damn, of all the programs this university offers, English was the last one I thought *he'd* want to pursue. "It was good." My tone doesn't match his excitement, and it comes off more mechanic and bland than I thought. I continue walking, memories flashing over me. "It was long time ago, so I don't remember too well." The truth is college years were filled with so many arguments with Mama and so many financial problems that I'm glad they are over and well behind me. Back then, I didn't have the money that I have now, and every expense had to be meticulously calculated in my budget. Heck, even to go out with the girls I had to make sure I could afford it or else I had to start talking to some random dude at the bar in the hopes he'd pay for my drinks. It was a big blow to my dignity having to rely on a total stranger to pay on my behalf, but it'd have been a bigger one telling my friends I couldn't afford it. All the girls I used to hang out with had a monthly allowance much bigger than my mom's salary, but I was just too proud to tell them the truth. Or maybe just too fearful they would reject me? Who knows…

"That's all?" he asks, maybe a bit disappointed at the lack of details. "It doesn't seem like you enjoyed it."

Well, I never got to use the degree at the end. Yes, to improve my English it was great, but apart from that, college for me was pretty useless. But I refrain myself from telling him that. Instead, I just smile and say, "If you enjoy English literature, you'll like it."

"And you don't?"

Oh boy, the question… I fill my lungs in a deep breath, considering thoughtfully his question. There's so much I want to say, and yet so little at the same time. So I settle for a quick, vague answer. "I do like literature, but beautiful prose doesn't pay the bills."

He nods, even more intrigued. "Care to expand?"

Gosh, I don't even know him, why would I bother so much answering personal questions to a total stranger? "It's a long story," I end up saying. "We'd need much more than a few minutes to talk about it," the words roll off my tongue, and I blame it on his magnetic blue eyes and carefully measured manners. Fortunately, I manage to think of a question of my own to focus on him instead. "What is your appointment for?"

"My application to the English program was rejected," he announces, with an ounce of humor that I fail to understand its reason. "I'm hoping Mr. Lewis will reconsider it."

"Do you have a plan?"

He seems to revel in my curiosity and takes an atrocious amount of time to answer.

"I do," he finally blurts out.

We start walking alongside the restaurant which Josianne and I will be having lunch at in a few minutes. As I come to think of it, I stop in front of the entrance doors and peer through the floor-to-ceiling windows, trying to see if I can find her already waiting for me inside.

"Are you looking for someone?" he asks, stopping too and following my gaze.

"Yes, I'm having lunch here with a friend."

And sure enough, I find Josianne, sitting on a table for two in the middle of the restaurant, glancing at her watch as she waits for me patiently, two glasses filled with water already on the table.

I also check my watch and gasp at the realization that I'm running late.

"I have to go," I tell him, the disappointment in my tone totally unexpected. I clear my throat, making sure to have a steadier one. "My friend is already inside. Just keep going straight and then turn left. You should see a newer-looking building with the admission office inside."

"Thank you so much for the chat." His tone, low and gentle, catches me totally off guard. He pauses for an instant, his lips slightly parted as he considers whether or not to say something else. And just like two idiots we stand in front of each other in total silence, our eyes pinned on one another. I've always been blunt and cheeky with men, and yet, right now, I find nothing but shyness in me. "Well, have a good lunch."

My heart falls a little at his words, but I force myself to compose a polite smile and give him a nod in appreciation. "Good luck at your appointment," I tell him, wondering why he didn't ask for my name or number. Maybe he wasn't interested in me after all, but just in my English degree.

Goddammit woman, ask him for his number yourself!

Before I can even decide whether or not I should see him again, he turns his back on me, and starts giving a few steps ahead. However, he stops and looks again in my direction. As he catches me still staring at him, I feel the heat of shame beaming on my cheeks. *Dammit!* "Will I see you around?" he asks out of nowhere.

I hesitate for a moment and find myself drawn in the deep blue of his eyes. Yet, as I look at them, I find two things I don't have: innocence and honesty.

From an English graduate to an escort and brothel keeper, I'd never have the stomach to tell him what I have become. It's stupid because I wouldn't mind telling the truth to most men—most men are dirty and morally corrupted anyway, but I don't see any of it in him. Maybe I'm wrong, but I'm not interested in finding out the truth.

Sometimes ignorance is bliss and it's best our little interaction ends on a positive note.

"I don't think so." Despite my heart tightening, I know this is the right thing to do. I push the door of the restaurant, and wave at him for a silent goodbye until the door shuts in front of me, taking with it the sight of him.

This is the right decision.

After all, it'd be a total waste of time developing a friendship with a college student.

Scanning around the restaurant, my eyes land on Josianne, and I force myself to put my little encounter with that boy behind, yet the impact he caused on me is just too peculiar to forget.

"Would you like a table, Miss?" the waitress asks.

"Oh, um, I'm good thanks," I answer, pointing toward my friend, before making my way toward Josianne.

* * *

After some small talk and jokes about our time as college students, the laughter has turned into an awkward silence. Josianne takes a sip of her orange juice, meticulously looking at me as I do the same with mine. Then, she puts her drink in front of her place setting and for some reason, starts playing with the base for a few seconds before saying, "Look, I really have to talk to you." Her tone switches from playful and welcoming to serious and grave. "It's a delicate situation, but the dean asked me to do so since he knows we are friends."

"Oh," I utter, my brows rising in surprise. "Alright, I'm listening."

Josianne takes a few more breaths before exhaling loudly. "There's an investigation going on because we think some of the girls are becoming…" she lets her words trail off, clearly embarrassed to say the rest. "Well, you know."

"Escorts? Sex workers?" I ask, given the fact she is too ashamed to say those words herself.

"Yes," she murmurs. "They came from very modest families and all of a sudden they start coming to campus in Bentleys, wearing Gucci, posting pictures in yacht parties, and vacationing in Capri."

I take another sip of my drink before I answer. "Seems like a good upgrade to me."

"Roxie," Josianne protests, given the fact I fail to see the issue here. "This campus is not a place for recruiting."

"I don't recruit," I riposte immediately. "The girls I manage have to come directly to me."

"Is there anyone you work with that gives them your contact details or the name of your agency?"

I ponder for a moment. There are definitely girls who are recommending my agency to their friends all the time, but it's not like I'm actively asking them to go on campus and distribute business cards. "Not that I'm aware of." As I observe the worry laced on her features, I add, "But, seriously, I'm not understanding what the issue is here. What they are doing is totally legal. I don't get your concern."

"Fine," she hisses, before finally disclosing the rest. "Those women aren't even finishing their bachelor's degrees, and we are talking about twenty to thirty students per year dropping out."

I just shrug, still failing to see the issue. "Students dropping out is a normal part of life," I tell her. "A bachelor's degree is no longer a requirement to become successful."

"So you think it's appropriate, what they are doing?" she asks, her prejudice lacing her tone. I look at her with shock in my eyes as if she doesn't know what I do for a living. "Never mind."

"Look," I begin, aiming to build a bridge between us. "I understand you're worried that they get mistreated, that they are ruining their lives, and so on." Josianne observes me attentively as I proceed, "But at the end of the day, it's *their* lives, not yours. Plus they are young and it's easy money, so I get the appeal."

"That doesn't make it right," she refutes back, slightly annoyed at our divergent opinions. "We don't want any recruiters on our campus. I don't know who they are, but one of my students told me she was referred to your agency here."

I heave a sigh, pondering her words. "As I already said, we are not recruiting," I tell her once more, hoping she'll understand once and for all I've got nothing to do with it. "If I have a few girls who start referring my agency to their friends, that's not my problem nor is it my job to keep tabs on them."

Josianne blinks twice, clearly tensed at my inflexibility. "Can you at least ask them to stop?"

"Stop doing what?" I ask. "Talking to their friends?"

I'm so over Josianne and her attitude. I have dealt with so many people like her, including Mom and my sister. At the end of the day, it all boils down to jealousy. They are getting old, they aren't making as much money as those drop-outs, and they are feeling resentful. While the drop-outs are living their best life, flying private, and enjoying themselves, Josianne is making less than eight thousand euros a month after spending seven years studying hard. If Josianne wants to go to Capri or St. Barth on vacation she has got to save up, while those girls spend nearly all year long at those places. My agency manages all the bookings, the fees, the photoshoots, and even mentors them. Some clients even compare me to Madame Claude, with there being the big advantage that I'm operating legally from Amsterdam.

"Tell the dean that Roxanne Feng isn't recruiting anyone, nor are her employees," I tell her, hoping to close this subject once and for all.

"Who ordered the salad with avocado and cashews?" the waitress asks, stopping at our table and holding a plate on each hand.

"I did," I answer as she places the dish in front of me.

She then puts the mashed potatoes and grilled steak in front of Josianne and gives us a quick smile. "Enjoy," she says before returning to the bar to attend other clients.

We start quietly eating our food, the tension between us vanishing as we give the first bite.

"This is delicious," she praises, the bite of meat still in her mouth. I give her a smile in return and keep focused on my own food. "I'm sorry to have had to talk to you about that subject. I know you are a good person."

As Josianne keeps talking, my attention is instantly drawn to the man that has just come inside.

Holy shit! It's the guy I met earlier. He crosses the restaurant, heading directly to the bar. As he passes through a few men, I notice how tall he is compared to them. Then he sits on one of the stalls and orders something from the waitress.

"Roxie?" Josianne asks.

I feel tempted to go to the bar and talk to him. I don't even know him and that's totally stupid of me, but he was so easy to talk to that I want to know how his appointment with Mr. Lewis went. The fact he's so pleasant to look at might also contribute to it. Yeah… It's hard to turn my gaze to somewhere else, I've met many men in my life but there's something about him, about his energy, his charisma, his presence, that makes him stand out. Maybe it's his charm, or his manners, or the way he holds the cup of coffee as he drinks his espresso, or the way he smiles at the waitress as he talks to her that makes him so attractive. As I keep observing him, I notice the waitress leaves and then walks back over to him with a piece of paper and a pen. He nods to thank her and writes something down… Well, it must be his phone number to give her. If I were her, I'd have totally asked him for it. I mean, if I were ten years younger and not doing what I do for a living.

"Roxie?" Josianne repeats.

I blink twice, my attention returning to her who seems to be containing a laugh. "What?"

"Are you listening?" I take a few seconds to answer, so Josianne turns around trying to figure out what is holding my attention for so long. "What are you looking at?"

"Nothing," I answer, giving a sip of my juice.

"The boy over there?" she asks, sounding surprised. "Do you know him?"

"Not really," I murmur, my eyes still pinned on him.

"He's cute, but way too young for you, my dear."

I frown instantly at her comment. "I didn't even say anything."

Josianne snorts at my serious expression. "Relax, I'm joking." She takes her cutlery, cuts a bite of her steak, and puts it on her mouth, chewing as she thinks something through. "I'm sure college students aren't your type, anyway."

I flash her a smile, not knowing what else to say and fork another bite of my food in silence. From the corner of my eye, I can see him standing up and reaching for his wallet to pay for his espresso. He hands a bill to the waitress who thanks him and he starts heading out.

Instantly, my heart turns the alert on, screaming at me to stand up and to go talk to him before he heads to the door and leaves. How am I going to see him again if I don't even have his number?

Roxie! What are you thinking?

Josianne is right. It's pointless for me to do that. He's a college student in his early twenties, and most likely just gave his number not to me, but to that young waitress.

I'm trying to focus on my plate or on whatever she is saying, but my heartbeat is pounding faster as each one of his steps getting closer to that door.

Please, wait for me, I find myself thinking.

I can't help following him with my gaze. He doesn't look in my direction, his steps are steady and confident and sure enough he reaches that door, passes through it, and leaves my sight once and for all.

My heart feels tight like I'm already regretting not having done anything. I should have gone over there and talked to him. Even if it was just to say hello and ask him about his appointment. Maybe it'd have ended there, but at least I'd have known if he managed to get his issue sorted out.

Suddenly, Josianne puts down her cutlery and leans forward. "Are you okay?"

No, I'm not okay. Without thinking twice, I instinctively take the napkin off my lap, stand up, and put it on my chair. "Give me a second."

Then, with a rush of adrenaline running through me, I hasten myself to leave the restaurant. As I cross the door, a fresh breeze reminds me I let my jacket on the back of my chair, but I don't care. My gaze travels across the campus, scanning through the many faces of men and women as I search for him. My eyes dart right and left, but I don't see anyone standing out, no one that looks like him. I walk a few more steps toward the parking lot, and check the cars.

Yet nothing.

I heave a sigh, filled with a mix of regret and relief. Regret because I wish I'd have at least known his name. Relief because maybe it'd have been a mistake.

After spending a few more seconds looking around, I walk back inside the restaurant, sadness washing over me. To my surprise, as I get in, I find the waitress standing in front of our table and talking to Josianne. She's most likely asking for the bill or ordering something else.

"Ah! Here you are," Josianne promptly says, her voice fortunately not too loud. The waitress turns, looking at me as I reach my chair. "What was that?"

"Nothing, I, um, I thought I saw someone I know and wanted to say hi." I take my seat and put my napkin back on my lap, feeling quite self-conscious at my stupid escapade; I literally left my friend and went outside to follow a college student I don't even know. What the heck? How can I be so pathetic?

"Did you manage to talk to him?" the waitress asks.

Her question is so intrusive and unexpected that it makes my heart skips a beat. "*Him*?" I repeat given the fact I didn't say it was a *he*.

"Well, I know *he* wanted to talk to you."

I furrow my brows in confusion. "What do you mean?"

And to my greatest shock, she takes from her apron a folded paper, handing it to me. "He told me to give you this because he had to go."

My lips part wide to breathe, and without waiting any further, I open the sheet and read:

I didn't want to bother you since you are with a friend, but I need to see you again. I hope the feeling is mutual.

Whenever you're free, drop me a message at 971028134.

Cheers,

Andries

Oh jeez! I must have blushed a sharp shade of red as I read this letter. Somehow, I read it in my head with his voice instead of mine. The word *need* coming from his lips sounds so delicious that I chew my bottom lip. *I need to see you again,* I picture him whispering those words to me. *I hope the feeling is mutual,* he says, his lips brushing against my ear, and then my neck, and it makes me feel all giddy inside and stupid and…

Argh! Get a grip, already!

"What is it?" Josianne asks, pulling me back from my reverie. And as my eyes go up, I didn't even notice that the waitress had already left our table. "I'm getting worried about you. Is everything okay?"

"Yes, of course," I reply, flashing her a smile as I close and shove his note inside my purse. Andries; so that's the name of the young man I met earlier. And I finally have his number too… I drink some water and try to finish my food, but I'm just too stupidly excited to keep eating. I have been with so many men, and yet that little interaction with him makes me feel like an inexperienced teenager.

"So you are not gonna tell me what that note says?" Josianne presses on.

The audacity, my goodness… She might even end up being his prof if he does his major in English. It's more than obvious that I won't tell her. "Sorry, but that's confidential."

"Alright," Josianne mutters, visibly displeased as she leans back on her chair. Her eyes remain fixated on me as I fork another bite, studying me attentively. "You are not gonna see him again, right?"

I freeze instantly at her question. I can't hide the shock in my eyes as I look at her with parted lips. "Why not?"

"Why would you do that? To pitch your girls to him?"

Does she really think so little of me? "Why are you so bothered?"

Josianne cuts eye contact, looking at her plate for a moment as she thinks what to say. "Because," she begins, swallowing the lump on her throat. Then as her eyes meet mine again she finally blurts out, "I don't want any more students involved in your agency. I'm sorry but this isn't right. They are young and impressionable."

"I get it," I hiss. "You really think this place is a target of ours? Let me be clear, it isn't. We don't pitch students to become clients or escorts."

I can feel the tension rising again between the two of us as she processes my words. We might have been friends since college, but she's always been very against my career choices, and sex-work in general. But also it's worth saying she's more my sister's friend than mine. "I hope so."

After lunch, I get into my car like a kid, fluttering on cloud nine. It's absolutely stupid, but I can't help it. It has been such a long time since I felt anything regarding another fellow human. But my joy is quickly overturned when Poppy starts calling me. Work. I have forgotten about it for a moment. I barely stop thinking about work, but when I think about my interaction with Andries, I manage to escape to another reality where work doesn't exist. I put my AirPods in my ears and answer the call while starting the car.

"Hey, how was lunch?" Poppy asks.

"It was good," I answer, remembering my discussion with Josianne. "Listen, make sure no one is recruiting at the universities, and tell the girls to be more discreet while they are on campus," I instruct her, since I know a few of the girls who are still studying. I can already picture them bragging to their friends about their income. "Jealously is vicious."

"Oh, is there a problem?" Poppy keeps asking, visibly surprised.

"I'll explain it to you later on," I say as I start driving to get out of the campus.

"Okay," she replies, before proceeding with my schedule. "So Karl will pass by your place at eight p.m. to pick you up for that event tomorrow night and will drop you back home at midnight. And Isaak will see you Saturday and Sunday."

Jeez, I'd totally forgotten how my weekend is already completely booked. And instead of looking forward to it as I usually do, it feels…well, it feels really like *work*.

"Okay, perfect."

* * *

It's late evening and I'm more than ready to finally get home. Reaching the condo, I park inside the garage, and then get into the lift, pressing the button to take me to the highest floor—to my penthouse. No one has ever been here except my sister. Let's just say it's like a little refuge from my daily work. Despite Karl's insistence, no client has ever been upstairs, and I intend to keep it that way.

As I step inside, I'm welcomed by the black and white tile of the hallway and the intimate lights from the ceiling which turns themselves automatically on. I breathe in the perfumed air, before dropping my purse and coat on the hanger. Then I take off my heels, and let out a sigh in relief as I walk barefoot toward the living room. The street lights coming from the floor-to-ceiling windows catch my attention, reminding me how lucky I am to live here. I grab the landline and make a quick phone call to the concierge.

"Is the spa available in an hour?" I ask once they answer.

"Of course, Ms. Feng. Would you like us to reserve the sauna for you?"

"Yes, please," I say, feeling already pampered just by his smooth voice. "And, by the way, is Gigi available for a deep-tissue massage?

"I think so, should I book her for after the sauna?"

"Yes, thank you."

"Is there anything else I can assist you with?"

"No, that's it," I tell him. "Thanks."

After hanging up, I put on some jazz music on the speakers, and go to the kitchen where I take from the fridge a new bottle of Sauvignon Blanc. I pour myself a glass and close my eyes savoring the spicy notes of green bell pepper, jalapeño, vanilla, nutmeg, and clove. The saxophonist fills the air with an incredible groove and I start instinctively swinging as my body follows the rhythm of the music. I couldn't have chosen a better playlist to enjoy this wine. I reopen my eyes, and survey the penthouse as if it were the very first time I am here. I bought this place two years ago, and yet, from time to time, I look at it with deep admiration. Not really admiration for the sumptuous and refined modern interior design, or the breathtaking view of the Royal Palace and the National Monument on the Dam Square, but truly admiration to my commitment in pursuing my own business in the field I wanted. Even in this country, the stigma surrounding sex-work is prevalent and I have lost many friends and acquittances for embracing such a lifestyle. Society expects women to feel shame and guilt to profit off their own sexuality, and when they don't feel either, they are marginalized and treated like they don't deserve basic decency. This is why I love what I do, the agency I created represents not only women but also give them protection and fights for their own interests when negotiating terms with clients. It's like a modeling agency, except it's not fashion brands who are calling us but politicians, bankers, and businessmen.

I cross the dining room, the floor-to-ceiling windows bouncing back the street lights, and head to the library where I still have my favorite books on the shelves. There, almost instinctively, I take an old Chinese edition of *The Selected Poems of Li Po*, Mama's favorite poet and one of the few books she gave me. As I come to think of it, she gave me this book when I got accepted at the English program at the University of Amsterdam. I can still remember how proud she was… I'd never forget that day. Out of curiosity, I open randomly to a page of the small book to read the first poem my eyes lay on. I chuckle rolls off my lips at the title, "Drinking Alone." Couldn't be more appropriate for the occasion.

I take my wine jug out among the flowers
to drink alone, without friends.

I raise my cup to entice the moon.
That, and my shadow, makes us three.

But the moon doesn't drink,
and my shadow silently follows.

For some reason, my mind replays the talk I had with Andries earlier today. "*Beautiful prose doesn't pay the bills,*" I remember telling him. And how true that is. How many poets can afford to live where I live now? I don't know many. Li Po for sure wasn't one of them.

I shut the book and put it back on the shelf, leaving this frivolous literature behind. Then I go to my dressing room and start planning my outfits for the weekend.

For a moment, I fell tempted to save Andries' number in my phone and text him. But for what? We are from two different worlds, living two very different lives, and I'm pretty sure it's better to keep it this way. That boy doesn't deserve the heartache.

And neither do I.

CHAPTER 5

V.D.B estate, August 27, 2021
Andries

It's Friday. And yet she still hasn't texted. I know I shouldn't expect much after a simple encounter, but as I watch the staff getting everything ready around the terrace for the evening, I can't help but let out a sigh in disappointment. I wanted so badly to invite her to the party. Her presence would have made it much more tolerable, but now it's already six p.m., so it's obvious she's going to gonna make it.

"What do you think? Pretty cool, huh?" I hear Dad asking as he comes over and stops beside me. In silence, we observe the staff testing the fairy lights that are hanging over the terrace. When they turn them on, I nod, liking quite a lot the golden glow and the intimate atmosphere they create.

"It looks nice," I say for the sake of politeness.

"You don't seem very happy though," Dad points out, his eyes now pinned on me as if he's trying to read my deepest thoughts. "What's wrong?"

I cut eye contact, my gaze drifting away for a moment, unable to hide my discontentment. "I'm fine."

"What's troubling you, son?" His question is laced with genuine curiosity and interest. "If it's because of a girl, she isn't worth it." I roll my eyes at his pathetic comment.

"It's just the nostalgia of moving to Amsterdam soon," I tell him instead. "I'm okay."

"Cut the bullshit," Dad answers with some unexpected humor. "You never felt any nostalgia when you left for a year." *Touché*. "So what's her name?"

"Dad, not everything in life involves a girl." Or in my case, a woman. "It's nothing really."

"Good," he utters, with an air of satisfaction as he nods pensively for a few seconds. I look at him more attentively, my eyes narrowing at his lips twisting into a smirk. "Because I invited Tatiana over."

"What!" I snap in total disbelief, my heart skipping a beat at the news. Holy fuck! "Flower-girl is coming?" I ask, my tone laced with shock and disapproval.

"Her name is Tatiana," Dad rectifies. Yet I can't help but run a hand through my hair and huff at his attitude. "What do you have against her? I don't get it."

A gush of air rolls of my lips, and I shake my head repeatedly, not bothering to conceal my displeasure. Of all the people in my high school, he really had to invite the one person I didn't want him to. "She's not my type," I tell him for the thousandth time.

"No one seems to be," he rebukes. "How come you've never introduced me to anyone you're seeing?"

"Fine, next time I'll introduce you to my one-night stand." I don't have any, but that's just a way to shut him and his deplorable remarks.

"Don't be stupid. You know what I meant."

Suddenly, the sound of an engine approaching leads my attention toward the roundabout close to the back entrance of the estate. This is usually the main entrance for guests, as it's the closest one to the terrace. From where I stand, it's not hard to spot the cars entering into the driveway, crossing the gardens, and parking just before the massive set of stairs that lead to where I am standing. I walk a bit closer to the balustrade, my eyes alighting on a red vintage Jaguar convertible. My lips twist into a smile up to my ears, recognizing the driver.

I immediately run out of the terrace, racing down the stairs as fast as I can in his direction.

When he finally opens the front door, my eyes land on the one and only friend that matters.

"Dan!"

He shuts the door behind him, walking in my direction with his usual air of superiority. "My man!"

I can't help but shake my head in amusement as he takes his cognac leather gloves off, but leaves the sunglasses on his face. Dan O'Brian has always been the most stylish of the group, especially with his love for vintage cars, overcoats, drinks and cigars. Despite having seen him just a week ago, I open my arms to welcome him with a big hug.

"Thank God you came," I say, giving him a few pats on the back. "This is gonna be the most boring party in the world."

"As soon as we have a good burgundy we will be fine."

I snort at his comment. "We'll need much more than that." Then leaning over him, I lower my voice and say, "My dad invited flower-girl."

Dan bursts out laughing. "Well, I'd imagine she's counting on you to pop her cherry."

"Fuck off," I push him playfully.

But Dan keeps laughing. "C'mon, Andries, don't be so hard to get."

While we keep teasing each other, we walk up the stairs and I lead him to the terrace, showing him where guests will be gathered for the evening. Dan greets my dad with a warm handshake, and after they exchange a few cheerful pleasantries, I invite him inside to the living room to give him something more proper than the cheap cocktails the bartender will be serving tonight.

Once I close the door behind us, Dan takes off his cashmere blazer, pulls the sleeves of his linen shirt up to his elbows, and sits comfortably in one of the armchairs.

"I heard you're moving to Amsterdam in two weeks," he begins, while I'm already heading to the bar cart to pour him a glass of his favorite Pinot Noir, a Grand Crus from Clos de la Roche. I know, let's not judge this man too harshly for drinking a burgundy without pairing it with proper food, but Dan has been into wines since I can recall and I'd be the last person on earth calling him out about it. "Why didn't you tell me? I'm hosting a burlesque party on the eleventh at my place."

I heave a long sigh, not surprised at his statement. Dan knows I'm not into parties—especially not *his* type of parties. "I appreciate the invite, but you know I'm not into that."

"Nonsense!" he snaps, before jumping over to where I'm standing. "You're gonna be a freshman! You have to loosen up a bit."

Despite his excitement, I remain unimpressed. "It's not my scene, but I'll see what I can do," I make that up, before handing him his drink.

"Are you missing your monk life or what?"

A snort escapes me, but I find myself pondering a decent answer at his question. "It's a big contrast with yours that's for sure."

"Honestly, though, aren't you happy to be back?" he presses on.

My gaze drifts away for a moment as I recall my life in the Amazon and Tibet. "I don't know, I liked being away." I freaking loved it! It was a solitary life, filled with meditation, reading, writing, and tranquility. A perfect year that ended up too abruptly thanks to my overbearing parents.

"Why did you come back then?"

A side smile stretches the corner of my lips at his question—Dan has always been blunt, and despite my being away for a year, he hasn't changed one tiny bit. "Let's just say Pops can be pretty convincing," I decide to answer.

"Well, I don't know about you, but I'm super happy you are back," he says, putting a hand on my shoulder. "And that you're moving to my city."

A few knocks on the wooden door halts our conversation abruptly and I shout to come in.

"My apologies, Mr. Andries, but your grandmothers are here," one of the housekeepers, Claudia, announces.

"They are only here for dinner," I tell Dan as I notice the worry on his face. "C'mon, let's go."

* * *

Fortunately, dinner goes fast enough thanks to Dan and his usual jokes. We manage to leave the dining room by ten p.m. but only to go to the terrace and greet the guests who have arrived and are now mingling with friends old and new. For the split of a second, I'm swept away at how the terrace has changed since this afternoon. Strings of fairy lights are hanging above our heads, glowing amid the dark night, while the live band music is playing some of my favorite jazz songs. A big bar stands on one side serving cocktails, and waiters go around the terrace offering glasses of champagne and canapés. It's full of people, some that I recognize, others not so much. But one thing is sure though, it feels like Elise and her friends must've invited half of our high school to come here.

"Is this prom or what?" Dan says under his breath as he recognizes a few familiar faces from high school. "Who sent out the invitations?"

"I did!" Elise snaps behind us, and we literally jump at her high-pitched tone. "Do you have a problem with that?"

"Well," Dan scans around the terrace, before looking back at my sister to answer. "It feels very high school-ish. I could've given you a hand with the guest list."

Elise just scoffs in return, unimpressed. "You do realize most of the guests are either in college or already working, right?"

I can't help but snort at the usual banter between these two. I met Dan at my fencing club when I was ten years old and realize he was also attending the same school as I. He might be five years older, but he's always been my favorite buddy to hang out with. Despite repeating at least two years of school due to his bad grades and behavior, Dan took over his family business in Amsterdam and is now also in college for some odd reason.

"Good evening, everyone!"

Holy shit! I recognize that voice! My gaze goes to where everyone is looking at, and to my biggest embarrassment, I see Dad on stage where the musicians are, a microphone in one hand and a flute of champagne on the other. The music has now faded away and I can't help but wonder what is Dad doing over there.

"I hope you're all enjoying the party and the exceptional groove played by those fine musicians," he continues, clearly reveling in this little moment of attention. The crowd cheers and raises their glasses to him, and Dan is no exception.

"I'd like to raise a toast to my oldest son and daughter, Andries and Elise, for both starting business school this fall."

"What!" Elise bursts out, looking at me as if I knew something she doesn't. "Is this for real? Did I get in?"

I shrug, totally confused. "I've got no idea."

"I'm extremely proud of you both and especially Elise who didn't even take a year off." While Dad has managed to make people snort and laugh at my own expense, I just wet my lips on the champagne, ignoring his unfortunate comment. This is so typical of him—putting me down while uplifting the perfect Elise seems like his favorite hobby. One more reason for me to change to English without even telling him. "She'll actually be the youngest of her class, so congratulations darling. I know you're gonna kill it." Elise is grinning like never before, totally smitten at the praises of our dad, and clearly on cloud nine while he continues his speech. "And I apologize to have kept your acceptance letter to myself until now." Fortunately, Dad looks at the musicians and nods at them, most likely as a signal for them to start playing a song. "Let's celebrate!"

The saxophonist starts playing and the rest of the musicians follow suit setting a festive mood over the terrace. Guests either start dancing or mingling between themselves and the vibe falls right back to what is was before his intervention. When Dad leaves the stage, Elise is quick to go and meet him. From the corner of my eye, I watch her opening her arms wide and embracing him tightly, they then start chatting like besties, and I know at this point I can't compete in that department. I've never been into displaying affection to my dad. And neither has he.

"Have you seen who's here?" Dan asks, his tone dripping with amusement.

Oh shit. On the other side of the terrace, my gaze zooms in on the slim brunette with a floral dress that Dan had been pointing at, surrounded by her friends, a glass of champagne in hand. While her friends are talking and laughing, she seems bored, glancing across the terrace as if she's looking for someone.

In the fraction of a second, I turn around, ready to run away, but Dan holds me just as fast.

"What the fuck?" I whisper, because he isn't letting me go.

"You're gonna say hi to your guests, buddy," he says, a smirk spreading on his lips, as he keeps standing in my way.

What a motherfucker he is. No wonder Dad likes him so much.

"Tatiana!" Dan calls, waving a hand in the air.

Fucking idiot! "You're gonna regret this," I snap between clenched teeth.

"I couldn't resist," he replies with sarcasm, before he turns me back to face Tatiana and pushes me forward while he walks in her direction.

I roll my eyes, hating this moment more than anything else.

"Wow," Dan utters, his tone always so ironic when we approach flower-girl and her friends. "You look absolutely stunning tonight." Tatiana lowers her gaze, giving him a big smile in return, and the desire to kill him is growing by the second. "Don't you think, Andries?"

I press my lips tight, containing the urge to punch him while he's having the blast of his life. "Of course," I say, reminding myself she's the daughter of one of my dad's most important suppliers. I swear, if her family wasn't so close to mine, I wouldn't have bothered to stay here.

"You look great too," she comments, looking at me, her tone always so soft and sweet. She tucks some strands of hair behind her ear, and then adds, "How was your backpacking trip?"

"It went very well," I tell her for the sake of politeness. "It was very eye-opening, to say the least."

Suddenly, Dan drops an arm around my shoulders, a goofy smile hanging on his lips. "Care to elaborate?"

I want to say a lot and nothing at the same time. "It was a very contrasting experience." I pause for a beat, choosing carefully my next set of words. "I spent six months in Columbia, first in Medellin, then Bogota, and then in the Amazons. And then I flew to Tibet." I see a waiter passing by, and I call him, taking a flute of champagne from his tray. I'm going to need much more than a single glass if I'm going to spend the whole evening here. "And you? How did your first year of college go?" I ask Tatiana.

"Oh, it went great. I've been doing an internship at the headquarters at the same time." Her family is the biggest producer of crops and dairy products in the country, and, not surprisingly, have a century-old business partnership with the Van den Bosches. "Your dad told me you are also gonna pursue a bachelor in business?"

If everything goes according to plan, Mr. Lewis should be able to switch me to English, but no one needs to know that. "Yes, that's correct."

While Dan is taking over and telling us some of his improbable stories, my attention goes toward my dad who just stepped outside from the main door and is now going down the first set of stairs that leads to the driveway and gardens.

Well, that's odd. All the dinner guests—which are only family members—arrive and leave by the front entrance, not the back one. What on earth is Dad doing there by himself?

"Excuse me," I say, before walking a few steps ahead until I reach the balustrade.

There, I see a black sedan entering into the driveway, crossing the fountain roundabout, and then parking right in front of my dad. While the driver exits the car, I see another man leaving one of the back seats, and my dad goes to greet him, shaking his hand. Meanwhile the driver opens the other rear door, helping someone else to get out and the two men go to meet her.

My eyes zoom at my dad as I watch him welcoming a slim and elegant woman with short blonde hair, styled like Marilyn Monroe, and wearing a long black sleek qipao, falling to the ankle.

"Is everything alright?" I think Dan is speaking to me but I'm too focused on the blonde woman that is now shaking my dad's hand. She looks so freaking similar to the woman I met yesterday on campus though. My dad looks totally smitten, of course, who wouldn't be?

Unfortunately, from where I'm standing, I can only see one side of her face, and I'm just too far away to discern any feature.

"Andries?" Dan repeats as I turn my head right and left, trying to avoid his hand as he waves it up and down in front of me. "Planet earth is calling Andries. Hello?" The three of them are now standing by the stairs talking and the more I look at her the more intrigued I am. How come the woman I met yesterday would be here? She didn't even send me a text. It's impossible! But she was clearly at least half-Asian, and this woman is sporting a traditional Chinese dress....

"What are you looking at?" Dan asks as he finally follows my stare. "You know you just left me hanging, right?"

"Who's that woman over there talking to my dad?" I ask him. "Do you know her?"

Dan looks in my direction, narrowing his eyes. "I don't know, but she's hot." My dad is now inviting them inside the house and I can only conclude they are going to his office, which is located on this side of the house! "One thing is for sure, she isn't going to college." I hurry myself to walk past Dan and head to the closest door. "Where the hell are you going?" I hear Dan barking behind me.

Quickly enough, I get back inside the house from the French glass door that gives access to the living room, and run through the hallway as fast as I can, until my eyes lay on my dad and his guests.

"Dad!" I call, before he can open the door of his office. "Finally, I found you." I slow down my pace since I'm close enough to them, and run a hand on my hair to make myself more presentable.

"Oh, you were looking for me?" His brows are furrowed with confusion, as if trying to figure out why I'm here.

"Yes, of course, I wanted to ask, um, where do you stock your limited editions of Jenever?" My gaze can't help but shifts to his right, and goddamn it, this is the woman I met on campus! What is she doing here? My heart feels like it's about to explode with excitement and it's near to impossible not to smile when we look at each other. Her lips are of red matte, contrasting beautifully with her pale skin and the black satin of her dress. Now that she's all glammed out, she's even more beautiful than I recalled. Is she a model or something? Her short blonde hair is wavy and brushed on one side and with her cheongsam, she reminds me one of those glamorous divas of the old Shanghai. "Oh, sorry, I'm so rude. I didn't know you had company." And just because I have looked at her for way too long, my attention goes to the man on her side, and I extend my hand. "Andries van den Bosch," I say, putting on a smile to greet him.

"Oh, it's an honor meeting you, Andries," the man answers, shaking my hand. "I'm Karl Townsend, I work at your dad's company."

"In which department?" I ask, feigning interest.

"Sales," he answers with an enthusiastic tone.

I give him a nod of understanding, and my gaze returns to the reason of my being here. I extend my hand to shake hers, but she takes a long second to do the same.

"I'm Karl's friend," she says after a few instants of silence.

I can't help but smile as I finally hear her speak again. Holy shit! This isn't a dream. She's really here, standing in front of me in my family estate! "And does Karl's friend have a name?"

She doesn't seem pleased for me asking, and I find it even more amusing. After a few more seconds of total silence between us, she finally says, "Roxanne."

I repeat her name in my head because it's just as unique as she is. "Any surname perhaps?"

"Just Roxanne."

Before I can reply, my dad steps in. "You should go and ask Claudia, she knows where they are." That's his way to ask me to leave.

"Alright, I will." My attention falls back to Karl and I give him a quick nod of the head. "Pleasure meeting you, Karl."

"You too," he answers, doing the same.

I look at her one last time and try to memorize every single feature of her face as I do so. "Roxanne."

Her beautiful almond eyes are still focused on me, as if she's mentally photographing me. Yet Roxanne doesn't say anything in return, all she does is a polite nod of the head, along with a timid smile, but her gaze says much more than words could ever do. I have traveled the world searching for peace but it's in her eyes that I have found it the most.

I hear my dad cleaning his throat, and while Roxanne seems to be terribly embarrassed at her behavior, a sharp shade of red settling on her cheeks, all I do is smile even more. This moment right here is the reason why I know I have to talk to her again tonight. "Alright, thanks Dad. Have a good meeting."

As I turn my back on them and walk in direction to the terrace, my smile stretches up to my ears—while I didn't speak much to her, it was enough to know her name and that she isn't his girlfriend.

Reaching the terrace again, I stumble on Dan, who's mingling with a group of friends. "Where were you?" he asks, already dragging me to somewhere quieter.

"I know her name," I say, squeezing his shoulders tight before roaming around, excitement bouncing inside my chest.

Dan does his best to keep up. "What are you talking about?"

"The woman I met yesterday, she's here. She's a friend of Karl Townsend—an employee at my dad's company."

He frowns, totally confused. "Wait—who did you meet yesterday? And where?" Dan asks immediately, a mix of outrage and enthusiasm in his tone. "What's happening?" I chuckle, amused at his growing curiosity. "Spit it out, man!"

"I met that woman yesterday on campus, her name's Roxanne," I tell him, unable to contain the pride in my voice. "Have you ever heard a name so beautiful and mesmerizing?"

"It's pretty dope, yeah." Dan nods, thinking something through. "Roxanne what?"

"I don't know."

His eyes widen in surprise. "You don't know? So how are you gonna find her again? The campus is pretty big."

I put a hand on his back as we keep strolling along the balustrade and say, "I have to get her number tonight."

"What?!" Dan stops in his tracks, looking at me with shock in his eyes. "Forget it—she might be his girlfriend, that's a dead plan."

"No, she is just a friend. If she was more than that, he'd have said it."

But Dan puts a hand on my shoulder, as if he were about to deliver some bad news. "Look, there's no way in hell you gonna get her number tonight, forget it."

I shoot him an arched eyebrow. "You wanna bet?"

"Andries…"

"What? Let's make a bet." I show him the palm of my hand, ready to shake his and do the bet.

Dan ponders for a few instants. "Alright, if I win, you go to my burlesque party."

"Jeez!" I drop my hand just as fast.

"Hey, you said you'd give it a thought," Dan reminds me. "I'm telling ya, it's gonna be the best party you've ever been to." I can't help shaking my head instinctively as he speaks. "Plus I'm gonna invite a few friends I know who are writers." I heave a long sigh, not impressed at all. "C'mon, you can't move to the capital and not attend."

I assess his offer carefully. "Alright. But if I win, you take care of flower-girl for me."

Dan looks over my shoulder, most likely to where Tatiana is. "Fine, but you need to get her number tonight. *And…*" he says, a finger in the air. "It must be her giving it to you, no one else."

Oh fuck, Dan knows me so well it hurts—I was thinking of simply asking Karl for Roxanne's number in exchange for a promotion or something. It'd have been so simple and easy. But I'm sure I can come up with something else.

"Deal." We seal our bet with a handshake and once we are done, I start putting a plan together. I need Roxanne to come here to the terrace but without Karl. Well, let's think for a moment; knowing my dad as I do, he only invites his employees to the family estate when they've done something extraordinary for the company and he wants to give them a promotion or a raise himself.

Oh shit! I've got a brilliant idea!

I glance at my watch—it's been only ten minutes since they went into my dad's office. Dad never starts talking business right away. He usually offers his guests a drink to begin with and then they spend some time doing small talk. This should work. Reaching for my iPhone, I call the landline in my dad's office. The ringtone goes on, and on…

"Yes?" Dad says as he answers the call.

"Hi Dad, can I speak to Karl for a moment, please?"

"To Karl?" he repeats, his voice just above a whisper.

"Yes, didn't you want me to start mingling with your top employees?"

"Yes, but—"

"I need to speak to him," I interpose. "I won't take long, promise."

I hear nothing but a loud rush of air from the other side of the line. "Mr. Townsend?" Dad says, his voice far from the speaker.

I clench my fist in victory. This might work!

"My son would like to talk to you."

"Hello?" Karl is finally speaking and I waste no time getting straight to the point.

"Did my dad already speak to you about your promotion?"

"Eh…" My question seems to have left him totally speechless.

"So?" I press on.

"I'm afraid not," he discloses, his voice low and barely audible.

"Listen—he invited you today for that, but I don't think he was expecting you to bring a friend along."

"Oh, um, I see… and what do you suggest?" he sounds shy and vulnerable and I can tell he's really looking forward to talking about his performance at the company tonight.

"If you want him to cut the bullshit and start talking about your promotion, you'd better be alone," I tell him, straight and clear. "I'll send one of the housekeepers to take your friend out on the terrace. I think it'll be more appropriate for you."

"Well, um, that's very kind of you." He sounds genuinely pleased. Well, of course he is. There's nothing worse for a hustler like him than for his friend to become the center of attention and discussion. "Thank you so much."

"You're most welcome. Good luck," I finish the call with my heart thundering anxiously inside my chest. Fuck! In a few minutes, Roxanne will be here at the terrace by herself. Funny how such a boring event turned out to be the most exciting one in such a short period of time.

"So?" Dan asks as he walks back toward me.

I reach him, and rubbing my hands together, I say, "So make sure Tatiana is well taken in care of because Mr. Andries is gonna be busy."

"Uh oh," he utters playfully. "Am I gonna lose my bet?"

"I'm getting her number tonight," I tell him, already on cloud nine. "This woman…" I shake my head with a smile. Before I start dwelling any further, I focus on searching for Claudia, my most trusted housekeeper, and instruct her to bring Roxanne to the terrace. Once Claudia goes to my dad's office, I head to the living room and go to serve myself a glass of burgundy—a small gesture to celebrate my upcoming victory against Dan.

I haven't felt this excited since I left home over a year ago and what a great feeling it is!

With my glass of burgundy in hand, I open the French door that gives direct access to the terrace, but my heart jumps into my throat and all the noise fades away when my eyes alight on her.

I remain quietly leaning against the doorway as I observe the most stunning woman I've ever seen standing by the balustrade, a glass of champagne in hand. What a view, my goodness! Her black, sleek dress molds perfectly to her curves, accenting her waistline. Her short blonde hair plays gently with the breeze of the evening, and her red lips are just as full and kissable at the distance as they were when she was standing close to me. She takes a sip from her glass, before her eyes start scanning attentively through the crowd with a hopeful smile until they drop to the floor, and she lets out a sigh filled with what seems to be disappointment.

I step onto the terrace and when I get close enough to her, I say, "Now that's quite a surprise!"

Her attention perks up as I watch her intently, and she lifts her head in my direction, a smile stretching across her lips.

"Looks like the universe is conspiring in my favor," I add, taking a sip from my glass as I mentally cheer at my good karma.

"That's one hell of a surprise, indeed," she answers, her tone polite but contained.

As I stand beside her, I feel Roxanne much more reserved than when we initially met on campus. Maybe it's because we are surrounded by people, who knows. One thing is for sure; I have to persuade her to leave this party with me and go to somewhere quieter where we can be left alone, only the two of us. "Aren't you bored here?"

Her eyes meet mine again, but she frowns in confusion. "Excuse me?"

"Spending the evening by the balustrade and not talking to anyone? I mean, most people here are boring anyway but still." I try to keep a nonchalant attitude, but her sweet perfume fills my lungs and it becomes harder than I thought.

"Oh, it's fine," she tells me immediately. "I'm just doing Karl a favor. I hope it goes well for him."

A small smile forms at the corners of my lips. "Ah, yes, what a lucky friend he is." *At least, he's got your number.*

"We've known each other for a long time," she says, like she's trying to justify her friendship with him. "He's very hardworking. He'll go far."

"Yeah, he seems to be a good hustler." I give a quick sip on my burgundy as I consider for a moment the question that is on the tip of my tongue, but deciding against it, I instead ask, "How come the two of you are just friends?

Roxanne nearly spits out her own bubbly, before she stares at me, astonishment written on her lovely features. "I beg your pardon?"

And that's enough to make me grin. "How come—"

"I heard the question," she interposes. "Why on earth are you asking me that?"

I just shrug in return. "Because I can't believe he never tried to be anything more than just a friend." I pause, observing her for a moment. "Unless he's gay, of course."

Roxanne, on the other hand, exhales loudly, her eyes darting down as she tries to conceal her annoyance. "It doesn't matter why."

"Oh, c'mon," I chide. "Why are you keeping something so simple a secret?"

She taps her fingers on her flute, thinking something through. "I'm not interested in being anyone's girlfriend," she fesses up. Then, looking at me, her confused gaze zooms at the growing smile on my face. "What?"

"That's something I can relate to." Leaning closer to her, I point my glass toward Tatiana, and say discreetly enough, "You see that girl over there with the flower dress?" Roxanne starts narrowing her eyes, focusing on Tatiana who's standing on the other side of the terrace with Dan. "She's had a crush on me since she was fifteen, and since then my dad hasn't stopped pushing me to date her."

"She's pretty," Roxanne comments politely. "Why have you never given her a chance?"

"Well, the official answer is that I'm not interested in being anyone's boyfriend and I know that's exactly what she wants." My eyes rest on hers again and I find myself smiling at her attentive and curious gaze. "But the truth is she isn't my type."

"What's your type, then?" I wasn't expecting her to pose such a question, and it's hard not to chuckle a bit. "I mean, because I might know someone who is."

My eyes lock on hers, and it's getting hard to keep on a proper conversation, but I make a conscious effort to do so. "Well, I like them older, more mature, less naive and shy, and…" My smile turns into a devilish smirk as I think over my next set of words. "Preferably with short blonde hair looking like a femme fatale who's about to eat me alive." Roxanne huffs at me, head shaking in amusement. "Do you know someone like that?"

She keeps shaking her head, before wetting her lips on the bubbly in a failed attempt to contain her laugh. "You are very funny, aren't you?"

"I try, I try…" Her eyes are glowing with amusement, and her laugher is everything I needed right now to lower my voice and say, "Why don't we leave this crappy event behind and go somewhere else?"

She sucks in a breath, her eyes widening at my question. "You can't be serious."

"Why not?"

I watch her gaze drifting away as she tries to come up with an excuse. "Because I'm here for a friend, and as tempting as it is, I won't be going anywhere with the son of his boss." Her tone is prim and proper and it just makes her even more charming.

Oh, so that's why she is much more on her guard now? "I'm sure Karl would understand," I tell her already taking her champagne out of her hand and giving the two glasses to the waiter that passes by.

Roxanne gapes at my audacity, her brows furrowing on me. "I won't go anywhere," she insists as I take her hand. "Andries!" But I'm already leading her toward the exit of the terrace when…

"Ah! Here you are!" my dad says cheerfully as he walks toward us, emerging from nowhere, accompanied by Karl.

What the fuck are they doing here?

Karl stares suspiciously at both of us and more precisely at my hand still holding hers. "Roxie, it's getting late, shall we?"

"Roxie?" I repeat, unable to take the amusement off my tone.

She frees her hand from my mine, smoothing her dress, and starts to follow Karl and my dad as they head toward the exit of the terrace. "Goodbye, Andries."

Before she can leave my side though, I reach for her wrist, forcing her to face me one last time. "You are leaving without giving me your number?"

"I said goodbye." And yet, she isn't moving.

"I'm wounded." While my tone is pretty amused, in reality, I'm truly shocked she isn't giving it to me. I mean, I gave her mine yesterday.

"Oh I'm sure you'll manage."

After releasing her, I remain standing like an idiot watching her joining my dad and Karl as they take the stairs to go down to where their car is parked. I swallow the lump on my throat, still processing what just happened.

"So…" Dan lets his word trails off as he comes in and stands beside me, he's already drinking another glass of burgundy, and looks totally delighted. "Should I send you the invite to my party to your new address in Amsterdam or here?"

I go stand by the balustrade and from there I watch Roxanne and Karl bidding farewell to my dad and then getting into the black sedan. The engine starts roaring and a few seconds later, my gaze follows the car moving away until it disappears from my sight. "I can't believe she didn't give me her number."

"First time a woman told you no?"

"First time," I mumble, my eyes still on the horizon.

"Well, that's worth celebrating."

CHAPTER 6

Roxanne

We might have left the Van den Bosch estate, but his presence hasn't left my mind. Oh jeez, what happened to me? I was literally about to go off somewhere with a total stranger. And to do what? This was work for fuck's sake! Work! Karl is paying me to accompany him, not to run away and get all cozy with his boss's son. How unprofessional!

"That was an incredible night, wasn't it?" Karl's smooth and pleasant voice breaks the awkward silence that has filled the space between us since we left.

"It was lovely, yes," I say, matching his tone. Without waiting any further, I ask, "Did your meeting with Sebastian go well?"

"It was great, yeah, he offered me a new position at the company, so I'm happy."

"That's amazing," I cheer him up excitedly, giving him a light touch on his arm. "Congratulations, then!"

Karl just smiles at me in return, before he voices a quick, "Thanks."

Nothing but the engine of the car can be heard as we continue the drive quietly for the next few minutes. Then Karl exhales louder than usual, and for some reason, he lays his pensive eyes on me.

"Can I ask you something?"

"You just did," I reply playfully.

But Karl remains just as serious. "Why were you holding Andries' hand?"

My heart falls to my knees at his question, I instantly avert my gaze and look down, frozen. "I wasn't." My voice is small, so I pause to gather myself and looking at Karl in the eye, I say, "That boy was just tipsy and trying to drag me out of the terrace with him so I was just stopping him."

His face remains stern without the trace of a smile to be seen. He brings a finger to his lips, looking pensively out of the window. "He seems to like you." He drops his comment like a bomb, and I don't know what to make of it. "Who wouldn't?" he chuckles at his rhetorical question, but I feel my heart pulsing hard inside my chest in anticipation at his next set of words. "Maybe that's not a bad idea, after all."

My brows rise up in surprise. "What do you mean?"

"Well, getting closer to him," he says. "It's a great contact to have."

"I'm not interested," I interpose straight away.

"Don't see it like that." He shifts in his seat, turning his body toward me. "One day he might be my boss, who knows." But I cut eye contact, my gaze returning to my window, feigning disinterest. "This is not the type of person you meet every day at the bar, Roxie. He's the fucking heir of the company I work for. That's a great contact to have," he points out once more. "Did you get his number at least?"

"I didn't," I lie. "And I'm not interested in fomenting a relationship with him for the sake of advancing your career."

"That could have been a great opportunity though," he points out with some regret in his tone. Then a few beats of silence ensue, until Karl crosses the line. "Does he know you are—"

"Of course not," I interpose, cutting him off. "And don't you dare tell him. Otherwise—"

"Don't worry," he reassures straight away. "Your secret is safe with me." He motions locking up his mouth with his hand and throwing away the key.

I dip my head between my hands, rubbing my eyelids with my fingers.

"Are you okay?"

"Hmm," I mumble. "Just tired."

The car finally comes to a halt and looking out of his window, I notice we've finally arrived at my place. I'm about to kiss him goodbye when he says, "Poppy told me to get you home by no later than midnight. But…" he lets his words trail off, his eyes filled with lust, considering me. "Is there a way we can extend it?"

"Not tonight, Karl," I answer, my tone assertive but not harsh, just before leaning in and giving him a kiss on the cheek. "You've been invoiced for four hours of escorting service, nothing more."

"I know, but—"

"Not tonight. I'm sorry." The driver opens my door and seeing the disappointment on Karl's face, I say, "I'm really tired. Let's meet next week."

The corner of his lips slightly curve up at my comment, but the sadness in his eyes is still very present. I stroke his stubble slightly, trying to end the night on a better tone. And seeing how he shuts his eyes to revel himself on my touch, I decide to lean in and press my lips on his for a good night kiss. "See you in a few days," I whisper warmly.

Then I make my way out and head to my apartment. It might already be midnight but the truth is I'm not tired—I just didn't want to sleep with him, which is ridiculous since Karl is my best paying client.

Reaching my apartment, I take off my heels, heaving a long sigh of relief, and walk bare foot on the marble floor to the bathroom. There I take off my dress, my earrings, and my underwear.

"Why don't we leave this crappy event behind and go somewhere else?" I hear his question replaying in my head. His warm voice caresses my skin, sparking a vicious throb between my legs. I try to shut him out, turning the water on. Then I get into the shower, and let the drops fall on my skin like the rain. Here, alone between the four walls of my shower, I shut my eyes, and let my mind wander under the steam. If Karl hadn't walked in, where would Andries have taken me? To his bedroom? No, most likely not. Probably to the beautiful gardens that stretched for miles, maybe we'd have roamed around under the dark night while getting to know each other. Jeez, I didn't even remember to ask him if he managed to switch programs. But I do remember how I

left him so abruptly. I still feel a pang in my heart to have refused to give him my number. I know I did what I had to. There's no regret to be found in my decision. But here, alone in the privacy of my shower, I can let my fantasies go wild and picture the cheeky smile on his face as I'd have taken his phone and added my contact details. My lips instantly twist into a smile as I recall having his.

I could text him, just to wish him goodnight.

Oh gosh! A flutter hits my stomach at the idea. Fuck! It's so ridiculous! I spend all week long with men, why do I have to think about one when I'm in the shower? I take some of my rose-infused body wash and focus on the present moment, and get myself mentally ready for my weekend in the country side with Isaak. According to Poppy, he'll pick me up by ten a.m. which is early enough to make sure I don't occupy my mind with useless reverie.

* * *

It's Saturday afternoon in the beautiful village of Giethoorn. Rays of sunshine beam on the carpet and low table, keeping my tea and mini club sandwiches warm while I'm sitting on the cozy velvet sofa and reading *Anna Karenina* from Tolstoy—both a classic and a cliché but it's Isaak's favorite novel and despite having read it once in high school, he asked me to read it again so we could discuss it. I've never quite understood how a woman like Anna could sacrifice and risk everything for a man though. "*Love. The reason I dislike that word is that it means too much for me, far more than you can understand.*" A gasp of air expels from my lungs as I shift in

ROXANNE.

my seat and turn the page. Isaak is out to walk his dog, and I know between sex and cuddles, he loves to see me reading his favorite novel. It's like a fetish to him. Not sure if it's because he married a woman who couldn't finish the damn book or what, but it gives him a tremendous sense of satisfaction when he sees me focused on it.

I nearly jump out of my skin when the loud ringtone of my iPhone comes from nowhere, stabbing at the silent air that fills the room. I stand up and go pick it from my purse that is lying on the armchair. As I check who's calling, I notice it's a number I don't have saved in my contacts. Well, that's odd, but I'm just too curious not to pick it up. After all, it can be something important.

"Hello?"

"Roxanne *Feng*, now that's a beautiful surname," I hear someone with an amused tone saying from the other side of the line.

Holy shit! I recognize that voice! I suck in a breath, my hand reaching up to hold my mouth for a second.

"I can't believe it!" I snap, before I start storming around the room in a failed attempt to calm myself down. "How did you—"

"I asked Karl," Andries interposes, his tone playful. For some stupid reason, his joy brings a smile to my lips. "It was too easy."

"How dare you?" My mind is now filled with dread as I look at the front door across the hallway. Jeez! Isaak will be back home anytime soon. "You are so—"

"Persistent? Smart? Decisive?" Andries, on the other hand, seems totally delighted, reveling in my distress.

"Rude!"

"Alright, I'll take it as a valid option."

"What do you want?" I try to hurry the phone call, my heartbeat speeding up at the idea of Isaak walking in and hearing me.

"Have dinner with me." His tone is calm but decided. Actually, I realize it wasn't even a question! "What about Thursday?"

I huff instantly. "You are totally delusional. Is this how guys your age behave now?"

"Guys my age?" he repeats, his tone dripping with amusement. "You mean older men don't ask you out? Well, that would explain a lot."

"Not interested," I lie, but it's better that way. "Goodbye." And it takes everything in me to stop this conversation to go any further.

After hanging up, I remain motionless, processing everything that just happened. Did Andries really invite me to have dinner with him?

I chuckle at the idea of going out with a man for free. *Nope. Not happening.*

Since Isaak hasn't arrived yet, I decide to quickly give Karl a call to get to the bottom of it. The ringtone goes on, and on, until he finally answers. Once I hear his voice, I go straight to the point.

"May I know why you gave Andries my number?" I ask, nearly scolding. "The boy just called to invite me out, for fuck's sake!"

"He asked you out?" Karl sounds surprised.

"Yes! You didn't have to give him my number," I tell him.

Despite my anger, there's a beat of silence from the other side. "And what did you say?"

"I said no, of course!" I snap in a whisper, taken aback at his question.

"Why not?"

I blink a few times, trying to understand his attitude. "Karl, I get your motivations, but I'm not interested in helping you out on that."

"I see," he says, his words trailing off as he seems to be considering me. "What if I pay you to go and have dinner with him?"

"What?" *Did he lose his mind or what?*

"You don't understand; in a decade or two, Sebastian is gonna step down as CEO and his son will most likely take over." *He can't be serious! So that's what he has in mind?* "Imagine if he is your friend by then!"

How can I tell him that I don't care in a nice, polite way? "If you want I can ask him to go and have dinner with you?" I propose instead, since he's so interested in getting closer to the son of his boss.

"With me?" he repeats before bursting off in laugher. "He isn't interested in me, my dear, he's interested in *you*."

"In me?" I repeat in a murmur, finding myself lost for words at his statement, but my heart does a little somersault in response.

"Of course in you!" Karl replies with mirth. "What else would he invite you for?"

It takes some strength in me to say, "Yes, but I'm not interested." My words are there, but the conviction in them is totally non-existent. Before Karl try once more to persuade me, I take a deep breath, and clear my throat making my tone more assertive. "Don't ever give my phone number out again without my permission. Are we clear?"

He lets out a sigh in annoyance, but doesn't protest. "Yes, ma'am."

"Perfect. Thanks!" I hear a key turning on the locker of the front door, so I hurry myself to end the phone call. "Well, I've got to go. Speak soon." Then I bury my phone inside my purse and head back to the couch, cracking open the novel I was reading.

"Slow down, Bob!" Isaak shouts as his French bulldog runs in my direction, ready to jump on me for a bit of attention. I play along, greeting Bob and talking to him. But Bob seems to be a bit limited in the language department so I look at Isaak and ask him some questions.

"How was the walk?"

"It was great, we saw another bulldog there so Bob was all excited." Leash in hand, Isaak slowly paces in our direction, his tall posture always so impressive, before disappearing into the kitchen. His dog follows suit, knowing he'll find food there.

I heave a long sigh of relief when Bob finally leaves the couch, and smooth my dress out. Then my eyes drift back to the novel and I continue my read.

"So how is the reading going?" I lift my head to meet with Isaak's enquiring face, a tulip glass in hand filled with Jenever. He gives a first sip, sitting beside me on the armchair. I've known him for five years, and literature has always been one of his favorite subjects. Maybe that's why he's remained one of my long-lasting clients. Instead of taking me to social events like Karl does, Isaak has always preferred romantic face-to-faces where we can listen to music, read, go on treks, and talk about literature.

"It's going alright," I say, my voice soft. "I should be done in a few days."

He considers me attentively. "If it's too boring, we can just watch the movie."

I snort, shaking my head. "It's alright, I've read worse."

A small smile spreads across his lovely face. "You aren't fan of the plot, huh?"

"It's just…" I try to find the best words to put on, reminding myself it's his favorite novel, but it's not that easy.

"Go ahead," Isaak demands, sitting back on his armchair, his face laced with curiosity. "Tell me the truth."

"Well," I begin cautiously. "I like Levin and Dolly, but I just can't sympathize with Anna, so it's hard for me to connect and enjoy the whole story."

His eyes widen in surprise. "Why don't you like her?"

"I think she's pathetic," I tell Isaak, my bluntness catching him off guard. "Everything she does for Vronsky, I mean, it's clear this affair was going nowhere. The boy was there just to have fun, with barely any risk for him. She, on the other hand, risked everything—her social position, her financial stability, her marriage, her honor, the custody of her child."

He takes a sip as I speak, clearly engrossed in the subject. "The things one does for love," he says, pausing for a beat. "Who can blame her?"

"This isn't love," I correct him, before I could even think. "It's lust, pure escapism from a dull high status life." Despite my harsh opinion, Isaak seems to revel in the conversation, his eyes twinkling. "I'd rather read about a hard working woman who makes her way to the top on her own than a rich woman destroying herself for '*love*.'"

"So you think she should have stayed and been miserable?"

"Vronsky himself told Anna their relationship would lead to misery. We always think the grass is greener on the other side, but that's not always the case," I tell him.

I keep observing Isaak, his dark-brown eyes drifting away as he processes my words and it's in that moment that it hits me—maybe Isaak is considering a divorce from his wife, and he relates much more to Anna as a character than I do. After all, *he* is the one having an affair, not me. He's the one risking his marriage and everything it entails by being with me. But the big difference is that he's paying me for the fantasy of being his lover. Anna and Vronsky were allegedly both equally in love with each other.

"By the end, it'll make sense." His voice is soft, and he finishes his drink before standing up. "We'll talk more once you're done." He then walks toward me and leans just enough to pin a chaste kiss on my head. "I'll be right back."

Oh jeez… As he leaves the living room, my heart squeezes a bit at the idea Isaak could've caught feelings for me over the years. That's one of the problems with long-term clients, they usually mistake my performance as a girlfriend with reality.

CHAPTER 7

Andries

I check my iPhone once more to make sure it wasn't a connection problem or that I hadn't run out of battery, but nope. It truly was Roxanne who'd hung up on me. I'm still laughing at my screen and at the two minutes conversation we just had—the funniest two minutes of my day actually.

While everyone is getting ready for the fencing class, I remain wondering why she is playing so hard to get. I mean, if that Karl hadn't reappeared on the terrace during my party, she was most likely down to go with me to a quieter place and God knows how the evening would have played out.

"Andries?" I hear Dan calling from the other side of the locker room. "Are you ready?"

I glance around the room, noticing we are the last ones. While he's already fully equipped, with his white jacket and breeches on, I'm still finishing putting mine on.

"One minute," I tell him, before shoving my phone into my bag and taking my jacket instead.

"Still thinking about that chick, huh?" I can't hide the growing smirk spreading across my face as he says so. "Damn, forget her, man. It's the second time she's rejected you now. Like just move on."

"That's the problem," I disclose as I put my gloves on. "I don't want to."

Dan huffs, shaking his head while we take our respective foils and masks. "There are tons of women out there. No need to waste your time with that one."

We head outside the locker room and cross the hallway, holding our foils in one hand and our masks in the other. Dan pushes the door onto the vast gymnasium and we find our team already lined up and in position and Coach Edgar, standing tall as he gives the first instructions.

My attention goes to the other side of the gym where a few young women are sitting. Some are wearing their fencing uniforms while others are dressed casually. And to my greatest surprise…

"What's flower-girl doing here?" I snap in a whisper to Dan, who's already looking at one of the girls.

"I don't know," he says, but it sounds like a lie. "Maybe she came here to see you."

Dan hastens himself and leaves my side to go and join the rest of the group. I try my best to avoid looking at Tatiana, but I feel her gaze following my every move.

Damn it! I'm sure it was Dan. How else could she have found out that I was here?

I reach the rest of the team, greet the coach with a quick nod, and we finally get started.

* * *

The class might have taken around fifty minutes, but it was hard to remain focused when you have cheerleaders on the bench. How come Coach Edgar didn't mind them? Fortunately, now that the class is over, I can't wait to head back to the locker room, get changed, and just go home. After taking off our fencing masks, Dan and I shake hands with a few other lads, before following them toward the door.

Suddenly though, I feel him putting a hand on my shoulder, stopping me in my tracks. "Where are you going?" I hear Dan asking from behind me.

I turn around and say, "Well, I'm gonna change."

Dan shakes his head in amusement, and abruptly grabs my arm pushing me in direction to the bench. "Don't be so rude," he snaps amid a quick snort. "Flower girl wants to talk to you."

"Fuck off," I retort, trying to stop him, but Dan is already draping an arm around my shoulders to make sure I can't escape.

"Jessica, Tatiana!" he shouts, most likely to embarrass me. *What a fucking asshole!*

I'm left with no option but to smile at them for the sake of politeness. The last thing I need is for Tatiana to tell her dad how mean and rude Andries van den Bosch is. Heck, the old man wouldn't wait a second to go and rant about me to my own dad. Guess that's what happens when your pops is close friends and business associates with flower-girl's dad.

"Hi Andries," she says with her usual sugary tone once we reach them. "What a great performance that was. You're really talented."

I press my lips tight to suppress a laugh. Dan, on the other hand, just snorts at her stupid comment.

"Have you heard that, Andries?" Dan is already teasing. "You had a great performance with your foil."

I huff, shaking my head at this dumbass and his joke.

"Thanks," I answer, not knowing what else to say or do. "Um, are you also a fencer?" It's the first thing I thought of. "I've never seen you here before."

"No, but Jessica is so I came here to see her."

"Right," I mutter, already dreaming of running away.

"I'm starving," Dan comments, and he's finally switched his arm support from mine to Jessica's. "Should we go and eat something, the four of us?"

"Sounds great!" Tatiana doesn't hide her enthusiasm. And at this point it's clear Dan and Jessica had pre-arranged this little meet-up.

I glare at Dan, who pays no attention to it, and knowing I've got no choice in the matter, I give Tatiana a pleasant smile and voice a quick, "Sure."

Not surprisingly, the restaurant we head to, Hap Hmm—which has been dishing up traditional Dutch cuisine since 1935—has a table for four already waiting for us.

Since Dan and I are regular patrons, the owner himself shows up to welcome me back after being out of the country for a year. The place is just as cozy as I remember, with its rounded white tables, gold-colored velvet booths and brown leather chairs.

A good lounge playlist makes the environment even more pleasant and I can't help but wonder what Roxanne is doing tonight. Is she heading out with friends like I'm doing? Is she spending the evening in Amsterdam too? Jeez, if only I could go and have a drink with her.

After we are all seated at our table, a waitress comes in, handing us our menus. While everyone is attentively checking the specials of the day, I take my iPhone discreetly out of my pocket, open the messaging app, and type: *Are you in Amsterdam tonight?*

I look for a few seconds at the question, wondering if Roxanne will reply or just ignore me. Well, there's only one way to find out…

After choosing the recipient and pressing *Send*, my attention goes to Tatiana, who's sitting beside me

"Have you ever tried the steak with pepper sauce?" she asks, leaning slightly toward me.

"Yep, it's pretty good," I tell her. "Actually, that's what I'm gonna order."

A few minutes ensue before my iPhone finally beeps with a new notification. Oh gosh! My heart bounces with excitement as I take it, unlock the screen, and check the new message.

I'm not. Goodbye.

But I froze just as fast after reading her answer. For fuck's sake, why is she playing so hard to get for a simple meetup? I lock the screen, and shove the phone back into my pocket upon hearing Dan calling my name.

"Are you ready to order?" he asks.

I notice the waitress standing beside him, a notepad and pen in hand and everyone around the table looking at me.

"I am." My gaze drops to the menu, and for some reason, my appetite for the steak is gone.

* * *

While I'm physically present at the table, my mind has been far away, ruminating whether I should text her back or not. Part of me want to, but the other one wants to follow Dan's advice and move on. My hand is inside my pocket, more precisely on my phone and the indecision is killing me.

I hate that feeling of holding yourself back from texting someone when that's all you want to do. Her little game doesn't make sense though. Why is she avoiding me like this? What's holding her back?

Heck, fuck it!

Amid the boring dinner, I decide to take my phone out and discreetly text the woman I can't stop thinking about once again: *Are you seriously gonna decline a simple coffee with me?*

I press *Send*, not expecting an answer any time soon, but at least it's said and done.

To my greatest surprise, before I can even shove the phone back inside my pocket, I hear a few beeps and a notification pops up.

You said dinner over the phone. Not coffee.

My eyes widen at her statement. *So does a coffee work?* I ask her straight away, excitement bouncing hard inside my chest.

And then nothing.

Three dots miraculously shows up on the chat, letting me know she's typing something. I can hear my pulse throbbing in my ears as I keep waiting for her answer.

C'mon! Send the damn text.

But the three dots disappear causing a pang to my heart. A gasp of air expels from my lungs, and I lean back on my chair, trying to be patient.

I have to think first, she finally answers.

Fuck. I press my lips tight at her message, my stomach tightening in frustration. It's just coffee! What does she have to think about? I take in a deep breath, refocusing.

It's coffee, I text back. *Not a marriage proposal.*

"Andries?"

I look up at Dan, who seems to be ordering a digestive or something.

"Do you want a glass of Jenever too?"

I remain silent for a moment, my mind still dwelling on her replies. I've never met such a difficult woman before. What is she so afraid of? "Eh, yeah. Why not?" I'm definitely gonna need a drink to prepare myself for her next answer. As I come to think of it, our back-and-forth feels like I'm negotiating a million-euro deal.

The notification sound nearly startles me, but I can't bring myself to check it right now. I've got the feeling she's gonna decline, and I don't want to face her rejection without a glass of Jenever in hand to help digesting the news.

"You've been so silent," Tatiana points out, her voice so small I can barely hear it. "Is everything okay?"

"Just work," I tell her, making that up, before I lock the screen and put the phone face down next to my plate setting.

"Oh," she utters, her chestnut eyes widening in surprise. She shifts in her seat, turning her body toward me. I notice she's sporting a casual dress with a deep v-neck which isn't usual for her, plus her brown hair is pulled back in a high ponytail giving an unobstructed view to her cleavage, but I refocus my attention on her gaze. "You are also doing an internship at your dad's company, right?"

"Yep," I promptly say, my fingers playing with the base of my empty wine glass. "Are you still working at yours?"

Tatiana nods, a polite smile spreading across her lips, but there's some sadness lacing her features too.

"Do you like working there?" I press on, forcing myself to continue making eye contact.

"It's alright," she says, shrugging. "Dad's so happy to have me there though." She tries to cover her sadness with a bubbly tone, but it's just too obvious.

"So that's the end goal?" She cocks her head to the side in confusion. "Working at your dad's company to make him happy?" The question simply rolls off my tongue, and I'm already regretting it when she breaks eyes contact, frowning.

"Eh…"

"Your glass of Jenever, sir," the waitress informs as she steps in, placing the glass in front of me.

I thank her, and without further ado, take a first gulp while Tatiana remains speechless, her eyes down on her lap as she ponders my question.

"Don't feel obligated to answer," I tell her.

Tatiana gives me another polite smile and a nod in agreement, before her attention switches back to Jessica.

With her being busy with her friend, I decide to get some courage and face Roxanne's answer once and for all. I unlock my screen, take a deep breath in, and check the notification.

Fine. 1 coffee. 10 mins. I can do Monday, Sept 6, at 5 p.m.

Holy shit! My lips twist into a smile up to my ears as I read the first part. *And then you delete my number.* But I drop it right after reading the rest.

1 coffee. 20 mins, I decide to reply.

And what about the last part? she texts back.

I exhale a bit louder than usual, annoyed at her request. Fuck. I can't believe she really wants me to delete her number. But why? Anyway, after meeting her again on Monday, I'm pretty sure she's gonna forget about this nonsense. *Deal,* I say. *Let's meet at the Van Rijn, then.*

Okay, see you Monday.

I heave a long sigh, before cheering at myself to have made it. I take another sip of my drink, unable to hide my growing smirk. It might take a whole week, but at least I'm finally gonna sit down and see her again.

Two hands abruptly landing on my shoulders pull me back from my thoughts. "Are you ready to make a move?" Dan asks.

I glance around the table and it seems like everyone is ready to go. Well, this dinner didn't end up as boring as I thought it would. "Always."

CHAPTER 8

Amsterdam, September 6, 2021
Roxanne

I should've said no, plain and simple. And yet, for some stupid reason that is beyond my comprehension, I didn't. A gush of air rolls off my lips as I stroll through the street where Van Rijn is located. I've been to this restaurant-bar a fair amount of times—after all, it's pretty well-known—but I've never felt this anxious before. Maybe because I'm normally paid to have dinner there with clients, all I hope is that no one from work is gonna be there today. My heart rate picks up as I step inside the establishment and am greeted by the hostess who recognizes me instantly. To my surprise though, it isn't as busy as usual, and I find a lot of empty tables around. I pace slowly across the restaurant, until I go to the lounge area where a black grand piano stands in the middle. Green velvet armchairs and small black tables surround the piano and the glass wall at the end provides much-needed light.

I stop in my tracks when my eyes land on him, perched at a corner table behind the piano and against the glass window. Andries hasn't seen me yet, since he remains focused on the book he's reading. His locks of thick brown hair fall on the edge of his brows and his eyes are slightly narrowed as he turns the page and continues reading with a seriousness I find particularly mesmerizing. It feels like I'm sneaking into his private world and the idea of it is more alluring that I'd like to admit.

He's sporting a navy blue sweater, sleeves rolled up to his elbows, paired with slim jeans and white sneakers; casual elegance as its finest. Even the way he's sitting on that chair is worthy of being photographed.

Enough, woman!

I straighten myself, take a deep breath and slowly start walking in his direction, wondering how I will break the ice between us after our awkward phone call.

As I get close enough to his table, I say, "So, did you manage to get into the English program?"

His lips form a slow, sexy twist and his eyes sparkle when they meet mine again, but he doesn't say a word in return. Instead, he shuts his book closed and puts it aside on the table. "Hi Roxanne," he answers, his voice curling around my name with sultry confidence. "Have a seat." He gestures me to sit in front of him, so I push the green velvet armchair, lowering myself into it. Before I can say something else, though, he waves at the waitress that is passing by and she stops at our table.

"Espresso?" he asks, looking at me.

I just nod, still a bit perturbed he didn't answer my question.

"Two please," he says to the waitress, before she gives him a quick sharp nod of the head and leaves our side.

An odd silence settles between the two of us, and while I'm shifting in my seat trying to avert my gaze, Andries just leans back on his chair, his eyes pinned on me as if he's reveling in my uneasiness.

"So?" I decide to press on, since his gaze remains pinned on me and I can nearly taste the amusement in it.

"Today was actually my first day of college," he announces. "And I'm glad I'm marking the day with you."

"Oh," I utter, unable to not smile at the compliment.

"And, um, yes, Mr. Lewis accepted me into the English program," he says, "so I guess we are also celebrating."

I suck in a breath at the news. "That's amazing, then!"

Before I can proceed, though, the waitress steps in with our two espressos and places them in front of us.

Once she walks away, we both lean in, and I instinctively rest my forearms on the table as I watch Andries take a first sip of his coffee without adding any sugar. Looking him in the eye, I put on a humorous tone and ask, "Why are we celebrating with coffee, then?"

His brows rise up in confusion "Why?" he repeats, his voice laced with sarcasm, before checking his watch. "Well, maybe because we have only eighteen minutes together and sadly I don't think that's enough to open a bottle."

"Maybe not a bottle, but we can certainly drink a glass." And with that said, I turn around, call the waitress, and once I have her attention, I order two flutes of bubbly.

"Did you ask what Champagne it is though?" a worried Andries interposes immediately.

I can't help but frown at his question. "Eh, does it matter?"

"Would you rather sip on mediocre bubbly that leaves a bad after taste in your mouth, or indulge in a crisp, refreshing high-quality Champagne?"

He sounds dead serious about it and the look on his face is enough to make me bite the corner of my mouth, so I don't laugh. But my stomach gives it away, and I let out a snort. "I guess the later."

"Excuse me?" he says a bit louder to the same waitress I spoke to a few seconds ago. She leaves the counter, and walks back to our table, a slight annoyance in her demeanor. "Two glasses of Dom Pérignon, please."

"We only sell Champagne by the bottle, but we have an Australian sparkling wine by the glass."

My jaw drops at the idea it was Australian sparkling wine that I was about to give to the heir of the Van den Bosch family and I can't help but laugh at the thought of it.

"See?" Andries says, his face softening amid my laugher. "That doesn't seem much like Champagne to me, now does it?" His attention returns to the waitress and he proceeds, "We'll take the bottle then."

"Andries, no!" I interpose immediately, my amusement switching into worry. "We only have time for one glass."

"I know that." And he gives a sharp nod to the waitress that retrieves back to the bar. "I met your friend, by the way," he adds casually, before finishing his espresso.

I blink twice in confusion. "My friend?"

"Yes, um, Professor Josianne van Aartsen? She's my English Linguistics teacher."

"Oh, yes," I answer, a slight worry in my tone, and then lowering my voice, I ask, "Did she recognize you?"

His lips twist into one of his signature sexy smile. "It's hard to tell, but, um, she was constantly looking at me, so I don't know. Probably."

"It's hard not to." Holy shit! I bite my tongue but it's too late, Andries is already smirking at my comment. "I mean, you're tall, blue eyes, kinda cute..." I let my words trail off as it feels like I'm only digging a deeper hole right now.

Andries reclines himself on his chair, crossing his arms over his chest in amusement as he keeps watching me. "So if I'm all of that, how come you have been avoiding me like the plague?"

I knew he'd ask me that, so heaving a long sigh, I say, "Because I know what this is all about." He shoots me an arched eyebrow, and I find myself torn between developing my statement or not. "I'm just not into it."

"I'm not interested in getting laid," he states firmly. "That's not who I am."

"Oh, really?" I can't help but scoff at his answer as I finish my espresso. "So what were you dragging me out of the terrace for?"

"To be with you," he says, like it was the most obvious thing in the world.

I chuckle, shaking my head at his attitude. "And to do what?"

"To talk, of course."

"Yeah, right," I mutter, unconvinced. "No man ever wants to just talk."

From the corner of my eye, I notice the waitress approaching our table with the bottle of Dom Pérignon and two flutes, and a colleague of hers bringing an ice bucket with a stand.

"Well, I'm serious. I just wanted to get to know you." He sounds rather honest, but I mean, he can easily be a professional liar. Who knows? I've known men my whole life and some are particularly good liars. "And to spend time with you." The waitress and her colleague are now standing in front of us, and as we watch her opening the bottle of Dom Pérignon, our conversation fades away for a bit. There is a discreet popping noise as the bottle is opened, then a crackling, fizzing sound as the bubbly is poured and the effervescence whooshes into the glass. She then gives us our respective flutes and put the bottle into the ice bucket. "Enjoy," she says, before walking away with her colleague.

With the glass in his hand, Andries resumes the conversation. "So, yeah, all I wanted was to be in your presence, Ms. Feng."

His charming tone makes me laugh. *What a player he is.* "Well, I don't usually do that either."

There's the trace of a smile forming at the corner of his lips. "Looks like you are making an exception today," he points out, raising his glass in a toast. "To exceptions."

I'm sure this is a game to him—scoring an older woman so that he can go and brag about to his friends. Let's be real, he's just a rich kid in college wanting to have some fun. That's all this is about. Actually, he'd have been a good fit as a client to one my girls. But that would imply exposing Karl and myself and I'm not gonna take the risk.

"To you, Andries," I say instead, raising my glass. "And to you having managed to switch to English."

We then take our first sip in silence, and I must say, while I have drank enough champagne to last my whole life, the bubbles feel like crystalline pearls on the palate, and it tastes intensely bready with crisp apple and melon characteristics throughout. Absolutely delicious!

"Better than sparkling wine?"

"I think so," I tell him, wondering if I made some moaning sound as I drank.

"Perfect." He then reclines back for a moment, taking in the view. "Now care to develop why you didn't like getting your bachelor's in English?" My jaw nearly drops at his question, and before I can say a word, he adds, "You said it was a long story."

His question catches me totally off guard. "Did I?"

"*We'd need much more than a few minutes to talk about it,*" he repeats word for word, exactly what I had told him on campus.

Oh shit. This is so damn personal! I pause for a moment, thinking of an answer that doesn't reveal too much. "Well, let's say most career options that I had back then weren't great," I tell him sincerely, brushing over every personal detail I can think of. "The thing is, a degree in English isn't gonna land you a well-paying job, but I don't think you care about that, so…"

"I want to be a writer," he discloses. "I know it's a risky career decision, but I've written for as long as I can remember and I don't see myself doing anything else."

"Writer? You mean, for a magazine or something?"

"Poetry or play would be my go to," he says. "But I could also do literary fiction."

"And does your dad know about that?" I ask, a drop of humor in my tone.

"Of course not," he replies just as fast, a devilish smile gracing his lips. "He still thinks I'm gonna get a degree in business and then join him to manage his company." Andries then pauses, clearly thinking something through. "Wait—You don't work at my dad's company, do you?"

"Oh no, only Karl does." Silence settles between us and I'm pretty sure in that instant, Andries is waiting for me to disclose what an English graduate does for a living, so I take another gulp of champagne to find some courage and say, "I'm a librarian."

His brows rise up in surprise, before he blinks twice. "Really?"

It's actually what my sister used to do before her current job, but he doesn't need to know that. "I mean, I used to but now I'm working at one of the oldest bookstores in the country."

"That's super cool," he sounds genuinely excited for me. "Do you like it? Tell me about it."

"Well, the pay could be better," I tell him, remembering my sister's rant when she accepted the offer. She thought the pay would be at least double than what she was making as a librarian since it's commission-based, but unfortunately the bookshop makes hardly any sales these days. "We have first editions and rare collectibles you won't find anywhere else, though, so yeah, that's pretty cool."

Andries nods pensively, before pulling his iPhone out of his inner-pocket. "What's the name of the bookstore?"

I do my best to conceal my uneasiness as I try to come up with an excuse, unfortunately, only the truth seems to come out, "I, um, I don't think it's appropriate telling you where I work."

I'm expecting him to insist or even laugh at my answer, but to my surprise he just shrugs. "Alright, I guess I'll have to use Google to find out."

A quick scoff rolls off my mouth. "Let me guess, you gonna visit every single bookshop in the city to find me?"

Andries arches a sculptured, dark brow while I mute my chuckles behind my hand. "Not everything is about you, *Roxie*," he says, amusement thick in his tone. Then he finishes his glass of champagne and takes the bottle from the ice bucket to refill our glasses. "I just wanted to check those rare editions and collectibles you were talking about, that's all." I actually feel bad for not telling him the name of the bookstore, he seems to be someone who enjoys reading, but I simply can't risk it. "I can even go in on your days off if you are that worried."

For a moment, I forget to listen, and my mind is solely focused on his features and the shape forming on his beautiful lips as he speaks. This man could've been a model. I'm not even a photographer but I'd have loved to snap a few pictures of him, especially with this sweater matching the deep-blue of his eyes. Lucky Josianne who will get to see him so often.

"Are you thinking of changing jobs?" I blink twice as my mind process his new question. "If the pay isn't that good, are you thinking of leaving that bookstore?"

"I don't know, um, I'm actually saving to buy it." Holy shit! Why did I even tell him that? "I mean, I might have to apply for a loan, but I'd love to own it at some point." Not even Lili knows about my plan. Is it because of the alcohol that I'm speaking so freely or what?

"Do you think you can recover your investment?"

No idea. "I think so, the place is just badly managed and advertised," I tell him, despite knowing perfectly well how unprofitable independent bookshops are. "It could be so much better than what it currently is."

"How come you care so much about that bookstore though?"

His question squeezes my heart instantly. I know the answer, oh yes, but do I truly want to tell him about it? After all, I've never spoken about it to anyone. "Well, um, Mama and I used to go there when I was little." My voice is small and nearly quivering at the end as memories wash over me. "She loved that bookstore so much that she actually ended up working there for twenty-five years until she got back problems and had to retire a few years ago." I take a deep breath, trying to keep my composure, but each time I speak about Mama, a mix of emotions emerges from the bottom of my heart. "I know she'd have loved to buy it."

"That makes sense," he says, his eyes pinned on me, an appreciative smile spreading on his lips. "I can help you if you want."

"Absolutely not," I snap straight away.

"Why not?" he insists, his tone even. "I can lend you the money if you are having trouble getting a loan."

"It's very kind of you, but I'm sure I'll be able to get it on my own." The truth is I already have the money and I intend to buy the bookshop this year to offer it to Mama and Lili for Christmas. All I have left to do is talk to the owner and make the offer. I hope he's not as attached to that bookshop as we are.

"Is your mother from here?" he asks, his glass of Champagne already in his hand to give another sip.

I observe him attentively as he finishes his second glass, and lean in, I rest my forearms on the table and bring myself closer to him to murmur, "How come you have been asking me so many personal questions?"

He meets my inquisitive gaze with a delicious smile, his eyes even sparkle a bit and he also leans forward to get closer to me. "I told you," he says, matching my low tone. "I want to get to know you."

My lips part slightly at the warmth in his voice, and just for the sake of making this moment last, I wet my lips and ask, "But why?"

He keeps staring at my eyes like he could see my soul, and when it feels too much, I avert my gaze for a second, but his smile keeps getting bigger. "Because I like you, silly."

He says those five words without an ounce of shyness, as if it was obvious. *He barely knows me, but he likes me? What does that even mean?*

The ringtone of my smartphone breaks through the air, and recognizing the song, I know it's someone at the agency calling. "I'm sorry, um…" I reach for my purse and dig into it, pulling my phone out. Poppy's name flashes on the screen, and as I check the time, I realize we have already been here for half an hour. "Andries?" My eyes travel up to meet his and as we look at each other, I can tell he already knows what I'm about to say. "I have to go."

"Time's up." Despite the humor in his tone, the sadness and disappointment in his eyes causes a pang to my heart.

As if he could feel it, he immediately cuts eye contact, searching for the waitress, and then gestures for the check. Afterwards, his attention falls back on me and he says, "If you are in a hurry, you can go."

"Oh no, I can wait for you." In that instant, I wish I could tell him that I'd love to meet him again, that we could be friends and I could help him in his studies, given the fact I graduated from the same program. It'd be good to have friends outside my work-related network, and have someone who isn't part of that world. But the way his presence makes me feel— so vulnerable and exposed—isn't a good indicator to see him again. Do I really want to never see him again though?

Enough!

When the waitress comes over with the leather black check book and the terminal, I take my credit card as fast as he takes his. "Don't even try," I tell him. "The champagne was my idea, I'll pay for it."

He snorts, shaking his head in amusement. "Your idea was cheap sparkling wine, lady."

Since the waitress doesn't really know what to do with our hands extending our cards, I look at her and say, "It's on me."

"Absolutely not," Andries replies, focused on her. "I'm the one who ordered the bottle, remember?" Then turning to me, he adds, "And I'm the one who invited you."

"No, I'm the one who told you to meet me at 5 p.m.," I retort just as fast.

"But I chose the place," he interposes.

The waitress lets out an exasperated breath, still holding the check book in her hands. "What if you guys just split it?"

"We might be Dutch but that's no reason to go Dutch," Andries replies, before turning to me and saying, "I insist, truly."

"And I also insist," I tell him.

We hold each other gaze as if it was some sort of competition, until we finally crack laughing. "You can pay next time," Andries offers.

Yeah right… He knows perfectly well I had asked him to delete my number and that this is technically our last meet-up.

"We'll split then," I tell the waitress with a sharp nod of the head.

She smiles in return, most likely in relief that our little back and forth is finally over and proceeds to open the checkbook and do the math in her head.

"It's a hundred and twenty euros each, please," she states, before typing the amount on the terminal.

I simply tap my card on the wireless section and the payment goes through with a beep.

Andries huffs in displeasure while I smile proudly at him. "It's a fair middle ground," I say, knowing he's having none of it.

"Yeah, right," he mutters while paying his part.

We then stand up and make our way out. Despite my high heels, I feel tiny walking beside him. I mean, I know Dutch men are tall but damn, he's like a tower next to me.

"How is the weather up there?" I tease as he opens and holds the door for me to pass.

He cracks a beautiful smile, showing his perfectly aligned white teeth. "Always pleasant, and down there?"

"It's getting windy," I say once I step outside and face the fresh breeze of the evening. I tighten my coat around me and rub my hands together. Jeez, it's really getting cold. We should've stayed inside and had dinner, it'd have been so great.

"We should've had dinner," Andries laments as we start walking on the sidewalk.

"What?" How come he was thinking exactly the same thing as me? When he's about to repeat what he just said, I stop in my tracks and search for his gaze. "Andries," I say, my tone heavier than usual. He also stops and once I have his undivided attention, I continue. "Can you delete my number now?" Shock and confusion plasters his lovely face and it makes me feel horrible. He had just admitted he liked me and now I'm behaving like a monster. "I hate to do this, but we have an agreement."

"Sure," he mutters, his brows furrowed and his lips pressed in a straight line. He takes his phone out of his pocket and meeting my gaze again, he adds, "But first you're gonna have to look me in the eye and tell me you felt nothing at all between us."

I can't prevent my jaw from gaping at his request. I blink twice, totally lost. "I, um…"

"Just say it," he continues. "If everything was in my head, then I apologize for any inconvenience caused and I'll gladly delete your number and never bother you again."

Holy shit! His coldness is like a knife to my chest. "I…"

His eyes remain fixed on me as I try to finish my sentence. "So?"

The truth is I'm struggling to say the words he wants me to say. I did feel a connection between us, I'd be lying if I tell him otherwise. Yet, I have already lied to him so much…

"It's not that hard, is it?" he presses on, searching for my gaze. "Just say you felt nothing for me and I'll delete your number."

"I can't see you anymore," I decide to say instead, tilting my head back to meet his eyes.

He takes a step forward, closing the small gap between us, peering down at me. "Why not?"

His voice is low and warm, laced with genuine interest, and if I don't cut eye contact right now, I'd be just too damn tempted to tell him the truth. "I'm, eh… I'm not available."

He scoffs in return. "You've got a boyfriend, huh?"

Tell him yes! For fuck's sake, tell him yes! "I'm just not available," I repeat. He runs a hand over his hair, heaving a long sigh, most likely in frustration at my vague answers. "I'm sorry."

To my greatest surprise, I try to silence my pain by pressing myself against the warmth of his body and give him a hug. When I wrap my arms around him, Andries freezes, not knowing what to say or do, and it only makes things worse. So I release him, feeling I crossed some line, and decide to just go. "Goodbye, Andries," I say with a frown before walking away.

CHAPTER 9

Andries

Wow. Did she really just give me a hug and say goodbye? Like… for good? What the hell was that? This doesn't make any sense. My head is spinning, and not just because of the champagne.

I remain where I am, standing not too far from the restaurant, still under a wave of shock. Though the sudden abruptness of my ringtone pulls me back from my thoughts. Looking at the screen, I heave a long sigh, before answering the call.

"Are you on the way?" Mom asks immediately, her tone slightly worried. "We are already here."

"Oh shit!" I curse under my breath as I recall that this evening I'm supposed to move into my new apartment. "Eh, yeah, I'm nearly there, five minutes."

"Okay, hurry up, we don't have all day."

After hanging up, I refocus on retrieving my bike and then enter the location of the "perfect apartment" my parents found for me into the GPS. Luckily it seems to be just nine minutes from here. Yes, I'm moving today and no, I have never been there. Mom said it was perfect, and I trust her taste—especially above my father's.

Reaching the building, I'm pleased to see the historic facade, its beautiful ornamentation, and its double bay windows with balconies at the front. Since it's located right in front of the canals, the view from upstairs must be superb.

I call Mom to let her know I've arrived, and she instructs me to take the lift to the top floor. The building isn't too high—with only four floors—but it looks quite modern inside as if it has been renovated recently.

Once I arrive on the last floor, the elevator door opens and I realize I'm right inside the apartment. I furrow my brows in confusion as I see Mom, Dad, Dan, and another guy in suit I don't recognize.

"Hey!" Mom walks in my direction to welcome me.

"What is Dan doing here?" I wanted to say to Dad, but it felt inappropriate to treat him that way in public.

"Glad to see you too, pal," Dan snaps with sarcasm, feigning to be hurt.

"He came here to welcome you, of course," Mom answers, locking an arm with mine as she walks me into the open layout. "By the way, don't worry about the elevator—we just deactivated the PIN so you can set a new one. And there's also a secondary steel door that has a bolt lock. Pretty cool, huh?"

"And what if the lift doesn't work?" I ask.

"You can always take the stairs," my father comments, before we exchange a quick hug and a pat on the back. "How was your first day? Good?"

"It was decent," I tell him, wondering if he knows I switched programs.

I start taking in my surroundings when Mom decides to introduce me to the leasing agent who then gives us a full tour of the place.

"The entire apartment has a dark wooden herringbone floor with underfloor heating, a beautiful lighting plan, built-in speakers, home automation, alarm system, luxury bathrooms and kitchen and various custom-made closets," he states as we cross the kitchen, living room, and then take the stairs to go to the second floor of the apartment, leading us to the bedroom.

The room is of good size, smells brand new, and has an attractive high ceiling and gas fireplace. I notice my luggage is already here, standing by the closet, and it feels so damn weird. How could I have forgotten that today was move-in day?

"The high windows offer views over the canal houses and the high altitude gives you some good privacy," the leasing agent explains as he opens one of them to show off the view from the balcony.

The ensuite bathroom is fully executed in natural stone and features a spacious walk-in rain shower, separate toilet and double sink unit. I nod, liking everything I have seen so far.

"So what do you think?" Dad asks, a slight impatience in his tone as he paces toward me, his hands plunged in his pockets. "Your mom said you'd rather live in a historical building than in one of those ultra-modern flats closer to campus like your sister. Did she nail it or not?"

"It's great," I say, genuinely pleased. "I really like the area and the building itself is beautiful."

"The other two rooms have been converted into a gym and a study per your request," the agent says to my mom.

"Well, sounds like home," Pops comments. "My parents weren't that generous when I went to college."

"Sebastian," Mom chides in a low voice.

We go downstairs and head to the ample living room where the leasing agent explains me how the alarm system works, the security around the house, how to set up the PIN to access my floor, and explains a few more things regarding the garage—where I can park my car and store my bike safely. Once everything is said and done, we bid farewell to the agent, and only my parents and Dan remain.

"So, shall we go have dinner?" Mom asks, visibly excited. "Your sister is also coming."

"Oh, we have dinner planned?" I look at Mom and Dad, my tone surprised. "I didn't know that."

"It's a last-minute thing," Dad interposes as he gathers his coat. "Your mom's idea."

"It's to celebrate your move to Amsterdam," she states with a bright smile I can't match. She then puts her hands on my shoulders and staring right into my eyes, she observes me attentively. "Aren't you excited?"

"Yeah, I am," I reply, trying to put on a more enthusiastic tone. But after facing the weirdest rejection of my life, it's hard to be in a festive mood.

***

It's dark and cold when we leave the building, but nevertheless, we start walking down the sidewalk since the restaurant where Mom made a reservation is only a few minutes away. She starts strolling ahead with Dad, her arm interlocked on his, leaving Dan and I behind. And for some reason, Dan starts slowing down his pace even more as if to give us more privacy.

"So?" he begins, his hands plunged inside his coat pockets to keep them warm.

"So what?" I reply back, walking at the same snail pace as him.

"Why did you arrive so late?"

"I went for coffee," I say, my tone even.

"Alone?" he presses, looking smug.

I chuckle at his insistence. "Maybe not," I answer, keeping it short.

"Something tells me it has to do with the woman who was at your party…" he lets his sneaky remark hang in the air and I can't help but stop in my tracks for an instant as I process what he just said.

"How do you know that?" I finally ask him, searching for the truth in his gaze.

Dan stops, and, lowering his voice, he says, "Well, news certainly spreads fast in this family."

"We had coffee yes," I tell him. "But I don't want to talk about it." And I start walking again, quickening my pace.

Dan follows right behind and eventually catches me. "Why not?"

"Because it's…" I look in front to my parents who are still way ahead of us and my attention returns to him "… private."

"Fuck off!" Now it's Dan stopping in the middle of the sidewalk. "I always tell you everything."

But I keep walking on my own, ignoring his indignation. "That doesn't mean I want to."

Since I'm still walking, Dan finally decides to stop his tantrum and strides in my direction. Once he stands beside me, his face becomes unusually serious. "You gonna need me to keep Tatiana at bay? Remember she's also attending business school."

"Fine!" I hiss, knowing where he was heading with his point. "She asked me to delete her number."

"Wow," he utters, his eyes widen in shock. "But why?"

"I don't know." I take a deep breath out, my patience running thin. I hate speaking about something that literally just happened not even two hours ago. "She acted very weird, like she gave me a hug and then told me goodbye with the intention to never see me again, which is fucking strange because…" I stop mid-sentence, the rest being too personal to say.

"Because?"

I ponder whether or not tell him the rest, but Dan already knows so much, I don't think at this point it'll make any difference. "I think there's really something between us," I fess out. "And she's just afraid of that."

"Don't worry," he says, giving me a quick pat on the back. "You gonna meet plenty of older chicks at my party Saturday night."

ROXANNE.

I huff, shaking my head at his reply. I knew he wouldn't get it. "Dan, I don't—"

"Oh yes, you do," he interposes just as fast. "You lost your bet against me, so now you are going."

* * *

Dinner was entertaining and agreeable, mainly thanks to my sister and Dan. They managed as always to monopolize the conversation, make my parents laugh, and distract me from drifting away for too long. Once we get out of the restaurant, my parents start walking in front of us, their pace faster than ours, most likely in a hurry to retrieve their car and go home. Since the car is parked close to my place, we all instinctively follow them. While Dan, my sister, and I are strolling behind my parents, Elise takes the opportunity to intertwine her arm with mine, most likely to bring my attention to her.

I glance at her and catch a smirk on her face like never before. "What do you want, Elise?" I ask immediately.

"Don't you have anything to tell me?" Her tone is laced with humor and as I pay close attention to her expression, it's clear she's up to something.

My intuition makes me shoot a glare at Dan, but he shrugs his shoulders in return, giving me an "I don't know" kind of look.

"Dan, do you mind?" she asks, making us stop in our tracks.

"Okay, okay, I got it." Dan starts walking alone, his pace quicker so to give us some space.

"What's going on here?" I ask again.

"Is there any reason why I didn't see you at any courses today?" she asks, her voice low enough not be heard by anyone else but me. "We are supposedly taking the same classes, you know."

Shit. It's obvious sooner or later my sister would find out I've switched programs. There's no point in denying it to her, so I decide to be frank and tell her the truth. "Yeah, I switched to English."

"You did *what*?"

"Shhh!" I whisper at her loud tone. We then resume walking like nothing happened, keeping a good distance from Dan—although, he already knows I switched. "I never wanted to go to business school, that was Dad's idea, not mine. I applied to English, and I decided to switch before the year started."

"Oh, wow," she utters, visibly confused, but also… impressed? It's hard to tell. "That's great, honestly." She sounds genuinely happy for me and the thought of it appeases me and even brings a smile to my lips. "Good for you to follow your path." She gives me a quick squeeze on the arm in appreciation as we keep strolling.

"Thanks," I reply. Then, after a few seconds in silence, I ask, "Please, do you mind keeping it to yourself for now? I'll tell him when I'm ready."

"Sure," she says, her eyes on me. "Don't worry, your secret is safe with me."

Despite reassuring me, I'm not sure if I can trust her, but I guess I don't have much choice in the matter. Only the future will tell.

CHAPTER 10

Amsterdam, September 7, 2021
Roxanne

I didn't sleep well last night and despite my extra-large cup of coffee, I sit on my office chair barely awake. I tried all the tricks in the book to sleep—from chamomile tea, zen music, to melatonin supplements—but my mind was ensnared with hundreds of ridiculous scenarios regarding something I could never have. Fortunately, someone knocks on the door which pulls me back down to earth. Before I can say anything, Poppy steps inside, an apprehensive look on her face.

"What happened?" I ask immediately.

Poppy strides in my direction, and standing beside me, she leans down and puts on a small voice. "It's about the cabaret."

My attention is immediately perked. "What about it?"

Poppy seems uncertain and I know at this point whatever she's about to say, it won't be good. "It looks like the owner wants to sell it to someone else."

"What!" I snap instantly, my sleepy mood switching into an angry one. "That's not possible! That was a closed deal."

"Well, the paperwork wasn't yet signed, so…" she trails off.

Fuck, fuck, and fuck! There's nothing worse than starting the day with such bad news. "I need to talk to Karl," I tell her.

"He's actually waiting outside."

My eyes widen in surprise. "Oh, please let him in."

She gives a sharp nod of the head before leaving my office. I recline on my chair, heaving a long sigh in frustration. I can't believe it! I've wanted to buy that cabaret for as long as I can remember, and Karl was the one working on the deal, since he's supposedly good friends with the owner. How come the owner now wants to sell it to someone else?

As soon as I hear a knock on the door, I look up and find exactly the person I need to talk to, standing on the doorway.

"Karl," I greet, rising from my seat as he strolls into my office. "I hope you're bringing me some good news."

"Eh…." He cocks his head to the side, looking at me with confusion in his gaze. "Didn't Poppy tell you?"

"Yes, and you told me that sale was a closed deal," I remind him straight away.

He paces slowly in my direction, his hands plunged into his pockets. "I thought that too, but the owner has got another seller—a big company from Paris that wants to expand their cabaret portfolio."

My chest heaves, blood pumping rapidly through my veins. "You said he was your friend and the only reason he was selling his cabaret was because you insisted!" I can't keep the aggression from my tone. This smells very fishy to me.

"I know, I know," he utters pensively and to my surprise he stops in front of the aquarium sitting on a cabinet and starts observing the fish. Talk about fishy. "Maybe we can work out a good arrangement."

I cross my arms over my chest, my eyes narrowing on him. He's got an agenda. I knew it. So typical of him. "What do you want?"

He opens the package containing their food, and then drops some of the pellets into the tank. "I heard you met with Andries yesterday," he begins cautiously, his focus on the fish.

"Have you been following me or what?" I ask, a slight worry in my tone as I approach him. "How come you know that?"

He observes the fish with satisfaction as they eat their food, the trace of a smile settling on his lips. "I just have people who happened to be at the right place at the right time." His eyes never leave them and I know in that instant that the cabaret deal is being held hostage by none other than Karl himself. He finally turns his attention to me and then says, "Let's be real, you guys didn't really go to an incognito place."

"I'm not seeing him again," I tell him, my tone clear and assertive. "I just met with him so he'd delete my number."

"Roxie, Roxie," he tuts, shaking his head in disapproval. Then he lays his hands on my shoulders, searching for my gaze. "Why can't we reach an agreement that is beneficial for both of us, mmh?" He quirks a tight smile and looks down at me, his eyes serious.

"I'm not playing those games, Karl," I tell him, matching his tone, and I give a few steps back from him.

"Look, I'm a reasonable man."

I scoff at his statement, and his eyebrows jump up questioningly.

"Can't you and him just be friends?"

"You know perfectly well he doesn't want us *just to be friends.*"

"I'm pretty sure he'll content himself to hang out with you." I shake my head in disagreement, but Karl proceeds, "I mean, it's not every day he's in the company of a woman like you."

I heave a long sigh, before staring right into his brown eyes and say, "Not. Interested." I walk past him, not stopping until I stand by the window of my office.

"A pity," I hear him lamenting behind me. "I could've secured the buying of that cabaret you wanted so much."

I turn around just as fast, my attention perked. "*How* and *when* can you secure it?"

"Today, if you pay two million."

"*Two* million?" I repeat, outraged. "Last time we spoke with him it was one point three."

"The French offered him two point five, Roxie," he answers, his tone even. I brace myself at the idea of dropping two million on a cabaret. The investment should be quick to break-even but still, it's a big chunk of money. "Look, I'm not the owner, I'm just the godfather of his son, but if you are willing to keep Andries in your loop, I can make a phone call and get it closed at two million for you."

I remain silent, processing everything he just told me. That cabaret would be the perfect tool to attract new clients, and I could start diversifying my revenue streams. If all it takes to seal the deal is to hang out with Andries one more time, then why not?

It seems like Karl is reading my mind, because he then says, "There's a party Saturday night called 'Red Light District', hosted by his friend Dan O'Brian. Why don't you just go there and see what happens?"

Jeez! So this was his plan all along? "How do you know about that party in the first place?" I can't help but ask.

"Because I speak to people, Roxie," he answers, remaining quite vague. "I know what's going on around the city."

I stand still, pondering further his offer as I look out of the window. Even if I wanted to be friends with Andries on my own, Karl will eventually find out and use my relationship with him to get what he wants. I don't know exactly what he's got in mind, but I don't think it's prudent to go along with his plan.

I turn around and to my surprise, I find Karl standing right beside me. "I don't think it's a good idea," I tell him, crossing my arms over my chest to mark my decision.

"Being friends with the heir of one of the most important families in this country and who happens to be the son of my boss *is* the definition of a good idea."

"A good idea for *you*," I point out.

"It's a partnership," he insists. In reality, it's more an exchange of favors. I'm pretty sure Karl isn't innocent regarding the new price tag for the cabaret. He's just making my life difficult so he can get what he wants. And what he wants is to make sure I keep his boss's son under my thumb. Since I'm not answering, he continues, "Look, when you started your agency who was the first client helping you out?"

I heave a long sigh, knowing exactly where he's heading with that. "You," I mutter.

"When you couldn't get a business loan, who made the phone call?"

"You," I repeat, averting my gaze.

"Who became friends with the owner of the cabaret you love so much just so I could persuade him to sell it to you?

"I get it," I snap. "I know you've always been supportive."

"All I'm asking is for you to keep that boy on your radar." Karl makes it seems like it's no big deal, but I know him all too well. It always starts with something small and innocent, and soon enough, that escalates into bigger and bigger demands. "What does he like to do?"

His new question feels totally random, but I ponder it for a moment. "He likes, um, poetry."

Karl blinks twice, totally astounded by my answer. "Poetry?"

"Yes," I say, suppressing a chuckle. The look on his face is priceless, though.

"Well, your sister works at a bookshop, take him there."

"What if he falls in love? What am I supposed to do? Break his heart?" I ask so he can see where I'm coming from. "He's young, he's gonna fall hard."

"Tell him you just want to be his friend, it's called communication."

I roll my eyes at his advice. "Yeah, right, as if it was that simple."

"It is, Roxie, it's actually *that* simple."

CHAPTER 11

The last thing I wanted to do tonight was go to Dan's stupid party. It represents everything I hate—loud noise, annoying music, and shallow people—overall a complete waste of time and energy. But I lost my bet against him, so here I am facing the consequences of my own actions. At the very least, I hope he's got some good liquor. Deleting Roxanne's number was hard, but not as hard as deleting the text messages we'd exchanged. The last words she said are still haunting me, and the fact she never told she felt nothing between us isn't helping either. But at the end of the day, Dan is right—I've got to move on, and stop thinking about a woman who clearly isn't into me.

The front door of Dan's house finally cracks open and a joyful brunette in a red corset with a short lace skirt greets me.

While I have no idea who she is, she, on the other hand, checks me out from top to bottom with lust in her eyes.

"Welcome to the Red Light, Andries," she says, her voice sleazy.

I frown at her answer. "How do you know my name?"

"Dan told me to take care of you," she purrs, leaning against the doorway, a smile spreading across her red lips.

"Eh, thanks." I return the smile awkwardly, not knowing what else to do.

She wets her lips, and in the blink of an eye, snatches my arm, pulling me inside. "Don't be so shy," she teases, locking her arm with mine once we get into the house.

There's a difference between shy and uninterested, but I prevent myself from telling her that.

She closes the door behind us, then helps me to take my coat off, and goes to store it in one of the wardrobes.

As I take in my surroundings, sensual music plays across the hallway matching perfectly well with the intimate atmosphere created by the strings of red lights. Most girls I lay my eyes on are dressed in cabaret attire—red or black corsets, lace, froufrou dresses, with feathers in their hair, black heels, and fishnet stockings. It feels like I stepped inside the Moulin Rouge or something. Despite it being a private party, it still looks more tasteful and dignifying than our deplorable, real life red light district.

"Andries!" I hear Dan shouting from the other side of the hallway, he then leaves his guests and comes forward to welcome me. I give a quick smile to those gazing at me, most likely wondering who I am. "Good to see you, man!" he says as we exchange a quick hug and a friendly pat on the back. "Welcome to the best place to be this evening." His cheerful tone makes me smile, although I'm not really in a festive mood. "What do you think? Pretty cool, huh?"

"Well, the vibe is really red," I comment as I take in my surroundings.

"It's burlesque, duh!"

"You told me it was burlesque but with poets in attendance, not courtesans."

"Oh, relax, they are probably seated in the living room," Dan brushes off. He then takes a glass of bubbly from a passing server and hands it to me. "Here, take some champagne to relax."

I give a first sip, and a sudden question crosses my mind. "You didn't invite Tatiana, right?"

"Flower-girl? Fuck no. But I did bring some really beautiful and experienced women for you to try your hand at." He then leans slightly closer to me and pointing with his glass, he says, "You see those two women over there? They are dancers at Casa Rosso. Come, I'll introduce you." He's about to go and speak to them, but I grab his arm right away to stop him.

"I appreciate it but I'm just interested in meeting the poets and connoisseurs you talked about."

Dan heaves a sigh, most likely in disappointment. "Ah, yeah. Well I'm gonna check on them regardless." I release him and he just goes and mingle with the two women he was talking about. Shaking my head, I decide to ramble around the house and enjoy the scenery. I enter into the living room, which has been transformed into a small red theater. It's entirely dark except for a few red lights flashing on and off. There are velvet tufted chesterfields spread across the room with matching red lamps on the low tables, creating an intimate, boudoir vibe, and at the very end, some sort of stage with a wooden chair in the spotlight.

"It's nice, isn't it?" My attention turns to my right side and I find the girl I had met at the entrance, a glass in her hand.

"What's going on there?" I ask, pointing at the stage.

Upon my question, the red lights turn off and the room becomes pitch black.

"Oh, let's have a seat, the show is about to start," she says, before snatching my hand and dragging me to the only available seat on a sofa, close enough to the stage. I sit tightly between two other women, and the girl I'm with sits on my lap without even thinking twice. At this point, I'm wondering if she's being paid by Dan to entertain his guests. Truthfully, it wouldn't surprise me.

For any other guy this would be heaven on earth, but I'm squeezed to the bone on this tiny sofa, and I've got no idea who this girl—her ass pressed against my crotch—even is.

All of a sudden, everyone starts clapping and cheering but my view is totally obstructed by her locks of hair to see what's going on. A new music starts playing and after a few beats, a female singer start singing the lyrics of "Diamonds Are a Girl's Best Friend" by Marilyn Monroe. At this point, I imagine someone must be on stage performing, so I lean slightly forward, turning to my right, and find an angle with unobstructed views to the stage. There's definitely someone there dancing, but the position isn't comfortable enough to stay like that for the whole show. After a while, I just give up and recline against the sofa, heaving a sigh. Fuck it. The show must be trash any way. The crowd starts singing along the singer when she reaches the chorus and some people even clap along. Mercifully, the girl gets up from my lap and excitedly goes on stage upon being invited by the main performer. My eyes widen in shock when I notice the female performer is actually wearing an under-bust corset, a matching choker necklace, and a thong covered with fake-diamonds. The two of them start chanting together and the guests keep cheering for more. I finish my drink and thank God there's a waiter passing by to give me a new one.

"She's beautiful, isn't she?"

The voice sounds familiar and as I look at who's sitting beside me more carefully, I can't help but chuckle at the whole thing.

"You?" I ask, trying not to sound too stunned, but I can't believe I didn't see her before. "At Dan's party? Now that's a surprise…."

"Oh," Roxanne utters, reveling in my astonishment. "Sorry, I didn't know it was you."

Yeah, right. I'm torn between staying here or trying to find another seat to watch the show from, but I don't want to give her the impression her mere presence is bothering me to the point I need to change seats, so I decide to suck it up and remain sitting beside the woman who bluntly rejected me just a few days ago. If there's someone who has got to leave this sofa, it's her, not me. "May I know who brought you here?" I decide to ask, my tone coming off more annoyed than expected. There's the trace of a smile settling on her lips as if in amusement. "Let me guess—you came with Karl again?"

"I came with the girl who's performing actually," she answers, pointing at the stage. "And you?"

I feel tempted to ask her if she knew I was coming, but there's simply no way in hell she could know about it. "I was told there would be poets and connoisseurs of literature in attendance, but looks like I was misled," I tell her, speaking close enough to her ear so that she can hear me.

"Not at all, I am here."

It takes everything in me not to laugh. "Really? You?"

"Well, yeah, I have a degree in English, remember?" Despite her question, I can't help but notice how close we are, to the point her legs are touching mine. I try to distance myself from her, but there's barely any space left.

"That doesn't mean you know about poetry," I riposte, knowing perfectly well that the amount of people who know about poetry are quite limited, even for English graduates.

Since the music continues raging in the background, Roxanne keeps leaning close enough to my ear and says, "At the bookshop we have rare editions of books from poets you have never heard of."

A quick chuckle escapes me at her overly confident assumption. "I've read nearly everything out there."

"Really? What about Verlaine?"

"Of course," I snap immediately. "He's a classic figure of the symbolist and decadent movement!"

"We have one of the first editions of his complete work in display."

My eyebrows rise up in surprise and I can't prevent my mouth from gaping. "You serious?" Roxanne just smiles, reveling in my complete astonishment. "And it's for sale?"

"I'm afraid it isn't," she replies, her face softening.

Fuck! A first edition of Verlaine's work and it's not for sale? What kind of bookshop does that? But I refrain myself from releasing my frustration on her, so instead I just say, "A bookshop with books that are not for sale, makes sense."

"They are part of our display since they are over one hundred years old," she explains.

"I'm sure we can reach an agreement."

"Or maybe we can't." While she seems to be enjoying her little game, I just try to remain as nonchalant as possible. "We actually have a section of banned poets, those whose work was considered too rebellious or provocative. Ever heard of Bei Dao?"

"No, who's he?"

"A Chinese poet who's part of the Misty Poets from the twentieth-century. He was the founder of *Jintian*—an influential literary journal in China which was banned by the communist party. As the founder, he was then forced to leave China in exile."

"Wow," I utter, fascinated by everything she just told me. "How do you know all that?"

"I'm Chinese on my mom's side and I enjoy reading classic works from the culture."

"And you are also fluent in Chinese literature?"

"I'd say I know enough, Mama was a teacher before moving here and she loved reading everything from the classics to contemporary. Poetry included."

I shift in my seat, trying to appease my excitement. But damn, it's hard! Chinese literature *and* banned poetry? How come we don't have a banned poetry program in school? Just sign me up now! "What can I do to get access to those books?" I ask immediately, my heart rate already accelerating at the idea I could be reading banned poetry soon. "I really want to lay my hands on them."

"Those poems are in Chinese anyways, so you wouldn't understand anything," Roxanne says, shrugging.

"Maybe you can translate them for me," I tell her. "I can pay you for that."

"That would take hours!" she points out just as fast, disregarding completely the last part. "I have other customers to take care of."

"What if I pass by after hours?" I insist.

She blinks twice, her face laced with confusion. "Wait— You want me to open the shop exclusively for you?" she asks, surprised.

I shrug, not seeing what's the issue with it. "Yeah, a lot of shops do private viewings. Just let me know the fee and I'll pay you."

"Um," her eyes drift down for a moment and it seems like she's assessing my request. "Fine, I guess that's the least I can do after how I treated you last time we met." Wow. I'm quite astounded that she admitted it herself. "I'll text you the address and a date."

I'm internally shaking my head at her last words. This seems more like an excuse to dodge having me at her bookshop, so I take my phone out and ask, "Do you mind giving me the bookshop's name and address now, in case you forget?"

She blinks twice, before scoffing at my question. "You don't trust me, huh?"

I give a nonchalant shrug. "I just want to make sure I can go and check those rare editions and the banned poets. That's all."

The show seems to be over and everyone is clapping, while the music becomes softer and less intrusive.

"Oh! I was looking for you!" Dan yaps as he steps in, and our attention immediately shifts to him. "There's a writer I'd like to introduce you to. He's not a poet but he writes short stories that have been published."

"Can you give me just a sec?" I ask him, before giving a quick look at Roxanne.

"I just sent you a text," she announces.

I frown in disbelief. Yet, as I check my phone, I see the new notification pop up. Wow. How come she retracted her decision to never see me again so quickly? "Okay, um, thanks." I then stand up and looking at her, I simply say, "Well, it was lovely seeing you again."

"The pleasure was all mine, Andries."

My gaze locks with hers for a moment, and it feels like neither of us truly wanted to stop the chat we were having, but Dan is quick to grab my arm, forcing me to turn around and walk away.

"Don't tell me that woman was the one you had coffee with and asked you to delete her number?"

"Yep, that's the one."

"Fuck," he mutters. "I swear I didn't know she was coming."

"That's alright," I reassure him, following him.

We stop in front of a group of three people mingling between themselves, and Dan is quick to jump in and starts the introduction. "Patrick, this is Andries, the poet I told you about." Dan then looks at me, putting a hand on my back. "Andries, this is Patrick—a published writer who also graduated from the same English program at the University of Amsterdam."

We shake hands and start doing some small talk about his work, how he got published, and so forth. "I was also lucky to get an agent who had faith in me," Patrick explains. "I can totally recommend his literary agency if you ever need."

I thank him and we quickly exchange contacts. A few minutes later, when the conversation starts fading away, the group parts way, and I take this moment alone to unlock the screen of my phone and check the text message Roxanne sent me: *You can keep my number. Let's meet up soon. X*

Thanks, I look forward to it, I decide to say in return. It's short, polite but definitely not flirty, and that's exactly how I'll behave with her from now on. I'll go to her bookshop only and exclusively as a client and with zero intention of pursuing her like I did before. Speaking of which, from the corner of my eye, I can see Roxanne heading in my direction. A natural swing of her hips that is hard not to notice accompanies her, as well as a glass of bubbly in a hand and a charming smile gracing her face. I must say, she looks really exquisite in that red qipao dress. Maybe too exquisite... Seeing her approaching, I avert my gaze, take a quick sip on my drink, and turn my back slightly on her, ready to walk out of here.

But it's too late—she just stops right beside me, and starts making conversation. "Hey," she greets softly, "how has your evening been? Are you enjoying the party?"

"It's been pretty good," I say for the sake of politeness, my tone dry. The last thing I want after being rejected by her and forced to delete her damn number is to come across as too friendly. "And yours?"

"Great too." I nod, then start glancing at my watch, ready to leave. "Are you…" she narrows her eyes on me as if searching her next set of words, "mad at me or something?"

"Mad?" I repeat, slightly surprised at her chosen word to describe my indifference. "No, why?"

"It feels like you are trying to avoid me."

"I'm just keeping my distance," I tell her sincerely.

And before I can inform her I'm going to go home, she says, "We can be friends, you know."

"Oh, can we?" I ask, my tone suspicious. "If you wanted to be my friend you wouldn't have forced me to delete your number in the first place." I couldn't keep it to myself.

She frowns for a second, considering me, and then finally decides to open up. "Because I know all you wanted to do was have sex with me."

I can't help but burst out laughing at her shameless and pretentious statement. "*That's* what you thought? Well, that's where you are wrong," I reply, still quite amused. "I just felt there was something between us and that's why I wanted to see you again." As I say those words our eyes lock for a quick moment and it seems like I can see her soul. "And I'm still convinced there is something between us since you never told me the opposite."

"Maybe we can be friends then?" Her voice is small and slightly nervous, quite different from the self-assured woman of just a few seconds ago. "I can help you out with your English degree and, um, we can schedule an evening for you to go check out our collection of poetry?"

"Sounds reasonable," I tell her as we start walking out of the living room.

We make our way toward the hallway and once there another question kicks in. "Can I ask you something?"

"Of course," she says right before bringing her glass to her lips.

The hallway is less crowded, the music much lower, and it feels much better to have a conversation here. "Why did you change your mind about me?" My words hang in the air, crisps and sharps, and I catch a few by-passers, watching.

Her eyes widen in surprise and I know at this point she wasn't expecting such a question to be made.

She heaves a long sigh, her eyes drifting to the floor as she processes what I just asked her. "Well," her eyes meet mine again, and damn it, each time I look at them it feels strange and uncomfortable. "I didn't like the idea of never seeing you again."

Why her answer makes my heart race faster, I'm not sure, but I take it as a simple friendly compliment and smile. "I'm gonna have to go," I say, opening up one of the built-in wardrobes to take my coat. "Whenever you are free to open the bookshop for a private viewing, let me know."

I put my coat on, and close a few buttons while I pass her, heading toward the front door.

Roxanne follows closely behind. "Okay, um, but you are already leaving?"

Reaching the front door, I turn around to face her, and I find the mix of disappointment and confusion in her gaze quite surprising.

"Well, yeah, it's getting late."

"Okay, sure," she utters, forcing a polite smile.

While last time we met she gave me a hug and then walked away, now it's my turn to walk away first. Should I give her a hug like she did? A kiss on the cheek? Nah... After how she treated me last time we met, I don't feel like doing any of it. So I just take her free hand and give her a quick shake. "Have a good evening." Then I open the door, and finally get out, leaving the noisy party and Roxanne behind.

CHAPTER 12

Amsterdam, September 13, 2021
Andries

"A handshake?" Dan repeats once more, flabbergasted.

Jeez, I knew I shouldn't have invited him to come over at the coffee shop where I'm studying in. Next time I'd go to the library—he must be allergic to that place.

"A handshake," I say again, before closing my book, since I feel like he isn't gonna leave any time soon. I take another sip of my coffee and decide to open up and share with him what's been troubling me. "This is so damn weird though," I blurt out. Dan shoots me an arched eyebrow in return. "She was acting super unavailable and now she texts me saying she wants to be my friend." Yep, Roxanne didn't waste time texting me this morning so we could schedule our evening at the bookshop. I was positively surprised, of course, but one must admit it's kinda suspicious.

"Well, maybe she realized that her strategy was causing some serious damage, so she backtracked."

"A strategy?" I repeat, slightly confused at his chosen word. "I was super honest and upfront with her, why does she need a strategy to begin with?"

"Because you are the catch of the century for a freaking librarian," he says, stealing one of the cookies the waitress had brought to our table. "What were the odds of her meeting a guy like you?"

"Oh, fuck off!"

I leap off my chair and I'm about to leave the table when he then pleads, "Let me explain." A gush of air rolls off my lips and wanting to give him the benefit of the doubt, I sit back. "I think—and that's just my theory—that this chick pulled the hard-to-get strategy first to keep your attention, and then when she saw you didn't text her for a whole week, and simply deleted her number like she asked, decided to change tactic."

"She wants to meet tomorrow evening," I fess up. "It feels surreal." Meeting Roxanne in a bookshop surrounded by rare editions of poetry seems too good to be true, which is why I'm feeling a bit weirded out.

"Wow," he mumbles, leaning back on his chair. "Talk about a change of heart."

"Yep…" My eyes drift away for a moment as I think something through. One thing is for sure—if she really had a change of heart as she and Dan told me, then it means she knows there's something between us; a connection that pulls us together. But is it only friendship that she really wants from me? I guess there's only one way to find out.

All of a sudden, I'm pulled right back on planet earth thanks to the loud ringtone of my iPhone. Jeez! I good reminder that I should put it on silence while being here. Looking at who is calling though, I hesitate for a moment, but decide to answer it nevertheless.

"Yes?"

"We've got to talk," Elise snaps immediately on the other side of the line. And before I can even ask her what's going on, she goes straight to the point. "What am I supposed to say to Tatiana regarding the fact you aren't attending business school? She's gonna find out sooner or later, you know."

I shift in my seat, straightening my shoulders. "Did she ask you about that?"

"Indirectly, yeah," Elise fesses up, her tone laced with worry.

"What did she say exactly?"

"She asked me if you were enjoying business school and then said we should meet someday at the library to do group study."

I tap my fingers on the table, pondering a proper answer to her dilemma. "If you come across her again, and she asks the same question tell her you don't know and to ask me directly." Knowing Tatiana as well as I do, she'll never invite me directly to do a group study, let alone approach me.

"Okay, I will," she says, sounding like she's in a hurry or something. "I've got to go, bye."

While I hang up and put my phone back inside my pocket, Dan doesn't seem to stop staring at me.

"Is everything alright?" he finally asks.

"Yeah everything's fine. Besides Tatiana trying indirectly to figure out why I'm not attending business school via my sister."

He heaves a long sigh, his eyes drifting for a moment before he asks, "Do you want me to take care of that?"

I look at him, considering his offer. "No, don't worry. I took care of it. But if she asks about it, tell her you don't know and to ask me directly."

"Got it," he says, pausing for a beat as I finish my coffee. "And, um, does your dad know already?"

"Of course not," I reply, my tone coming off more aggressive than I thought. After all, I'm fully aware this news will come as a bombshell, no matter who delivers it. "But I know sooner or later I'll have to tell him."

"Well, the later the better…"

I nod, a sigh escaping as I try to relax at the thought of facing my dad. "The later the better, indeed."

CHAPTER 13

Amsterdam, September 14, 2021
Roxanne

We decide to meet each other tonight at eight p.m., and thanks to this little accomplishment, tomorrow evening I'm meeting Karl and his friend to finalize the cabaret purchase. Lili should be home in ten minutes, which will give me time enough to ask her for the key to the bookshop and to take her car there before Andries arrives. After all, as a librarian working for a low-wage, it wouldn't make sense for him to see me driving a Porsche.

I heave a long sigh as I wait in front of her apartment, a mix of excitement and apprehension pounding hard in my chest. I feel the urge to light up a cigarette, but as I'm about to do so, I hear someone coming into the building—and I'm pretty sure it's her. So I put the pack of cigarette back inside my purse and patiently wait for her to get to the fourth floor.

"Hey," I say when I see my tired sister struggling to climb the last of the stairs.

"What are you doing here?" she asks immediately, an ounce of annoyance in her tone.

Given how tired and irritated she seems to be, I decide to start with some small talk first. "I just wanted to see you how you were doing."

She walks in my direction, key already in hand, and I step aside, letting her put the key inside the lock.

"Yeah, right," she mutters in disbelief, before the door cracks open and we get in. She puts a finger on her lips, shushing me. "Mama must be in her room, sleeping," she whispers. "Let's go the kitchen."

We cross the hallways as silently as possible and after getting inside the kitchen, Lili pushes the door behind us, sighing in relief.

"So," she begins, her voice not too loud, as she walks toward the fridge and gets from there a bottle of Sauvignon Blanc. "What brought you here on a random Tuesday evening?"

She knows me well. "I wanted to know if you were doing well."

"I'm perfect, and you?" She stands against the counter, the bottle in hand and her eyes on me. "Still managing that agency of yours?"

I knew she'd bring the focus of the conversation back on me and my job. I normally shut her down with vague answers, but since today I need a favor from her, I decide to tell her truth. "Well, if you must know, I'm buying the most famous cabaret in Amsterdam. The signing is happening tomorrow."

"I see," she mutters under her breath as she takes two glasses from the cabinet and places them in front of each other. "Looks like you're gonna stay in the industry for a while then."

"I honestly don't see the problem with that." It saddens me that she still feels the need to bother me about the industry I work in. Maybe it's Mama that makes her feel the need to be so judgmental. The truth is I do like the industry that fills the red light district, and it's hard for her to understand that. In her mind, any woman working in that industry—even the most respected and highest paid— should be ashamed of their lifestyle. But I'm not. And this bothers her and Mama way more than they'd like to admit. "The cabaret is very well known, profitable and it'll help me diversify my revenue streams."

"So with all these revenue streams, I assume you are officially retired from your previous job, right?" she asks, her attention on filling our glasses with wine.

"Retired?" I repeat, not really sure I understand the meaning of her question.

"You know, as an escort."

Should I tell her yes? I know I told her I was done with it when I came here for Mama's birthday, but should I keep saying that now? One more lie wouldn't really hurt, would it? "Well, kind of, yes. I just have three clients that I am seeing off and on," I decide to disclose. She pours the wine, totally mute, her lips in a straight line. "Plus, I've been with them for years so they are more than just regular clients."

"I know about it—the divorce of your Karl from that former actress and model is all over the news," she says under her breath, but loud enough for me to hear it. "Don't you see the wrong here?"

"That's none of my business though," I tell her, hoping to close this subject once and for all. Jeez! I should've kept it to myself. "I'm not the one who made the vow. Can we move on now?"

"Fine," she hisses, but finally takes the glasses and paces in my direction to give me mine. "Well, cheers."

She raises her glass and I do the same. Except she doesn't know what to cheer about.

"To you, lil sister," I tell her, clinking her glass with mine.

She smiles without much of enthusiasm before she takes her first sip.

We keep quiet as we drink, enjoying this peaceful moment, until I finally break our silence. "By the way, um, do you mind if I hold a private viewing of the bookshop tonight?"

She blinks twice, before squeezing her eyes in confusion. "What do you mean?"

"A friend of mine is a poet," I disclose. "And I told him I was working at your bookshop. He wants to check the rare editions of poetry you have on display."

"A poet?" she repeats, astonishment laced all over her face. "And you gonna pitch him your services in my bookshop or what?"

"I don't know," I tell her sincerely. "He's an English student I met on campus the other day. But I've got to get to know him more before deciding if I should introduce him to one of my girls."

"The poor boy," she says as she shakes her head, heaving a sigh. "Why are you wasting your time with him? He might be broke and wouldn't be able to afford any of them."

Given the fact I don't want to disclose Andries' identity to my sister, I simply say, "He was wearing a Patek Philippe limited edition pilot's Calatrava 5522." Lili seems to have no idea what this is, so I explain, "It's a very discreet and unpretentious watch but it's worth fifty grand. I think he can pay a few thousand bucks for a girl if he's feeling lonely."

"Have you ever thought about, hmmm, having some decency and morals for once and let that young man out of your scheming?" she sounds irritated, nearly annoyed. "You already have so much money with all the clients your girls are bringing. Why do you need to prey on a college student?"

"Because he's the perfect profile. We are customizing the girlfriend experience package and—"

"Argh! I don't want to hear that," she cuts me off, rising a dismissive hand. "I hope one day you'll see the damage you are doing."

"We are meeting at eight p.m. tonight," I say, refocusing on what I came here for. "I promise I'll leave the store in the same state I found it."

A gush of air rolls off her mouth, and her gaze drifts to the floor, considering my request. "Fine, but you need to come back here and give me the key by no later than eleven."

"No problem," I answer, giving her a quick pat on the arm. "Thank you so much for doing this."

"He's gonna find out sooner or later that you're no expert in literature though."

I knew she had to give her two cents on the matter, like she did with everything. "I still remember a lot from my college years, I should be fine," I reply, while I do a small victory dance in my head.

"You could've been a great librarian," she says with some nostalgia in her voice.

"We've already had this discussion before." In fact, we've had this discussion almost every time we've seen each other over the past fifteen years. But seeing my sister struggling with money and paying her bills while holding an English degree is a good reminder that a degree doesn't equal good pay. There are no wealthy librarians. And despite my love for books, I quickly realized I'd rather be comfortably wealthy than a librarian long time ago.

CHAPTER 14

It seems like I'm the first to arrive in front of the antiquarian bookstore. Located in a small, narrowed, pedestrian street downtown, it's no wonder I'd never been here before. It's the kind of place that only a local would know about. Since I'm new to living in Amsterdam, there was no way I'd have heard of it before now. The modest brick building seems to have been restored a few years ago, but the façade has kept its original architecture and seems well kept. The floor-to-ceiling display is filled with old editions of hardbacks, and by the titles, I can see they are all classics from a variety of genres.

I stand close enough to the door and putting my hands on each side of my eyes, I try to peer through the glass and get a clue of what the inside looks like.

"Need some help sneaking in?" I hear Roxanne saying from behind me.

I turn around, my face already beaming with joy, but I'm suddenly taken aback at how cute she is in normal attire with flat shoes. I mean, if we can consider a vintage flare skirt normal attire.

"Oh, that's a very different outfit from the burlesque party," I point out teasingly.

"Well, I don't work in high heels and a qipao."

"To be honest, I like seeing you wearing flats. You look really cute in them."

"You and your compliments…." And yet, she can't help but smile despite shaking her head at me. "Thanks, though."

I stand aside, and she opens the door, inviting me in. "Welcome to paradise," she says, before turning the lights on.

As I step inside and take in my surroundings, I realize the bookshop is absolutely exquisite, and much bigger than I imagined. In fact, I thought it'd be something tiny but no, it truly looks like a small museum of ancient art, except here the ancient art is the display of first editions and rare books. This truly feels like a small piece of paradise for someone who loves classic literature as much as I do. There's an antique walnut table at the center of the room and a rug under the oak laminated floor, a spiral staircase going to another floor right behind the table, and a few leather armchairs spread around the room. Some books are presented in display cases most likely due to their rarity, while most of them are behind the mahogany antique bookcases with glass doors that cover the walls. Everywhere I look I can only see shelves filled with hardcovers that are visibly dated of a few decades or even centuries. The warm light isn't too harsh and creates a very studious and serene atmosphere.

"This feels like home," I tell Roxanne, peering at every book in the display glasses like I'm in a museum.

"Oh, yeah, I love how classy and antique this place feels," she says and I now understand better the vintage outfit and haircut.

"Oh, you even have a first edition of Roland Holst's work?" I ask, pointing at the book on display that is dated from 1910.

Roxane walks over and standing beside me she takes a look at the cover before nodding. "Yep, but those books aren't for sale."

The fact that there are books here, in this tiny, random bookshop, that are over a hundred-and-ten years old makes this place so damn interesting.

"Now come over, I'm gonna show you my favorite room." She crosses the room and I follow closely behind until she opens a wooden door on the left, not too far from the staircases.

"And this…" she says as she turns the light on stepping into a small room. "It's the censored literature room I told you about."

"Oh, wow." I walk into the new compartment which is maybe just slightly bigger than my dressing room, with a rug covering the floor and a table in the center, and start perusing the titles standing on the shelves. "How much time do we have here?"

Roxie glances at her watch, quite amused at my question. "Um, well, I guess around an hour or two."

She then starts scanning through the shelves until she stops at the "Chinese Literature" section—which includes two big bookcases filled from floor to ceiling. She zooms in on one shelf in particular, searching more rigorously for a specific title until she pulls out a brown leather-bound hardcover. It's written in Chinese characters I obviously can't understand it, so I wait for her to say something.

"This is a selection of poems from Bei Dao, the poet who had to go into exile," she explains as she opens the book first on the index page and then to a particular poem. "I have a few books from him at home, but in English. If you'd like, you can borrow them." Before I can even thank her for her kind gesture, she seems to be already engrossed in the ink of the pages. "This is one of my favorite poems, it's called 'All'." She shows me the Chinese characters and while it looks beautiful I've got no idea what it is saying.

"Would you translate it for me?" I ask.

"Sure," she mumbles, her eyes returning to the page. She reads it in her head first and after a few moments, she starts,

"*All is fate,*
All is cloud,
All is a beginning without an end,
All is a search that dies at birth."

Her voice is melodic and truly magnetic as she reads it. If I could touch her timbre it'd feel like velvet, fine-grained, and smooth.

"*All love is in the heart,*
All past is in a dream,
All hope carries annotations."

As she continues, her eyes focused on the prose, I lean slightly on the table, totally smitten at having someone reading me a poem. What were the odds of a woman reading me Chinese poetry in Amsterdam? I don't know, but I don't think this is a coincidence.

"All faith carries groans,
All explosions have a momentary quiet,
All deaths have a lingering echo."

I wish I could snatch a picture of her right in that moment, her head slightly tilted down as she holds the book wide open between her hands, her vintage outfit matching perfectly with her blonde hairstyle and the shelves surrounding us. Once she closes the book, the air around us feels somehow more solemn.

"That was beautiful," I tell her quietly, not sure if I meant her or the poem, or both. "Is there a way I can buy it?"

"Thanks," she says, her eyes now on me. "This book is just for display," she informs. "The ones with a red dot on the back-cover mean *not for sale*."

"What if I buy it, but let it be on display?"

Her eyes narrow at me and she presses her lips, most likely in annoyance. "You can't take no for an answer, can you?"

I shrug nonchalantly. "You know, there's a lot of private collections being displayed in galleries and museums," I tell her instead.

"But you don't even know Chinese," she retorts.

"Well, I might need a translator to read me the rest of the poems but—"

She scoffs in return, and looking me in the eye, she just spits two words, "Not interested."

"Why not?" I ask, giving a few steps forward. As I stand close enough to her, the smell of her perfume permeates the air and my heart speeds up at the first intake of the aroma into my lungs. "Is it that bad to read poetry out loud?" I glance around the room, before my eyes fall back on her. "There's no one here except us."

"You like poetry, or me reading it?" she asks, staring at me like I'm a child she's trying to scold.

"Both, but at this point more the latter." The temptation to wrap my hands around her waist, tug her against me and then kiss her glossy lips is terrifying, and at the same time, deeply alluring.

One side of her mouth lifts into a semblance of a smile as if she can see through me. "What are you thinking?"

I mimic her smile, and I can't help but feel the heat rising as our gazes lock on each other. Kissing her now would be the perfect moment. But Roxie blinks twice and cuts eye contact, turning toward the shelf to put the book back in its place.

"Well, there's still a lot to see," she says afterwards, and yet, I'm still ravaging her in my head and wondering what her lips taste like. "So what if we go and check out the rest?" Her question hangs in the air as she starts walking around the room.

CHAPTER 15

Roxanne

Being in the bookshop alone with Andries feels like being reunited with an old friend after being apart for years. The longer I'm with him, the more captivated I am. He's like a kid at a toy store, his eyes gleaming at each new shelf he lays his eyes on.

"Oh jeez, you have so many incredible books," he points out as he takes an English edition of Baudelaire's masterpiece, *Flowers of Evil*, from a shelf of the "French Poetry" section. "I love Baudelaire. The first time I read his poems I was around fifteen, spending the summer in France."

"Wow," I utter, unable not to picture a young Andries chilling at the beach in the Côte d'Azur and reading a book he randomly picked at the villa he was staying at. "Do you know French though?"

"I speak it fluently actually," he says, flicking through the pages of the hardcover. "Oh! This one is one of my favorites." He clears his throat and then starts reading out loud a part of his favorite poem, "*Her eyes fixed upon me, like a tamed tigress, With a vague, dreamy air she was trying poses, And by blending candor with lechery, Her metamorphoses took on a novel charm—*"

My cheeks flush as I listen to the sensuality of the words and the more he reads, the more I understand that this isn't a typical poem. "Okay, enough of the French poets." I take the book out of his hands, and put it back on the shelf. "Now I understand why you were so captivated by Baudelaire."

Andries shrugs. "There's something about his work that resonates with me. I can relate to his struggles and—"

"Ah yes, between drinking and having sex with beautiful women, what a hard life this French man had…."

"Baudelaire considered drinking as a way to escape reality because he couldn't bear it," he retorts, jumping to his rescue. "I too used to drink way too much."

"That's what teenagers do, though."

"Or because there's something else underneath," he points out while picking another book from the shelf, his attention divided between me and the new title he has in hands. "Sometimes it's to cope with the struggles of life."

I can't help but scoff, head shaking at his response. But Andries frowns looking at me with confusion in his gaze. "Oh, c'mon, what kind of struggle can someone like you face in life?" I ask, failing to see his point. "I know what it's like having to count the money to afford one damn cocktail on a Saturday night."

He turns completely to face me and shuts the book with one hand, his features deepening. Did I strike a nerve or what? "Do you know what it's like to be judged by everything but by the content of your character, Ms. Feng?"

The formality and seriousness of his question makes me freeze on the spot—it came so unexpectedly that I remain totally silent as I search for an answer.

"That was my life before I left for Medellín," he proceeds, his smile evaporating as he revisits those distant memories. "People just hung out with me because of what they could get from me." There's so much sadness in his tone that it squeezes my heart and I notice how pensive he has become as he says those words. "No one knew who I was—myself included—but I felt deep down I wasn't the person my parents and my upbringing forced me to be. Regardless, no one cared to know the real me." He takes a deep breath in and out and I can tell he's trying to keep his emotions under control. It feels like there are bruises he hasn't totally healed from and without knowing it I just reopened them. "Even when I left for a year, trying to make sense of this world, my dad forced me to come back to go to business school." He chuckles at the thought of it while shaking his head, before his eyes fall back on me. "I never in my entire life wanted to attend business school. Do you think my parents care though?" Despite the seriousness of the moment, his piercing blue eyes make it all too hard to concentrate. "Do you think they care about the poems I have written since I learned how to write?" A quick chuckle escapes him and then he adds, "They most likely burned them all as I never found my notebooks again."

Before I can step in and present an apology, he says, "I'm sorry but if you think my life is perfect because I didn't struggle financially, then you are very mistaken."

"I didn't mean to sound offensive. I'm sorry, it's just… like, you are young, handsome, rich…" I let my words trail off, but it's clear that Andries wants me to finish my point. "You can get anything you want in life."

"I know that," he replies without an ounce of doubt. "And that's the problem."

My brows rise up in confusion. "How so?"

"You just literally judged me based on everything but the content of my character," he points out and I can't help but feel terrible to have done the exact same thing he just accused his surroundings of doing. "What I feel, what I like, what I struggle with… No one has ever cared. If not even my own parents care, I'm not expecting anyone else to."

I'm momentarily taken aback by his answers and the maturity of the subject, and, as I come to think of it, despite having all these issues with Mama, I know how much she loved to share her passion for literature with my sister and I, which might explain why we both ended up graduating in English.

"So that's why you left for a year?" I ask him.

"Yeah, I wanted to be free to do and be what I want, and I think that trip was very liberating." He pauses for a moment, a wistful smile gracing his lips. "Until my dad pulled me right back into his vapid and unsatisfying world."

"Your dad seems quite the opposite of you, no?"

"Oh, yeah, he loves to organize parties, dinners, outings. He's a true social butterfly, believe me." There's something in his voice that makes me smile. "I'd rather be surrounded by this," he says, pointing around the shelves filled with books, "than by people."

"I totally get that," I tell him, and deciding to open up a bit, I say, "When I was younger, I craved validation from my peers at college, especially those who had more money than me. But now? Now, I just want peace and serenity."

"There's nothing like peace and serenity, is there?"

I nod, my lips twisting into a smile as I look at his cerulean eyes. As I keep staring at him, Andries doesn't avert his gaze. On the contrary, he tucks a lock of hair behind my ear and continues observing me attentively as if reveling in what he's seeing. He's inches from me, and I can't help but wilt under his presence. His sweater molds perfectly around his athletic body and it's kind of hard not to notice how toned his arms are.

I must say, it's kind of rare to find a man that is both athletic and enjoys literature. Isaak definitely sacrificed the former.

Silence fills the air between us but tension rises as I catch his eyes staring at my lips.

My head tilts down as I feel the heat beaming on my cheeks from him staring at me for so long. I feel tempted for a moment to close the small gap between us and kiss him. But I can't—I mean, I *shouldn't*.

All of a sudden, though, I feel his fingers lifting my chin up and the embarrassment is total when I meet his blue eyes again. Oh gosh... My belly flutters and my heart races in anticipation of what could happen next.

"Thank you for listening to me," he says under his breath. "And for sharing this evening with me."

The warmth and humility in his tone is causing a frenzy of fire to storm through my body. His presence is like a magnet, and I want nothing more than being pulled closer to him. But is this what I'm here for? No! I'm here because Karl asked me to be, and I can't forget I'm just doing a favor for a client.

"Let's have dinner tomorrow night," Andries continues, his tone always so inviting, until I realize it's not a question.

"Dinner?" I repeat, unable to contain the shock in my tone.

"Yeah, why? You don't eat?" he asks, a teasing smile playing at the corners of his lips.

"I do but…" I feel undecided whether to be upfront with him or not, but it's best to. "Andries, I don't do this."

He shoots me an arched eyebrow. "*This*?"

"Dates. I don't do dates."

"It's not a date," he retorts.

"No?"

"You know what, why don't I bring dinner and we can eat here tomorrow night?

My mouth hangs open at his offer. "You want to have a picnic in the bookshop?"

"Eating surrounded by books and poetry is much better than in a restaurant," he argues. "I'll take care of everything. Trust me, it's gonna be amazing."

I grin at him before lowering my gaze as I ponder his invitation. I feel like declining, but why shouldn't I see him just one more time? He seems so damn excited that I don't want to be a killjoy. Glancing around the bookshop, I can totally picture eating either on the table or even on the floor if he brings a blanket.

"Okay, but something easy to eat like a pizza or a sandwich," I decide to say. "And I can only make it Thursday evening."

His face brightens up instantly with a huge smile. And I'm not quite sure what to make of it.

* * *

"One last meeting with him and that's it," I think to myself as I get back inside my sister's car, a Ford Focus 2014. Tomorrow the cabaret will officially be mine, so there's no more reason for me to see him afterwards. Andries is not a client, and not even a prospect, so why would I spend more time with him?

Because you like him....

I heave a long sigh, wondering if I should even meet him again on Thursday. And if I do, where will this lead us? *"Maybe we can be friends, then?"* I remember asking him at his friend's party.

I scoff at how stupid that question was. Friends don't feel tempted to kiss each other, for fuck's sake! We both know there's some kind of attraction between us. It's undeniable. Being around him is tempting me to do things I shouldn't want to. He's a freshman in college, young and naive, and has literally no idea what I do for a living. If he ever finds out, I'm pretty sure he won't hesitate to terminate whatever relationship we have. Maybe it's better I just cancel our dinner. It's doomed from the start.

Arriving in front of my sister's building, I park the car exactly where I found it, and hurry to get inside as fast as I can. Once I'm at her doorstep, I call her on her cellphone, once, twice, until I hear a squeak on the door lock.

A tired Lili sneaks in between the doorframe. "Damn, girl, it's past midnight."

I wince at her rebuke, knowing she's right. "I'm so sorry. I wanted to give you the key and, um, I also need to talk to you for a sec."

She heaves a sigh in frustration, before opening the door wide to let me in.

We go to the kitchen like we did a few hours ago, and once Lili closes the door behind us, she heads to one of the cabinets and takes a glass from there. "So how is your poet doing?" she asks, before pouring some water into her glass. "Did you eat him alive yet?"

"Ha ha," I answer back. "He bought two poetry books. Here's the money and the titles in case you want to register the purchase tomorrow morning." I put the money on the counter along with a paper with the titles written in it and her car key.

"Oh, thanks." She then pauses for a beat, observing me as she drinks. "Do you think you'll see him again?"

I wince at her question, unable to say no. "Um, well, we're meeting the day after tomorrow at eight p.m. at the bookshop."

"Again?" she snaps in a whisper.

"I'll pay you a fee."

"What if my boss catches you, huh?" she rebukes immediately. "I could get fired."

"I'll close the shop properly and I'll be careful, don't worry," I say as I try to reassure her as much as possible. "What if I pay you a hundred bucks for each opening?"

Blowing out a ragged breath, she assesses my request for a moment. "Alright, I'd definitely appreciate some extra cash. Mama needs some new clothes and the landlord is raising the rent next month."

"I can advance you some—"

"No, no, no," she interposes, cutting me off. "I already owe you five hundred. That's enough. I'm fine."

"I'd rather have you owing me money than having you living on the streets."

"What a big exaggeration, I'm saving as much as I can for the winter. I will be fine."

I open my purse and plunge my hand inside, trying to find my checkbook. "How much is the rent gonna be?"

"He's gonna increase it to sixteen hundred starting next month. It was in the contract anyway so I can't do much."

Shit. And the bills are not even included. Winters in Amsterdam can get very cold and she'll definitely need to spend more in electricity. I take my checkbook and a pen out of my purse, and write down her details. "Here," I say, handing her the check. "That should be enough for the coming winter."

After glancing at the check, her eyes widen in surprise and she gasps. "A thousand euros? Like, I can't accept it."

"Li—"

"No, it's too much. I can't." Since I'm not taking it back, she puts the check on the counter next to her car key. "I'm gonna find a new job."

"You already have a job."

"Like a part-time thing. Maybe I'll start teaching Dutch or Chinese online."

"How?" I ask, and before she can give me an answer, I add, "You leave for work at seven and come back at seven, and then you spend the rest of the evening taking care of Mama. I don't see how you're gonna find time for that."

"I wake up at seven and leave for work at eight," she corrects me like it's a big deal. "And sometimes I come back at six."

"Even still, look at yourself. You're tired, with eye bags that would scare anyone." I take a step forward, observing my exhausted sister more attentively. "Have you been exercising? Eating properly?"

"My job is demanding," she snaps defensively.

"Then your boss should pay you properly too."

"He can find a new storekeeper in no time if I ask him for a raise. A younger chick, freshly out of college, who would work for less than two thousand bucks a month."

"Why don't you work for me?" I ask her once more, even though I've tried many times. "You could be my new assistant."

"You know why," she chips.

There's no point in insisting, so I just say, "Alright, but if you ever need a new job, that one is reserved for you."

Instead of thanking me like any decent person would, Lili crosses her arms over her chest, an inquisitive look on her face. "And what would happen to your current assistant? Would you fire her?"

I'm quite stunned at her question, but decide to be as honest as I can. "I'll give her a good indemnity and let her go, yeah. I don't need more than one."

"That doesn't sit well with me...."

"See? That's why you don't get ahead in life. You care too much about people you don't even know."

"I'm not like you, Roxie."

"Well, maybe you should be!" My sister's eyes widen in shock at my high-pitched tone. The room falls into a freezing silence as I take a few breaths, trying to calm myself down. "You could live like a queen, you know." My tone is now lower and less aggressive and for once I decide to tell her everything without holding back. She spent her whole life criticizing me, so now it's my turn. "You and Mama could live in a superb condo with a gym and a pool, and a concierge in the best area of the city. Mama could have new clothes for winter from quality brands, aqua gym lessons for her back, a daily nurse to take care of her, and you could take her to good restaurants with fresh ingredients and decent service, instead of those cheap franchises." Despite my ranting, her face is devoid of any expression as if she's just quietly processing everything I'm telling her. "But instead you prefer to work as an underpaid sales clerk in a failing bookshop for a guy who would gladly take a new chick in if you ever dare to ask him for a raise." Jeez! I finally said it.

"Because there is something called dignity, which I have and you don't," she counters back.

"Dignity?" I repeat, scoffing at her. "Being underpaid is the opposite of having dignity, Li."

Her gaze drops to the floor for a moment as she considers me. "Fine, I'll ask him for a raise. We'll see how it goes."

"And you should get a better place," I tell her as I gather my things. "You should have your own bathroom. You're twenty-nine for fuck's sake. Why on earth are you still sharing a bathroom with Mama?"

"You know how much it costs having two full bathrooms and two bedrooms in Amsterdam?" she asks me, her tone defensive. "You haven't been checking."

"You could afford it. It's all in your hands."

"Are you done?" She cracks the door wide open, stepping aside to invite me out. "I've got to wake up early."

"Sure, thank you again for your help." I start walking out of the kitchen, but as I cross the doorway, I stop in my tracks. Thinking something through, I look at my sister one last time and say, "I love you, Lili, and I know you deserve much more in life."

CHAPTER 16

Amsterdam, September 15, 2021
Roxanne

There are few things in life that taste as good as closing a business acquisition. Owning this cabaret has been a dream of mine since Karl first took me here twelve years ago. I was still young and impressionable, but despite everything, I remember telling him how one day I'd own this place. Instead of laughing at me, he told me he'd help me to get there, but once I had the money to buy it, I decided to start my own agency instead and the cabaret became a second thought.

Looking around, I couldn't be prouder of what this place has become. Bar Rouge is an intimate Parisian restaurant, bar, and nightclub all in one; a place where Asian food and erotic performance fuse in perfect harmony under the strings of red lights. Now that the paperwork has been signed, we thank the former owner and our respective lawyers and bid them farewell. We escort them outside and wave at them until they get into their cars and drive away.

Finally alone with Karl, we get back inside the empty cabaret, that is open just for us, heading to the bar.

"Happy?" he asks, already sitting on one of the stools.

I sit beside him, resting my arms on the counter. "Very much so."

He then looks at the bartender who came earlier than usual and orders a new bottle of champagne. "We're gonna have a blast here tonight."

"I don't doubt it." I spin around on my seat, and take in my surroundings. It's still early so the cabaret isn't yet open to the public, but I can already picture the red lights, the music, the dancers performing, the festive atmosphere… "Jeez, I still can't believe it's finally mine." Looking back at Karl, I give him a pat on the arm, and then say, "Thank you for helping me out."

"You're most welcome," Karl replies in a whisper.

The bartender comes back, opens a new bottle of Dom Pérignon in front of us, and we clap cheerfully when he starts pouring the champagne in the two flutes he'd placed on the counter. We take our respective glasses and hold them in the air.

"Well, to the new owner of Bar Rouge," Karl begins, his tone joyful and supportive. "I wish you much success with this new venture."

"Thank you," I reply, matching his tone before we clink our glasses and take the first sip.

"How is Andries doing?" His question takes me totally off guard, and I nearly spit my bubbly.

What am I supposed to tell him? And why is he asking me that? "Um, he's okay, busy between college and poetry."

"You met him yesterday at the bookshop, right?" Karl presses.

I narrow my eyes at him, confused at his curiosity. "Yes, I did. But why do you want to know that?"

He doesn't answer straight away though. First he slowly takes another sip from his glass, enjoying the bubbly, until his attention finally returns to me. "His dad's gonna pick a new head of global sales at the end of the year, since the last guy decided to jump ship," he discloses, a mix of excitement and apprehension laced in his tone. "Do you think you can give Andries a word on my behalf next time you see him?"

Absolutely not! "You just got a promotion, didn't you?"

"Yeah, but that guy wasn't supposed to leave so soon." He takes a deep breath in and then exhales louder than usual. "That's an opportunity I don't want to pass up."

I chuckle as I realize something. "That's why you wanted me to hang out with him, huh? So that I could lobby on your favor."

"Well, I told you it'd be a beneficial friendship..." His answer is all I needed to know and it takes everything in me not to throw the rest of my drink on him. "Look at us— you, owner of the biggest escort agency in the country and now one of the best cabarets, and me the next head of global sales at Van den Bosch Industries. We're gonna be richer than the Van den Bosches themselves!"

"It's gonna be hard to beat, though," I mutter as I try to keep my anger under control. "You know, with their generational wealth and all that."

"I know, I was just kidding." He pauses for a beat, observing me with a side smile on his lips. "But if you can get me this promotion, I'll make sure to compensate you properly."

"Such as?" I ask, feigning interest.

"Anything you want," he answers, finishing his flute. "I'm open to splitting my bonus with you."

A gush of air rolls off my lips, the excitement to spend the rest of the evening with him totally gone. "Look, I can talk to Andries but I can't guarantee anything."

His side smile turns into a smirk, and for some reason, he starts checking me out from top to bottom. "I'm sure you can make yourself very persuasive."

I've heard enough! I stand up from my seat, finish my glass and gather my belongings. "I'll give it a try," I tell him, my tone coming across more aggressive than I had wanted to.

"Where are you going?" Karl asks as he sees me getting ready to leave. "Tonight's our night isn't it?"

"It is, but I'm gonna have to hang out with Andries again, and if he is not the one paying for that, then someone else is."

Karl snorts at my answer, and plunges a hand inside the inner pocket of his blazer. "Fine, how much is it?"

"It's not about money, I'm afraid, but something else."

He blinks twice, his face stunned. "Are you serious?" he asks, searching for an answer in my gaze. "You're gonna withhold sex like my wife used to?"

"Our sexual relationship is gonna be on hold, yes," I tell him, keeping my tone as professional and dry as possible. "That's the price to pay for me hanging out with someone so that they can be of benefit to your career."

"Fuck," he spits out. "So it's either having sex with you or asking Andries a favor to get me the promotion?" Karl seems to be landing on planet Earth just now. "Is this for real?" He runs a hand through his dark hair, completely lost and confused. "Why can't I have both?"

"Because life is about choices," I tell him right away. "I can recommend another girl to you if you want."

"Fuck," he repeats, his eyes drifting away as he processes everything I just told him. "And how long is this gonna last?"

Honestly, after Karl held the acquisition of this cabaret in hostage so that he could have leverage on me, it made me lose all respect and affection I had for him, and those two are bare minimums for me to have sex with someone.

"Until someone gets that promotion," I tell him, knowing perfectly well that by then I might terminate our contract altogether once and for all.

"What if you fail and I don't get it, though?"

"Don't worry," I lean closer to Karl and then whisper, "I can be very persuasive." And leaving him at that, I turn and make my way out.

CHAPTER 17

Amsterdam, September 16, 2021
Roxanne

Karl might believe sex is just on hold until he gets his promotion, but the truth is I don't intend to have sex with him ever again. I'm just not ready to tell him the truth though. It's not that he was a bad lover or anything, but he crossed a line the day he walked into my office and tried to dangle the cabaret as a carrot in front of me. Despite having to hang out with him from time to time, I feel so much better knowing at the end of the night, I won't have to do anything sexual with him. My thoughts are completely washed over when my eyes lay on a tall young man, standing by the door of the bookstore, holding a pizza package in his hands and carrying a backpack on one shoulder. My heart melts, seeing the effort he has put into the picnic. The fact he spent time planning and arranging this is something I deeply appreciate.

When he looks in my direction, his face lights up with a big smile causing a flutter in my stomach. I smooth my skirt, making sure it's in place as I approach him, then I take a deep breath and compose a polite smile.

"I see you came well prepared," I tell him, my heartbeat steadily rising. "Do you need help?"

"I should be good," he says as I unlock the door and welcome him inside. "Thanks."

Once we get into the store, I lock the door behind us, already wondering what he brought for the evening. Then glancing around the bookshop, I ask, "So, where would you like to set up the picnic?"

He walks around the room until he finds a space against the wall at the back that is spacious enough. "What about here?"

I can't help but shoot him a stare and then chuckle. "We are sitting on the floor?"

"Nah," he answers, opening a small compartment from his backpack, where he removes a blanket. I help him to stretch it wide open on the floor and the fabric seems thick enough to sit comfortably on it. I notice there are two cushions, one on each armchair, so I go and take them while Andries is sorting out the rest.

When I come back, I realize his backpack isn't a regular one, but a wine cooler bag with space for a bottle and two glasses. I had never seen this before, and when he takes the bottle out of the cooler, I can't help but smile as my eyes lay on the legendary black bottle of a Krug Clos d'Ambonnay.

"Champagne and pizza?" I tell him, seriously impressed. "That's an interesting take."

"Yeah, I read somewhere this champagne is the perfect pairing for a truffle pizza." He sits on the blanket, his back against the wall and I sit beside him. Having a picnic with Andries on the floor of the bookshop my sister works at is wild beyond imagination, but so damn fun. His black sweater contrasts beautifully with the cerulean of his eyes and his cologne permeates the air, making it quite hard to ignore it.

While he's already working on the bottle to open it, I can't help but try to discreetly open the box to check the pizza.

"Don't be so impatient," he playfully scolds, pushing my hand away.

His tone seems like the one of a parent rebuking his child, and laughter erupts at the thought of it.

When the bottle is finally open, Andries fills each glass with perfect precision like he's used to it. Not even a drop falls away. He gives me a glass and as I look at him taking his, I'm still not over the fact that this young college student managed to lure me into having a picnic with him.

"Well, cheers, to an amazing evening surrounded by the finest books," he says, raising his glass to clink with mine.

As I take my first sip, I can't help but let my eyes linger on him and more precisely at how perfect he is. If I wasn't so embarrassed to have a picnic in my sister's bookstore, I'd have taken a few pictures of the evening to keep it to myself.

"You wanna start?"

I blink twice, his voice puling me back to planet Earth. Looking at his hand, he's holding a slice of pizza on a paper plate, offering it to me.

"Oh, thanks." I take the plate and I can't help but salivate at the incredible scent coming from the truffles, so I decide to get started and take a big bite, throwing all my ladylike manners out of the window. I shut my eyes, letting myself savor this delicious pizza. "Hmmm..." Earthy, musky, umami-rich; the flavor profile of the truffle is like nothing else. It's a heady scent that if you find yourself hooked will turn you a bit googly eyed at just the mention of it, like the cologne of someone you fancy...

I can hear Andries chuckling, and then asking, "How is it?"

Reopening my eyes, I notice he's been staring at me for quite a bit, but I'm just too high on the truffle to mind. "Absolutely delicious," I mumble, trying to swallow before I can talk. "Honestly, this is such an incredible pairing."

"Was it worth trusting me?"

I feel the heat beaming on my cheeks at his question. "Maybe," I say, my voice small, before wetting my lips on the bubbly. Andries is still staring at me, a pensive look on his face, and the more I ease myself around him, the more I feel tempted to get closer to him and do things I shouldn't even think of. But damn, I can't help thinking how lucky his future girlfriend will be for having someone so attentive and dedicated like him. *Jeez! Why am I even thinking about that?* I shake myself out of my reverie and try to focus on the reason for my being here.

"Before I forget, um, I spoke to Karl recently and it seems like your dad is looking for a new head of global sales..." I begin slowly as he stops eating, looking at me attentively. "Do you think you can put in a word for him? He's really interested in the position."

"Sure, I can do that," he says as he resumes eating his pizza.

"Thank you." I lean in and give him a peck on the cheek in appreciation. Why that makes my heart race faster, I'm not sure. I feel my cheeks turn slightly rosy, but I brush it off rather quickly.

His face lights up immediately, with a smile spreading up to his ears as he revels in my unexpected display of affection.

With this ticked off my mind, I decide to change the subject to something we had spoken about before. "So, tell me, if your dad is the social life of the family, is your mom more like you?" I ask, before wetting my lips on the bubbly. "You didn't speak much about her last time we met."

"Ah, yeah, she's a loner like me," he answers, while finishing his slice of pizza. "And she also reads a lot, except it's not literature, but appeals."

I frown at the last part. "Appeals?"

"Yeah, she's a judge at the court of appeals in Utrecht, so that's her kind of literature."

"How did you fall in love with poetry if none of your parents were into it?" I continue.

He heaves a sigh, thinking more deeply about my question. "Actually, I think I started writing poetry before even knowing what poetry was."

My brows raise up in surprise. "Really?"

"Yeah, I wanted to write down what I was going through, what I was experiencing and feeling, and I guess that's how it started."

"I'd love to read your poems," I tell him, maybe slightly embarrassed at the request to read something so personal and intimate. "And I sincerely hope you'll become a published poet one day."

"Thank you," he says under his breath, his head bowing slightly in appreciation. "Actually, I never shared them with anyone."

Oh jeez, that makes me want to read them even more! "Why not?"

He shrugs, before taking a sip on his glass. "I never met someone who wanted to read poetry." His words carry some melancholia that makes my gaze freeze. "And my family certainly isn't interested in it." My heart aches for him. The fact no one in his family has ever been supportive of his writing must have been so isolating. "What about yours?"

His question catches me off guard and I find myself tensing at the subject. "They are no longer together," I say simply, hoping to end the conversation there.

But Andries seem to have something else in mind. "May I ask why?"

Damn, I was definitely not expecting that this evening we'd be talking about my parents. "Well, Mama got older…" I let my words trail off, clearly unprepared to be talking about their divorce. Even though it has been a long time ago, I still feel a certain uneasiness talking about it. Andries remains attentively fixed on me, so I search for the best words to put on. "One day Dad just decided to leave," I fess out. Andries has been so open about his life with me, maybe it's time to open up and do the same. "He sent Mama a text message and she started reading it as she was going down stairs to check the mail. She slipped and fell hard on the floor, suffering several spinal cord injuries." My heart squeezes at the simple memory of it. "I witnessed everything: the tears, the screams, the anger, the pain. But she wasn't crying because of the fall, it was because of him. It was a text from Dad telling her he had fallen in love with another woman and had decided to move on with his life. He never came back. Not even to pick up his clothes or to tell us goodbye." *This is so freaking private. Why am I even telling him all this?*

"That's so fucked up, jeez," Andries blurts out, his face laced with a mix of sadness and annoyance as he processes everything I just said. He stares absently at the floor before his eyes return to me. "So that's why love has never been in the picture for you?"

My heart nearly hurdles into my throat at the word *love* coming from his mouth. "Yeah, I think it's fair to say I didn't have the best role models at home." I pause for a moment, finish my glass, and then say, "Plus, most men I've met are cheaters and liars anyway, so why bother? I'm just saving myself from a heartbreak."

Noticing that the glass in my hand is empty, Andries casually holds my glass over my hand and refills it. It might not be a big deal for him, but feeling his hand over mine doesn't go unnoticed. "Not all men are cheaters and liars," he casually points out.

"But enough of them are," I retort. Seeing how his gaze is still fixed on me, I decide to delve further. "When the looks fade away, when the passion switches to boredom, when the kids come into play, believe me, most of them are." And leaving him to that, I take a new sip of this delicious champagne.

"What if you fall in love, though?"

I nearly spit out my drink upon hearing him. "I won't," I answer decidedly. "I'm in control of my own life and feelings."

To my surprise, he chuckles with a certain joy, and then his head leans back against the wall, looking at me with a smug expression. "That sounds very naive to me."

"Excuse me?" *I can't believe he just said that!* "What do you know about love in the first place?"

"Well, I know that falling in love is something worth experiencing at least once in a lifetime."

Fucking poet.

I instantly huff and shake my head at his observation as I eat my slice of pizza in silence, a question forming in the back of my head. "Have you ever been in love?"

"Not yet," he answers, his eyes still pinned on me as if he's thinking something through.

The way he remains steadily looking at me is starting to make me feel quite self-conscious that I'm the only one still eating. "So how do you know it is worth it?" I ask, discreetly throwing the crust of the pizza in the box.

His lips form a slow sexy twist and his eyes sparkle when they meet mine again. "I grew up with living proof of it."

I feel paralyzed by his voice. His words carry a heaviness that enchants me, and the more I get to know him, the more I want to stay in his life and see if... *No! Stop!* I wet my lips, unsure what to think of this moment.

"Why so quiet?" he asks, his tone warm and low. Amid the silence, he leans closer to me, staying just inches from my parted lips, and my heart nearly jumps out of my chest at the idea he could kiss them.

His gaze drifts slowly down and before he closes the small gap between us, my hand goes to his chest as I try to stop him. "Andries…"

"Mm?" His thumb slowly caresses my cheek, and I feel my heart warming at the gesture.

"I don't think we should do this." The conviction in my barely audible voice is totally lacking.

His lips remain inches from mine as if teasing me and I know perfectly well that if I cave to this, it's gonna be harder to stop afterwards.

"Do what?" he asks, his eyes on my lips like they are the prey. I find myself totally drawn to him, my body aching to feel his touch, his mouth… Oh gosh, my pussy throbs at the thought we could do so much more than just talk.

I'm going to regret this. I'm sure I'm going to, but in the heat of the moment, my hand goes around the back of his head and I pull him toward me. "This." Shutting my eyes, I let myself revel in the heady sensation of feeling his lips pressed on mine. A low growl escapes him as I deepen the kiss, my tongue stroking his, and my body pulses with an electric current at the taste of his warm mouth.

His hands wrap around my waist, and he pulls me closer to him, sitting me on his bulge. Oh gosh, my skirt goes up and the feel of him pressed against my panties makes my heartbeat speed up. I don't think it has ever pounded so damn fast.

Before I can even think, he starts pulling my blouse up and I mechanically raise my arms in the air, helping him out.

"We shouldn't," I mumble, once I'm left only with my bra on. Yet his skilled mouth finds its way to my neck, where he traces languorous kisses all the way down to the valley between my breasts. I shut my eyes, wet my lips, and let my hands run and tug his hair. "Ahh…" My head is spinning with lust and I feel myself drenching at the hardness of his growing erection. "Andries, we shouldn't be doing this," I repeat, aiming to bring back some common sense.

"Why not?" he asks as he returns to my neck.

"I'm way older," I breathe beneath his touch, his mouth now sucking and nibbling my flesh and I shiver, feeling the warm slickness ache between my legs.

"Not a valid reason," I hear him saying before he presses his lips on mine again for a lingering kiss. His tongue is hot and demanding, flicking in my mouth and playing with my own, leaving me totally helpless. My clit is throbbing, pleading to have his mouth there.

"Andries," I moan between his kisses as I waver between resisting him or not.

"You have no idea how much I want you." Oh, I do have an idea! I can feel his cock pressed against his pants, hard and ready for me. This is all happening so sudden that I don't know how to react. Ten minutes ago we were just talking and now I'm without my blouse sitting on top of his boner, flushed cheeks, my wetness coating the fabric of my panties. What is happening to me?

"I don't do one-night stands," I tell him, trying to find yet another excuse to put an end to this madness.

But everything seems in vain to discourage him as he says, "Me either."

Before I can lean into him for another kiss, loud footsteps erupt above us and the blood in my body runs cold immediately.

I shush him, trying to remain as silent as possible to focus on the emerging noises.

"What the fuck was that?" Andries seems just as worried.

"Holy shit!" I say in a whisper as I come up with a realization. "I think the owner lives upstairs!"

Andries gapes at my answer. "Are you serious?"

"Let's go," I instruct, already standing on my feet to make my way out. I put my blouse back on, and take my purse, while Andries gathers his backpack before we hurry to make our way out. We head to the back door of the store, which is closer to us than the front door. And after I manage to open it, we step outside, finding ourselves in a dark alley. I'm glad I kept the door keys with me, jeez! Then I click the door shut again and lock the door just like it was.

"That was wild!" Andries comments, running a hand on his hair. "Do you think it was really the owner?"

I can only hope that whoever that was doesn't go downstairs now. I need Lili to take the leftovers and throw them away before he can see them. Gosh! My sister is gonna kill me. "I don't know, but that's a good reminder that I shouldn't spend my whole evening with you," I snap, pointing a finger at him.

All of a sudden, though, he reaches down and takes my hand, pulling me against him. I gasp at how quick his move is. "A good reminder that you should come to my place and finish what we started."

I scoff at his cocky answer, head shaking. "Yeah, right..."

I release myself from his grip and take a step back, but he takes a step forward, and I find myself caged between the wall of the building that stands behind me and Andries.

"Why not?" His voice is low, filled with lust, and before I can even give him a reply, his mouth finds its way back to my neck, making me moan in response.

"I've to wake up early tomorrow," I manage to mumble, even though I don't sound very convincing. I shut my eyes, my lips parting as I revel in the ardor of his kisses, his hands are now under my blouse, roaming on my back and pressing my body against his. And with each passing second I'm in his embrace, I feel closer to heaven than earth. "It's best I go now."

He looks me in the eye for a second, a mix of confusion and desire lodged in his gaze. Quickly enough, he takes one of my hands and presses it against his boner, making me gasp at the feel of him. "You gonna leave me like that?"

"Andries!" I protest, shoving my hand off of his.

"What?" He snatches my legs and in the blink of an eye wraps them around his hips, pressing his hardness against my core. "Come to my place," he demands, his hands on my ass to hold me in place against the wall.

"We shouldn't have done what we did," I chide. My arms are clasped around his neck for support, and my ankles hook at his lower back. "I told you I just wanted us to be friends."

"And we are."

I shoot him an arched eyebrow at his statement, and he answers pressing his groin against me.

"Ah!" I couldn't have hated and loved this moment more.

"It's not like we are together," he breathes, before his lips are on mine again, and everything else fades away. Despite being fully dressed, he starts grinding against me as if we were naked. My eyes are shut and it feels just too good to tell him to stop. "Ah!" My breath is ragged and loud against his mouth, and the simple feel of his manhood between my thighs makes me see stars. My head falls back against the wall; I'm just too high on lust to even process what is going on. All I hear is the sound of our heartbeats panting in fury, the rhythm of his thrusts against me, and the desire of feeling each other translated into moans and whimpers.

"I want you so damn much." He marks every single word with intensity while thrusting against me. "Let me take you to my place."

I don't have the strength in me to speak, I'm too drunk on him to even protest.

"Roxie?" he says my name with so much need and sensuality that I can't help but keep my eyes shut, thinking about everything we could do here or at his place. To my greatest disappointment, he stops and releases me, and I find myself standing on my two feet again, except my thong is so wet that it is beyond embarrassing. He takes my hand in his and then leads me toward the street. "Let's go home."

"I can't," I say, already missing the warmth of his body pressed against mine. "You are such a wicked temptation, my god…"

"A wicked temptation?" He stops in his track, turning around to face me. "Are you hearing yourself? I want you, you want me, let's go home and finish what we started."

It's so easy for him to say that. He knows he's getting under my skin, and the more time I spend with him, the harder it will be to stop. But maybe just tonight we could…

No! I have to give the keys back to my sister. I promised her I would, and I even took her car to come here.

"Andries, this is wrong on so many levels," I manage to force the words out. "If I sleep with you, I'm sure I'll love it, but I'll also regret it."

He looks at me totally flabbergasted. "Why?"

"I know you don't care about our age gap but…"

"Oh, gosh!" He rolls his eyes, head shaking in disbelief. "And you? Do you really care about it? We have like just twelve years difference. Even my uncle and aunt have a bigger one."

"That doesn't make it right." And before he can resume walking toward his car with me, I add, "Andries, look, let's be honest here, we both know where this is gonna take us." I pause, observing him for a moment. "You even told me you aren't into one-night stands."

He chuckles, his head shaking at my words. "You are afraid, aren't you?"

I frown at his question. "Afraid? Of what?"

"Of falling for me," he says, our eyes locking on each other. "Or of being in a relationship, I don't know, but it feels to me you are afraid of something."

"Maybe," I answer, my voice small, but I can't deny there's definitely some truth to it. "I told you I just wanted us to be friends."

"And we *are* just friends." He heaves a long sigh filled with genuine frustration, and runs a hand through his tousled hair, trying to calm all the sexual tension down. "When will I see you again?"

"I…" *I don't think we should see each other again,* but I find myself unable to say those words. Even if I should, I'm just incapable of telling him that, so instead, I say, "Once you have your first poetry book all done." Which should have a similar outcome.

"That's a good motivation to get it done in a week or two, you know."

"Joke aside, I need time," I tell him, my tone more serious.

"I got it," he hisses.

Looking at my car, which is parked not too far from where we are, I ask, "Do you need a ride?" I pass through him and start making my way toward my car.

Andries then starts walking again, but this time without the same urge and eagerness.

"I also took my car," he informs.

"Oh," I utter, quite surprised. "Is this because you were convinced we'd end up at your place?"

While I'm finding my comment pretty amusing, Andries on the other hand doesn't seem to think so. "You are just delaying something that is inevitable." His words are delivered with so much gravity and conviction that my gaze freezes on him. He opens the door of his car, which happens to be parked right next to mine and my heart is already feeling tight at the idea he's leaving. "But if it matters to you, I will wait." I remain quietly observing him as I stand beside my car. There's nothing more to be said and he knows it. "Well, have a good one."

I feel tempted to go give him one last kiss so that I could keep his taste on my lips, but he's already lowering himself into the driver's seat.

When I hear his door shutting, I know it's time for me to do the same.

Getting into my car, I focus on turning the engine on, and despite already missing his presence, I know this was the right decision, and I couldn't be prouder of myself for having gone through with it.

***

"*You are just delaying something that is inevitable.*" His words replay in my head like a broken record while I'm heading back to Bijlmer to return the car and keys to my sister. What do they mean though? Does he really believe there can be something between us? Like a relationship? I shake my head instinctively at the simple thought of it.

Reaching the parking lot in front of my sister's building, I park the car in the same place I found it and hurry to go upstairs and give her the keys.

When I reach her front door, I call her, and glancing at my watch, I hope she isn't asleep yet.

Fortunately, I hear footsteps approaching and then someone unlocking the door from the other side.

Lili peers out, and then opens the door wide, standing in the doorway. "Look who's here…"

"Hey," I greet, my voice low so not to wake up Mama. "I just wanted to give you back the keys."

I give them back to her and I'm about to turn around and leave when Lili asks, "How is the poet doing? Did you pitch him your services yet?"

At her question, my iPhone starts vibrating in my hand so I just turn it face up to check the screen. It's a new text message from Andries: *Going to bed now. Thank you for the evening. I miss you. X*

"I don't think I'll ever see him again," I announce, shoving my phone back into my purse.

Her brow frowns at my statement. "Why not?"

"I think he's falling in love," I say, keeping it short and hoping to close the subject of this discussion.

"Oh," she mouths, leaning against the doorway. "And you didn't know he was taken?"

"I mean, he's falling for me," I correct.

"For you?" she repeats, totally flabbergasted. "The poor man." She pauses, heaving a long sigh. "I agree, you should put an end to this, then."

Trying to change the subject of our discussion, I ask, "Um, by the way, where does the owner live?"

"I think he lives next to the bookshop or something," she casually replies. "Why?"

My jaw falls at her answer. "You didn't think it was prudent to let me know that?"

"But why?" Lili stands stills, straightening her posture. "What happened?"

"We heard footsteps above us, it was scary as fuck."

"Oh, damn. And did anyone see you?"

"No, I don't think so," I tell her sincerely. Then lowering my voice and putting on a more friendly tone, I say, "But we left a few leftovers there."

She sucks in a breath, looking at me with eyes wide open. "What?"

"We had to leave in a hurry," I explain immediately. "We were in the back of the room and we started hearing noise from upstairs, so we left from the back door."

"It's the last time you go there," she snaps, pointing a finger at me. "I'll pick up the mess you left there, but I can't risk you being caught."

"I know." My gaze drops to the floor for a moment, a gush of air rolling of my mouth. "I don't intend to see him again, anyway."

"Good."

"Well, thank you for everything." I give her a quick hug and then a kiss on each cheek.

Lili holds my arm for an instant, her eyes observing me attentively. "Are you alright?"

"Yeah, just tired from all the commotion," I say, keeping it short. "Well, have a good night." The truth is my emotions and feelings are in a big knot and I've got no idea how to untangle them.

As I retrieve my car, I realize the insanity of what was about to happen—I was literally about to have sex with a college student! I huff and shake my head while turning the engine on. Before putting my hands on the steering wheel though, I look once more at Andries' text message. And despite knowing I should ignore it, I decide to text him back.

Hey, I'm going to bed now, I type, my heart tightening at the lie I'm writing. *Thank you for the evening. It was great. Good night. X.*

Afterwards, I get myself out of the parking lot and head downtown again. A sigh escapes my lips, thinking about the amazing evening I spent with him. And yet, the more I think about it, the more I realize we shouldn't have crossed the line.

This isn't gonna go anywhere.

I have an agency to focus on, a new cabaret; the last thing I need is to start catching feelings for a much younger man that knows nothing about the real Roxanne. This evening was a mistake, plain and simple. An amazing one, but still a mistake. This was my last time meeting him. If Karl needs someone to hang out with the son of his boss, then I'm afraid he'll have to do it himself. I already asked Andries to give a word to his dad for Karl's promotion, so I've already done my part.

After texting Andries, I open the chat with Karl and say, *Hey! The evening was a success, and I asked him to talk to his dad about appointing you for the promotion.*

Minutes later, while I'm driving back home, my phone pings with a new text message from Karl:

Great! See you Saturday night! X

CHAPTER 18

Amsterdam, September 19, 2021
Andries

There are nights when I can't sleep because the words float behind my eyelids until I write them down, and then there are nights when it feels like walking through mud to simply finish a sentence. Tonight is somewhere in between, where I know there is a story in me I just haven't been able to grasp, so I'm just writing nonsense until the dam inside me finally breaks. Except, it's been hours, and it still hasn't broken.

Maybe it's because I can almost feel the city buzzing with life outside, and although I don't want any of it, part of my mind is still a little bit fascinated at the way everyone else lives their lives around here. All the other students seem to compartmentalize their studies and personal lives, while I can't seem to separate who I am from what I love. How can medical students go and smoke until their lungs burn with it, and how can international students with tight budgets spend thousands on bottle service when they should know better?

I've long since vacated my studies, leaving my laptop behind and simply writing freehand in a notebook, sitting on the bed, against the comfortable pillows. Sometimes it's just better to write on pen and paper instead of digitally; it feels more organic, more personal.

It's almost nine p.m., and I've forgone lighting the fireplace tonight, choosing instead to work by the glow of the flicking, atmospheric bedside lamp. Through the windows, it's dark enough that I can't see the passersby I know are walking below, but the lights from the occasional boats on the canal assure me they are there.

There's a lot on my mind when, in reality, I should be mostly focused on my studies. If I was going to go against the grain and be an English major instead of going to business school, I better damn well ace every class. At school, not much can distract me, especially not Dan and his parties, but here…

Here there is Roxanne. And she is somewhere in this city, probably not even thinking about me, while I write and rewrite descriptions of our first kiss over and over. Recounting the moon in her blonde hair and the dust motes floating in front of her eyes inside the bookshop, the air smelling of parchment and ink.

I'm a fool to have tried to have sex with her on the first night, but at least I'm self-aware. That has to count for something, right?

I'm ready to pour myself a glass of red wine and call it a night when I hear something coming from my study. Realizing it's my phone, I hop up to grab it, plucking it from my desk. My heart falls a little when I see it's Dan and not Roxanne, but it's a silly emotion.

"Hey, Dan," I greet, putting the screen against my cheek.

"Why do you always sound so down in the dumps when I call?" he asks, voice slightly raised over all the noise in the background of wherever he is. I can pick out music, the laughter of women, and the clinking of glasses.

"I only sound that way when you're calling me past normal speaking hours. What's up?"

"Has anyone ever told you you're an old man trapped in a youthful body? Anyway." Dan pauses, his tone becoming conspiratorial. "You should come to the cabaret where I'm having dinner. I think it'd interest you."

I walk back to my bed and sit on the edge. "No."

"Andries, Roxanne is here. With Karl."

I freeze in the middle of hanging up the phone, bringing it back to my ear rapidly. "What did you say?"

"Roxanne and Karl just walked in and got a table at the front of the stage. They're the only two at the table, and they're sitting close together."

My heart feels heavy. It's like my constant thoughts about her had somehow conjured her back into my life, except in a way I'd have never wished. "She told me she and Karl were just friends."

Dan hums. "They don't look like friends, dude."

"I'll consider it," I grit out. "Send me the address and maybe I'll come."

The message comes almost immediately, as if Dan had it typed and ready to send before he even called me. As soon as I tap the address to bring up a map, the heavy feeling in my chest intensifies. It's in the red light district. That fact makes me at once want to go even more intensely, and at the same time, more reluctant than ever to make the trip.

I want nothing to do with the area. As much as it's blown up in the media as some place of wanton debauchery, the trope isn't completely unwarranted. It's a place where sex becomes entertainment, something to be bought and enjoyed like any other transaction, whether it is with an escort or watching an erotic cabaret show, which is what I'm sure Dan is doing right now. I don't want to view sex that way, ever, and I certainly don't enjoy thinking of Roxanne watching some arousing cabaret numbers with Karl. Or anyone, for that matter.

On the other hand, I'm not going to let my distaste of the area dissuade me from getting to the bottom of whatever is going on. Just a few days earlier, I had been making out with her, my hands between her breasts and her tiny frame against mine. How can she be dating someone else when she said she wasn't? It just doesn't make sense, and I won't be able to rest until I force it to.

* * *

The cab that picks me up is nearly silent as it coasts across the cobblestone roads. It had taken me less than thirty minutes to change into a shirt and jeans and prepare myself for the trip, but now that I have almost arrived, a lot of my confidence in this confrontation has drained away. I don't want to smother Roxanne, but I feel like I have a right to know what's really going on.

Inside, my first impression is that everything is red, red, and more red. It's a Parisian-themed cabaret, but it's leaning heavily into the red-light district vibe. As my eyes adjust, I can see that it's less gaudy than I had originally assumed, with dark wooden tables and bar tops, metal gas lamps, and the low drone of a brass quartet playing in the corner. The place is packed to the gills, but I can see Dan waving enthusiastically from some place close to the stage, so I push my way through and make my way to him.

The female guests are dressed in what I'd consider club-wear—everything is clearly expensive and well-made but showing enough skin to be a tad tacky. The employed ladies are a different story. They are walking seductive distractions, with heels high enough to make a less experienced wearer wobble, silk structured corsets and one-pieces, headdresses that look more like works of art, and some with feathered fans nearly half the size of their bodies. As I walk, I notice them dragging these fans across the bodies of patrons as they speak to them, a shivery touch that seems to offer a promise of more to come, even if they are just there to look at. They are experts, and I'm sure they have plenty of returning customers to prove it.

The show hasn't started, so the intricately dressed employees are still mingling by the time I reach Dan's table. I stop in my tracks as I examine the other people at the table with my friend; Dan, Jessica, and–

Elise? What! My sister Elise?

I bypass Dan in a rush, grabbing Elise by the wrist and bending over to hiss into her face, "What the hell are you doing here? You are seventeen."

Elise yanks her arm out of my grip and tilts her chin up stubbornly. "And you're eighteen, so what's the difference?"

"The difference is," I tell her, still crowding into her space, "I'm legally an adult."

Elise shrugs one shoulder, pulling up the strap of her shirt when it slides down, never unlocking her gaze from mine. "Mind your own business then, Andries the adult."

I start to lecture her more, but Dan lays a hand on my arm, his grip just barely letting me know that he'll pull me back if I don't chill out. "Relax, man. I'm taking good care of her. She's safe with me and Jessica."

"That doesn't make it better," I tell him, but I take the hint and back off. Elise looks triumphant, but I studiously ignore her now. I'll deal with her later.

"Where is she?" I continue, and Dan points a finger toward the stage, and there, two rows back, is Roxanne and Karl.

I try to be a rational person and look at the complete picture with a calm view, but something thunderous and new is waking up in my chest and I just can't. Something about seeing her, sitting close enough to Karl that their shoulders touch when one of them leans over to speak, makes me feel...*jealous*—something I've never experienced before in my life. Elise, Dan, and everything else suddenly become secondary to this.

I know these feelings are over the top, especially for a woman I've only just recently gotten to know, but something inside of me, almost primal, can't help but think, *Mine.*

I'd been spending so much time with her at the bookshop, helping her find the right titles, discuss poetry, and sort through collections, that I was sure a burgeoning romance was blooming between us. She laughed with me, gave me that genuine smile I had never seen until we were alone, and gushed about her favorite authors and books until she was nearly blue in the face. She had opened up about personal topics she wouldn't normally talk about all while eating greasy pizza on a blanket... I bet that Karl had never seen anything other than the perfectly polished Roxanne he had beside him now.

I ignore Elise's protests and sink down into a chair at their table, not acknowledging Jessica's hesitant greeting or Dan's smartass comments. Pulling out my phone, I send Roxanne a message and then wait impatiently for her to receive it, my eyes boring a hole in the back of her head.

Are you and Karl enjoying yourselves? It looks like it from back here.

It takes her a second, but finally, I see her pull her phone out from her clutch, reading the message before whipping her head around to look at me.

She narrows her eyes and goes to put the phone away, but I send her another quick text.

Outside. Now.

When I start to stand, Dan clears his throat, and I look down at him. It's then I feel the awkward tension that has fallen over the table ever since I sat down, and it makes me cringe a little. I didn't mean to ruin my friend's night, even if he was escorting my underage sister about town.

"Let her go, Andries. That one isn't for you," Dan advises me, his usually amused voice somber.

"You don't know what you're talking about."

He looks torn and shakes his head. "I do. More than you know. Just leave her alone for now, and if you have to be near her, just be her friend. You two are not going to work out the way you think you are."

"Then why did you call me?" I ask, throwing up my hands in exasperation.

"I was hoping seeing them would dampen that flame, not stoke it higher. Just let her go, man."

"No, you wanted me to handle this, then I'm handling it." I start to stomp outside, but stop, feeling a touch guilty for the darkness I had thrown over their good time. "Don't wait up for me. Go ahead and drink or whatever you're wanting to do. I'll be back."

As I push through the crowd, I feel the three of them watching me carefully, but I don't give them the satisfaction of turning around. There is only one person I want to talk to in this moment, and it's the woman I just witnessed walking out the back door, her phone clutched angrily in her perfectly manicured hands.

Roxanne.

She's going to give me the truth tonight, because I'm done playing nice to win her affections.

* * *

Beneath the anemic lights of the alleyway behind the cabaret, Roxanne is as beautiful as ever. Her mere presence elevates the place beyond what it had been before. Even if she looks ready to slap me in the face.

Part of me wishes she would. I'd take anything from her besides the dull aloofness that is written all over her features.

"I have to say, Andries, I didn't expect to see you here of all places." She pulls out a thin box of cigarettes from her clutch and lights one, the smoke spiraling to the heavens. And God help me because all I want is to snatch it out of her mouth.

"I could say the same for you, Roxanne."

She raises her eyebrows as she takes another drag off the cigarette. "You have a strange opinion of me, then. I happen to enjoy cabarets."

I lean against the brick wall of the building, figuring that this wasn't going to be the quick, fiery confrontation I had imagined. She is all too relaxed, the movements of her body languid and slow as she crosses her arms, waiting for my response.

"There's a bit of a difference between the classic cabaret and the kind that are glorified strip clubs," I tell her, and she narrows her eyes.

"You sound very judgmental right now. It isn't a good look on you."

I chuckle sarcastically. "You know what isn't a good look on you? Kissing one man and then ending up at some pornographic cabaret club with another less than a week later."

"You and I are just friends. I don't particularly like that you're assuming you have some say on anything I do or who

I spend my time with." Something flashes in her eyes, anger or annoyance, but it's gone as soon as it appears.

"Are you admitting you're here with him as a date?" I ask.

"Don't put words in my mouth." Roxanne drops the cigarette and grinds it beneath her heel, ash smearing on the concrete. "And frankly, it's none of your business what I do, or where I go."

Outwardly, I don't move, but it feels like an arrow lodges itself in my chest when she says that. I know we don't have any sort of title, but everything up until this point had felt like a relationship building between the two of us. Had I really read into everything so wrongly? We kissed. Several times. And made out. Heck, we almost had sex. Surely that isn't just a thing between friends.

"God forbid you be held accountable," I scoff. "Am I just a game to you?"

"No," she bites out. "You're my *friend*, like I just said. But tread carefully, Andries. You're acting like an asshole, and I'm not friends with assholes."

Her words stoke a fire in me, and I don't mean to sound as angry as I do when I speak. I just can't help it. "Roxanne, I know you think I'm the bad guy here, but I'm getting the impression all this time you've been spending with me is because you and your *date* Karl were just using me to get him that promotion he's been going on about." I push myself up off the wall and step a little closer to her. "And while I might be a lot of things, Roxie, I am not a pawn or a fool."

I can tell I've struck a nerve because she straightens. "Not that it's any business of yours, but Karl is just a friend. Don't flatter yourself. You haven't come up as the topic of conversation at all."

She's close enough that I can almost smell the intoxicating scent of her perfume, but I keep my resolve, scoffing. "I don't believe you for a second. Not with the way you're speaking to me right now."

Her haughty expression falls, but only for a second before the mask is back up. It's like she's a totally different person from the woman I've been spending my time with. Like I don't even know her.

"You're wrong, Andries, and I'm only hurtful because you started it."

"If I'm wrong," I lean even more into her space, bending over at the waist until we are at eye level. "Then prove it."

Roxanne smirks, an expression in complete opposition from the hurt in her eyes. She reaches out and drags her nails lightly down my cheek before sweeping past me. "I don't owe you any proof. Goodnight, Andries."

Her departure is so sudden that even when I whip around and try to grab her arm to stop her, she's gotten away, back inside the cabaret and back to Karl. I pace the length of the alley, trying to regain my calm, hearing and feeling the bass from the cabaret music reverberating under my feet.

If I leave now, she'll know that she's rattled me, and the last thing I want is to appear as a quitter, or a man that can be easily brushed off. I have no interest in the show, and even less interest in watching some erotic nonsense with Roxanne and Karl sitting together and enjoying it at the same time. Would he touch her leg, or whisper in her ear? The thought makes heat rise up on the back of my neck.

I open the door back into the club, maybe a little too forcefully, causing the glasses on the nearest table to rattle. I walk back to the table where Dan, Jessica, and Elise are, sitting back down in silence. Dan and Jessica look apprehensive, but Elise just looks bored with me, which is fine. I want to pretend my sister isn't here anyway, as I'm not thrilled with her being so young and attending things like this. If I ignore her, I won't have to think about it.

I can tell Dan wants to ask me how it went, but he keeps sliding glances at Jessica and Elise, ultimately deciding not to mention Roxanne, so he moves the conversation in a different direction.

"Have you ever been to a cabaret before?" he asks, sounding genuinely curious. He is a great actor.

"To a normal cabaret, yes, but considering where this one is located, and how the performers are dressed…" I wave at one performer, who's leaning over another table with the pale, white globes of her ass barely concealed by her one-piece lingerie. Not totally out of place for a cabaret show, but it gives me a clue how over-the-top this one might be. "I assume this isn't like a *normal* cabaret."

"It's much better," he assures me, waving over a server to get a drink for me. "Just relax and try to forget about whatever nonsense you've gotten yourself into."

"Easy for you to say," I mutter, but I try to take his advice, anyway. The lights are starting to lower, and I know showtime is about to begin.

It's exactly as I had expected, but I guess I still hadn't been completely prepared for it. It's not that I'm puritanical in any regard, but I hadn't been completely aware of how steeped in sexual energy this cabaret would be.

Tonight, though, I just feel exceptionally uncomfortable with my sister beside me and the woman I was starting to grow fonder of with each passing day a few tables away with another man.

The dancers on stage, bedecked in red lace and gold appliqués, move in a hypnotic, almost snake-like fashion, the music they move to a perfect mixture of throbbing rhythms and inviting melody.

When they disrobe, flesh flushed, and on display, I clench my jaw and try even harder to ignore my sister, which inevitably makes me focus on Roxanne again. She's swayed toward Karl, and I can see her face in profile, her smile sugary and self-assured. I clench my fists under the table, locking my eyes back on the dancers, bare-breasted and sensual. I try to imagine myself touching one of them, fingers and palms cupping and stroking, but every time I find myself believing in the fantasy, they turn into Roxanne beneath my touch, before evaporating into smoke.

I have to get out of here.

I tip back the drink Dan had ordered me, letting the entire pour cascade down my throat and burn like liquid fire in my stomach before pushing my chair back and standing.

"Excuse me," I tell the table simply, avoiding Dan's questioning looks as I slip, half bent over as to not disrupt the show, through the crowd and out of the cabaret.

I tilt my head back toward the sky and take deep lungfuls of cool night air, ready to be home among the four walls I had found comfort in lately, but before I can hail my waiting driver, Dan sidles up beside me.

"You're missing the show," I comment, not turning to look at him.

"Yeah, but I thought you might need me more, so I took a quick break." Dan bumps his shoulder into mine until I finally pay him my full attention.

He grins, before saying, "You're lovesick."

I want to argue, but he's probably right. "Maybe. If so, then I'm being ridiculous."

Dan, as much of a jokester as he is, switches gears and becomes more serious as he continues. "You need to just cut the whole thing with Roxanne off and move on. You two are in completely different places in your lives and she obviously has an entire life and group of people around her already. Don't waste your time trying to carve out a niche with her when there are sweet, available girls that you'll have so much more in common with."

"I don't want a mirror of myself, Dan. I want someone different. Someone to challenge me and make me grow, someone who will show me different aspects of life I never would have seen otherwise. Roxanne is that for me."

"You're going to fly too close to the sun and get burned here, Icarus," Dan warns. "Women like Roxanne aren't looking to be teachers, they're looking for a partner that meets them at their level. You're still a student, dude, and you're still finding out who you're going to be in life."

"That's why I'm so into her. The fact that she's established in life, comfortable in her skin. I don't want some simpering eighteen-year-old, I want a woman who knows who and what she wants out of life and out of partners." I drag my hand through my hair, frustrated. "I've never been so immediately attracted to anyone in my life."

Dan is quiet for a moment before replying. "Do you think if you sleep with her this obsession will sort of die out?"

"It's not about the sex," I assure him. "It's about her as a whole."

He shrugs. "I'm just saying, man, that there is a fine line between attraction and obsession. Don't step too far over that line or you're going to get yourself in trouble."

I slide him a glance, both annoyed with him and full of a grudging affection for my stalwart friend. He doesn't pull the punches when he gives advice, but he's only telling me all this because he's looking out for me.

"She was angry enough at me tonight that she might not want to see me again, but I'm convinced there is something between us, and it isn't just one sided. But do me a favor. If you notice me getting too intense, tell me. I don't want to ruin a good thing by being too…"

"Too much like yourself? Got it," Dan jokes, and I elbow him, and we both start to laugh.

"Go back in and enjoy the show, and for the love of all things holy, please keep an eye on my sister," I tell him, jerking my chin toward the cabaret. "I'll talk to you tomorrow."

"You sure you don't want to come back in with me?"

I shake my head. "No. I've got some things I need to work out in my head. Alone."

CHAPTER 19

Amsterdam, September 20, 2021
Andries

For as agonized and determined as I had been to join the English program, I'm now completely and utterly hopeless at paying attention in class with Roxanne on my mind. The lecture hall is enormous and old, sweeping wide, the wood of the desks rubbed smooth and shiny with age. I usually sit closer to the front to prove that I'm paying attention, but I knew it was useless today, so I lingered in the back, trying and failing to ignore the weight of my phone in my pocket.

With my book spread out in front of me, I try my best to keep up with the professor, making scant notes here and there between checking my phone screen for message alerts. I'm not absorbing anything in class, but maybe if my notes are coherent enough, I won't fall too much behind. If that doesn't work, I can always copy notes from my classmates.

After getting home from the cabaret last Saturday night, I had tossed and turned for hours, unable to get the evening off my mind. Roxanne had never spoken to me like that before or ever been angry with me either, and it ate at me minute after minute. I considered calling her at least a dozen times over the weekend, but I refused to admit defeat in this matter. I'm in the right, she is in the wrong. Still, my patience is running thin, and I wonder how much longer I can stare at the blank phone screen before I break down and call her.

I want an apology. *Need* an apology. Her behavior is atrocious and selfish, and it almost seems like she is in denial about our connection. She clearly doesn't have any strong feelings for Karl, but the fact that she was there with him is more than I can calmly accept. Why hadn't she invited me instead, or if he had invited her, why did she accept?

The lecture hall is full enough that no one notices my obsessive phone checking, but I'm so sick of my compulsions that I'm ready for class to be over anyway. Counting the minutes down doesn't make time go faster, though, it just makes me more impatient.

I have taken to tapping my pencil on my desk anxiously when my phone finally vibrates silently with five minutes of class left to go. I fumble it out of my pocket, heart soaring and then immediately crashing back down to earth when I see it's Elise texting me, and not Roxanne. Fuck.

The weather is beautiful today, let's go for a walk after you get out of class. I'll meet you outside.

I don't want to go for a walk with my sister. I don't want to do anything but go back to my apartment and wait on Roxanne's hypothetical message, and if it never came, close myself in my office and write until I had purged all these negative emotions. But logically, I know walking with Elise is the better choice, if only to get some sunshine and distract my mind.

I'm already zipping my messenger bag up and swinging it over my shoulder when class is dismissed, and as promised, Elise is waiting outside the lecture hall for me. She's wearing a sweet, fond expression as she hugs me in greeting as if I wasn't aware she was at an erotic show two nights ago just like I was. The idea still makes me shiver uncomfortably. It's almost impossible to imagine my sister enjoying something like that.

"You look exhausted," she comments as we walk out onto the concourse.

Campus is tucked perfectly into the city, but there is still enough green grass and beautifully paved pathways by the water to enjoy between classes. The sun is out, sparkling on the water, and while the air is cool, it's nicer than it has been in a few days. Elise is right; it feels good to stretch my legs and breathe in the fresh air.

"Something like that," I answer finally.

She watches my face for a moment while we walk before speaking again. "Why did you leave so early last Saturday night?"

"I found the entire evening... distasteful."

She shrugs one delicate shoulder. "I thought it was very soft, considering the material."

"It was a combination of things, as I'm sure you know. You're just fishing for an explanation from me." I slide her a suspicious glance.

"Are you still mad at me for going?" she asks carefully.

"Why Elise, you're being so very polite today considering how snotty you were Saturday night? Do I only get your respect when we aren't among friends?" I'm only half-joking, but Elise has the good sense to look a little chagrined, the corners of her mouth turning down in a frown.

"I was afraid you were going to make me leave," she explains after a few moments meekly.

"I won't lie, I'd have liked to." I shove my hands in my pockets as we stroll. "But rest assured I won't say a word to our parents about it. From my side, you're free to do what you like, same as me."

She smiles at me in return, most likely in satisfaction, as we continue walking. "Speaking of you and what you like to do... What have you been up to? Have you been...um... meeting new people?" Elise is clearly trying to get me to talk about Roxanne, in a roundabout way, but still not asking outright.

"If you want to know, sister, speak plainly."

"Fine," she huffs. "Who was that woman that you went outside with, and who you were staring at all night?"

"She works at one of the antiquarian bookstores in town. She and I have been... spending time together, I guess is how you would describe it."

"In a romantic sense?" Elise presses.

"Maybe, maybe not. I'm not sure, though if you had asked me before Saturday, I'd have said yes."

Elise hums in thought, considering her next words carefully. "Don't be angry, bro, but I don't think that woman —or any woman who you just meet about town—is worth the obvious grief you are going through. You're a Van den Bosch. If that's not enough for her, then she's an idiot."

"Don't speak about her like that," I snap, before quickly reining in my temper when Elise flinches. "Sorry. It's just that I feel this undeniable connection between us, and I can't help but be inspired to follow it."

"Look, Andries, don't take this the wrong way, but this woman is what, a librarian, you say? A bookstore owner? She doesn't sound like the kind of woman that would integrate into our family very well. I saw that she was with the same Karl that came over to our estate, but what our dad's employees do is none of our concern. You, on the other hand, are very much someone I am concerned about."

"Elise…" I start, but she cuts me off.

"On the other hand, if you are craving the company of one of the fairer sex, there is the perfect girl right here on campus with us!" Elise sounds conspiratorial, smirking at me, and I fight not to roll my eyes.

"Tatiana?" I ask, containing a laugh.

"Yes!" she exclaims. "See, we're on the same wavelength, and you must've been thinking about her in some capacity if you were that swift to know who I was talking about. She's the perfect fit for you, bro, and she's almost already part of the family with as much as her dad spends time with ours!"

"They aren't spending time together as you put it. They are doing business together, so I find it hard to believe you actually consider Tatiana almost part of the family." I sigh, pinching the bridge of my nose. "She's a lovely girl, Elise, but she is just not for me."

"You're only saying that now because you're smitten with someone else." Elise waves her hand in a dismissive gesture. "But as soon as this little infatuation of yours fades and you give Tatiana a chance, you'll see how much better it can be to be romantically connected to someone who meshes seamlessly into your life."

"I don't want seamless," I insist. "I want it to be real, I want it to be almost electric in its intensity, and that's what I have with Roxie. Not Tatiana."

Elise has a calculating look on her face, and I immediately regret using Roxanne's name, even if it was the shortened version of it. I don't think my sister would go as far as conspiring with our dad to get me to court flower-girl, but watching her make a mental note of the name, I realize I could be very much mistaken.

My siblings are all perfect examples of what Van den Bosch's children should be, but Elise especially fit the family mold perfectly. She is Dad's favorite, and he dotes on her like she can do no wrong. In return, she feeds into anything he asks of her, more than willing to take over the role of the eldest child if I continue to spurn my place in the family. Or, she might be working behind the scenes with my parents to make sure I find a good, respectable match to keep the family name pristine.

"Did Dad set you up to do this?" I ask her bluntly, and she startles, looking at me with wide eyes.

"No! Why ever would you think that? We're just talking, sibling to sibling."

"Really? Because I feel like you're mining me for information. Why else would your 'perfect match' for me be a girl that our parents would surely approve of and not a friend or classmate of yours?"

Elise stops, stepping in front of me so we're eye to eye. "Because Tatiana *is* perfect for you. She is bright, bubbly, and positive. She will balance out all your…" Elise wiggles her fingers to indicate me. "Eccentric, brooding writer habits."

My mouth twitches. I don't want to laugh, because I'm not sure if I completely believe her, but I can't help chuckling anyway. "Brooding writer habits?"

She steps back to my side, this time linking our arms as we stroll. "Oh, you know. Constant frown, long-winded way of speech, always holed up in your apartment, dark circles under your eyes…"

Feigning offense, I touch the area under my eyes. "Dark circles?"

"I'm teasing. I'm sure they're just because you didn't get much sleep last night."

"Something like that," I agree.

We walk in silence for a while after that, just enjoying the weather and each other's company, but eventually, Elise speaks up again, this time sounding more serious than before. "Andries?"

"Hm?"

"Have you told Dad that you switched programs yet?"

My stomach sinks, thinking about my switch to the English program and how much I've been dreading bringing it up to our dad. I should have done it immediately, but the longer I waited, the more difficult it became. I swallow before shaking my head.

"Ah, no. I haven't, and I don't plan to for some time at least."

"Oh," Elise says simply.

"I don't mean to sound blunt, but I really need you to keep your mouth shut about this, Elise. It's my burden to bear and my story to tell. Promise me."

She lifts her hand to her mouth and mimics zipping it up like a zipper. "I won't say anything, I swear. You can count on me for this."

I blow out a breath, relaxing a little. "Okay. Thank you."

For the rest of the walk, we just chat about school and all the things it entails, and the subject of my love life is finally closed. This thing I have with Roxanne feels personal, something secret that I hold close to my heart and that I'm not yet ready to share with the world. I'm not sure why, but it feels like if I speak of it openly, it will crumble apart before my eyes. Our friendship is fragile and new, and now, very strained. I hope it can be fixed, because I can't wait much longer to know the truth of where we stand.

I don't tell Elise any of that, though. If she isn't spying on me for our parents, I don't want to burden her with my drama and distract her from school. If she *is* spying, Roxanne is certainly something I don't want my parents to know about.

I look down at my sister and the slight smile on her lips, her eyes slightly squinted against the light shining off the canal, and feel thankful for her suggestion to spend time together. It brought up some difficult questions, yes, but she is still my family, and she was right. The weather is beautiful today.

CHAPTER 20

Pass by the bookshop before I close, I need to give you something. With my sister's message in mind and a thundering heart inside my chest, I open the door of the bookshop, just twenty minutes shy before she closes. I did ask her why I had to come over, but she didn't say anything else in return.

The bookstore has a familiar scent, a combination of tea tree oil and whatever candles Lili has decided to burn that week. She always manages to keep the place smelling inviting. Nothing overpowering, just enough to make sure when you walk in, it's calming. It was something my mother started years ago, and Lili continued after she left.

When I walk into the store, though, my heart tightens as I remember the evening I spent with Andries. Oh gosh! I can't let my mind drift back to him. I have to chase him out of my heart for good. Jeez! This bookstore has always been special to me, even before he came here. In fact, when I was a teenager and my mother started working here, it was like a treasure hunt, always searching for the next book that would transport us to some distant world.

It's fair to say my sister and I received our education from these shelves. The best education possible, really. The fact that being so well read also helped me with my clients is more than just a little ironic.

As I cross the store, my eyes focus on the very place I kissed Andries for the first time and the thought of it brings back memories of him. His lips on mine. How good he smelled… how good his arms felt holding me while we kissed with more passion than one-sided lust. Again, it was something I rarely experienced.

Stop it!

I force myself out of my reverie and smile once my sister comes into view as she stands behind the counter, closing the cash register and making notes. I approach her quietly not wanting to distract her.

"The poet came here," she announces out of nowhere, and she rolls her eyes in a not-so-subtle manner. She's either annoyed or thinks Andries and I are still seeing each other. "He left something for you, since you weren't here."

"What did you tell him?" I ask immediately, my curiosity sparked.

"That I was your sister and worked here part-time," she answers, her tone even, as she slides a brown paper package across the desk at me.

It's wrapped in a thin string and looks like a package transported from the past century. Square and thin. "Do you know what it is?"

"Nope." Her words are curt, and her attention returns to whatever she's doing. Basically it means: *I don't care.*

I thought she'd ask me a bunch of questions about it, but I'm glad she doesn't.

As I look to the package in my hands, I can't help but think again about Andries and when I told him we could see each other again after he writes his first book of poetry. Maybe it's a sample of what he's been working on. And that's exactly this side of him I'm definitely falling for. A man who looks like a stunning model and can also write complex prose. At least for me.

Tucking the package under my arm, I'm tempted to try to talk to Lili more, but without any warning she turns and walks into the back. Not a word. And I'm not about to get into it with her. The front doorbell tinkles and an actual customer walks in so I know I need to make myself scarce. Plus, I can't help but wonder what's inside the package. The way Andries acts is like no man I've ever known before.

By the time I walk out, Lili is hovering near a customer and answering questions. She does a great job running the place and making sure that the store has things that will draw the eye in the window. I have so many ideas about how to do more with the place, but it's not a good time. It'll be eventually.

With a bit of time on the walk home, I decide to quickly text Andries, letting him know that I've picked up his package and I'm heading home to open it.

Thank you! I'm glad you received it. His response is almost cryptic when it comes a few minutes later, but then he adds, *You're an inspiration, more than you know.*

If he only knew… He's been in my mind more often than all my clients combined. And it's been impossible to spend one day without his memory haunting me.

Once I stop seeing my clients and turn this chapter of my life, maybe I should tell him the truth about me. Would I have the courage though? One thing is sure, when that day comes, Mama will be quite pleased. Maybe pleased enough to let me back into her life a bit. *Maybe…*

Reaching home, I take off my shoes and coat, and head to the kitchen to pour myself a glass of Sauvignon Blanc. Then I walk onto the living room, and sit comfortably on the couch his gift in one hand and my wine in the other. After putting my glass on the low table, I tear apart the brown paper package and find inside a leather-bound notebook. Curious, I open it and read the first page:

Roxanne,

Love knows many shapes and forms
Not always following the norms
How can love be wrong if it feels right?
How can I see light and you only see the night?

I want more than you're willing to give
I wish you'd stop being so resistive
My heart cries tears without end
Because you won't allow yourself to be more than a friend.

— Andries van den Bosch

I raise my eyebrows in surprise, barely believing what I'm reading. Oh my gosh! Are these his poems? The poems he's been working on since we met? They're good. Really good.

> *A dancing heart*
> *A smiling soul*
> *Worries that depart*
> *Irrationality taking control.*

> *My dear, that is what you do*
> *To a man who is in love*
> *Hoping you will feel it too*
> *Because being with you is all I can think of.*

Holy shit! This is so private and intimate that I don't even know how to feel. A man making me feel emotions like this is so far beyond what I'd normally expect that it's hard to believe he truly wrote those poems for me. And yet, he did, and I jump right onto the next one:

> *On the outside I remain quiet*
> *But my soul is preparing a riot*
> *Seeing you in undeserved arms making a mistake*
> *Makes my loving heart shake*

> *All I feel when I observe this*
> *Is watching a woman I miss*
> *And the only thing my mind can see*
> *Is that it should be me.*

I wonder if he wrote this poem the day he saw me with Karl at the cabaret. Of all the men I met in my life, none ever gifted me a book filled with poems they have written themselves. As I come to think of it, I don't think any man I know even is capable of writing such beautiful prose. I take another sip on my glass and continue reading. There're more beautiful rows of words that follow, and quickly I can see that he's been pouring his heart out onto the pages. And it's all directed at me. It's slightly overwhelming.

My life for the past decade has been me involved with multitudes of men, but nobody has ever gone so far as to write anything so special and intimate for me besides a love note. I've been given cards with thoughts in them that could be cut right out of a porno film, but this is so different. It's raw, honest, vulnerable, and so like Andries. As I keep looking at the words written on the sheets, I grow more confident that my decision to end my contract with Karl should extend to Isaak and Charlie.

Just as I'm flipping another page, my cell phone rings. It's Poppy, and it'd be odd if I didn't answer. Plus, as much as my heart is plunging into my chest, I need to tell her to take the final step toward what I intend to do.

"Hey, Poppy, how are you?" I never greet my assistant with anything but professionalism.

"Sorry to call you so late, but I just wanted to confirm that Charlie will pick you up this Friday at six p.m. for the opera."

"Ah, yes, thank you." For some reason, I don't feel the same excitement I used to when Poppy would announce my next outings with clients. The idea of stopping to see them altogether have been in the back of my head for a while now, actually since the day I put my relationship with Karl on hold. Or was it since the day Andries and I made out at the bookshop? Maybe a combination of both… "Erm, Poppy?"

"Yes?"

"Can you please book a driver to wait for me at Charlie's place right after the opera?"

"Eh, but you are supposed to spend the night there, no?" She generally knows my itinerary and she's right, that part of the evening will be expected. Unless I don't charge him.

"Not anymore," I answer, swirling my wine before I give another gulp. "We won't invoice him for the evening, though."

"Okay, um, is there a problem?" She sounds worried.

"That evening will be my last one with Charlie," I announce. "That's it."

"Oh, so, um, you want us to terminate his contract with you?" she asks.

"Yes, I'll let him know it's over after the opera."

"Okay, and for Isaak? Are you still meeting him this Saturday?"

Oh shit! Isaak!

We only meet once a month and always at his secluded property in the village of Giethoorn, and yet, it feels like it was just yesterday that I was last there with him. "Not this weekend, Poppy," I tell her. "Tell him the one after."

"Eh." She seems to be confused at my request. "Don't you think you should call him though? You have known him for years, it's best you have a word with him first."

I consider her advice for a moment. "You're right, I'll call him."

After my phone call with Poppy, I take another gulp of my wine and get myself ready for my next call. Isaak won't be happy about me canceling his monthly meeting. Or anything else I need to tell him about.

Once he picks up the line, he greets me with so much joy that I feel slightly bad at what I'm about to do. So first I make some small talk to get him warmed up, and only then I say, "Look, um, unfortunately this weekend I won't be able to make it. I have some prior family commitments and need to postpone." It's always been so much easier to lie.

"Oh, alright, should we see each other the weekend after, then?"

He has no idea this is coming. And it's really time to pull the Band-Aid off and make sure I tell him directly. Poppy shouldn't handle this one. "Well, I actually need to talk to you first during the week. Face-to-face, I mean."

"Oh, wow, sounds serious. Should we meet at a coffee shop or something?" he asks.

"Eh, I was thinking a place where we could talk—only the two of us."

He pauses on the line. I know the man, and his wheels are definitely turning quickly trying to figure out what's going on. Thankfully he doesn't probe any further. Always a diplomat.

"I know the manager of Chris Coffee, what if we meet there at two o'clock before they open to the public?"

Perfect. "Sounds great, yeah, what day of the week?"

"I can do next Thursday, does that work?" he says.

"Perfect, thank you so much, I'll see you next Thursday, then."

Hanging up the phone there's a sense of guilt, quickly replaced with a sense of relief. Now all I have to do is wait a week and then it will all be done. I know my clients aren't going to be happy about my decision. Heck, I don't even know if I'll have the courage when the time comes to go through with it. But there's something in me, something I can't really explain, that believes it is the right thing to do.

CHAPTER 21

Amsterdam, October 1, 2021
Andries

After the first few days of radio silence from Roxanne, I knew I was going to obsess if I didn't do something about it. Still, my pride wouldn't allow me to just call her, so instead, I had put my phone on silent and thrown it into the drawer of my nightstand, forcing myself to ignore its presence. During that time, I put together the best poems I could craft and gifted my notebook to her. What a disappointment it was when I entered the bookstore and only her sister, a woman named Lili, was there. Two days have passed since Roxanne told me she had received my gift and yet nothing has been said until now. Maybe she didn't like it, maybe she even hated it. Who knows…

Over the past two weeks, I've run the gamut of emotions, from heartache to anger, and finally settling into an even sense of annoyance. At first, I felt that Roxanne owed me something, either her time or an explanation, but by now, I have come to terms with the fact that no matter if she and I had started down the path of romance, we are still little more than acquaintances.

Would it have been meaningful for me if she had at least sent me a message after the cabaret? Of course. But I couldn't force her to care, and maybe I had cared too much.

I'm ready to let it fall by the wayside, but the universe seems to have other things in mind, and it manifests in a constant buzzing from downstairs. I ignore whoever it is for a moment, hoping they'll go away, but when the buzzing gets louder and louder, I finally give up. Tugging a shirt over my head, I stomp to the intercom and seeing that's my sister, I'm left with little options but to let her in.

A few minutes later, the elevator door opens and Elise comes in, and without saying a word, she shoves her iPhone into my hand, pushes past me, and flops down on my couch. What the heck?

"Elise…?" I start, but she points to her iPhone, protected by a Tiffany blue case.

I look at the screen, and it reads *Dad*, with an active call that has been going on for twenty-five minutes. He's still on the line. Shit.

Elise points at the phone again, more forcefully this time. I reluctantly lift it to my ear.

"Hi Dad…"

Before he says a single word, he heaves a sigh on the other end of the line. "Why the hell haven't you been answering my calls? Your mother and I have been worried sick."

"I was taking a break from social media to focus on schoolwork," I lie easily. Well, it isn't a total lie. I'm working on some things for school, but it isn't business school like he'd assume. If I tell Dad I've been working on my poetry, he'll scoff dismissively, and I'm just not in the mood for that.

"That's all well and good, but speaking to your parents isn't social media. I expect you to at least answer once in a while, Andries."

I'm not too concerned with Dad's opinion on my hiatus from electronic communication, but I do feel a twinge of guilt knowing that Mom had been so worried. "I apologize. If I need to go dark for a few days in the future, I'll at least tell you first."

Dad harrumphs, but lets the anger drop out of his voice. "Fine. Look, I'll drop the subject because I actually need a favor from you, son."

Oh no. That can never mean anything good. I break out in a cold sweat, a million possibilities running through my mind. What if he wanted to see my grades for my *business* classes, when in reality I was taking none?

I swallow, keeping my tone even. "What's up?"

"I need you to escort someone to the opera for me tonight, someone special."

Fuck, I think I know where this is going. "Dad, my studies…"

"Oh, don't sound so downtrodden. I'm not sending you with some old spinster or anything like that. It's–"

"Tatiana, right?" I interrupt.

Dad is shocked into silence for a few seconds before catching back up. "Yes, actually. How did you know?"

"It just seems she continues to come up in conversation, somehow," I say sarcastically, sliding a glance at Elise, who gives me a smirk and a finger wave from where she's reclining. I clench my teeth in annoyance.

"Fate can do that sometimes, bringing people into our lives again and again who we are meant to become close with," Dad says, not missing a beat.

I groan. "Will you allow me to say no?"

"For all I do for you, son, you shirking this small favor would be quite disappointing to me. I need you to take Tatiana to the opera. It's only for a few hours and it'll be good for you to get out and take in some of the arts around Amsterdam."

I'm glad he can't see my face because little does he know I've been entrenched in the arts since I arrived here. I'm in the English program after all. "I'm not interested."

"You don't have to be. You just have to show up."

"So why ask me if you've already made the decision for me?" I snap. "Why not just command me?"

Dad sighs. "You're my son, Andries. Not a dog."

"The question still stands," I say, not backing down.

"Honestly, son, I hoped you'd be happy to go, and even if you weren't thrilled, I assumed you'd at least be responsible enough not to argue about it. The opera is an ideal place to network and meet people who share similar interests for when you graduate."

"Don't turn this into something it's not. It's all about making me spend time with Tatiana, either because you and Elise are plotting to get us to become a couple or because her dad insisted I be her date. Both options have nothing to do with me or my future."

"Andries," Dad all but groans. "A classy, beautiful woman is an amazing boon for any man's future. Especially one as sweet and intelligent as Tatiana. Trust me when I say women with a good heart are few and far between in our social circles."

"She's a friend at best, Dad. I can't force myself to have feelings for her," I insist.

"You haven't even given her a fair chance," Dad quickly interjects. "She's been in love with you for as long as I can remember."

"But I haven't," I protest just as fast. "She can be in love with me all she wants. I don't feel the same."

From his voice, I know he's pinching the bridge of his nose in frustration. "Look, I'm not asking you to marry her. I'm just asking you to take her to the damn opera." Dad's running out of patience, I can tell by his hurried tone and the gush of air rolling off his mouth. Plus, in normal circumstances, he'd have never used foul language with me.

I feel tempted to simply hang up the call right now, but keeping my tone firm and polite I say once more, "Dad, I'm not interested in taking Tatiana to the opera or to anywhere else for that matter. *I'm studying...*" Total bullshit, but he'd never buy into me skipping out on Tatiana just to sit at home and read poetry. My studies, on the other hand, he actually cares about.

"Any man would be interested," he says incredulously. She's such a charming, stunning young lady."

"Well, not me," I reply. The thing is, Dad isn't wrong. Tatiana is everything he says; charming, lovely, intelligent...

but she lacks the passion and fire for life and its secrets that I'm attracted to in a woman.

There is silence from Dad's end of the line, and I begin to believe he's just going to hang up on me when he finally speaks again, this time sounding resigned. "Alright, look, her dad and I are really close business partners. This is a very simple thing you can do for me that ensures I maintain the best relationship with him."

"I know..." Does he truly believe I forgot? He tells me that every single month! "If you are asking me as a favor from father to son, I might be more open to considering it than if you're just trying to play matchmaker like everyone else."

"Fine. If that's the way you need to view it, I won't complain. She's got two tickets and she'd be delighted to go with you."

"But why didn't she call or text me herself? She has my number." If Tatiana had really wanted to go with me, she could have asked, and as long as I didn't get the vibe that she wanted it to be a romantic encounter, I'd have probably accepted. When our parents get involved, though, it makes me want to dig my heels in and refuse.

"Because she's got manners and she doesn't want to bother you," he snaps, reaching the end of his patience. "Can you do me this favor, please? I'll give you a bigger allowance next month."

Little does Dad know, I'm also nearly out of patience, watching Elise kick her feet in the air as she flips through one of my notebooks that had been sitting on my coffee table. If she had also minded her own business and made an excuse for me, I wouldn't be having this conversation right now.

"Is the allowance a payment for me to be her date? Because if so, it makes me feel like a gigolo having to take her out," I grit out.

He scoffs. "Oh, for fuck's sake! Stop being so difficult! A gigolo is paid to have sex. I'm just asking you to go with her to the opera."

"I'm not an escort either." And right now this is exactly what he's doing: paying me to take Tatiana out. Like a high-end male escort. And it's fucking pathetic and disgusting. "Can't you for once take my side on this?" I ask, despite already knowing the answer. "I'd like to know that you would stick up for me and the little self-respect I now have left."

"It's the last time I ask you for such a favor, I swear." At least for once he sounds sincere. "If her dad asks me something like that again, I'll advise him to speak to Tatiana and have her deal with you directly."

"Don't worry, I'll talk to her," I tell him. "She can't always be leveraging your business relationship with her dad to get what she wants."

"I doubt she's doing it in bad faith," he argues. "She's just shy."

"Yeah, right…" I roll my eyes at how deluded Dad can be. That's why Elise can manipulate him so well. Does he truly believe both of these girls are that innocent and with no agenda? "When is the event?"

"Tonight at eight."

"What?" I glance at my watch immediately. "That's in like two hours!"

"I know, it's a bit last minute. But if you had answered your phone then this wouldn't be a problem," Dad explains, sounding exasperated. "But I got you a driver."

"Fine, I'll call Tatiana and tell her I'm picking her up." I'm pretty sure she's already getting ready by now, knowing all too well I wouldn't decline the invitation coming from my dad.

Dad lets out a relieved breath. "Thank you, son. I truly appreciate it."

I hang up, heaving a sigh in annoyance while I throw Elise her phone back, which she catches easily. I'm not interested in the opera on the best of days, but now that I'm being forced to go with Tatiana, I'm even less interested. Ugh, what a waste of my time.

* * *

I know flower-girl is gonna expect more from me. She always does, but she's simply as bland to me as a blank page. Still, I'd hate to disappoint her, so when she walks out of the building where she lives, I play my part and smile at her, making a show of looking her over, taking in her dress and the way it flows over her body. I don't want to be here, but if I'm going to do this favor for my dad, I might as well play the part to the best of my abilities.

No one would ever say that Tatiana wasn't a beautiful woman, and as she descends the stairs to where I'm waiting outside the car, she's obviously using that beauty to her full advantage. Looking at me through thick, dark lashes, she smiles gently, just a subtle pull at the corner of her mouth. Her dark brunette hair has been pulled back into a low chignon, with expertly curled pieces pulled loose to accentuate her face.

Tatiana has features that lend themselves more toward cute than stunning, with large, wide eyes and a heart-shaped face, but she definitely knows how to do her makeup to make herself appear older than she is. She's put aside her normal flowing sundresses for the occasion and is wearing something in ivory. The dress is sleeveless, glimmering when she moves, and ends below her knees, with a slit up the back that is just inches from being problematic. She looks perfect for the occasion, and more mature than I've ever seen her.

I'm still not interested, but that doesn't mean I can't be nice.

I hold open the door for her as she approaches. "Hey, how are you? I was told you require an escort for the evening."

She rolls her eyes flirtatiously. "You don't have to make it sound like you're babysitting me."

Then why does it feel that way? But I don't speak it out loud. "Sorry."

I slide into the car next to her while she checks the contents of her clutch before touching up her lipstick in a small hand mirror. I can smell her perfume, something rosy, and it makes me want to roll the window down.

Now that I'm alone in the car with her, this is obviously nothing more than the date setup I have imagined it to be in the first place.

Tatiana breaks the silence. "I wanted to go with you specifically, you know. I could have found someone else to take me, but I wanted it to be you."

I cringe internally. "I'm flattered." I grasp around in my mind for a new subject. "I didn't check, this was so last minute for me. What show is it that we're seeing tonight?"

She brightens at the question, looking for anything to engage with me over. "*Anna Bolena*. It's about—"

"The life of Anne Boleyn, I'm familiar."

She purses her lips at the interruption but shakes it off quickly enough. "Do you like the opera?"

"I appreciate the art form for what it is, but it isn't anything I'd seek out on my own."

"I see." She twists the fabric of her dress in her fingers. "I rather like it."

I muster up a smile for her. "Then I hope you enjoy yourself tonight."

She scoots her body infinitesimally closer to me. It's a big move for the shy girl, so I allow it. I don't want to crush her spirit. "Oh, I know I will."

* * *

The Dutch National Opera looks much more modern on the outside than it does on the inside; a sprawling white building consisting mostly of mirrors and sitting right on the water. It's hard to believe that once you enter, you'll be transported to somewhere dark and intimate to watch the show.

Tatiana is glowing as I take her hand and help her out of the car. She's more than happy to link our arms together, her tiny hand tipped with seashell-pink nails resting on my upper arm as we walk in together.

From the outside, I'm sure we look like the perfect young couple. All my suits are tailored, and, while I am not a vain man, I cut an impressive enough figure that I'm aware of my charm. Flower-girl is almost bursting with excited energy, and I wonder how she'll even make it through the show without squealing. She really is thrilled to be on my arm.

Tatiana knows how to carry herself at these events, but I've known her for years, and it makes me constantly on alert for her excitement to deflate and be replaced with anxiousness. We decide to spend some time downstairs taking in the incredible architecture and seeing who else is in attendance, and in about ten minutes, we'll go to our private box so she can decompress from all the socializing.

That shyness is something I actually did relate to Tatiana about. Not that I'm shy, but huge crowds and hordes of people are not something I enjoy, so going to our seats early is perfectly fine with me.

Heavy, scarlet curtains, gold accents, and a hushed atmosphere is all just a prelude to the performance. The entire opera house, this one and all others like it, are an ode to the art that they host, and everyone present seems to sense the importance of it all.

I should be more of a fan of opera, since it's a culmination of music and literature, but it all falls a little short for me. Words on a page are clearer, more concise, and speak to my soul in a way other forms of art simply don't.

"It's amazing here," Tatiana says as we stroll arm in arm, her heels silent on the soft carpets that grace the flawless marble floors. "I'm glad you decided to come."

I want to tell her that I hadn't had much of a choice, but I refrain. It isn't her fault our parents are all trying to push us together. Though I suppose Tatiana is a more willing participant than I am.

I hum in agreement, but I'm quickly losing interest in the need to make our appearances among the masses. I want to make our way to the box and await the start of the show.

I start to lead Tatiana in that direction, and she is more than happy to follow, still captivated by everything else around us. We reach the bottom of the tall, curving staircase that would lead us to the next level when I freeze, stopping dead in my tracks. Tatiana jerks backward when she doesn't notice and continues to walk with my arm in hers.

"What is it?" she asks, surprised, but she might as well have been speaking a foreign language, because I'm not hearing a single one of her words—what must have been a figment of my imagination is descending toward us.

"Oh, the poet," the figment says, her voice all smoke and sultriness when she lays her eyes on me.

"Roxanne?" I can't stop myself from gaping as she makes her way down the stairs in her long black lace gown. It perfectly fits her wonderful hips and waist, hugging her curves lovingly, to the point that I'm ridiculously jealous of the pieces of fabric. Her blonde hair is brushed up in a high chignon like a fifties diva, exposing her delicate, pale neck, her lips just as red as the first time I'd seen her. She's such a vision. But I try to brush those thoughts away, focusing myself on some normal subject that doesn't reveal my shock.

"You, um, you also like opera?" I ask, immediately chastising myself internally for the inane question. I focus on keeping my posture straight and my attitude nonchalant.

The look on her face is curious, with just a dash of amusement. "Sometimes. And you?"

"It's alright," I answer, wishing I'm half as eloquent when I speak as when I write. "I came here with a friend who does, though. Roxanne, this is Tatiana, a friend of the family."

"Oh, you came with a friend?" Roxanne asks, surprised. Or maybe just feigning it as she secretly revels in my effort at hiding the impact she has on me. Still, I watch her size Tatiana up like an opponent in the arena of battle, all while Tatiana is oblivious, just smiling her sweet innocent smile. "Me too," she continues. "What a coincidence."

I raise my brows. "Karl again?"

"No, actually." She gives me nothing but a side smile, lowering her chin so she's looking up at me through her lashes. "His name's Charlie."

"Who's he?" I ask, but Roxanne has turned her attention to Tatiana, greeting her kindly, despite the tension I'm sure I see in her shoulders.

I admire her ability to seem aloof, but then she takes one step closer toward me and bends just enough to reach my ear. "He's a very interesting man who enjoys opera fiercely," she whispers. And I've got no idea how or why, but my heart tightens upon hearing this. How is it that she continues to make me feel this way even when telling me she's with another man?

Before I can formulate another sentence, an older man comes down the marble stairs behind Roxanne. He's tall, but lanky, with thinning hair and a confident expression. The man looks familiar, but not in any way I can place. He pays Tatiana and I no attention, his heated gaze fully fixed on Roxanne.

"Ah, here you are, my dear. I thought that you had gone and abandoned me," the man jokes, and Roxanne looks over her shoulder at him with clear fondness, but at least she shows none of the attraction to him that he obviously feels for her.

The man comes up beside Roxanne and snakes his arm around her waist, one long-fingered hand possessively on her hip. I clench my jaw, forcing my eyes off where he is touching her and back to Roxanne's face. She looks at me curiously, until she seems to realize what it is that is bothering me.

Instead of brushing him off, she tilts her head in my direction, and introduces me.

"Charlie, this is Andries, a friend and a talented poet," she says, and despite the fact that she used that dreaded word, *friend*, I feel a rush of warmth in my chest at her recognition of my poetry. Did she really think I was talented? Does that mean she read the poems I sent her?

"Oh Andries, how nice to see you again!" Charlie exclaims, seeming to recognize me before I did him. He must be my dad's age, or even older, and watching him paw at Roxanne makes me incredibly uncomfortable.

Then it clicks into place. I recognize him because he is one of my dad's clients. Of course, everyone seems to know Dad. I reach out my hand and he takes it enthusiastically, shaking my hand as if he had no idea how much I disliked him at this moment.

"You know each other?" Roxanne squeaks, looking between the two of us. Now I'm the one reveling in her astonishment.

"Yes, I know his dad very well," Charlie tells her as we smile at each other. "A brilliant young man if I recall. Are you enjoying business school?"

I freeze, looking at Roxanne, who only tilts her head slightly at the mention of business school. She knows I'm actually in the English program, but the last thing I need is my secret getting outed because she accidentally speaks up in front of Charlie. Thank God, she gives me no indication of telling on me. "It's great, yeah…"

Charlie sighs wistfully. "Oh, to be young and back in university. I'm sure your parents are very proud. Roxanne just said you write poetry too? Is that a hobby of yours?"

"Uh, yeah, something like that. A hobby," I answer, ready to change the topic. Roxanne gives me a curious look, but still doesn't say anything, thankfully.

A bell tolls over the sound system, letting us know that it's time to find our seats and wait for the show to start. It's both a blessing, because I don't have to answer any more of Charlie's questions, but it also feels like a curse having to leave Roxanne behind. More than anything, I wish it was just the two of us heading to my loge together, but we are both beholden to other people for the night.

"Come on," Tatianna says softly, tugging on my arm. "Let's go. I don't want to miss anything."

Reluctantly, I let myself be led away, but not without a curt goodbye to Charlie and a look filled with longing at Roxanne over my shoulder as I walk away. I have no idea how I'll make it through the rest of the night knowing she is here with someone else. But I bet it'll certainly drive me mad.

* * *

As the lights lower and the music begins, everything fades to silence, all ears focused on the performance. I'd have been too, even if opera isn't my forte, if it hadn't been for Roxanne.

I can only hope Tatiana is oblivious because otherwise, I can't imagine that she won't be offended by how easily my attention is being snatched away from her. Thankfully, she seems occupied enough by the performance that she doesn't look over at me too much.

A few minutes earlier, while we were settling into the loge, she had asked me about Roxanne, but once I had mentioned that I knew her from a shared interest in literature, Tatiana had quickly lost interest.

I, on the other hand, can't shut down my interest no matter how hard I try. It doesn't help that, if I squint, I can see Roxanne and Charlie in their loge, sitting much too close together for my sanity.

When Tatiana takes her opera glasses off her face for a moment, laying them on the edge of the box in front of us, I pick them for a quick glance at the other couple. I can feel Tatiana watching me, but I hope she can't tell exactly where I'm looking.

I regret my decision within seconds, at first appreciating how beautiful Roxanne is, but then feeling sick to my stomach when I watch Charlie run his hand up her lace-clad leg to her thigh. I clench the opera glasses so hard that I can feel the metal of them biting into my skin, and still I can't look away until I hear a small, "Could I have my glasses back?" from Tatiana.

Ashamed, I hand them back to her and give her a brief pat on the shoulder when she looks at me with her eyebrows drawn together in worry. Tatiana watches me for a few more moments before raising the glasses back to her face and returning her attention back to the opera.

I try to do the same, but no matter how hard I try to give all my attention to the singers on stage and the soaring notes pouring from their mouths, my eyes continue to drift back to the darkened loge where I know Charlie and Roxanne reside. Sitting close, touching, whispering in each other's ears… I'm consumed with frustrated anger. First Karl and now Charlie—how many "*friends*" does Roxanne even have?

On one hand, I get it. She's a captivating woman who stands out from the crowd. Mature, gorgeous, and interesting enough to hold a conversation with anyone she meets, so it's no wonder she keeps being asked to be the plus one at so many events. On the other hand, why does she keep accepting if she isn't emotionally involved with any of these men? Is she that desperate for company or entertainment? Because I can be that man for her, and between us, it'd be *real*. Authentic. Not some fake date for appearances.

I'm ready to crawl out of my skin when the lights come up to indicate the break in the show. Tatiana stands slowly, and I know I'll hate myself later for what I'm about to do, but I have to have some space to breathe if I'm going to continue being the appropriate companion for her, even if I'm about to hurt her feelings right now.

"Tatiana, I'm going to go get some air. Will you be alright by yourself for a few minutes?"

She looks surprised, and then disappointed, looking at the ground as she speaks. "I suppose so. I just don't enjoy being around these huge crowds without you."

I hesitate. "Do you want me to bring something back for you, so you can stay here?"

Her uncomfortable stance eases a little, and she nods. "Yes, that would be perfect, actually. A glass of sparkling wine, maybe?"

"Of course," I say, feeling awkward. I should reach out and touch her in some way as reassurance, but I just nod at her instead before pushing the heavy curtain aside and hurrying away.

I don't know where I'm even going once I'm free of the loge, following the hallway all the way to the end and then down a set of stairs tucked into the corner. Then another hallway, and another set of stairs, this one even more narrow and hidden than the last. I don't even notice my surroundings until there is nowhere else for me to go, and I'm in a sparsely lit corridor. Doors line the walls in equal intervals, and while the lights still burn in the ceiling above, there is an air of disuse about the place.

I step forward and open the first door, revealing a dark room. I flip on the light, and it sputters before coming on fully, illuminating a small dressing room complete with a full wall mirror in front of a counter, likely for hair and makeup.

Ah, this must just be an area of extra changing rooms for large productions. I feel like I'm the only one that has been in this corridor for years, and it's secluded enough that I feel comfortable sinking down onto a stool to get my bearings. It's the first bit of real solitude I've had since Elise burst into my apartment this afternoon.

I let my mind drift to all the things that aren't the woman I've found myself captivated by. School, my friends, my family… nothing seems to keep my mind busy for long before it drifts right back to Roxanne. What is she doing right now? Did she and Charlie leave for the night, heading for some smoke-filled lounge or even his hotel? I'm usually in sync with my busy mind, but tonight I detest it.

I'm startled from my reverie by soft footsteps in the hall, and I freeze, wondering if I have time to flee before someone catches me down here. It's not like I'm harassing performers or anything detestable like that, but surely this wasn't an area that the public was meant to find.

Before I can make my move, the silhouette of the person appears in the doorway, materializing into Roxanne herself. We both freeze in place, but it's her who moves first, chuckling in that low, sultry voice of hers.

"What are the chances?" she asks, sauntering forward toward me.

I'm quick to come up with an answer, wanting to hold her attention as long as possible. "The universe has a way of bringing fated lovers together, you know."

"Is that something you read or something you just came up with by yourself?" She reaches me and brings her hands up to adjust my collar. I'm almost positive there isn't anything wrong with it, but I certainly don't want to push her away.

This close, I can smell her, and it takes a herculean amount of control not to bury my face in that bare, silken throat of hers. "A little bit of both, I suppose."

"So humble," she says, breath brushing my cheek as she speaks. "So why are you down here hiding and not doting on your beautiful young lady instead? Tatiana, right?"

"Actually, I was getting away from her, and everyone else here."

Her hands are still on my collar, but instead of falling completely away, she slides them down my lapels and pulls me closer. "Does that mean you want me to leave?"

I wrap my hands around her delicate wrists. "You're the only person whose company I want at the moment."

"Well, that's all I have, Andries. A moment before I have to get back to my loge." She gathers her thoughts and at this point, it's evident she followed me down the stairs with the intention to talk to me. "I read the poems," she announces. "I loved them. Just like I loved every second we spent together, but that night at the bookstore… It was…"

"It was amazing," I say under my breath, matching her tone.

"It was a mistake." Her words are like a knife piercing my heart. It hurts so damn much that I frown, but I try my best to keep my composure. "I can't see you again, Andries. I'm not the right woman for you." I'm about to speak up, when she interrupts. "It's best I go now." She's about to turn and leave, so I hold her wrist, halting her.

"Stay here for a bit." My voice is nothing but a murmur.

She tugs her wrist from my grasp but takes the sting of the separation away by brushing a stray piece of my hair back into place. We are so close to each other, mere inches, but I want her closer still.

"Charlie won't accept me disappearing right out from under his nose. Plus, that is rude."

That irks the heck out of me. "Charlie is into hookers by the way. I'm not sure what kind of relationship you have with him, but if I were you, I'd go home and end the date."

She huffs, and I can see her stiffen in offense. "I don't do dates, I already told you that." She moves away slightly, and I clench my fists.

"Why are you guys here, then?" I demand, my voice still quiet.

"I could ask you the same about your lovely Tatiana," Roxanne responds, tilting her chin up stubbornly.

"Why do you even care? Are you concerned that I'll take her home to fuck tonight?" I ask, narrowing my eyes.

"You said you weren't interested in her." She crosses her arms and cocks her head to the side as she waits for my response. "Unless, of course, she managed to get her way after all. What is she now? Your fuck buddy?"

"She's just a friend I'm taking to the opera," I say, quite surprised at how aggressive she has become when talking about flower-girl. "She's a family friend like I said, and it'd be rude for me to refuse her, especially since I'll be seeing her around all the time. What about Charlie? I somehow doubt you two are *family friends.*"

"He's just a friend I'm taking to the opera." She gives me my very own answer, and I can hear the tension in her tone. I wonder why it's so important to her that I believe her if everything that happened between us is nothing more than a mistake. Is it because she wants to assure me she is still technically single? The idea makes wicked thoughts come into my mind.

This time I walk toward her, almost pressing her backward with my presence. But Roxanne is no easily swayed woman, and she stands her ground, arms still crossed.

"What about when the two of you leave here tonight? Are you just friends leaving the opera? Or more?" I demand.

"None of your damn business," Roxanne snaps.

Finally, I've crowded her so much that she has to look up to meet my eyes, and I can see her stiff posture waver at my nearness. I drag my knuckles over her cheek, and her breath hisses out quietly. "Promise me you won't do anything with him," I murmur. "You deserve so much better."

"And how do you know that?" Her voice is thin.

"Because I know you," I say, leaning in until we are sharing breaths, just a single movement away from touching lips. I'm terrified, elated, triumphantly confident and overrun with desire. Those lips are so close, inches from mine. If I could just taste them again…

Roxanne's eyelids flutter as if she's going to make the final move before our lips touch, but then her eyes snap open again and she looks toward the door. "I… I should go back upstairs…"

Before she can run away, I cup her face in my hands, forcing her to look me in the eye. "Stop worrying about anyone else, and start worrying about yourself. What do *you* want, Roxanne?"

With the quietest moan, almost as if she is chastising herself before letting go, she grabs my lapels again and pulls me into a kiss. The first second is shock before I'm able to savor the feeling of her mouth pressed to mine. It's her that kissed me. *Her*. Just like the first time we kissed, and that's proof enough to know she wants me as much as I want her. This isn't my imagination fooling me around.

I lose myself then, in the rush of her quick tongue in my mouth and the soft sounds she makes, her face cupped in my hands while she drags her nails over my scalp. My mind splits in two, one half calculating my next move while the other half is lost in the kiss.

I back her up until her hips touch the makeup counter, and I lift her so that she can sit on it. Then I shove the length of her gown all the way up and step forward so that I'm between her bare legs and she locks her ankles around me. It's ridiculously erotic, and all of my sense threatens to flee. I force myself to concentrate on just kissing her, just soaking in the taste and feel of her, but I want more. Jeez! I need so much more. She wraps her arms around my neck, her lips never leaving mine, while her crotch keeps pressing against my bulge. Our kisses are short and hurried, filled with rapture and need, as if we wanted to make the most of our time here.

I finally begin to run one hand down her back, trying to find the damn zipper, when a harsh sound shatters the moment. Roxanne pulls back with a gasp.

"That's my phone," she says simply.

I don't move away from her, returning to kiss her neck right before she pushes me back and slides around me. I want to grab her wrist, but she's already reaching into her clutch and checking the phone.

"Fuck," she breathes. "It's Charlie. The second act has already started." She opens her mouth to say something but shakes her head before it comes out. Finally, she says, "You should get back to Tatiana too."

"Roxanne, wait!"

But she doesn't even hesitate, and before I can ask her to do otherwise, she's run away. Back to Charlie, back to their loge, and away from me.

CHAPTER 22

Roxanne

I'd have loved to have given the opera my full attention, but it's simply impossible. Not when I can still feel Andries' hands on my body and his mouth on mine. How can I have been so foolish? Sure, the dressing room was secluded, but anyone could have walked in on us.

I have tried, really tried, to not let this poet get under my skin, but each time I see him... it all goes through the window. At this point in my life, I didn't believe that any man would hold my attention long enough to make my heart skip a beat, but he somehow managed it. At first, it had been his looks—that height, and his pillow-soft lips—but beneath the surface, he's even more addicting than his appearance let on.

Despite telling him that it was a mistake, I don't regret kissing him at the bookstore. It was sweet and lovely, but once I realized that such a kiss would make him feel like we were more than friends, I knew I should let him go completely to avoid any more misconceptions.

Somehow, though, he continues to show up wherever I am, all that serious energy rolling off him whenever he is near me, and tonight he looks so damn incredible in his suit that I should have known I was in trouble.

The universe has a way of bringing fated lovers together, you know. Andries' one-off comment replays in my mind over and over again, bothering me more than I let on. Why were he and I circling each other like sharks around the city now, when before it had just been a pleasurable distraction from my reality? Andries had been someone I could share my love of literature with, open up about my family and myself, but now this tension between us had nearly ruined all of that.

Then, just to make it worse, I'm the one who kissed him in the dressing room. What was he supposed to think now? I must be the queen of mixed signals.

I know why I did it, though, and it makes me a little ashamed of myself. I kissed him because I was burning with jealousy over the girl he had brought. The adorable, fresh-faced, incredibly young Tatiana… Andries had already mentioned how much she wanted him as her boyfriend and seeing the two of them in person really drove the point home. She clearly desires him at her side, and they even look perfect together. Except for the fact that Andries can't take his eyes off me, and with how seriously he has taken our bookstore make out session, he definitely isn't going to make out with me in the dressing room and then go off and do the same with Tatiana. It just isn't in his nature, I'm sure of it.

And yet, no kiss can prevent him from taking Tatiana home to fuck out of the public eye. He can flirt and give me those intense looks while he is out, but for all I know, he could be sleeping with her every single night and I'd be none the wiser.

I know it's hypocritical to be thinking about the two of them as Charlie escorts me out to the car, but I can't help myself. Why was I here with Charlie, a man over double Andries age, when I could be with the poet himself? Oh yeah, because being with Charlie means a paycheck. Being with Andries only means heartache.

We are nearly at Charlie's car when he asks, "Are you cold? I have your jacket here."

Startled out of my reverie, I look over at him. I should be cold, it's freezing out here, but my mind is so scattered that I hadn't even noticed.

"Yes, thank you Charlie," I say politely, taking the jacket from him, his fingers brushing across mine as I do. His touch makes me feel nothing, but he's oblivious.

Charlie opens the car door for me as the valet brings it around, some cherry red supercar that I hadn't bothered to learn the model of, and I slide into the uncomfortable seat, hiking my dress up as I go.

I'm numb to this lifestyle, I realize. These things that would have impressed me when I was younger seem meaningless now. If I had to choose the last time I really felt happy, it was back at the bookstore with Andries. Carefree, happy, and surrounded by my first true love in life: books. My business is beyond successful, my personal clients would pay almost any amount to be with me, and anything in the world could be mine if I really wanted. But all I wanted, all I craved, was something real, not hidden beneath a patina of glitz and sex.

Between shifting gears, I feel Charlie reach over and lay his hand on my knee, moving it slowly upward and taking the hem of my dress with it. Any other time, this would be my cue to turn on my escort persona and lean into his advances like he's the most irresistible man in the world. Tonight, though, I just can't make the change, and in my heart, I know exactly why.

I am done escorting.

My business makes plenty on its own, and I'm so tangled up in these feelings for Andries, that it isn't fair to my clients, anyway. I'll focus on the management of my agency only and leave the field work to the rest of my girls. I discreetly text my driver, confirming he'll be at Charlie's house when we arrive so I can make my escape. A part of me feels bad because Charlie surely thinks that I'm going to join him for the rest of the night, but no part of me will accept going upstairs with him tonight.

We arrive outside his apartment, and Charlie leans over the center console to reach me, hand raising to my face and eyes closing as if he means to kiss me. I put my hand out and stop him with it on his chest, and his eyes pop open in surprise.

"What's the problem?" he asks, perplexed.

I swallow hard, knowing that this is a monumental thing I'm about to do and it's something I decided almost on the spur of the moment. Still, I know I'm doing the right thing. "I have to tell you something, Charlie," I begin, my tone a mix of serious and polite.

He sits fully back in his seat, waving his hand for me to continue.

"This is my last night seeing you in this capacity." I square my shoulders as I continue. "I'm stepping back to better run my business, but when I made this decision, you and I already had this appointment on the books. I'm not going to invoice you for it though."

Charlie blinks a few times, processing the dump of information. "I've been seeing you for forever, Roxie. Is it something I did?"

I shake my head vehemently. "No, no. This was a personal decision I made solely on my own, a few days ago, actually. I just wanted us to have a good evening before I broke the news."

"This is *terrible* news," he mutters, more to himself than me.

I reach out to touch his hand gently. "I'm very sorry, Charlie. You have always been good to me, and I appreciate the time we spent together."

I open my door, ready to leave the car, but he grasps my arm, looking back up at me. "Come upstairs. One last hurrah."

I shake my head again. "No, I'm done. But I can set you up with one of my best girls. You only need to ask."

"I'll pay you triple to come upstairs with me tonight. I want to tell you goodbye properly."

The businesswoman inside of me is interested, but no matter what, my heart simply won't allow me to sleep with him tonight. I pull my arm out of his grasp before patting his cheek with my open hand, smiling at him fondly. He really has been a good client, and I'll miss his conversation, even if I'm glad to stop sleeping with him.

"Goodbye, Charlie. Call me if you want me to find you someone else in the upcoming weeks."

Despite hearing Charlie shouting a few nasty words at me, I don't look back as I flee to my driver, who is already waiting for me on the curb.

Once I shut the door behind me, I'm able to let out an enormous sigh of relief. I have finally done it, and for the moment, I'm free.

* * *

I tossed and turned for the entire night, finally falling into a fitful doze around two a.m. This morning, my mind is still buzzing with the decisions I had made, and the ones looming in my future.

As much as Andries is the catalyst for my choices, I knew I had to make them for my own wellbeing too. Because still, after everything that had happened, I wasn't even remotely considering a relationship with him. It was too much, too fast, and I didn't date as a personal rule. Desiring Andries was one thing, but being serious with him was another beast altogether.

Still, I wished he had at least messaged me when he reached home, but I suppose this is his bit of revenge from the night at the cabaret. Ignoring me, just like I had ignored him.

If I had been certain that he had gone home by himself, I'd be more comfortable playing the long game with him, waiting patiently until he either came crawling to me or we had another clandestine meeting out in public. But there's one variable that makes me more impatient than I wanted to be: Tatiana.

Andries mentioning how he was going to fuck her could have been a quick, meaningless comment, but why would he hold himself back when she was so close to literally throwing herself at him? Tatiana is gorgeous, in that innocent, vulnerable way that so many men like. I can't really fault Andries a single bit if he takes her home, dressing room kiss or no.

The more I think about it, the more it consumes me. Would he read her poetry in bed? Brush her long, shining hair off her bare shoulders? No, there's no way he took her home last night, but until I know for sure, I feel like I'm going to obsess about it. So I decide to do something so totally out of character that it's almost comical.

I text him first.

How was your evening with Tatiana? I can't help but press *Enter.* Yes, I know, it's ridiculous. I shouldn't care. But I just need to know.

To my greatest surprise, he replies a few minutes later.

Lovely. And yours with Charlie?

I huff instantly. Lovely is the exact same word I used to describe Tatiana. Did he take her to his apartment and fuck her? Of course he did. He's a freshman in college, living in Amsterdam on his own. Who was I kidding? She must have jumped on him as soon as they left the opera. The way she looked at him, jeez, she was nearly eating him alive.

From where I'm sitting on my bed, I want to throw the phone across the room and forget that Andries even existed, but my brand-new obsessive nature gets the better of me.

Excellent, I text him back, before pulling a pillow over my face and screaming into it. I hate him. I hate what he's doing to me. This has to just be a passing mania because I can't live like this forever.

It takes Andries just enough time to text back that I wonder if he had hesitated, but when the message comes through it says, *Would you rather call me so we can talk instead of this stilted texting?*

I smirk to myself as I type, *I thought all you college kids only communicated through text and hated talking on the phone?*

His answer pops up just a few seconds later: *I rarely have thoughts that are short enough to fit into a text box, so it isn't my favorite form of communication. If you want to continue this conversation, you obviously know my number. Give me a call.*

I contemplate it. If I call him, then that is me making another first move, my third time in the past twenty-four hours if I count the dressing room kiss and me texting Andries first. Except this time, he offered to talk on the phone, so was he technically making the move this time around? These little, minute details suddenly feel so important to me.

I don't call him right away. I get up and out of bed, brush my teeth, apply a face-mask, wait for it to dry, and take a long, luxurious shower with some of my favorite music playing. I lather my hair, trying to wash the thoughts of the poet out of my mind. If I don't call him at all, then that will really show him his place. I was no young Tatiana to come crawling to his door, begging for a place in his bed. He is the one who has to crawl to me.

And yet, I try to think about what my reaction would have been when I was Tatiana's age. Was I still so sweet and naïve then that I wouldn't have felt shame prostrating myself in front of a man for his attention? Would the victory of having Andries pay me attention be enough to ease the sting of embarrassment for coming to him, asking for his touch, and not the other way around? And furthermore, what is it about this man that has me so fascinated that I can't shake the thought of him?

Andries knows nothing of me as a professional escort or owner of my own escort agency. He only knows me for my personality, even the little bits of it I had ignored until I started spending time with him. I never thought I would want to seek the company of a man to find peace. Normally the only way for me to decompress is to spend time completely alone, far away from men of any sort. Sex was work, kissing was work, even dating was work. But it isn't that way with Andries. I just know it. Fuck, I'm going to call him. There are so few shreds of my pride left anyway, it doesn't even matter.

I pull my favorite silk robe on and slide down into a chair next to the window overlooking the city, where a fog hangs over the streets and the water, forming a blanket of gray. Before I can second guess myself, I tap Andries' contact and call him.

"Good morning, Ms. Feng." Andries almost sounds smug, like he already knew I'd call him. "How are you doing today?"

"Hey," I respond, a bit lost for words now that I actually have him on the phone. "I'm good, and you?"

His laugh is low. "I've never been so well."

I swallow once. Twice. Trying to get some moisture in my suddenly sand-dry mouth to ask the next question. "Is she there?"

"She?" he asks, playing innocent, as if he didn't know exactly who I meant.

"You're really going to make me elaborate?" Since he doesn't answer back, I heave a long sigh and finish my sentence. "Fine. Tatiana…"

"Oh, I think she's still sleeping," he answers, so very nonchalantly.

"What?" I can't believe it! He really slept with her? Something in the back of my mind told me it'd happen, but his off-handed confirmation of her spending the night has my head spinning. I should have never called. "She slept at your place?"

Andries hums to himself, almost as if he is considering not answering. "She might have. Does it bother you?"

He doesn't deserve an answer, the self-assured asshole. But I give it anyway. In for a penny, in for a pound. "Yes, it does. You kissed me yesterday, remember?"

"I seem to remember you kissing me first, and then I just kissed you back."

"Exactly!" I exclaim. "And that was reason enough for you to not take her to your place."

"Wait, kissing now means we are exclusive?" He sounds pensive, but I have a feeling it's sarcastic. "I wasn't aware of that, you know, given the fact I've seen you with two different men since our first kiss in the bookstore."

"That's not fair. I didn't kiss you and then immediately go home with someone else like you did last night," I snap. Andries is silent, not responding to my angry outburst. I take a few deep breaths until I have myself under control. "So, you really slept with her?"

"Why don't you come over to find out?" he asks, a mischievous hint to his voice. "I think it'd be better."

What! Absolutely not! "Andries—"

He doesn't give me the chance to finish. "I'm serious. I just texted you the address."

"I never said–"

"Oh! And I've got news for you about that favor for Karl," Andries continues, not giving me any room to speak my mind. "See you soon."

He hangs up, and I pull the phone away from my face, staring at it in shock. To hell with Andries and his nonsense! I shouldn't play into his game. I'm too old for this shit. I'm not meeting him again. Enough! No man has ever meant anything to me. And the poet won't be the exception.

I won't go. There is absolutely no way I will go. The only reason I could conceive of going while still maintaining my dignity would be to show up, tell him he's ruined any chance of having a friendship with me because of his smug, asshole attitude, and leave immediately afterwards. I don't know where he gets off thinking that I am at his beck and call. No man controls what I do. I control them.

There's something tugging at the back of my mind, though. Why would he invite me over if Tatiana was there? As much of a jerk as Andries is currently being, I feel certain that he wouldn't stoop to inviting me over to be face-to-face with his lover to potentially create an altercation. Under the bravado, I'm sure there is a sweet, thoughtful man who is acting out because I hurt him first. But there was no way I could have known he'd see me with both Karl and Charlie. The chances were abysmal, but it came to happen, anyway. Which meant Andries really had moved on to sleeping with Tatiana instead of his stubborn perusal of me, or he was using the possibility of fucking Tatiana as bait to either make me come over or to make me jealous.

I hate that it is working. I'm beyond jealous, and just a hair away from leaving to go confront him in person.

I don't make the decision right away, brewing coffee and fixing my hair to try and make the time stretch farther and farther, but nothing seems to ease the galloping desire inside of me to accept his invitation and go to see him. If I go there, I'd have to make him realize this was a one-time thing, as I'll never be at the beck and call of another person. But if I go to see him, at least I'd finally know the truth about him and Tatianna.

An image of Andries, shirtless and in jeans, opening the door to greet me arises uninvited in my mind. I know, with no question, that he must be beautiful naked. He is so tall, his skin sun-kissed just enough, and he has the body of a swimmer or runner; lean, strong, and cut. Andries is young, and fit, full of vibrant youth and life. I can't even remember the last time I had taken someone like that to bed. Someone who could keep up with me, again and again.

I finally decide that the only way to cleanse Andries from my mind is to go to his place and take what I need from him. Whether it be an assurance that he isn't sleeping with Tatiana, a promise for us to never speak again so we could both move on, a plan to remain strictly friends and never lovers, or… God forbid… sex. The longer I wait to take what I want, the more I'm able to build him up in my mind as someone perfect and nearly unattainable. Dammit, I'm Roxanne Feng, no one and nothing is unattainable to me. Especially not a man.

Stubborn and decided, I don my shoes and head out the door.

***

Of course, Andries lives in an incredible top-floor apartment, with views of the canals. Does this man have any obvious faults, or is everything so perfect just to drive me insane?

I don't need to buzz, since the door downstairs is already open but once I arrive to his floor, I fight the urge to fidget as I wait for him to open the door for me. Seconds seem likes hours, but finally, he opens it for me, looking as good-natured as I have ever seen him. He's not fooling anyone, though. I know the broody poet is under there.

He isn't half-naked like I fantasized, but the gray sweatpants and fitted white t-shirt are still distracting enough to pique my interest. Andries is barefoot, his usually perfect hair slightly mussed, and it's so domestic and comfortable that I want to be part of his world right then and there. I want to be walking around this opulent apartment, barefoot and in one of his white shirts. Drinking coffee in bed with his head pillowed in my lap, the blankets a mess around us. I want it all. For now, though, I have something to figure out first.

"Roxanne," he nearly purrs. "Come in, I'm cooking, so just have a seat and I'll be right over."

I slip my shoes off by the door as soon as I see the dark wooden floor, gleaming and immaculately clean. I'm pleasantly surprised to find the floor is warm as I make my way into the kitchen, where Andries is standing at the stove, something sizzling in the pan in front of him. I can smell spicy peppers and onions.

"Smells nice. What are you cooking?" I ask politely, not sure where to start with him, especially since there's the distinct possibility there's another woman somewhere in the apartment.

He looks over at his shoulder at me, emphasizing his powerful jaw. How can he look so young sometimes, but so masculine and mature at others? "Just breakfast…an omelet, specifically. Would you like one? What do you eat?"

"No… If you have any extra, that's fine, but don't make anything special for me." There are three stools at the breakfast bar, and I slide onto one of them to watch him cook. He doesn't engage me in conversation, so I just watch how he works, and how his body moves, shoulders flexing as he scrapes at the pan with a wooden spatula. I've never seen him so relaxed.

I should let this moment exist for what it is, but I don't have all day to wait for him to address the elephant in the room. "Is she here?" I ask directly, steeling myself for the answer.

He doesn't even turn to look at me this time. "Oh yeah, she's just showering."

I make a strangled sound in response, head jerking toward the stairs where the bathroom must be. Andries finally glances back at me and barks a laugh. "What a face! I'm only teasing. I'm not so much of a rake to have two women in the house at the same time."

I flush red with anger, clenching my fists so I don't throw the nearest thing I can grab at the back of his head. "Fucking asshole!"

He laughs again. "Jealous, Roxie?"

"Shut the hell up, Andries," I groan, rubbing my temples and trying to get my pulse back to normal. "So you and her —"

"Don't worry," he interposes, cutting me off. "I dropped her at her place after the opera. Your pride can remain intact." I'm glad he can't see me flinch at how accurate that statement is. He continues, "And Charlie?"

I have a brief urge to lie, just like he had done with me, but I'm desperate for honesty now, and I don't want to stall this conversation. "Same. I wasn't going to sleep with him with your taste still in my mouth, don't you know that?"

He stills, and I see him shut the stove off and pull the pan aside, off the heat, before he turns to face me, blue eyes narrowed and intense. "So does that mean you have... feelings for me?"

I tilt my chin up, heart galloping even faster now. Fuck, I feel like I'm sixteen again and admitting a crush to a boy at school! "Maybe…"

"Just maybe?" Andries stalks around the counter, making his way to where I am sitting on the stool. He pauses at the corner, leaning on it with his hip and crossing his arms, still too far away for me to touch.

"Fine," I say. "I have feelings for you, yes." I have to force the words out through clenched teeth. They are so foreign, so forbidden to me. "There I said it. Are you happy now? Is your ego satiated?"

"I'm just tired of these games. Does that mean you really want us to be exclusive, or are you going to tell me this and then I'll see you tomorrow with Karl at a street fair or Charlie at a cafe?"

His question makes me tense, but I try to ponder it as much as I can. "Well, it bothers me seeing you with another woman, so…" I sigh. "That is very hard for me to admit. I rarely feel jealously, so don't downplay my confession."

One corner of his mouth pulls up, and I can't decide if that tiny smirk is dangerous or amused. "So you don't want to share me?"

"Exactly," I grit out. "Don't make me say it again."

"Great, I don't want to share you either." He comes the rest of the way to me, moving like a lion on the hunt, and before I can blink, he's hovering over me, both of his hands resting on the marble counter on either side of me, bracketing me in.

I have no time to respond before he's kissing me, and I'm awash in relief that it's him that kissed me this time and not the other way around. It's almost as much of a relief as knowing Tatiana isn't upstairs. I have been so on edge, so doubtful about these bizarre feelings for this younger man that I might have combusted on the spot if he didn't prove how much he needed me.

And prove it, he does. Andries has the softest lips I have ever kissed, and all the vigor of a man who is filled with want and desire. When his tongue sweeps into my mouth, I hear myself moaning, and am shocked at how quickly he has me feeling helpless. Hell, I'm shaking against him as he moves closer to me until his chest is pressed against mine. It is a catharsis, kissing him and knowing we are alone, no one around to catch us, no rules to abide by. Inside, I feel warm and liquid, pliable under his touch.

I know, logically, that Andries does nothing lightly. He is the most serious person I know, and he pours all that seriousness into seducing me, and arousal, something that is almost a stranger to me now, spreads its wings in my chest and unfurled through me in slow degrees. He cups my face in both of his hands like I'm something precious and breakable, his tongue exploring the cave of my mouth and holding me in place while he does so, as if he wouldn't be satisfied until he knew every little piece of me. Then his hands slide down to my shoulders and grasp around my hips, pulling me forward on the stool until my ass is perched on the edge and my back arched, torso flush with his.

He moves his mouth across my jaw, down to my neck, biting with just the smallest amount of force at the tendon there. I try to touch him, try to put my hands under his shirt, but he is unmovable, and his grip on me firm. Like if he let me go, I would evaporate.

"Andries," I try, but his mouth has found my collarbone, and then the swell of my breasts in the V of the soft cotton shirt I had thrown on before leaving, and he isn't stopping to answer me.

"Let me undress you," I say, voice strained. He grunts, almost animalistic against my skin, but after a few seconds, he gives me some space, backing up just enough to yank his own shirt over his head before he bats my hands away from the hem of mine, sliding it over my head for me. He is the master of this situation, and every move he makes proves it to me.

With Andries, I'm just Roxanne, a woman who desires a man, not a professional. Though I have to admit there are a few perks to my previous job, and the absolutely over the top lingerie is one of them. It's all worth it to see Andries freeze and look at me in my scarlet lace bra that leaves almost nothing to the imagination, my nipples dark and visible through the whorls of lace, and my cleavage pushed up to perfection. He takes in three heaving breaths as I stand, shimmying my jeans down my legs until I'm left in just the bra and matching thong. I make a show of turning around and bending over to extricate my feet from the jeans so he can see my ass, before turning back around and balancing myself once more on the stool.

"Do you like what you see?" I ask, tilting my head slightly and drinking in the sight of him, almost frozen in place as he looks at me.

The poet is suddenly a man of few words as he doesn't bother answering. He just shucks his sweats, standing before me in a skintight pair of black, silk briefs only for a second before he is on me again.

This time I hold him still, grabbing a handful of his hair as I kiss those pillowy lips to my heart's content, nipping and licking at him as his hands roam around my body restlessly. When I release him, he claims my mouth again only briefly before he restarts his descent downwards.

He has a beautiful body, just like I knew he would, his waist trim and hard, compact muscles shifting as he kneels on the floor in front of me. There is very little hidden on him; I can see his collarbone, the ripple of muscles in his back, and the definition in his legs. He's a work of art, and once this first time full of furious passion had passed, I would worship this moment slowly and carefully.

He starts at my breasts, hands pulling the straps down my shoulders while he kisses the swell above the bra cups, slowly moving toward the center. Every bit of my need seems to be concentrated on my nipples as he takes his time until I'm ready to grab him by the hair and put his mouth right where I want it. Finally, *finally*, he nips at the aching tips through the lace of the bra before wrapping his lips fully around one nipple and sucking hard, before moving to the other. I shudder, my whole body tense with sensation. I don't even register him unhooking my bra and tossing it aside until his mouth returns to my bare flesh, tongue making concentrated circles on my nipples, the feeling of it all centering in my belly. I barely recognize the noises I'm making.

When he takes his mouth off of me, he speaks for the first time since he started kissing me, but only to say, "Hips up."

I quickly comply, and my panties fly off to the side somewhere. He doesn't take his time undressing me, I notice distantly, more focused on getting me naked as quickly as possible.

"Tell me if I'm being too rough," he says, voice hoarse with lust. "I have… I've wanted this for too long to be exceedingly gentle."

"I don't want you to be gentle," I tell him. "I just want you, Andries."

With a growl, he grips my thighs hard, fingers dimpling the soft flesh there, and wrenches my legs apart. I have to grab the counter behind me for balance. Andries looks me over, eyes fixated between my legs, for long seconds. If I had been a less experienced woman, I might even feel embarrassment for how soaking wet I am for him, but I had nothing to be ashamed of, and I wanted him to know how much he affected me.

"You're so fucking beautiful," he breathes. "More beautiful than I could've ever dreamed. Fuck."

"And you—Ah! Andries!" I gasp, unable to finish my sentence, because as soon as he finished speaking, Andries leaned forward and put his mouth on my core with no preamble. It was so sudden, it left me breathless.

"Tell me what you like," he says between licks. He covers every inch of me with his tongue, dipping it into my channel before stroking it right back to my clit and everywhere in between. It's incredible, but chaotic, so I acquiesce to his request, burying my hand in his hair and moving him exactly where I need him.

"Here," I whisper. "Suck."

He pulls me even more against his mouth, taking my directions perfectly as he wraps his lips around my clit and sucks. Every nerve in my body comes to life like blazing little stars, adding more and more to that ball of pleasure building in my belly.

From the way we are positioned, I can look down and watch him eat me out perfectly, my hand still on his head guiding him while his fingers dig into my hips, even as I start to roll them toward him as my climax nears. I can't look away from the sight of his head between my legs, just like I can't help the desperate little cries spilling from between my lips. I grab onto the counter hard with one hand, the other never letting go of Andries and I grind against his face, too far gone down the road to orgasm to turn back now.

"Don't you dare stop," I command, and he moans against me.

Chest heaving, legs shuddering, my orgasm explodes inside of me like a small bomb, shock waves rolling through me as I continue to hold Andries against my pussy, until finally it ebbs, and I can unclench my fingers from his hair.

My body is limp as he surges upward to kiss me, and I can taste myself on his lips and tongue. He scoops me into his arms, and I lock my hands behind his neck as he carries me up the stairs, presumably to the bedroom.

In the back of my mind, I'm so satisfied by my climax that I want to give him the same. I want to suck him and let him lay back while I take care of everything, but Andries is on a mission to make love to me, and I'm going to have to relinquish the driver's seat, at least for now. And that is more than fine with me. I'll pamper him later.

I have little time to take in the gorgeous bedroom, fire burning in the fireplace and the windows overlooking the city and canals that let in the perfect amount of light. He lays me down on the fluffy comforter like I'm made of glass, but I sit up before he can stop me, palming his impressive erection through his boxers. To my surprise, it makes him shake like a leaf in the wind.

"I want to make it last, Roxie, but once I'm inside you, I will not last. I've wanted you for too long," he admits.

"Don't worry, it will be perfect." I work my fingers under the waistband of his boxers and push them to the ground, running my hands over the hardness of his legs until one hand could finally grasp his cock. He's hard as stone, long and thick, curved just enough to make things interesting. I scoot to the very edge of the bed, but I'm only able to snake out my tongue and lick him once, tasting salt and precum, before he hisses and steps back.

"No, I want to last, and I won't if you do that."

"Fine." I sigh, reclining backwards and crooking a finger toward him. "Come here, then."

It's like a slow dance from there, Andries crawling over me, settling himself between my legs, resting with his elbows on either side of my head as he kisses me. I can feel his manhood pushing against me when he unconsciously thrusts his hips forward, and it makes me more and more impatient. This is clearly special to him, and to me too, so I don't rush him as much as I want to.

Finally, right before I'm about to reach down and take him in hand myself, he shifts his hips and lifts one of my legs over his shoulder, positioning himself right outside my entrance. I let out a shaky breath and nod when he looks down at me, a questioning look on his face.

He wraps one arm around my head so he can cup my face in his hand, our eyes locked together as he pushes into me slowly, oh so slowly. Every second seems monumental to him, and he watches me as if he's committing my reactions to memory, until finally he's fully inside me, his hips bumping into mine.

"Roxanne," he groans.

"Andries," I answer. "Make love to me."

It'd have been simple for him to make this moment quick, and I wouldn't have even minded. He had already made me come hard enough when he had put that wicked mouth between my legs, so this moment is all his. I should have known better, though. Andries does nothing by small degrees, including sex it seems.

His first few strokes seem almost tentative, and I can feel the muscles in his thighs quivering each time his hips meet mine. There is no rhythm initially as he comes to terms with the feeling of me wrapped around him. He's just started to pick up speed, a crease of concentration forming between his brows, when he stops abruptly and pulls out.

"Did you…?" I ask, but he shakes his head.

"No, but it was a close call. Give me a second."

I pull my leg from over his shoulder, so we are laying torso flush to torso again. He rests on his forearms while I caress his body with my hands, taking advantage of the first quiet moment between us since he had first kissed me in the kitchen, even as I ache from the emptiness where he had pulled out. His skin is so soft beneath my fingers, and I make a mental note of the way he gasps when I graze his nipple or the hollow of his hipbone. His barely-held-onto control might frustrate someone else, but I love every bit of it. Just another sign of how important I am to him, and how fierce his attraction is.

Time is tenuous here, so it could have been either minutes or hours before he shifts his body again, and I feel his erection jutting against me. I wrap my legs around his body, locking my ankles together at the small of his back while he wordlessly grasps his cock, guiding it back in place before thrusting home. My nerves sing as he sinks deep.

"It's so good," I say quietly, sensing how incredibly stiff his entire frame is. It's as if a single gust of wind would blow him to pieces. "Your cock was made for my pussy."

He bites my shoulder, pushing into me hard. "If you keep talking like that, this is going to be over before it even begins."

The feeling each time he bottoms out in me is a flutter of pleasure, building to what I know will be an avalanche. Again, though, his pace stutters and he pulls out. I'm about to protest, my pussy throbbing with how badly I want him back in me, when he slides the thick head of his cock between my folds in the opposite direction until it glides over my clit. It's like a starburst of pleasure, and I suck in air at the unexpected feeling.

"You like that?" he forces out between his teeth.

"Oh, yes. Do it again."

Andries obliges, positioning his hips in slight movements, so he strokes his member over that little bundle of nerves again and again without slipping back inside me. It doesn't give me the bone-deep satisfaction like when he's fucking me in earnest, but the exquisite feelings are sharp and intoxicating.

I thrash my head side to side, spine arched as I press myself into him, loving this while also desperate for more. When I crack my eyes open to look at Andries, his expression is smug, even while he forces himself to concentrate. He's driving me crazy, and he knows it.

"Your legs are shaking," he says, almost too calmly. "What do you need, Roxanne?"

"I need," I pant between strokes. "You inside me. Please fuck me, Andries."

With a strangled noise, the slippery pressure ceases, and I feel him nudging at my entrance again before he plunges into me once more. My body sings in ecstasy at being filled again. Andries doesn't move right away, taking time to suck my nipples into his mouth again while he regains composure. Right before he fucks me, he captures my mouth in a hot, frenzied kiss.

"I'm not going to be able to stop this time," he groans before sweeping his tongue back into my mouth.

When I pull away to catch my breath, I assure him, "I don't want you to."

Since he had warned me how close he was, I slide my hand between us and rub circles around my clit as he fucks me in tightly controlled thrusts, his entire body tense and shuddering as I had ever seen a man, but he was determined for me to come again before he followed me.

The forceful, perfect roll of his hips feels amazing as he fills me over and over, and the added sensation of me touching myself makes it so intense that I know it won't take me long, either. I tell him as much, my voice a strained whisper. Each time he bottoms out in me, I'm pushed closer and closer, until finally—

"I'm coming," I gasp. "Oh fuck, Andries, I'm coming."

He lets himself go too, thrusting wildly until he comes, teeth clenched and groaning my name over and over. Once he has emptied himself, he collapses on top of me, the echoes of both of our orgasms wracking our bodies as we lay together.

Reality creeps in slowly. Andries raises himself up and then pins soft kisses on my face, first on my forehead then on my eyelids, moving down to my cheeks and jawline while remaining motionless inside me. "Was it good for you?" he asks, his face now up again to look me in the eye.

I smile lazily, pushing a lock of sweaty hair off his forehead. "Incredible." His lips curve up for a moment before he closes the small space between us, pressing his lips on mine in a kiss filled with so much ardor that it makes me quiver.

"Thank God." He rolls off me onto his back, scrubbing his hands over his face before sighing.

I raise myself up on my elbow to watch him. "Did you expect otherwise? You are a very attentive lover."

He looks blankly at the ceiling, collecting his thoughts for such a long time I begin to get chilled, so I wrap myself in a blanket and continue to wait, until finally he closes his eyes. His expression is so serious that I feel a stab of worry.

"What's wrong?"

He shakes his head, but when he opens his eyes again, they aren't clear of concern like I had hoped. Something is up with him.

"It's nothing," he tells me, trying to sound nonchalant, but I can hear the note of tension underneath it all.

I search his eyes with mine, trying to decipher what could be bothering him immediately after the incredible moment we had just shared. Could he be upset with me?

"Was it not good for you?" I ask nervously. If it turns out the first real, truly desired sexual encounter I've had in so long wasn't good for my partner, I don't know what I will do with myself.

He makes a disbelieving noise, but when he sees my own expression he gathers me into his arms and pulls me close. I can smell his sweat and the warm, amber smell that is specific to him.

"Don't be insane, Roxie. You were incredible."

I push against his chest with my hands so I can look into his face again, even as he tries to shy away from eye contact. "You aren't going to get out of being honest with me by flattery. Tell me what's going on."

Andries inhales deeply, chest swelling. He looks like a man preparing for his own execution, not one who just had sex with the woman he had been relentlessly pursuing.

"Promise me that you won't judge me."

A million panicked thoughts run through my head. Could he already have a significant other? Or some sort of sickness he has now passed to me? I know we didn't use a condom, but since I've got an IUD I didn't think twice about it. I push the thoughts away, knowing Andries isn't the sort of person to hide something so serious. He cares about me. He wouldn't hurt me.

"I promise," I whisper.

Andries gathers his nerves, breathing slowly before locking eyes with me, determined and unafraid. "You were my first."

I laugh, but he doesn't. It feels like my stomach falls to the floor. He can't be serious.

"That can't be true," I say, shocked. "There's no way—"

"I never wanted anyone before you," he insists, his eyes on me as he observes my expression. "And I wanted you so badly I knew you were the one I wanted to be with first."

"Oh, Andries…" I'm totally speechless, not sure what to think of it, I cover my face with my hands, brain shorting out and refusing to accept this information. "This is a lot to process."

He sits against the headboard, looking at me from there, some locks of his hair falling on his forehead. "You wouldn't have slept with me if you had known I was a virgin."

"I never said that," I riposte, before sitting beside him. Truthfully, I have no idea what I'd have done, or if I'd have been so desperate to be with him, but something tells me it wouldn't have changed as much as he'd like to think. "It... I... I don't think it'd have changed anything, except I would have wanted it to be more special for you."

He grabs both my hands in his, looking at me seriously. "Nothing in my life has ever been as special as the moment we just shared, Roxie. Never doubt that."

I suck in a shuddering breath and nod. "I won't." I swallow, wanting to fill the silence. "How did you stay a virgin for so long? I mean, look at you." Andries rolls his eyes, a smile tugging at the corner of his mouth as if he knows what I'm going to say. "You're gorgeous. When you walk by, women turn their heads to watch you go, and you clearly had that Tatiana girl trailing after you like a marionette. You're gentle, intelligent, and what woman doesn't love an anguished, angsty poet?"

He tucks a strand of my short hair behind my ear. I'm sure it's a chaotic mess right now. "I never wanted to give myself to a woman just to do it. What I'm trying to say is, I didn't want to have sex just to stop being a virgin, or just to see what it was like. I knew there would be a woman whom I burned for, and she would be the one I took to bed for the very first time. As soon as I laid my eyes on you, part of me knew, and as we started to get to know each other, I became certain you were that woman."

There's a lump in my throat when I respond, "I'm so happy, then, that it was me. But you could have told me."

His hand hesitates where it is stroking my cheek. "I didn't want to risk you changing your mind just based on that fact, and I didn't want you to treat me differently during sex because of it either. I wanted you, and I wanted it to be honest and real."

I can tell he's on edge, as if he's waiting for me to reject him now that I know about his virginity. He's been so unflinchingly open with me that I want to reward him somehow.

I raise myself up, and before Andries can catch on, I straddle his hips, balancing with my hands on his chest. He looks up at me in awe, eyes hitching on my tits. "What are you doing?"

"I'm going to show you just how much it doesn't matter that you were a virgin. Just lay back and let me make you feel good."

I'm sure he wants to protest, or tell me that it isn't necessary, but I've made up my mind and he isn't going to change it. I slither downwards until I'm kneeling between his legs, dragging my nails up his inner thighs until I reach his cock. He's getting hard swiftly, knowing what's about to happen.

"Roxie—" is all he's able to get out before I snake my tongue out and lick him from root to tip. He hisses, throwing his head back against the pillow. Now it's me who is feeling smug.

From the first touch of my tongue, Andries had been completely erect, even though it had been mere minutes since he had last come. I spend some time mapping the entirety of his hard length with my tongue, swirling it around the head each time I reached the tip. I can taste myself on him, mixed with his own unique taste, and I hum in pleasure at how much I enjoy it.

Each time I glance upwards, I can see Andries, raising up on both his elbows and watching me so intensely it makes me shiver. He's looking at me like he's never seen anything so fascinating, so erotic, and I want to put on a show for him. I don't want Andries to ever forget this moment.

He's so thick and long that I have to work myself up to taking all of his cock into my mouth and throat. I have to concentrate fully on my breathing to be able to suck him deeper, but the noises falling from between his lips make it all worth it.

At first, he moans and sighs my name in that sexy, deep voice, but once I'm able to take more than half of his cock down my throat, he is beyond words. I feel his fingers carding through my hair and his hips thrusting into my mouth in time with the strokes of my tongue. Finally, after long moments of patience and careful breathing, I'm able to slide his entire cock into my mouth and down my throat. It takes all of my willpower not to gag, but I'm rewarded with the twitching of Andries' beautiful body and the feral noises he makes.

Once I've proven that I can take all of him, I start to suck his cock the way I'm positive he needs, the wet sounds of my mouth on him filling the room. His grip in my hair is rougher, guiding me up and down his length, but I refuse to give up control.

When I hollow my cheeks, putting the perfect amount of suction on him, he utters a strained, "Fuck," and it's the signal I need to know that he's close to coming. I pull my mouth off him completely, gazing up his body, asking him,

"Are you gonna come down my throat?"

He has no words for me, just a fierce growl as I wrap my lips around him again gripping the base of his cock with one hand and stroking him while my tongue swirls around the tip, over and over until his legs are shaking and I can taste the salty pre-cum leaking out.

When Andries reaches orgasm, I feel him spurt against the back of my mouth, his body completely arched off the bed as if he's been electrified. He makes a single, helpless noise that immediately makes me feel like the most powerful woman on earth.

I don't pull away from him until he sinks back flat to the mattress, chest heaving. I drag the back of my hand over my mouth and crawl back up his body until I'm lying by his side once more, snuggling against him while he catches his breath.

"You're a sorceress," he says finally, voice gravelly as if he hasn't spoken in days. "It's the only explanation for what you've just done to me."

* * *

We spend the entire day together, never leaving the apartment. We order takeout after having a long, luxurious shower together, and eat naked in bed, wrapped in sheets and talking until our bodies and the attraction between them would allow no more chit chat.

The second time around, I try to take over, but Andries rolls me off of him midway through, his need for control overriding everything. I don't complain, because it's delicious and hot as hell, but I swear eventually he's going to let me take care of him just the way I want.

I sleep in his arms, content and completely satisfied for the first time in forever. My body seems to hum happily and I fall asleep counting his heartbeats, limbs all tangled together.

Sunday morning is more of the same, but even I get sore after a while, so Andries gets me off again, sitting on the marble bathroom counter with his head between my legs, before carrying my wrung-out frame to the bubbling, warm bath.

During lunch, he reaches his hand across the table and takes mine. I look up at him, and I can see he wants to ask me something serious.

"What is it, Andries?"

"I'm going to be in a fencing competition next weekend in Belgium. Come with me." He looks so hopeful that I almost immediately agree but stop myself. It's a big move, a vacation together, and I still have so much to think about and so much going on with my business.

"It's at the Royal and Knightly Saint Michael's Guild. It's the oldest fencing club in the world. I'd love for you to join us. Everyone else is bringing their significant other. I mean, except my sister."

My stomach clenches at the phrase "significant other" and at the word "sister," I pull my hand out of his. "I need to think about it. It's very short notice."

His hopeful expression shudders shut. "Is it really, or do you just not want to be seen with me? It's only a two-hour drive."

I can feel all the loving, warm, intimate energy of the last twenty-four hours slipping through my fingers, but I don't rush to fix it. I let it go, so I can hopefully think clearly. "I'll let you know later this week. I have to think."

Andries tears his eyes from me and focuses back on his meal. His fork stabs are rather angry. "Fine. Let me know when you make a decision."

"I will," I promise in a whisper, feeling awful, but still so unsure about what is happening between us. This sexual staycation is one thing. Meeting all of his friends and, God forbid, his sister is something else entirely.

I glance at his perfect face, his blue eyes clouded with doubt, and bite my tongue not to just agree and wipe the sadness off of his expression. He makes it far, far too easy. Silence settles between us as we keep eating our meal but as I remember he had something to tell me about Karl, I speak again. "By the way, um, did you say you had some news about that promotion Karl is trying to land?"

"Oh, yeah." He seems to be totally shaken out of his thoughts. "My dad called me yesterday morning and told me he had pre-selected five candidates for the promotion and Karl is one of them. He'll announce who has got the job in December, though. I can't obviously guarantee that he'll pick Karl, but the fact there's only five candidates left sounds promising."

I'm totally in awe that he'd already spoken to his dad about Karl's promotion and I can't help but say, "Honestly, thank you so much for doing this. After that situation at the cabaret, I thought…."

"I'd already spoken to him by then," he announces. "In fact I had spoken to him the following day after our evening at the bookstore." He pauses for a moment and takes a breath, his eyes never leaving mine. "So you can understand how I felt when I saw you with him."

I reach for his hand, covering it with mine and looking him in the eye, I say, "Karl and I are just friends, I truly meant that when we spoke outside of the cabaret. After dinner, I simply went home."

"Thanks for being honest with me," he answers, taking my hand and giving it a kiss. "I really appreciate it."

Oh gosh, a pang of guilt squeezes my heart at his words. If he only knew...

CHAPTER 23

Amsterdam, October 7, 2021
Roxanne

It's ironic that I'm going to end my relationship with Isaak in the coffeeshop he took me to the first time I went out with him. This place has been around for well over a hundred years, and the aging brick walls reflect the age. When I approach the place and see Isaak outside, he's lingering on a bench that's likely been there since the nineteenth century.

I decided to wear something demure today thanks to the weather. It isn't raining for once and I also don't want Isaak getting any wrong ideas. The thoughts of indecision are still percolating lightly in my mind. Am I doing the right thing by separating myself from these men? Isaak has been with me for five years and has given me opportunities I couldn't have even began to dream of when I was first starting out with my agency.

Plus, he's an excellent companion and lover. One of my favorites to travel with. Old enough that he didn't want sex all the time, but young enough that he still wanted to have fun. There's nothing worse than being on vacation with a client and the guy just wanting sex all the time and never leaving the hotel room to enjoy yourself.

"Good afternoon." He stands and kisses my cheek as he always does when we meet. His lips are soft for now, but I know that underlying that is a man who enjoys things that are hard when we're alone together. I glance at the door of the shop bearing a sign that clearly states it is closed.

He sees my eyes. "Don't worry. I know the owner." Of course you do. He knocks lightly on the door, and it is opened within moments, another older man nodding at us as Isaak leads me inside. In a Mafia movie I might be worried because maybe he's found out that I'm planning to break up with him and is going to take me in the back, but in reality, Isaak is just well connected.

The man rushes behind the counter and has two drinks already prepared, as if he'd began preparing them as soon as I'd walked up. He probably did. And of course mine is exactly what I always order: Pu-erh tea. When Isaak and I first started going out, he always made sure the coffee shops we'd meet at would have this particular tea just to make me smile.

"I'm glad you wanted to see me today." He nods at me, and I can see the sparkle in his eye that always seems to be there when he's around me. Long ago he revealed that he had feelings for me beyond the simple business transaction, which is why he became a long-term client. Emotion means that he will listen. "How have you been?"

Typically in between our meetups that happen only once a month I wouldn't reach out, but this is something different. And he's intuitive enough to realize it's unusual. I can see concern behind his eyes.

"I've been quite good. Making some big changes actually. I really enjoyed the novel we discussed last time we were together and managed to finish it." Having already planned it out, this will be my segue into the statement I need to make.

"I'm so glad!" He takes a sip of his coffee slowly. "One of the reasons I enjoy spending time with you is because of how much you enjoy literature."

He's flattering me on purpose. He knows something's going on.

"There was something quite reflective in it for me, and that's what I'm here to discuss with you actually." He leans forward, his eyes searching and trying to figure it out. He's always been a very intuitive man, but I know that he has no idea what I'm about to say. I'm having a hard enough time saying it myself, after all. "The affair between Anna and Vronsky."

He leans back. "Ah…yes, I was hoping you'd see the similarities there. For us, of course. What I appreciate so much about you is that you really see things." His hand moves forward but before he can take my hand I pull it away.

"Their affair ended. And I'm here to say that I'm afraid ours needs to end as well," I announce, keeping my tone firm but not harsh. "We need to stop seeing each other."

His eyes dart to mine, his gaze is almost incredulous. "What!? Roxanne… you can't be serious." Thankfully the coffee shop owner is in the back because I don't want anyone else to have to observe what we are going to say to each other. "It's... we've... I've known you for *years*. This is..." He's searching for words, but I can tell my declaration has taken him aback. Which is rare for him.

"It has nothing to do with you or anyone else." At least that part is partially true. "I've decided to move on with my life, and that means leaving what I do behind." He needs a bone, so I reach forward now and take his hand. "Thanks to you I've been able to set myself up to live a suitable life and will be comfortable while I figure everything out. But it's only fair to let you go now in a proper way. I hope that you can find it in your heart to understand."

He takes his hand away. "I guess... I just thought there was more between us." His eyes dart down, and I can tell he's almost ashamed about the fact that he's developed feelings for me. It happens a lot in my world, so I know that it's also much better to cut things off for him as well.

"You're a very special man to me and always will be. I just need to move on. I won't be seeing anyone anymore professionally." There's no need to let him know about my personal life.

"Does that mean I can still see you... outside of work?" It's phrased in the perfect way to probe if he could still see me. Maybe keep a foot in the door. I have to shake my head and he turns his head, obviously upset.

"I need to cut things off. I'm sorry, but it's best for both of us." His eyes drop down to his cup of coffee and it's impossible to stay there and prolong his sadness. Plus, I'm not sad about my decision. Andries is the man I want to be with. Even if it means giving up the clients that have sustained me for years. "I'm going to go, and I'd appreciate it if you didn't contact me in the future."

He looks at me and there's a flash of anger. "So that's it? After everything? We've... I've..." His hand clenches on the table and he's stammering, obviously flailing in his mind. The tablecloth clenches in his hand. I can see the owner stick his head out of the back with a nervous look.

"I'm sorry, Isaak." At that, it's easy to stand up and walk out of the shop.

I take a deep breath when I get outside, and it feels like the air is suddenly clearer. Even though it's mid-afternoon, people are starting to crowd the sidewalks. I mingle between them, knowing Isaak won't follow me and make a scene amid the crowd.

There's a massive sense of relief, and as I walk and hear the hum of the city around me expand while the working class returns to their homes it is nice to window shop a bit. After all, I have nowhere to be. No men to correspond with, except for Andries. The freedom is both liberating and terrifying at the same time.

As if he knows I'm thinking about him, my phone vibrates and a text message from Andries appears:

Dinner at mine. I have wine and some excellent appetizers. A picture follows. Damned man intentionally sent me a picture of one of my favorite reds. He must want something. But it's also very flattering that he remembers the little things.

I'll be there in about an hour, I text him back.

Excellent. But too long. Send me your location and I'll Uber you.

I pause, considering his request, to which I then reply, *Fine, here you go.* And I send him my location.

It's somehow ironic that I've broken up with my last client and now I'm about to be whisked away to my new boyfriend's place. My boyfriend... What a name! It feels so weird and new at the same time, that I'm still processing it.

A few minutes later, I quickly get a ping on my phone, and it informs me a car is on the way. When I slide in the driver already knows where I'm supposed to be going. The smell of the car is brand new—just like my relationship.

Reaching the top floor, the elevator's door opens wide, giving direct access to his apartment. As usual, I take off my coat and shoes at the entrance, before dropping them into one of the closets of the hallway. His place is just as bright and incredibly clean as the last time I was here. As I take in my surroundings, I notice how contemporary the interior design is, but I know furniture, and the fact his couch alone costs more than some people's motorcycles says volumes. The smoky smell in the air tells me we're having something rich and sumptuous for dinner, so I quietly head to the kitchen, knowing that's most likely where I will find him.

My heart does a little somersault when my eyes lay on his tall figure, which stands in front of the counter and is focused on the steaming pot. Though my presence isn't noiseless, so Andries turns around, his face beaming with joy as our eyes lock.

"Hey," he greets, his voice welcoming.

My lips twist into a smile as I walk past the breakfast bar and then, standing on my tiptoes, I reach out for his lips.

The kiss is genuine but brief, and I find myself already missing the taste of his lips when they part from mine so that he can speak. "I'm so glad you could make it." His mouth spreads in a wide smile that makes my face fall a little. And it's hard to admit it, but I've missed him. "What have you been up to?"

Oh, you know, breaking up with one of my oldest clients. "Shopping, mostly. It was a day off." Thankfully he doesn't know any semblance of my supposed schedule.

He holds up the bottle of wine for me to inspect. It's, of course, French and it's exquisite.

"Already decanted." Without asking permission he pours me a glass and I take a sip, the tart flavor dancing across my tongue. Rich, oaky notes that warm me. I'm in the right place.

"So you're free this weekend?" It's said as almost a command, not a question but I quickly nod. If he wants to spend some time together with more wine, I'm happy to do so. "You know, for that fencing tournament in Ghent. We'll be spending the weekend there." His smile twinkles in his eyes and I know he's looking forward to a night or two in a hotel room.

"Oh yes, right…" My body goes tense as I remind myself we'd spoken about it last Sunday. Jeez! I didn't expect something like that to be the result of his sudden invitation.

"My sister and my friends will be there. They've been asking questions about my mystery girlfriend. All I want to do is show you off." He lets out a quick snort in amusement, but I don't think anything funny about it.

My body is suddenly chilled. There's a desire to be with him of course, but meeting his friends and family... And so fast? It seems like too much. "I don't think so."

There's something in his eyes. I've seen it before and it's almost as if he changes from light to dark when desire begins to burn there. He's definitely not used to not getting what he asks for, and that makes it fun to say no to him. It's a skill I've cultivated over many years, and he has no idea of that. He probably thinks I'm going to be the demure Asian princess and that's simply not in my nature.

"What do you mean, you don't think so? It'll be a great weekend, and the hotel is spectacular." He steps forward and now his body is close enough to me on the stool to feel the energy between us. "Just like this dress."

Now I know what he's aiming for. If he wants to get me to break down, he has another thing coming. I've been seduced by some pretty incredible men in my time. Giving him a coy smile, I say, "Glad you like it."

His body is looming over mine and now I can tell exactly what's in his eyes. He's not trying to kiss me. I think he has something else in mind. Fingers fall to my bare knees and it's impossible not to feel goosebumps break out. He leans forward with a sigh.

My thin frame isn't enough to resist his strong arms, and frankly I don't want to. The dress I wore for my encounter with Isaak isn't much because the weather is warm today, so it's barely there and my legs are bare as well. The lingerie underneath is only a wisp of lace. And now I can feel the heat between my legs as his lips touch my knee, sending a spark up toward my hips.

"Andries…what are you doing?" I say the words with a coy smile, but I know exactly what he's doing. The man isn't used to hearing no. Thankfully, unlike my former clients, he's doing something to convince me instead of demanding that I acquiesce to his demands with something as silly as money.

"Convincing you that a weekend away with me will be a very…fun…" his lips finally touch my inner thigh and his hands spread my knees wider, "…time." I'm used to men kissing me, but this is somehow different. Deliberate and glorious, like he has nothing else on his mind but devouring my body. I'm used to being the instigator, not the person being spoiled with physical satisfaction.

His lips trail up and I feel his hands join them, sliding up my dress to touch the very edges of my lace panties. Instead of tugging though, he leans in, and I feel his tongue slide up the thin fabric, sending a pulse of sensory joy straight up my spine. He inhales deeply and sighs, making me feel the vibration of his mouth.

Tugging at the sides I know exactly what he wants so I lift my hips, letting him finally take the panties down my narrow legs. My slit is already wet from what I know is about to come. Even though he's trying to convince me, I still have to stay coy but it's impossible when he tucks the panties into his jeans' pocket and moves back between my legs.

"Mmm…" he moans as his tongue finally touches my bare pussy and slides up slowly, making every nerve stand on end. My nipples spring to life under my dress. Jesus, he's so damn good with his mouth. "God, just imagine us in the presidential suite… lying on the bed, my body on top of yours." Fuck.

He knows that the way to my heart is the fantasy. The fantasy of actually having a man who loves me and wants to keep my heart with his along with my body. To give myself completely to one man isn't something I've ever contemplated before but now with his lips and tongue devouring me it seems so right somehow.

His mouth feels like it is everywhere. My lips are on fire, my hips grinding against his mouth and all I can think about is getting to the place he keeps denying me from. That pinnacle of pleasure. It's totally deliberate, I can tell. Fuck, he's such a skilled lover and that's one of the reasons why I need to say no. I can't tempt fate by letting him in.

"Ah… ooh… please… don't stop…." As the words leave my mouth his tongue stops moving, making the warm wave of pleasure that was about to crest fade away. Like it was never there to begin with. "Fuck… no…" I beg, wanting him to keep going. The bastard knows exactly what he's doing. And the one way to get me to agree to anything is to actually please me.

But every time I come close his mouth stops. He inserts a finger, and it only makes things worse, like he knows how to touch all the places that send me close to the edge but not over it. Delicious torture. Every time a drop of me leaves my body he laps it up eagerly and continues to moan.

"All I want…" he licks me again slowly "…is to hear…" Another slow torturous movement, this time with his finger moving. All I want to do is erupt; he's doing things to me that no man has ever done. "…Yes. Say it, Roxie…"

Finally my resolve breaks down. If this is an indication of how we will spend time together outside of the tournament, what woman would say no? "Ah…okay…yes…yes…" As soon as the words leave my mouth his tongue starts moving along with his finger, deliberate and steady.

He moans into my slit and my declarations of going with him become more as my hips begin to shake uncontrollably and my core starts to spasm with the release he's been denying me. "Yes! Ahhh! Yes!" As my body shakes across his face, almost thrusting onto his tongue the delicious release washes over me with a shiver that almost knocks me off the stool. His strong hands hold me in place as I gasp through my orgasm, which feels like it is lasting a lifetime.

As my shaking slows he kisses my inner thigh again and then stands up, his lips finding mine. I can taste and smell my scent all over his face and he smiles as I suck on his tongue. Now all I want is for him to take me into the bedroom and fuck me senseless.

"Excellent. Now we can have dinner." He walks around my still shaking body without giving me my panties back. Fuck.

The glass feels warm in my hand, and I can see it shaking. He has a hold over me I can't explain.

CHAPTER 24

Amsterdam, October 8, 2021
Andries

I have planned everything out as best as I can, never having booked an entire trip to impress someone before. No expense has been spared, but I know that money isn't what is going to impress Roxanne. It's going to take a lot more than that.

I'm still under the impression that her acceptance of my invitation was reluctant, and although it twists at my heartstrings to think she's still unsure of me, I can't exactly blame her. Our last weekend together had been passion-filled, lustful, and frantic—just like our dinner on Thursday—with there being hardly a single second to breathe. To me, it's everything I could have hoped for. To her, it was completely unexpected. I'm not a fool, and I know she hadn't wanted to fall for me, but the chemistry between us is far too undeniable.

That meant that this weekend in Ghent could set the pace for the rest of our relationship. If she enjoyed herself and found me to be a partner she could be with long term, then I'll have succeeded in my mission. If something happens to mess this opportunity up, I'll never forgive myself.

I made a reservation at one of the best hotels in town. Even though I know perfectly Roxanne can't be bought, I want to give her comfort and luxury, so our time together can be effortless.

Now that it's time to depart for Ghent, I'm experiencing an uncommon bout of nerves. I hide them the best that I can, pacing around my apartment for the full hour before she is due to arrive, but I can't help them from bubbling to the surface.

Just as I'm about to pull my phone out to call Roxanne, I hear the familiar buzz of someone wanting to be let in, and I press the button to allow her up. I wipe my palms on my pants and force my heart rate to slow. She is here. It's going to be fine. It's going to be better than fine.

She is stunning, just as she always is, dressed for the drive, in tall riding boots, leggings, and a leather jacket to match, and her blonde hair is haphazardly brushed behind on the back of her head. I hadn't seen her since she left Thursday evening, and before I could stop myself, I'm rushing forward and gathering her into my arms, ignoring the suitcase behind her.

She makes a small noise as I crush my mouth to hers, but she goes soft in my grip almost immediately, succumbing to the kiss. I'm already counting the minutes we have until check-in to see if I have time to take her to bed, just once, before we leave, when she puts both of her hands on my chest and gently pushes me back with a breathy laugh.

"It's nice to see you too, Andries. But shouldn't we get going?"

I try to pull her back in, but she evades me. "We have time," I insist, but she wags a finger at me.

"No, we don't. You're gonna be mad at yourself if we don't have time to unpack a little before dinner."

I pursue her around the apartment until I finally catch her, and she dissolves into helpless giggles as I pull her down to the couch with me. I kiss her neck before she rolls away, smoothing her hair down and standing up.

"Andries! You texted me saying to hurry up! Now let's go!" She crosses her arms, but when I tilt her chin up with my finger for a single kiss, she allows it. She tastes like mint and the barest hint of coffee.

"Alright, but once we check-in, you're mine," I growl against her mouth, palming her ass through her leggings before finally releasing her.

I carry her suitcase out to the car, already having packed all my things last night, and she follows, offering to help multiple times until I insist she get into the car. With the apartment locked up and all of our things loaded, we're able to get on the road.

It's a two hour drive, but the sun is out and the most fascinating woman on Earth is riding passenger. It's the epitome of perfection, and I can't believe how swiftly a rather boring fencing competition has morphed into a weekend such as the one to come.

Roxanne has pulled out her phone and is messing with the car's Bluetooth, a concentrated look on her face. "What kind of music do you like?" she asks while scrolling through what I assume is her own playlists.

"A lot of indie artists, and quite a bit of classic rock, thanks to my dad." I tap my fingers on the steering wheel, thinking about all the music my dad had introduced me to. "Honestly, I haven't listened to much lately besides instrumentals. I find it affects the way I write when there are other words I'm half listening to."

"That makes sense," she replies. "Do you care if I play some of my stuff, then?"

I give her a quick glance. "Anything you want, babe."

Little does she know, I mean that literally too. She could have asked me for anything at that moment, and I'd have given it to her.

"*Babe*?" she repeats, clearly amused.

"It just rolled out of my mouth," I tell her casually. "Why?"

She keeps staring at me, her lips curving into a pleasant smile. "I like it."

I reach down and give a little squeeze to her hand, before my attention returns to the road.

We listen to her songs for some time, but what I really want is to talk to her. To know her as well as possible. "Have you been to Ghent before?"

She shrugs. "I've been to Belgium, but I've never been to that city in particular."

"After this weekend, I think it'll be a special place for us both," I say, reaching past the gearshift to caress her leg.

She huffs but lays her hand over mine. "Your self-confidence knows no bounds."

* * *

Most of the fencers, Dan included, are staying elsewhere, all in the same hotel. Originally, I had planned to do the same, so I could be front and center for any partying that might go on after the matches, but once Roxanne accepted my invitation, I turned my room at the first hotel over to Elise.

For the two of us, I had acquired the presidential suite at Pillows Grand Boutique Hotel Reylof, somewhere far away from my friends and any other peers that might eavesdrop or interfere. I didn't even tell Dan, or anyone else, where we were staying, and I planned on keeping it a secret for the duration of our stay.

Ghent is one of the oldest cities in Belgium and the architecture leaves no doubts as to how old it really is. There are rows and rows of abbeys, cathedrals, guildhalls, and castles, the most fantastic of them along the Lyes River. It's not a place where the old had been torn down to construct the new, but instead, celebrated its history with some of the best maintained ancient architecture in the world.

Three enormous towers, the Belfry of Ghent, the Saint Bavo Cathedral, and Saint Nicholas' Church, overlook the city as guardians of stone and make it seem like walking back in time when you stand at the base of them. Most of the city was built keeping in mind Baroque and Gothic architecture, with miles and miles of pale stone and intricate designs. Having Roxanne here made me look upon the place with fresh eyes, thinking about the things I wanted to show her and experience with her by my side.

Our hotel is in the center of the city, where it sits like a beating heart full of people coming and going. It had been the residence of nobility, who had lived in the city in the 1700s, but inside the entire place had been restored and modernized. As we arrive, the valet takes our car while the other employees unload our luggage, and after a quick check-in, we are escorted to the suite. Roxanne is clearly used to this kind of treatment, never missing a step. Once we are in the elevator, with only a single bellhop with us, she looks up at me with a mischievous look in her eye.

"You planned this all by yourself?" she asks.

"Um, yeah."

She makes a pleased noise. "I'm impressed. Most college students can't even do a load of laundry, let alone sweep a girl off her feet with something as luxurious as this."

I snort at her comment, heading shaking. "Just you wait," I promise, and I can see her shiver delightfully.

By the time we leave from here, she'll have forgotten all about Karl, or Charlie, or anyone else for that matter.

The suite is decorated in shades of white, tan, and navy blue. The hotel employee must be able to sense something brewing between Roxanne and me because he takes the tip I offer and scurries away as quickly as he can. I slip my arm behind her back, and we check out the accommodations together, her leaning her weight on me comfortingly. She's so small next to me that it makes my chest clench. She's delicate, but at the same time, unshakeable.

"What time is dinner?" she asks, lowering herself into one of the leather lounge chairs in the living area, stretching her arms above her head.

"Six." I frown, thinking of Dan, Jessica, and Elise, and how much I want to keep Roxanne to myself instead of sharing her with them. "But we can skip it if you want. Order room service. Eat it in bed... naked."

She rolls her eyes. "Oh yes, the perfect first impression for your sister and friends, not showing up at all. You know we have to go."

It's just starting to hit me that I have her completely alone, finally, somewhere besides the car, and we have hours to spare until dinner. When she stretches, her breasts press against her tight black shirt, the lines of her neck and collarbone tempting me to put my mouth on them. My blood thrums in my veins, insistent and blazing hot. When I don't answer her, she looks over at me, and she stills in the chair.

"Are you okay?" she asks hesitantly. "You look... intense."

There are dozens of places in this hotel suite I could fuck her, and I plan to put them all to good use: the bed, the soaking tub, the walk-in shower, in front of the fireplace... but right now, I'm going to have her right in the chair where she is sitting as I don't even have the patience to move anywhere else. I have to be inside her, and it has to be right now.

"... Andries?"

I stalk toward her, and I watch as she presses her back against the chair, almost as if she's afraid, but I know better. As I approach, I yank my shirt off, followed by kicking my shoes away. Roxanne has been trying, ever since we first made love, to take control and fuck me her way, but I wanted her to know she was mine. I wanted to mark her with my teeth, my tongue, and my seed. Everything. All of it.

When I reach her, I press one of her shoulders back against the chair, pinning her in place. "Give me your leg."

She complies, and I tug the first leather boot off, and then the other, stopping to cup my now-raging erection so she can see it through my pants. "Do you see what you do to me?"

"Yes," she breathes, licking her lips unconsciously. She tries to move forward, but I hold her still, stripping the leggings from her so she's sitting before me in just her shirt, leather jacket, and black lace panties. It's so erotic, and I commit the image to memory.

"Let me touch you," she pleads.

"Soon," I assure her. "But undress for me first."

Despite her rapid breathing, she doesn't rush it, sliding her jacket off slowly before pulling her shirt over her head and letting it fall to the floor. Of course, her bra perfectly matches her panties. As soon as the shirt is gone, I'm on her again, kissing her mouth until I feel her tongue slide against mine. She's working my belt off, pushing my pants down, and then one of her hands is stroking my cock while the other grips one cheek of my bare ass, pointed nails digging in and pulling me closer.

Nothing has ever felt like her touch. Nothing. My entire body is hers if she wants it, but first I have to have her before I burn alive. She works my manhood expertly, smearing the pre-cum from the tip over the head and using it to ease her grip. I brace myself with my hands on the back of the chair while she does it, claiming her mouth, back arched so she can reach all the parts of me she seems hungry to touch and taste.

I can't take it much longer, even as I reach down to pinch her nipples through the lace, drinking in the sweet noises she makes as I do so. I want to do so *much* for her, but we are both rapidly losing control. I'll worship her with my hands and tongue later, but right now I have to be inside her.

Roxanne and I must be in sync because when I back up just the smallest bit, she sheds her underwear in the blink of an eye. I step out of the legs of my pants on the floor before surging forward, falling on my knees and wrapping her in my arms, the feel of her skin on mine complete and total ecstasy.

"I've missed you," I tell her, voice hoarse as she guides me toward her entrance with a hand wrapped around my cock. "Missed this."

"I have too, God help me, you're all I've thought about," Roxanne pants. She kisses my jaw, biting my bottom lip as she lines us up perfectly, and I sink into her in one steady thrust.

We don't speak anymore after that. Once I'm buried in her, I can't stop. I rut against her like an animal, and if she had been a lesser woman, it would have been too much. But this was Roxanne, my perfect mate, the woman made for me. With me kneeling and her legs wrapped around me, our height difference disappears, and I switch between ravaging her mouth, grazing my teeth against her long, pale throat, and pressing our foreheads together and gazing not just into her eyes, but into her very soul. My hips never stop, and she never fails to meet me thrust for thrust.

I fuck her with all my pent-up need from the past week, the slap of our flesh filling the suite along with her short, staccato moans each time I hit deep inside her. I lose track of time. My stamina is endless for her. Only her.

The leather of the seat is working against us, causing her to slide, so without ever pulling out of her, I maneuver us to the ground and onto the soft shearling rug spread across the hard wooden floor. I vaguely think that I should have lit the fireplace for this to be perfect, but there was no time—not when I couldn't think because I needed to fuck her so badly.

She moves her body like the sea, rolling into me in the perfect complement to my unhinged fucking. With her tucked so close against me, I can feel as she starts to tense up right before her pussy grips me hard. She's close, and the knowledge of it causes my balls to tighten up. I push forward even more until she's almost bent in half, hips bucking like mad. Distantly, I hear her calling my name to the ceiling, but it's drowned out by the blood rushing in my ears.

Her nails dig into my back a millisecond before she comes, her channel milking my cock and her smooth, controlled movements becoming wild, frantic. I'm right behind her, coming so hard I can't see straight, but holding onto her until the very last second. I won't let her fall away from me.

She cradles my head against her shoulder, an action so steeped in affection that it makes my heart skip a beat. We're both panting, trying to catch our breath and glistening with sweat. Maybe not lighting the fire was the right move.

"You've ruined me," she breathes, voice thready. "You've ruined me for anyone else."

I clutch her hard against me. "There will *never* be anyone else," I growl, meaning every syllable with every ounce of my being. "Never, Roxie, you hear me?"

"Yes," she whispers. "Yes."

* * *

Despite offering to skip dinner dozens more times, Roxie actually seems invigorated from our fuck session, instead of drained like I am. She's excited to meet everyone, her trepidation from earlier seeming to have evaporated into nothing.

"It's the orgasm," she says when I point out that she didn't even want to go, just a few days before. "It's like rose-colored glasses. Everything seems better after a good fuck."

The dinner reservation is at a small, but well-renowned restaurant called Roots. Jessica had insisted we sit outdoors, in a small dining area nestled intimately between two buildings and dotted with radiant heaters to keep the temperature pleasant.

Watching her change from the vixen I had just fucked in front of the empty fireplace into the most elegant woman I have ever seen is almost like magic. She curled her blonde hair into loose waves, pulled on a slip dress so dark green it's nearly black, and finished it with black Louboutins and ebony pearl earrings. She applied makeup as if in a trance, and when she finished, her long black trench coat draped over her arm for later, she looked like a completely different woman. But I'd know my Roxanne anywhere, no matter what she wore.

I care little for what I look like for dinner since all I really want is to get back to the hotel with my girlfriend, but given the fact she's dressed like a femme fatale, I dress to match her in a tailored black suit, white shirt, and no tie. We had showered after our interlude, and I was able to slick my now clean hair back from my face and proclaim myself ready.

"You look so incredible in a suit," Roxie comments wistfully from where she is perched on the edge of the bed. "I nearly fell down the stairs when I saw you at the opera. If you had been dressed like this when you brought up skipping dinner, I might have bought into it."

"It's not too late," I suggest.

"Yes, it is. I'm already dressed. Let's go."

As much as I didn't want to go to this dinner, seeing the way that everyone looks at the two of us with envy makes pride swell in me. I especially love noticing the men who look at Roxanne for extended seconds before turning their eyes to me in disappointment. No one can have her. She's mine, and I quite enjoy letting the entire city of Ghent know it. Hell, given the opportunity, I'd tell the entire world she belongs to me.

The restaurant isn't too far from the hotel, but it takes me a moment to find it with its unassuming facade. Some of Roxanne's excited energy has turned nervous again, so I slip a hand into hers after turning the car off and squeeze reassuringly.

"Are you ready?"

"No. Yes," she says, breathing deeply. "It's just… I know they expect Tatiana or someone *like* Tatiana. I don't want you to regret bringing me."

I grab her other hand and turn her to face me. "That cannot be Roxanne, the most confident woman alive who has the highest opinion of herself possible."

She smirks, the smallest bit, and it's a good sign. "Oh, I don't mind if they hate me. I only worry that it will go badly for you if they detest me. It's only your opinion I care about, and these are your loved ones."

"Love is a strong word," I hedge, and she laughs briefly before blowing out a breath. I don't completely buy into the idea that she doesn't care, but I'll let her have her pride.

I help her out of the car, and she leans on me, our arms locked together as we walk inside. I don't let it show, but I'm anxious too, because this introduction might be the most meaningful of my life.

I gaze down at my woman until she meets my eyes. "Let's do this."

CHAPTER 25

Ghent, October 8, 2021
Roxanne

To say it's an eventful day would be an understatement. First the drive into Ghent, then the mind-boggling sex, and now meeting Andries' friends and sister only hours after we finished fucking like rabbits. It's a lot, to say the least.

Being nervous to meet people is not normal for me, but this thing between Andries and I has been a whirlwind, and it's been only a week since we had done more than kiss. Now I'm about to meet his sister, and as much as Andries is clearly smitten with me, I know that this introduction can make or break our budding relationship. It frankly terrifies me, because if it goes south, all of this trust I had poured into him will be for nothing.

I have to believe in him.

The restaurant is small, and I'm happy to see that there is more room to breathe out on the patio area. The radiant heaters keep everything nice and toasty, and I'm pleased to shrug off my coat and fold it over my arm. A host takes it for me, and I link arms with Andries again to find our table.

I recognize the couple, Dan and Jessica, from the cabaret and some pictures Andries showed me of them. Dan has his tousled hair slicked back and is dressed similarly to Andries, and his lovely partner Jessica smiles warmly as we approach.

The third person I also recognize from the pictures, and it clicks in my mind suddenly that she had also been at the cabaret. This must be Elise, and while her expression is polite, there is a sharp, calculating awareness in her eyes as she looks me over from head to toe. It almost seems like a challenge, and I bristle, but when we reach the table, she's the first to stand and greet us.

Elise kisses each of my cheeks, telling me how lovely it is to finally meet me, and how enamored her brother obviously is. Dan snorts in amusement, but Andries looks completely blank, as if he wasn't sure what Elise would do next.

I thank her, turning on all my professional charms and Andries is quick to pull a chair for me to sit, beside him.

"I noticed you changed hotels," Dan comments.

"I wanted somewhere more private," Andries explains, not offering up the name of our hotel.

"I understand," Jessica says. "Staying with everyone we know in the rooms around us tends to feel like an ongoing frat party after a night or so. Not conducive to a romantic time away."

"You don't seem to mind, Jess," Dan teases.

"I'm used to it by now, unfortunately." She sighs.

We order appetizers and wine, making surface-level conversation about dishes and drink preferences. Elise pays me the most attention, watching every move I make, and every move her brother makes toward me. When Andries leans over to whisper something into my ear, her eyes narrow in the tiniest increment. Judgmental or cautious, I can't tell.

"So, Andries said you're a librarian working at a bookshop?" Elise asks.

I lie effortlessly. Bless my poor sister, the real librarian and bookstore clerk. "Yes, I love literature. It's what Andries and I bonded over initially."

"I'm sure he was happy to have someone to talk to death about books and all of that nonsense," she says, waving a hand dismissively in front of her.

"Actually, I'd started to find a lot of things stale. Andries reignited my love for poetry and books. He's so passionate, it's contagious." I smile at Andries as I speak, hoping to relax him a little once he realizes everyone is getting along. His grip on my knee lets up a bit.

"Passionate," Elise muses. "Indeed."

It wasn't that I expected the dinner to go badly, but I just hadn't expected it to be as seamless as it was. I know there was some fascination with Andries' mystery date, but after the shock of my presence had worn off, they seemed even more interested in the fact that Andries had a date *at all*. It surprises me, because Andries is beyond handsome, smart, and kind, but they insist he's an introvert who shuns all forms of socializing. He looks embarrassed at times, but I don't mind that part of him. It's just one thread in the tapestry of the man who I'm becoming more and more fond of.

Elise's questions are the most forward, but she never approaches rudeness, and once Andries launches into a story about how he and I have discovered we shared a favorite poet, an obscure man from the eighteenth century, and Elise sees the joy on his face, most of her tension toward me seems to melt away. It lets me knows she loves her brother, despite the arguments Andries had mentioned, and that made me respect her more in turn. I don't have any illusions that I'm a fitting replacement for the adored Tatiana, but at least there isn't any animosity between Elise and me.

After a raspberry tart dessert, we bid everyone goodbye, and I promise to sit with Elise and Jessica during the matches tomorrow. Andries is quiet at first once we are in the car, sliding glances at me as if he is just waiting for me to erupt.

"Did you have a good time?" he asks gently. "I know they can be a lot—"

"I had a wonderful time. Stop worrying."

"You're sure? Because you don't have to sit with my sister and—"

"Stop worrying." I reach over to squeeze his well-muscled leg. "Are we all best friends? No. But I think they find me acceptable, at least for a weekend fling."

I realize it's the wrong joke to make when his expression darkens. "A weekend fling?"

"No, no, I didn't mean that's what this is. I just mean your friends probably don't take us seriously, since you apparently never date." When he continues to frown, I unbuckle, ignoring all the traffic laws as I lean over the gearshift and press a soft kiss to his jaw. "What we have is all ours, love."

At the word *love*, his body language eases, and he breathes deeply. I slide back to my seat, watching him, affection blooming inside of me like a rose.

"Did you call me love?" he asks finally.

"I did."

His smile is up to his ears. "Will you do it more often?"

I laugh quietly, never taking my eyes off him. "I will."

* * *

Ghent, October 9, 2021
Roxanne

"I changed my mind. Let's stay in bed."

Andries chuckles at my statement, biting the curve of my bare shoulder and extricating himself from the naked embrace we are locked in. "I have a fencing match in less than an hour and you're supposed to watch."

"Fuck fencing," I groan.

"No, but I'll fuck you later if you behave and get out of bed so we can leave."

"Fine," I tell him, sitting up in just enough time to watch his bare ass as he walks to the dresser where our things have been unpacked. It's a travesty when he is fully dressed, but I have to admit defeat and go get dressed myself.

It isn't that I'm not excited to see him fence, because I am. It's just spending the day in bed with my boyfriend, where I can be my most honest self, is more appealing than any other earthly activity. He's right, though, and we're riding the razor's edge of being late if we don't hurry up.

I shrug on the designer wrap dress I've picked out for today, touching up my curls in the mirror and painting my lips red. Andries loves red lipstick, and since I'd be cheering him on, I wanted him to be able to pick me out from the crowd.

The Royal and Knightly Saint Michael's Guild isn't far from our hotel, but Andries is in a rush, and quieter than usual. I don't press him, but his demeanor dims my excitement for the event. As we pull in, he looks at me and blows out a breath.

"Can I tell you something?" he asks.

"Of course."

"I've never been nervous to fence in my life. But I'm nervous about losing in front of you. This is just a hobby to me, but right now it feels like the world championship just because you're here."

"Oh, Andries, don't think that way." He doesn't look convinced, so I have to think on my feet.

Clambering over the gearshift—which I'm beginning to hate, as much as it's in my way—I straddle his lap, much to his surprise, and put my hands on each side of his cheeks. It's intimate, and I'm not wearing anything besides my panties under the dress, and if the immediate bulge that I feel against my leg is any indication, he has noticed.

"If you lose, we'll go back to the hotel, and I'll nurse your imaginary wounds. You can just lay back and let me take care of you. If you win, you can have…" I grind myself against him slowly, and we both gasp. "Me. I'll be your spoils of war. What do you think?"

His hands flip up my dress until he's grabbing both my ass cheeks in a firm grip. "Why don't you give me a preview?" he asks, voice thick with arousal.

I consider it briefly, but one look at the time on the dash convinces me otherwise. Much to his shock, I open the driver's door and slide out, adjusting my dress as I go.

"Later!" I call to him, rushing inside before he can come to his senses. "I'll see you after the match!"

"Roxanne!" is all I hear before I'm inside, laughing to myself, even as I can feel my pulse between my legs. It really takes just the slightest touch from him to get me going.

There isn't much space for spectators inside, but I find Jessica and Elise easy enough. They've saved me a seat in the crowded, tiny viewing area, and it's a relief to sit down, knowing that we weren't too late for Andries to participate.

"Running behind?" Jessica asks, humor in her voice.

"Something like that," I answer, smiling secretly. Elise picks up on it, though, and wrinkles her nose.

"Ew," she groans, and I laugh despite myself.

After a few cordial questions, the two other women realize I know nothing about fencing and start to fill me in on the rules. Andries had given me a brief overview, but it was obvious he went mostly off instinct. Jessica and Elise make it much clearer for me, and by the time the adjudicators arrive, and everything is being prepared, I'm more excited than ever to see Andries fight.

The first couple of matches go so quickly that I have a hard time keeping up, going mostly off the reactions of the crowd to find out what is happening. By the third match, though, I've figured it out in my mind, and I'm able to better appreciate the graceful way the fencers move, bodies poised and controlled. It's almost like a dance.

Andries' match is the fifth of the day, his opponent an amateur fencer from Germany. With how anonymous the fighters appear in their uniforms and masks, it's easy to forget the real people underneath, but that all changes when Andries comes out.

He often reminds me of some sort of lion when we make love, fierce and nearly feral, and that attitude bleeds over into the way he moves here. He flicks his foil as he speaks to the judges, his mask under one arm. He had been in his normal clothes in the car, and seeing him like this is a jolt to my senses.

He's so ridiculously attractive, completely in his element. I'm bewitched. Everyone around me fades away until it's only Andries, his opponent, and me. Right before he puts the mask on, he turns, meeting eyes with me, and nodding once. It's time.

He had made it clear to me he wasn't a true professional, but if he had never said anything, I'd have assumed he was the best fencer on Earth, only because it was Andries and anything he did seemed so easy, so natural. He moves like an oncoming storm, with less grace than the competitors before him, but more fire. His opponent strikes, but is driven back, and Andries presses him hard. I'm gripping the railing of the viewing area until my knuckles turn white, afraid to even blink.

Andries pulls ahead, but then the opponent manages to come back. The other matches took minutes, and while this one certainly does too, it seems like hours to me. Rush, strike, parry, it all blurs together, but then—

Andries wins!

Jessica and Elise cheer, but I can only think of my promise from the car. He had won, and anything he wants from me, he can now have. I clap with everyone else, until he tears his mask off, his hair wet from sweat, flinging away from his face. Andries locks eyes with me, and in his gaze, there was a promise as primal and ferocious as anything I'd ever seen. His eyes say, *You're mine*.

My heart is hammering in my chest, and when I unconsciously lay my hand over it, Andries notices and smiles, sharp and predatory. An almost fearful excitement skitters up my spine while an ache begins between my thighs. These matches can't end soon enough.

CHAPTER 26

Amsterdam, October 12, 2021
Roxanne

Despite it being Tuesday, my mind's still replaying my weekend with Andries, more precisely the moments we spent together in his suite. Fuck! I can't believe I'm his first woman. This is absolutely insane. And yet, I heave a long sigh as I remember the feeling of his hands caressing my skin, his tongue between my thighs, and the heady sensation of having him inside of me. My heart starts pumping faster as those memories take over me, but I'm pulled right back on planet Earth at the sound of a knocking on my office door. My attention focuses on the door that cracks open and Poppy stepping in.

"Karl's here," she announces, standing by the doorway. "May I let him in?"

Oh shit! I glance at my watch, then straighten my posture and nod, waiting for Karl to come in. We've got to talk—that's not fair keeping him hanging and expecting that our relationship will resume like it was before. If I managed to end everything with Isaak and Charlie, then I have to be able to do the same with him.

"Karl," I greet as he finally walks in, looking sharp in a suit, his stubble and hair perfectly trimmed. He paces in my direction and I invite him to sit in one of the chairs in front of my desk.

"How was your weekend?" Karl asks, unbuttoning his jacket as he lowers himself in the chair. "I've heard you had a good time in Ghent."

I've got no idea who told him about it, but this is one more reason to end this relationship once and for all.

"We need to talk," I announce, disregarding his question about my personal life.

"About?" he says, leaning back on his chair.

I do the same on mine, and looking him in the eye, I say, "About us."

His eyes widen in surprise, and he leans forward, sitting just at the edge of his seat. "Us?" he repeats in confusion. "You mean…"

"I've decided that I'm gonna focus solely on agency management," I tell him. His features deepen, but I don't think he's connecting the dots, so I add, "Which means I'm ending our contract."

He scoffs in response, head shaking, and one of his hands starts rubbing his stubble as he process the news. "It's because of him, isn't it?"

"It has nothing to do with Andries," I answer, despite knowing all too well he's played a big role in my decision. "I think it's best we just remain friends."

"Wow," he utters, a wave of shock taking over him. "Jeez! After fifteen years, you want to break up?" The astonishment in his tone tightens my heart. And despite him being a career-focused asshole, I know deep down he developed some kind of feelings for me. "What the fuck?" he asks, leaping off his chair at the realization of what this entails. "No!" he snaps at me, as if he has any say in the matter. "Let's just renegotiate the terms, I'm sure we can find a good arrangement."

"Karl…" I say, trying to bring him back to reason.

"Roxie, look," he begins as he walks around my desk and then swirls my chair to face me. "I understand I haven't been that romantic with you lately but—"

"We are not in a relationship," I remind him just as fast, my tone stern. "You pay me to be with you."

"I'm going through a divorce, I really need you." His words remind me why so many clients decide to stick with the same girl instead of trying new ones. Once they've found someone who listens to them, they become loyal customers for life.

"I can recommend you someone else, I own an agency, remember?"

"But I only want you." He sounds at the verge of despair. "Look, I don't mind going through a dry period, but at least be present in my life."

I look him in the eye and despite seeing how hurt he is, I've got to stand my ground. "Karl, I'm sorry, but I'm revoking our contract."

He scoffs. "Fuck!" A gush of air rolls off his lips, sounding extra annoyed. "You had sex with him, huh?"

Unease pricks at the back of my neck, so I stand up, and walk a few steps away from him, but he follows closely behind.

"Answer me," he demands.

"It's none of your damn business," I snap in annoyance, turning around to face him.

"Jeez," he breathes, his jaw flexing at the realization of what is happening. "And I bet it was for free."

"Enough!"

I'm about to ask him to leave, but Karl storms in my direction and standing in front of me, he says, "You know how old he is? Did you ask him?"

"Karl, you have to go," I tell him, my tone even and polite. "Don't force me to call security."

"He's eighteen, Roxanne."

His words hit me like a ton of bricks, and I freeze looking at him like a total idiot. "What?"

"You never bothered to ask him, huh?"

While I try not to appear too stunned at the revelation, I can't help but obsess over that little detail. Eighteen? Really? Karl has to be lying. It's true I didn't ask Andries his age but I never thought he'd be under twenty. I mean, he spent an entire year traveling the world and living on his own. How could he possibly be that young?

"How do you know that?"

"I asked his dad when we were having that meeting at his estate," he discloses, reveling in my uneasiness. And to make me feel even worse, he then says, "Just to put things in perspective—you were seventeen when he was born."

I can't help but feel an icky feeling creeping up my spine as I recall everything I did with Andries. "*You* pushed me to hang out with him," I rebuke.

"I pushed you to be his friend, not his lover," he points out in defense. Then lowering his voice, he asks, "Does he know who you are? What you do for a living?"

"Enough," I snap, irritated at his queries. After all, I'm sure he's fishing for info so he can use it against me. Walking back to my desk, I grab my landline and dial the security line. "Security will escort you outside," I chip, wanting nothing more than to end this conversation once and for all.

Karl chuckles at my comment, head shaking. "Yeah, that's what I thought."

Fortunately a few instants later, a tall, bulky man is knocking on my office door and after entering my office, he stands beside Karl ready to escort him out.

"One last question," Karl demands, looking me in the eye. "What about your other clients? Are you gonna break up with them too?"

"I already did." The security man looks at me for instruction, so I give him a nod of the head, letting him know he can take Karl out of here. "Goodbye, Karl," I say as I watch my first and last client walk out of my office and also out of my life.

After fifteen years, it's a strange feeling knowing that I'm no longer an escort. I have officially no more outings or sex with men for money. A new chapter of my life has begun, and I'm pretty excited about it. It's actually quite freeing and I'm sure I won't miss any of it. There's one thing that I need to clear out though: Andries' age. I pick my iPhone and call him immediately. But once he answers and I hear his voice, I nearly forget why I should be mad at him.

"We need to talk," I tell him as I refocus on the reason of my calling.

"No need to be so stiff," he answers, his tone laced with humor. "You can simply say: *Babe, I miss you and want to be with you.*"

His good energy is infectious, and I can't help but laugh at his words. "Can I come by later on? Like around six or something?"

"Sure, you know where I live."

"Great," I say, keeping my posture straight even though he can't see it. "See you later, then." After hanging up, I can't keep the smile from my cheeks knowing I'm going to see him again in a few hours.

Don't be an idiot!

If what Karl said is true, this thing we're having is beyond icky and wrong! I should've known being with a young college student couldn't work out. Fuck! Eighteen? I lean back on my armchair and rub my eyelids for a moment to relax as I ponder what I'm going to tell him. Andries and I had a great time together, but I don't think I can look past his age. The difference is just too much. Well, if I managed to put an end to a fifteen-year relationship with a client just fine, I'm pretty sure I can do the same with a relationship that just started.

* * *

As the elevator's door dings and opens wide to Andries' place, the clatter of dishes and silverware, followed by the slicing sounds of a knife on veggies, permeates through his open layout, suggesting he's already up to something in the kitchen.

"Good evening!" I say, letting him know I've arrived.

"Good evening," Andries replies from the kitchen, his voice cozy and warm like a blanket in winter. "We're having cheesy chicken and broccoli pasta, I hope it's okay?"

His question hangs in the air as I take off my shoes and coat putting them along with my purse inside the wardrobe of the hallway. Then I make my way toward the kitchen, and lean slightly against the wall, observing him. He's sporting a white t-shirt perfectly molding his built-up back and wide shoulders and black shorts as he stands in front of the counter. It's a simple domestic moment, but I keep quiet without interrupting him and try to memorize every single detail as much as I can. It's something I have never seen in my parents' house, and it's so unfamiliar that I can't help but feel a little squeeze in my chest. Oh gosh, why did he have to be so young?

"Andries," I utter, my tone serious.

His head turns slightly around to check on me until his entire body follows. "Is everything alright?"

The fear in his eyes is so precious that I feel bad even to confront him.

I heave a long sigh, doing my best to keep my voice soft. "Why did you never tell me that you are only eighteen?"

His face deepens with a frown, and I can tell he wasn't expecting such a question. "Because… you never asked me."

"Because I thought you were twenty-something; I mean, you look way older."

His brows are furrowed with confusion as if trying to figure something out. "Why is my age a problem now?"

"Because I didn't know you were *that* young."

"Well, I'm turning nineteen on December 26th," he discloses. "And you are cordially invited to accompany me."

I scoff at his careless attitude. "You realize how bad I feel?" I walk over to where he's standing and looking up at him, I add, "I feel dirty knowing I had sex with an eighteen-year-old."

While I'm dead serious about it, Andries tries hard to suppress a laugh. "Really?" he asks in amusement. "If you feel dirty, maybe we can go for a shower?"

"Andries," I say, aiming to bring some seriousness back. "This is not funny."

"You are very tense, though." His hands go to my shoulders, and he starts massaging them. "Did you have a bad day at work or what?" He's quite talented, and the pressure he applies is just the right amount for me to enjoy and feel my tensed body relaxing.

I turn around, my back on him so that he can continue working on my shoulders and then my back.

"I see someone likes massages," he points out.

"Oh, yes," I purr, impatiently waiting for him to resume.

I push my ass against his front and feel his bulge forming in his pants, and coupled with his fingers digging gently into my flesh, it's enough to make my head swell in delight.

His tongue is warm against the nap of my neck and then close enough to the rim of my ear, he whispers, "Take off your blouse, babe."

"Fine, but just for the massage," I warn as I pull the blue, lace blouse over my head as quickly and smoothly as I can, and drop it on the counter beside us.

His breathing quickens, and a sigh escapes his parted lips. "Your skin is so smooth, I could write a poem about it so easily, and the mole, so tiny, but it's there, decorating your skin." He darts his tongue and laves around the mole I had no idea about.

"Mmh," I moan, shutting my eyes to revel in his touch.

Then he unhooks the bra clasp at the back and removes the strap slowly enough like I'm made of crystal.

I can feel my throat clogging up as his fingers knead my shoulders, moving slowly down to my back; he's humming a familiar tune under his breath, like he's being paid to do it. Hell, he's a god. My adorable, young god…

His fingers continue making wonders on my back, they are even better than the masseuse at the spa of my condo. Maybe it's the sexual tension, but I can feel my nerves loosening.

"Right there, yes," I moan as his fingers press deeper onto my skin.

"Can I use my mouth?" he quips sexily.

I shake my head, but with a small smile playing on my lips. "No, that's going to distract me."

He hums and moves upward toward the nape of my neck. "How?"

He knows what I'm talking about, but Andries likes to hear my thoughts, and to know what I'm feeling in every single moment. He just wants me to say the words, tell him how much of an effect he has on me. God! He's so adorable, and the fact that he's so attentive to every part of me fuels my desire for more. "Tell me, babe, how is this a distraction?" He asks again, his mouth tracing languorous kisses right below my ear while his arms go around my belly.

I pick one of his hands and drag it up to my breast. My nipples are hard and the swollen knob screams for attention. I hear a quick chuckle from behind me as he withdraws his hand. "As much as I want to put my hands around them right now, I need to focus," he says, his voice husky.

"You can also massage them, you know," I insist, my tone filled with need.

Without further ado, he sits me on the spotless counter that looks so pristine—even though he uses it every day—and then his warm mouth latches on my nipples and I whimper at the sensation. "Ah!"

He suckles my breast as a baby would, and hums as his tongue plays around my nipple; the vibration coming from his throat makes my insides curl, and I fist his brown hair, letting out a low moan as I arch my back, pushing my tits more toward him.

"I wasn't asking about this," I manage to say through gritted teeth, my eyes nearly rolling back.

"I know, but your tits have been begging, and I could hear them scream." He palms the right one and bobs his head on the other.

Then he clasps his hands around my waist and pushes my body against his, rubbing his hands on my waist as he kneads slowly.

"Do you feel that?"

"You're so good with your hands, I feel a lot better now."

His eyes dance with devotion, and before I can utter any more words, he plugs his tongue into my mouth.

"I'm not, babe; I just know your body like the back of my palm." He swivels his tongue around mine, then bites my lips. "Let's continue in the bedroom."

I want to tell him no. I didn't come up here to have sex; I want to talk and be logical about frolicking with a boy his age, but my body craves so much more than a massage, I throw back my head, giving him access to my neck, but instead of kissing it, he suddenly lifts and picks me into his arms like I weigh nothing.

"Andries," I protest immediately, finding myself being carried out of the kitchen in his arms. "What about the food?"

"Don't worry about it."

With my face at the crook of his neck, Andries carries me upstairs to his bedroom. The room is decked in low, glowing light and soft music blares from the speakers.

He drops me on the bed, before hovering over me and kissing me intently.

"I didn't come here to have sex, Andries. I want to talk," I force the words out, trying to cover my bare skin but the effort seems futile as his penetrating gaze burns into me.

He's silent for a short moment; his lips turn up in a smile before his head goes down to my breast. "I'm not going to be talking about my age when I should be fucking you. We can do that later," he hisses while pulling my skirt and panties down my legs. "Or never, because it doesn't matter." His eyes gleam with defiance and possessiveness. I want to protest and point out how wrong it is, but the feel of his tongue on my tightening knob blurs my sense of reasoning. He sucks hard and bites, soothing the spot his teeth had marked with his tongue.

When his tongue delves into my mouth, it isn't light or tentative, but demanding and fierce. It's like he's trying to tell me something, trying to convince me that there's nothing wrong with us wanting to be with each other. I melt into him and frame his chiseled face with my palms. His blue eyes have darkened considerably. I move my lips to his jawbone, and run my wet tongue on the contour of his jaw. He hisses a breath and parts my legs with his; I latch my lips on his neck and suck, then bite, just the way he did to me.

"Fuck," he groans, leaning into me, his rock-hard member brushing my thighs, and I sigh, closing my eyes as the sensual energy wafts through the air. The music has changed to "Hu Man" by Greentea Peng. It's a song I've only listened to once in his presence. He must have found it on my playlist or heard me humming under my breath.

"You're overdressed for this," I say, pushing him a few feet away from me. "Don't you think that's a bit unfair?" I ask cupping my tits in my hands. They are warm, and my dark areolas bring out the pinkness of my nipples.

"Want to play a game?" he inquires in a husky tone.

"Like what?" I ask, without missing a beat. Sex is always fun with him, and I know that whatever he's got planned is going to be explosive.

"Hmm…" He removes his shirt slow enough, revealing his sculpted torso, and damn, his little show wrecks my insides. I ache to be fucked right now against the sheets but today is different. It's like he's trying to prove a point. He wants to tell me that his age doesn't matter, that he can take care of me and make me happy.

He doesn't have to. I'm already head over heels. I can't even think straight— all I see is him, pleasuring me over and again.

He pulls down his shorts and my eyes can't help but zoom to his dick. It's hard and looks almost painful as the shiny head tugs upwards with his pre-cum dripping onto my thighs.

"Touch yourself," he says, his fingers pinching my nipples. "I want to see you shove your dainty fingers into your slit, with your hand on your tit, massaging it slowly while your hips move to meet your fingers, thrusting gently at first, then faster until you climax. Fuck, I want to see your juice on your fingers, babe." The challenge in his voice is clear. My heart clogs in my throat as he moves close and kisses me. He grabs my left hand, his eyes staring deeply into mine as he pulls it down my body, toward my pussy. "I've dreamt about you doing this; now I want to watch you come apart from your fingers, but with my name on your lips."

I exhale slowly, and my face flushes as the wetness between my thighs is near embarrassing.

To think that finding out he's way younger than me would help tame my reaction toward him. I was wrong to have assumed that I'd be able to make him see reason with me when I was in the elevator on my way up to his apartment. Seeing him here, naked and being all dominant skyrockets my feelings. The heat that runs through my veins turns the ache into a bit of pain.

Without uttering a word, I let him guide my hand lower, my eyes watching every movement as both our hands disappear between my thighs. I lift my right leg to give him access to my throbbing center.

My breath comes in shallow hitches as I plunge a finger into my slit, thrusting slowly. My lips slightly apart as I fight to control my uneven breathing

"Pinch your nipples," he coos, standing up to lean against the wall. His dick is rock hard and precum leaks from the reddened head.

My eyes nearly pop open when he takes his dick in his cupped fingers. With his gaze locked on mine, he thrusts into it.

"Fuck, just like that, babe. Yeah, fuck," he groans loudly, touching himself.

I add a second finger and shift my ass on the bed to give myself favorable access to my pussy.

"I want to hear my name on your lips," he demands, thrusting faster into his cupped fingers.

"Andries, please…" I rub my fingers around my clit patting the patch of hairs I had left just above the center. "Fuck!" My other hand holds onto the edge of the bed as I pump in faster and faster, closing my eyes as the feeling ratchets and my toes curl under a wave of lust.

An overwhelming need surges through me as I writhe my hips, moaning incoherently as my fingers pump in and out. He's close; I can see it from the way his movement slurs and his thighs press together as he tries to control his orgasm.

He is holding it in for me. I move the hand from the edge of the bed to my nipples, pulling my two tits as close as I can; I pinch the hardened knobs and almost drown in ecstasy when the overpowering climax hits.

"Fuck! ...Damn, Andries!"

I imagine him doing it to me, fingering my dripping center and sucking my nipples.

"Let me drive you over the edge, babe," he says in a low, commanding tone that provokes a whimper to escape from my parted lips.

He pulls my fingers out of my pussy and replaces them with his long fingers. When he curves one slightly to meet my G-spot, his thumb rubs my clit, and he's murmuring words under his breath; words that capture everything he feels about me. Fuck! My mind is blank and all I can feel is his fingers plaguing my senses as he keeps withdrawing each time I get close to come.

"Please, let me come, please…" I want to push him away and continue from where I stopped before he took over, but his eyes burn into mine and what I see there weakens me.

Desire. Possessiveness. Lust. Power. And dare I say… Love?

"Fuck, you're so wet…and so warm…and so fucking mine."

My walls tighten around his fingers, and I collapse against the sheets, moaning heavily as my body shakes in trance from my orgasm.

"That was so hot," he breaths, smiling widely.

My lips refuse to move as my body is still heated from the torrid of emotions I felt when he threw me over the edge.

He chuckles when I don't say anything, but his rich cologne tickles my nose when he leans into me.

"You're so beautiful, Roxanne." He tilts my head forward to gaze into him. I suck in a breath as his thumb rubs my lower lip, then he pushes it into my mouth, and I suck in gently, tasting myself on his finger.

His tongue and teeth make their way down until my belly button, then he takes it lower, nibbling at my waistline. I'm writhing, begging him to put his mouth where I most want it, but he ignores my pleas, and continues to tease me with his lips and fingers trailing over my body, except the place I want him to be.

"You smell amazing," he says against my naked skin, until he drags his lips lower, down to my moist center. His nose rubs against my center, inhaling my scent.

I thought he was talking about my perfume, but then I realize he's referring to the scent of my arousal. I can perceive it too, and, Lordy, it's thick in the air. He's driving me crazy with his teasing and he knows it.

"Ahhh!" I moan as his tongue jams into my slit. "Yes! Right there!" I throw back my head on the pillow as loud whimpers escape my lips.

Andries is fucking me with his tongue, and the feeling is incredible. He swivels it around my center, then thrusts it in over and again.

"Your right leg on my shoulder," he says, lifting my leg, and placing it on his shoulder. This gives him more access to my throbbing center.

"So beautiful. So pink and wet. Fuck!" he mutters against my fold, sucking it hungrily, like a starving man, then he reverts to nibbling like I'm some snack he can't get enough of.

I deign a look at him. His muscles are visible and a bead of sweat forms on his chest.

"I want to feel you, Andries, all of you," I breathe, tugging at his head to go faster. I angle my hips upwards to meet the onslaught from his mouth. "Please, fuck me, please…"

He chuckles and spreads my legs farther apart, then inserts a finger to join his tongue.

"Fuck! Damn it, babe!"

He makes a loud sucking sound and his finger curves slightly, brushing against my pussy wall. He teases the entrance to my hole with his finger, swirling the juice around my core.

"You taste so good. I can do this all day," he says, just as his fingers and tongue shove in and out, pleasuring me. I'm boiling inside and the throaty sounds I'm making fuel him. He holds my hips and buckles them against his face, digging in deeper and deeper with his tongue.

I'm almost at the edge when he slows down and sits on his haunches, his eyes dancing with mischief as he takes in my disheveled and flushed face. I'm feverish with need, and my center is throbbing. It's painful as the need to release pulsates through my body.

"Please, babe, I want to come on your face," I cry pushing up from the bed to tug his head back to where it's supposed to be, but he shrugs away and takes his dick in his hand, rubbing the pre-cum that has leaked all over around his hardened length.

"I'm gonna fuck you, now, and God, it's not gonna be slow. I'm so hard that it's hurting. I want you so bad, so fucking bad, babe."

"Oh gosh, yes," I breathe, spreading my legs further apart as he kneels in between them, but his eyes shift to his ensuite bathroom, and a smirk curves at the edge of his lips.

"Not here," he says, then he picks me up and walks me toward the bathroom.

There, he turns on the shower and we step inside, letting the warm water cascade down our bodies. He pulls me into him, then parts my legs with his, sliding in two fingers into my still moist center. I gasp as he rubs my clit, feeling myself drenched and so ready for him.

I exhale slowly, and shut my eyes, reveling in every movement of his fingers. He tugs my head upwards and brings our face close.

"Turn around and bend over, your palms on the wall," he commands, still fingering me.

I turn and stick out my ass toward him. "Are you gonna fuck my ass?" I ask, slightly scared that he'd say yes. But instead of an answer, I suck in a breath as his hardened member jabs into my slit.

"Fuck! You're so tight, babe…fuck!"

He moves slowly, trying to get me to adjust to his length. He is long and thick, pushing into me gently as if I could break.

"Harder," I plead.

That's all the push he needs. He pulls out and then, holding me by the waistline, plunges in with a force that makes me almost topple over.

"You like it rough, don't you?" he growls against my ear.

His balls slap my clit as he moves, while he thrusts faster and deeper with a rhythm that matches my heartbeat. I'm so close, but I don't want it to end; I want to keep fucking him and come all over his dick.

"Yes! Like that! Yes!"

His breathing is ragged as he pumps into me with reckless abandon. There's a smooth kind of friction and the noise from our joint bodies hangs in the air, dulling the sound from the speakers and the spray of water.

As I draw closer to ecstasy, the tempo he has set slurs as he tries to hit my G-spot.

"Yes! Ah! Yes…yes, right there." I angle my ass to meet his thrusts with a little movement of my thighs. His hands are on my hips and he buckles them against his length, driving me nuts with an overpowering need to combust.

He shudders and fucks me harder, then gyrates his ass once, twice, before pushing deep into me again. I'm wound so tight and the need to release claws at me, freezing my movement. He moves like a piston and throws his head back as his legs shake, his release rearing its head as his grip on my waist tightens and he jams into me, making me come at the same time as him.

"Fuck, babe," he growls. "I love you, God, I love you, Roxanne." He makes a rugged sound as his body spasms and his hot seed spreads inside of me. I wonder if he truly means those words or not, but given the situation, I prefer to simply ignore them.

His thrusts start slowing down until he stops completely, his lips tracing wet kisses on my back as he fights to control his ragged breath.

I keep quiet, reveling in the moment, the three little words replaying in my mind, but then he says, "Jeez, you keep raising the bar; I don't think I'll ever be able to keep up."

I chuckle at his joke, and it's clear he didn't really mean that he loves me, no—what he loves is what all my clients do—to have sex with me.

* * *

After a long, steamy evening, Andries and I find ourselves relaxing on his bed, still naked. While he's sitting against the headboard, focused on writing in his notebook, I remain beside him staring absently at this beautiful male specimen and replaying the whole evening in my mind. Does he really love me like he said or was he just high on lust? He didn't talk about it afterwards, so maybe at the end of the day it wasn't that meaningful.

"If I were the moon, you'd be the sun," Andries says, reading from his notebook. "Do you think it's lame?"

His question pulls me back from my thought and I blink twice, refocusing on him. "Mmh?"

"If I were the moon, you'd be the sun," he repeats, his face a mix of seriousness and indecisiveness that makes him so damn adorable. "Lame or cute analogy?" he asks again. But my mind keeps drifting away, and I can't help but wonder how such a young man can make me feels things I never did before. "Okay, I get it, it's lame, yeah, what a stupid idea bringing astrology into poetry."

"I really like you." The words simply roll off my mouth, but it just feels the right thing to say.

His lips part at my revelation and he keeps staring at me with shock in his eyes. "Well, that's good to know," he answers, clearly lost for words as our eyes lock on each other's. "I really like you too."

For some reason, I'm slightly disappointed he didn't say the same three words he said when he was coming inside of me.

"And I really like this," I continue.

He shoots me an arched brow. "This?"

"Whatever is going on between us, I like it."

Andries chuckles in return. "It's called a relationship."

"Well, I like it," I admit, letting my heart take the wheel. "And you are an amazing boyfriend. Even if I find the word 'boyfriend' funny. But that's something I've got to work on."

Andries lets out a quick chuckle, before he intertwines his fingers with mine, pulling me closer to him. "We can always get engaged and then you can call me your fiancé."

"Oh, don't be silly!" I protest, slapping his arm playfully. "I'll get used to the word boyfriend just fine." I cup his face into my hands and close the small gap between us for a lingering kiss. All of a sudden, though, the ringtone of my iPhone breaks through the room and I can't help but heave a long sigh in annoyance. I turn to the nightstand on my bedside and take my iPhone to check who's calling, but when I see the time flashing on the screen, I gasp immediately in horror. "Oh, jeez, it's getting so damn late."

"Do you live far from here?" he asks.

"Bijlmer," I lie. He doesn't need to know I live just a few minutes from here. Otherwise he might want to come over and finding out that I live in a penthouse would raise unnecessary suspicion. After all, it's way out of the budget for a bookshop clerk. "With my sister and Mama."

"Why don't you sleep here, then?" Andries suggests like it's no big deal.

"Are you sure it's okay with you?"

"Is it okay with me?" he repeats in amusement. "Yeah, of course."

"I appreciate it, thanks." I turn off my phone, having no interest whatsoever in talking to my sister right now.

"You can sleep here more often, you know," he points out.

I raise my eyebrows in surprise, taken aback at his invitation. "How often?" I ask, returning to sit beside him on the bed.

"Well, the bookshop isn't far from here, so you could just sleep here. Might be easier than commuting every day back and forth."

I can't keep the smile from my face as I hear him speak. "So you basically want me to live here?"

"I wouldn't mind," he answers, his blue eyes meeting mine. "Sleeping every night with you…sounds like a dream come true."

My eyes widen at his words. What a poet he is… I should know better by now. And yet, being this close to him and having this conversation causes my heart to patter against my ribs. "You mean, every single night of the week?"

"Yes, silly," he answers playfully, before pressing his lips on mine for a kiss. "Is this too much, too soon?"

I ponder his invitation; this would mean I'd be living here with him, like a couple. Jeez! From wanting us to be just friends to move together and live like a couple, what happened? "I can do part-time," I tell him, trying to find some middle ground. "A few days here and a few days home."

"Good," he utters. Then I lean into him, noticing his eyes glued to my nipples before he blinks, refocusing on my face. "That's already a victory for me."

The excitement of living with him makes me feel all giddy inside, and in a sudden move, I sit astride his lap, my arms wrapped around his neck. Gosh! I can already feel his dick on my ass cheek, the hardness crushing into me.

"You said you wanted to talk," he points out, most likely teasing.

"Later," I mumble, my breath fanning his face before I tug him into a kiss. "I want to feel you inside of me again."

His eyes go wide in faux amazement. I want to laugh at the expression on his face, but I rein it in and hiss in a sharp breath as he lifts me, then onto his dick that has tilted upwards.

I wonder briefly if I'll ever get enough of him. He's like a drug, and my insides scream as he pushes into me, taking me again.

"Close your eyes," he says in a low voice. "I want you to remember how I make you feel when you're alone and scolding yourself for being with me." His lips start tracing a line of kisses, warm and languorous, on my neck. "Feel what my body is doing to yours. They're so connected, and the emotions are seared in so deep it will take a million years to undo them." His mouth is on my neck, sniffing, then nibbling at the throbbing veins. "I want you to feel me inside of you, even when we're apart." He lifts me up and then in a quick move, thrusts back in again.

Fuck!

"Did you feel that?" he purrs.

"Yes, gosh. Do it again!"

He wraps his hands around my waist, lifting me and pushing me down again, repeatedly.

Fuck! I guess we can talk another day.

CHAPTER 27

Amsterdam, October 27, 2021
Andries

For the past two weeks, Roxanne has been sleeping at my place more and more often, and I must say, it's been absolutely fantastic to have her there. We might have our arguments from time to time, but she's super chill and perfect company for someone who enjoys quietness and literature.

"Isn't he exquisite?" Elise asks rhetorically, stroking the neck of her latest conquest—of the equine persuasion, anyway. And the horse is genuinely impressive, especially with the price tag that came with it. Pops always finds a way to keep her happy, after all, the little apple of his eye isn't going to go without anything she wants. "He's so good to ride. Like he knows what I'm going to do before I even use my legs."

"Very nice," I answer to placate her. We haven't seen each other since Ghent, and I know if I didn't come to see her at the barn, we might only see each other again on Christmas Day. After all, between Roxanne, my time spent at the library, and classes, there's just nowhere that I'll magically run into her.

I know she's here about four days a week so it's easy to assume I can catch her.

Strangely enough, she didn't say a word about Roxanne after the weekend we spent in Ghent, which isn't usual for her. And, as much as I hate to admit it, her opinion matters.

Before I can start probing my phone rings and Elise is too obsessed with her new horse to notice. Roxanne's name is on the screen. Odd, she'd normally just text, not call.

"Hey, love, how are you?" As soon as she hears me say the word *love*, Elise's ears perk up.

"Hey, um, I know we have plans tonight but I need to cancel." Her voice sounds strained, and I know that there's something more behind it. She sounds worried.

"Is everything okay?"

Elise glances over at me and looks concerned, mouthing words I can't understand and don't care about. I quickly give her a nod, refocusing on my phone call.

"What's going on?" I continue.

Finally she speaks. "It's Mama. She's in the hospital. Her back problems are getting worse, so my sister is with her now before she goes for surgery. I need to be there for her."

"Of course, I totally understand," I reassure her. "Don't worry about the dinner, focus on your family." If she was in front of me I'd want to pull her into my arms, but I hope that my words reassure her just like my arms would. "By the way, um, which hospital is it?"

"OLVG, East side," she informs me, her tone a mix of weary and anxious. "Well, I've got to go, I'll call you later."

"Sure, bye." Once we hang up, I can't help but ruminate about what just happened.

The odd thing is I know she's barely spoken to her mom in years. It's her sister who normally takes care of her, not Roxanne. I find it a bit strange that she's suddenly rushing to the bedside like a dutiful child. Could it simply be a way to break our plans tonight? No, she wouldn't be the type of woman to lie about something as important as her mother being sick.

Once we finish the call, I feel an urge to head to the hospital and be there for her, instead of staying alone at home, ruminating about it. Maybe going there and showing I care is the right thing to do. Part of me wants to swoop in and take care of Roxanne like no other man ever has.

"Trouble in paradise?" Elise asks with a smirk on her face. She knows the pressure I feel to make sure everything is good with Roxanne almost hangs in the air around me. But given the fact she knows my girlfriend, I decide to tell her the truth.

"Her mother's in the hospital. I think it's better I go."

She grins and pats her horse again.

"Andries to the rescue!" Her peal of laughter annoys me but something else burns the feeling away: the desire to be there for my girlfriend. I know she didn't invite me, but maybe she didn't because she thought I wouldn't care enough about it. I quickly jump in the car as it's a bit of a hike to get to the hospital. I've always hated these places. They're sterile, smell like death and the sense is always that people are sick everywhere.

I'd much rather take advantage of the private clinics I have access to, but I know Roxanne probably won't take advantage of one even if I offer. And I've never met her mother. It's a curious thing, but with my family I can understand it.

Arriving at the hospital, I pick up some flowers quickly in the gift shop. Always find an opportunity to make a good first impression. They aren't the ones I'd usually choose but there's no time to head to my usual flower shop. And since we are in Amsterdam, tulips are plentiful everywhere.

"I'm looking for Mrs. Feng's room?" I inquire at the front desk, and I'm directed to the third floor where there are admissions. The place isn't crowded as I walk around the halls, just the typical bustle of a hospital with workers in scrubs and the room is easy to find.

Roxanne is standing outside, and I immediately draw her into my arms. She seems slightly upset at first but then relieved to see me there. "I came right away. Is your mother okay?" Her affect is slightly different. Gone is the confident woman and it is as if she's been replaced with somebody else.

"She's okay. Already in surgery. Her back finally gave out and she was in a lot of pain. They took her nearly two hours ago. No word yet." Her head rests on my shoulder and I can tell she's comforted by me being there.

A younger woman who looks similar in facial features to Roxanne walks out of the hospital room. Unlike her sister, Lili has got long black hair flowing down her shoulders and is dressed quite demurely. She looks at me with confusion, as if she isn't recognizing me. Roxanne steps back and glances over. "Lili, you remember Andries from the store?"

Lili's eyes head to mine and I can see her probing a bit. She's beautiful like her sister but with high sweeping cheekbones, dark circles under her almond eyes, and a more tired hue. If I didn't know Roxanne was the oldest, I'd have thought Lili was the one in her mid-thirties. I offer my hand and she finally takes it. "It's great to see you again," I say, despite our first meeting was fleeting at the bookstore. The two women are such a dichotomy even though I know they are in the same family. Classic and elegant versus practical and urban.

It's awkward standing there with the two sisters. Lili and Roxanne don't seem to know what to say to each other, and I'm standing in the middle feeling like a third wheel. The sounds of the hospital are all around us, people in scrubs marching to and from and announcements over the speakers constantly.

My timing is perfect. A stretcher appears down the hall and given the way both women's heads turn I know it's their mother coming down the narrow lane. Roxanne looks relieved.

The stretcher is wheeled into the room and both women follow with me trailing behind. Now I firmly feel like an interloper and know that I should probably go. The funny part is the two women still haven't really acknowledged each other with words. They both take up residence on either side of the bed and look down. Their mother is round faced, short salt and pepper gray hair, and pale with her hospital gown covering what looks like a frail body.

Her eyes are open though, which might be a good sign. She turns her head and looks at both girls, but I notice that her hand only reaches out for Lili. Roxanne approaches the bed and instead of being offered, takes her other hand and squeezes it. "Mom, I'm glad you are awake. How are you feeling?"

Her eyes turn to me, and Roxanne lowers her head. "This is my friend Andries. Mom, Andries. Andries, Mom." I nod my head at her and she turns away immediately back to Lili.

Behind us a doctor with what must be an intern sweeps in and starts talking in a boisterous voice. "Surgery was a success! We managed to clean things up and she should be in a lot less pain now."

Roxanne looks at the doctor. "What about recovery? And will she be able to move around?"

"In a bit. She'll need at least a week here for recovery and then lots of physiotherapy, but I think she's in pretty good shape. In a few months she'll feel like a new woman." He glances around the room as if he can sense the tension. Doctors are probably used to that type of thing. Both women nod and Roxanne's mother closes her eyes. "But she also needs rest. She's going to be knocked out for a day or so."

I can tell that's a hint for me to leave. I take Roxanne's hand and squeeze it, noticing that Lili's eyes stray over to me touching her sister affectionately. "We'll talk tomorrow," I say in a low voice before pressing my lips on her forehead.

"Thank you for coming," she answers, matching my low voice. "I really appreciate it."

Despite being there for just half an hour, I'm glad it made a difference for her.

On my way home my phone pings with a text. *All okay with Roxanne?*

At least my sister seems to be keeping her nose into things. If she didn't, no one in my family would ever know anything about me, so I allow her to keep everyone informed. *All good. Out of surgery and recovering. I'll be heading back there tomorrow.*

CHAPTER 28

I hadn't spoken to Roxanne the following day, so after class I decide to head back to the hospital and surprise her. Assuming she will be there, of course. But even if she's not, at least maybe I can ingratiate myself to her mother. I want to get to know her family as best I can, even her sister.

Walking in I can see an older woman lying in the bed and when I knock on the door she turns to see me. "Mrs. Feng?"

She nods slowly, looking suspicious. "I'm a friend of Roxanne's. She told me you were here, and I thought she would be as well." Her expression suddenly turns stern but then relaxes when I offer her the flowers. It's the least I can offer to the mother of the woman I'm so in love with.

"They are beautiful. Thank you." She pauses, observing them attentively. "*When in April the sweet showers fall and pierce the drought of March to the root, and all the veins are bathed in liquor of such power as brings about the engendering of the flower.*"

I'm taken aback. "You're a fan of Chaucer?" I know she used to work at a bookstore, but I didn't expect the mother of my girlfriend to be so fluent in poetry.

She smiles. "I've worked at that bookstore for twenty-five years, myself. I'm Yao Feng, by the way." It's a genuine smile, and quickly I can tell that the fact I nailed the author of her quote has disarmed her.

"The apple doesn't fall far from the tree, then. My name is Andries, and I met your daughter at the bookstore." Well, not really, but we met there twice.

Her eyes narrow. "At the bookstore?"

I nod and she turns her head. It is strange that as soon as I mention her daughter and the store she clams up immediately.

"I'm a big fan of poetry. In fact, I'm an amateur poet. Even wrote something for your daughter."

She sighs and then turns back to me, nodding. "I appreciate a man who knows what good literature is." She is silent for a few moments and then offers more, "I used to teach literature, actually."

My eyes widen in surprise at her revelation. It's obvious that the whole family is into literature.

"Your daughter is incredibly knowledgeable. I can see where she gets it."

Her eyes turn to me, and she frowns. "You mean Lili, right? She's a wonderful girl, you two will get along quite well, I think."

I am taken aback slightly. "No, um, I mean Roxanne."

"Ah." She pauses, disappointment settling on her face. "Yes, I can see that you like her. But you should get to know Lili as well. Do you think she's attractive?"

Now it feels quite awkward. Like the mother knows I'm dating her oldest daughter but wants to set me up with the other one. What am I supposed to say? "She's very nice."

Trying to distract her I mention a couple of my favorite poets and she opens up quite a bit once I get her going.

After a few more minutes I can tell she's starting to grimace from being turned toward me. Suddenly a voice arrives that is familiar and almost scares me. "Mother, you should be resting."

I turn to see Roxanne with a stern expression on her face. I can't tell if it's anger at me or her mother. Or both. As she approaches the bed her mother turns her head, and her mouth closes firmly.

There is something odd about the dynamic between the two of them. I just can't quite put my finger on it, but I also want her to know how I feel. It's time to just open up and reveal it. After all, the situation with her mother can't be easy for her to be dealing with especially when there is strain between the two of them.

When I was alone with her, Yao was open and friendly and actually a joy to talk to, but as soon as Roxanne entered, she clammed up. Why?

I share a glance to the door with Roxanne, and she gets the cue. We both walk out of the room and go further down the hallway to speak more privately.

"Has your mother spoken to you since yesterday?" I decide to ask when we are finally left alone.

Her eyes fall. "No. It seems like no matter what I do she just doesn't want to deal with me. She hates me. I'm a disappointment."

This incredible cultured woman who's so educated is a disappointment? It just can't be possible. Something else had to be behind it, but that wasn't for me to probe into. I just want Roxanne to know that she has my support. "You are an amazing daughter, no matter what your mom says."

Her eyes meet mine and I can see she's grateful but still guarded. "I wish she could think the same."

I know I have to go and meet Dan for our scheduled outing, but part of me doesn't want to leave her right now. Not when she needs me. "I'm here for you, okay? If you need anything just call me. I'm just going to meet with Dan and can come back later if you want." I reach for her hand, and she allows me to take hers. In her eyes there is gratitude and when I pull her close and hug her, she doesn't resist. It feels good to know I can comfort her when she needs it.

"How come you care so much about me?" She looks into my eyes when we step back, and I know that I need to tell her. After all, why would I keep it hidden from her? She's the most remarkable woman I've ever met, and getting to know her mother just reinforces the fact that there's nobody else I want to be with. But the words I say next surprise even me, as natural as they sound being said to this incredible woman.

"Because I love you." At that her eyes go wide and her face floods with emotion. I've shown her many times how I feel but now just saying the words it feels like a massive weight is lifting from my shoulders. She knows it, and that's important to me. It isn't something I say lightly.

Instead of a response I see tears welling up and then she leans in and kisses me. It's a kiss with almost desperate overtones and I do my best to return it, trying to show her with my lips and my arms around her how much she means to me. Her body seems to melt into mine as her lips seek and search to seal the gap between us. It's not sexual at all, even though her frame against mine makes my libido stir. It's telling both of us that what is happening between us is more than just a fleeting encounter. I want more, and now she knows it. I want her. All of her. Flaws and everything she has to give.

Once the kiss breaks, I know she's conflicted, and I need to make sure she knows I don't expect anything in return. "Don't feel pressured to say it too. I just wanted you to know what I truly feel for you."

I see her eyes drop. The gesture would normally be seen as meekness, but I know with her it is simple gratitude. "Thank you so much for understanding."

"Of course, just say it whenever you are ready." I try to let her know with every fiber of my voice that I truly mean what I'm saying. Taking her hands, I bring them up to my lips and kiss them. My phone starts vibrating and I know it's Dan wondering where I am. I have to leave even though we are having a perfect moment.

"You are the most amazing man I've ever met, you know that, right?" Her voice is almost breaking, but she sounds honest and genuine.

I feel my heart warming at the compliment, and I know that continuing to explore her deeper being is a process I crave. I kiss her on the forehead gently and finally step away. Her hands linger on mine before they break apart.

Walking down the hospital hall, I see her walk back into her mother's room and feel confident that she knows where I stand. The fact that she keeps her family a priority even though her mom treats her so badly, is quite admirable to me. I'm not sure if I'd do the same if my parents treated me that way. This woman is one of the most remarkable people I've ever known.

CHAPTER 29

Roxanne

I take a deep breath before walking back into the room with Mama. Part of me is praying that my sister shows up soon. I don't want to deal with the discussion that we are bound to have... Or the lack thereof. She's excellent at making me feel guilt even without saying anything at all. And after what Andries just revealed my emotions are all over the place.

But Andries is gone and I'm alone again with a woman who won't even talk to me. Granted, it's the first time we are alone in a room without Lili being around. And I just had the man I'm dating tell me he loves me. Jeez! A man who has no idea who I really am and thinks I'm somebody else.

My mind is still racing as I get into the room, plus there's nobody else here and I know Mama isn't going to talk to me. She's been ashamed of me since I can remember. It's impossible for her to understand why I did what I had to do. Especially with my sister as the good dutiful daughter who works at a more dignifying job.

To my surprise, she looks over with her mouth tightly pressed and actually speaks. "That man deserves so much better."

The words bring a flash of anger. It's the first words she's spoken to me in over a decade. "You talk to me now?"

"Does he know who you are?" she spits out the last words like they are something evil. Insinuation flows from her tongue. I'm a whore in her mind. Like a common girl standing on a street corner back home where men pay ten dollars for whatever they want, and I just open my legs like a flower for anything. She has no idea how much money I've made and the type of men I've been with. All she can see is that Andries is from a good family and somehow I don't deserve that.

"I can't believe it, after ignoring me like I'm dead for over a decade, the first thing you say to me is that my boyfriend deserves better?"

"You're gonna end up breaking his heart, and that's hurting me. He's a good man. So yes, I have no choice but to speak to you because what you are doing is wrong." Her judgement comes from a place I know well. After all, she's been judgmental her whole life. Part of that is due to the way she was abandoned with me and my sister and had to make it on her own with two children in a foreign country. The irony is she doesn't realize that the very thing she's condemning me for is exactly what's kept me financially well off and prevented me from descending into something worse.

"Wrong? What's that supposed to mean?" I ask her.

"You're leading that poor boy on. How old is he? Twenty-two, twenty-three? Does he even know how old you are? If he expects having a family with you, the poor boy will be deeply disappointed."

"He doesn't care," I retort, my eyes flashing. "Yes, Andries is young but he's an old soul and we get along just fine."

"Does he know you have sex with men for money, though? I'm pretty sure he will care about it."

I take a deep breath, and trying to tame my anger, I say, "I'm no longer an escort, Mama. I have stopped doing it."

Her eyes go wide but I can still see the suspicion in her gaze as she looks at my face. She's suspicious of everyone and everything, probably even the nurses coming into her room to administer medication for her back.

"Pah. You need to tell him about your past to have any hope of a future, but you can't even bring yourself to be honest with the boy. And your brothel? Does he know about it?" The tinges of venom in her voice are tangible in the air, almost as if she's spitting in my face.

"It's an agency," I point out.

"Call it whatever you want. To me, a place where you sell sex is a brothel."

I huff, head shaking. In her mind I must have been lying there on a foam mattress spreading my legs for any man that walked in. She has no idea I've been around the world and stayed in hotels that cost more per night than our monthly rent growing up. That the men I've dealt with don't have to enter a red-light door and hope that the girl gives them a good time for cheap. She's got absolutely no idea what she's talking about, but she never cared about it, either way.

"Does he know about that, huh?" she repeats, since I didn't answer her. "That young man has got morals, Roxanne. I've no idea how you found him, but—" Finally I have had enough. The anger percolating inside me suddenly comes to a rush and boils over. I've dealt with Andries admitting that he loves me, I've had to push away the men who have provided for me, and now I'm getting nothing but judgement from a woman who turned her back on me twelve years ago. Finally the emotion breaks through me like a wave crashing over a sea wall and I need to defend myself. With her, it's almost impossible to do it.

"Enough!" I have to clench my fists and keep my voice down to a hiss, otherwise the nurses outside will hear. And it's hard enough for me to look my mother in the eye and actually fight back. Even though my profession for years has been asserting myself, she's the one person that can make me feel like a little kid again. "I've always been here for you even though you hate me! Can't you stop being so mean?"

I realize after the words come out of my mouth I'm being a bit petulant and not far off from stomping my foot on the ground like a child. But that's how she's making me feel. It doesn't even faze her as usual, and her eyes narrow into a familiar gaze that always withers my resolve like intense heat withering a flower.

"Mean? You sound like a child." Touché, Mama. "I'm not the one pretending to be someone I'm not." She lies back with a small groan, as if the effort of being mad at me has caused her pain. Guilt flies into my heart immediately. She's right, of course, like she usually is. I've spent years pretending to be somebody else for my clients, but the truth is even my real boyfriend doesn't know who I am. At least not the truth about my previous lifestyle and career. If he did, he'd most likely leave me.

A nurse quickly walks into the room and looks at me. "Is everything okay in here? Just doing a quick check." My mother doesn't respond and neither do I. She can probably feel the tension in the air between us. A decade worth of dialogue resolved within minutes with more harsh words. She walks to the bed and starts to check monitors and I take that as my cue to leave. There's no point in me being here anyway with my mother's desires made crystal clear.

Of course the worst timing in the world results in Lili walking in and I'm sure she can feel the tension in the air. Once the nurse has done her checks and leaves, Lili turns to me and asks, "What's going on?"

Mama barks behind me before I can even answer. "I'm telling her to break up with her boyfriend because she's a whore. He, of course, has no idea." Lili grits her teeth, I know she doesn't approve of my choices either.

"Mom, that's pretty harsh." A bit of relief washes over me when my sister defends me. Her attention then returns to me and she says, "But she's right, you know." Her words make my heart reel. I can't believe she's siding with her! "That poor man has no idea about you and who you really are. You're just lying to him."

A surge of anger floods into my body. Now it's two on one. Like it always has been. I can't even process what is happening when I'm supposed to be here supporting my mother after a major event. Now they are ganging up on my personal life. It's too much. "You two need to keep your opinions to yourself. I'm going to go now."

Without waiting for an answer, I turn and stalk out of the room.

Lili has always been the good one. I'm the bad seed. Even though now with Andries I have an opportunity to explore a life that I never thought possible. It's the right way to go, that's what every fiber of my being is telling me. The sad thing is that it means I can't be around my mother and sister anymore. It's a while until Christmas too, maybe I'll wait until then to have us all in the same room again.

CHAPTER 30

Andries

Reaching the Waldorf Astoria, I hurry myself to get to the Peacock where Dan is waiting for me.

The lounge is very serene, almost like a library except for the low hum of the people inside at each table. A deep blue carpet stretches across the floor and is just thick enough to feel comfortable under my feet. As I approach the table Dan stands up and gives me a warm embrace, with a few pats on the back.

Waiters in dark jackets hover attentively around the room, and before I can wave at a waiter to order, Dan steps in and says, "I've already ordered something for us. You'll love it." He's into tea so this is a pretty common occurrence for him. I'm sure there's something on the menu that he's found he wants to try out.

"Great, thanks," I say, taking a seat in the armchair, while Dan sits back on the couch.

"You're not usually late," he points out. As much as he's a good friend, he's one of those guys that is annoyingly punctual. Plus, I'm only five minutes late. So I let it go intentionally.

"I was at the hospital. Roxanne's mother had to have emergency surgery, so she was a bit worried about her," I disclose.

His eyebrows raise in obvious surprise. "So you're meeting her family now? Sounds serious."

"It is. More serious than I thought actually."

He smiles as the waiter approaches our table holding a tray. But when the teapot is left on the table, Dan frowns when he looks at what the man has brought us.

"I'm sorry, what is this?" Dan asks to the waiter, pointing at the teapot, visibly disappointed.

"Um, your tea, sir," he answers.

"I'm afraid not. I ordered a blooming tea?" Dan proceeds as a question even though I can tell he's irritated by the expression on his face.

"A blooming tea?" The waiter seems to have no idea what Dan is talking about.

"Yes, a tea with a flower that blooms once they are infused." He looks at the teapot with a disdainful expression. "There's only leaves in here."

The waiter is obviously confused. "Oh, um, I'm so sorry but I don't think we have that type of tea, sir."

Dan heaves a long sigh, his irritation growing. "Can you go back and check, please? It's not on the regular menu." The word *regular* is the indication that he probably found out about something he thinks is a big secret. Half the time he doesn't end up with what he wants anyway, but it never seems to dissuade him from trying.

"Sure," the waiter mutters, before disappearing from our sight carrying the teapots back to the kitchen.

"Gosh, and this is supposed to be a tearoom," Dan comments, before running a hand through his wild hair. "So," he begins, leaning back on the couch. "What were you saying?"

"I told Roxanne I loved her," I blurt out. I have to tell somebody—the fact I actually said those words to another woman is really weighing on my mind. Almost as if I'm confessing a crime.

His eyes go wide in surprise. After all, he knows I've never said those words to anyone before. "Oh wow, that's a big step." He leans into the table, and gives me a look that I'm used to. Evaluating exactly what I'm telling him but skeptical at the same time. "And, um, what did she say?"

"Well, she said nothing and just kissed me." It sounds slightly silly coming out of my mouth when I tell him.

Dan sighs. I know he thinks that I said the words way too fast. But when you know, you know. At least that's what's flying through my mind.

Finally he nods. "Maybe she needs time, you know. Don't stress it out."

"Do you think I screwed up?" I have to know what he thinks, otherwise I wouldn't have told him.

"Why would you think that?" he asks, his chin resting on his palm as he observes me.

"Because I told her those three little words and some people just freak out when they hear them," I tell him.

"Isn't she your girlfriend, though? Aren't you guys basically living under the same roof at this point?"

"Yeah, but, I don't want to scare her off." I pause for a moment, reminding myself of something. "She's never had a serious boyfriend before, so I don't want to rush."

"Now that's weird," he comments. There is a small hint of sarcasm in his voice. Suspicion too.

"What? That she never had a boyfriend?"

"Yeah, like how old is she again?" he asks.

I shrug nonchalantly. "Thirty-five."

"And she's *never* had a serious boyfriend?" There's some kind of accusation behind his words but I don't know what he's inferring.

"I don't see what the problem is. She has high standards and if anything, she just didn't meet any guy of her liking."

"Yeah, I don't know, that's weird to me…" He keeps his words trailing off, but I think Dan is just exaggerating.

Thankfully, the waiter approaches the table again, and this time it looks like he's gotten the order right. The teapot is still there, but this time it contains a large flower inside. It's yellow and orange and looks open and lovely. Dan smiles. He nods at the waiter, obviously satisfied that he got what he wanted.

"Your blooming tea, sir," the waiter proudly announces.

"Ah, fantastic, thank you."

The waiter picks up the teapot and pours the water inside the two cups. Immediately the flower folds in on itself and I have to lean over and watch as the water changes color to mimic the yellow inside the flower. I have no idea what to expect before I take a sip.

We wait a moment and then Dan is the first to try it out. "It's worth the wait. This is one of the most exotic teas around. And obviously you like exotic things." His eyes sparkle and I know he means Roxanne. And he's right, I do often like exotic things.

Taking my first sip I can see why his eyes roll back in his head. He normally exaggerates everything. Especially when it comes to the women he dates. According to him, they are all models, even if it's just on Instagram. But the tea is good. Sweet flavors, very distinct and open to my tongue. It actually makes me think of Roxanne and the scent of her skin and I can feel myself reacting physically to the taste as it floods my mouth.

"Now that's good tea," Dan sighs as he takes another sip.

All of a sudden though, my iPhone ringtone breaks through the quietness of the room and as I look at the caller's name, I can't help but frown in confusion. A few seconds later though, I decide to slide right to answer and put my phone up to my ear.

"Dad?" I say almost in disbelief.

"Andries!" Even hearing his voice over the phone is a bit odd. His gravelly tone is getting worse, most likely because of the cigars he enjoys so much. It's pathetic—he knows it isn't good for him, but he's too stubborn to care. "It has been such a long time; we haven't chatted." It's only been two weeks... "How have you been?"

"I'm great." Banal and basic, that's the name of the game with my dad. There are things he needs to know and things he doesn't.

"I've heard you have a girlfriend?" My jaw falls on my knees at his question. "Is it true?"

"How do you know that?" I ask, despite being sure it's Elise who told him. Sighing inwardly, I know exactly where the conversation is going to head. He's been dying for me to get with some pretty girl from a good family and settle down rather than live a lifestyle like Dan does.

"Well, your sister…" he confesses, letting his words trail off. "I'm happy for you, son," he interposes immediately before I can think otherwise. "I didn't know you liked them older, though." Fortunately his tone is more humorous than anything else. "Why don't you invite her here for your birthday? You could spend the week at the estate with her and then we could do New Year's Eve all together."

"Are you serious?" I ask, finding the invitation highly suspicious. "You really want to meet her?"

"Of course I do! You've never introduced us to anyone!" There's a reason for that of course, but he doesn't need to know that. My family is about the furthest thing from normal even considering our heritage and I bet most girls—with the exception of Tatiana of course—wouldn't even warrant an invitation. Roxanne is different, that's for sure, but that doesn't mean I want my father to meet her that soon. He'll recognize her immediately and I'm not sure how I feel about it.

"Your sister told me she works at a bookshop, is it true?" I can nearly taste the classism in his tone. No matter how hard Dad tries, he can't sound genuine for the life of him. I'm surprised he's not asking me about her college pedigree and where her family is from right off the bat. That will come when he meets her, I'm sure.

"She does, yeah, it's one of the oldest bookshops of the country and she intends to buy it," I tell him, slightly on the defensive.

"Does she have the means for that?"

I have to grit my teeth at that one. Already he's probing to see if she's financially stable. "She can get a loan."

"Loans need to be repaid though," he replies like he's the bank himself. "Is the bookshop profitable?"

"Dad, why do you even care about it, huh? She doesn't come from money, but she's absolutely amazing and is passionate about the same subjects as I." That's my way of saying *shut the hell up old man*, and I know he can tell from my tone that I don't approve of his line of questioning. As usual.

"I just want you to be careful."

"I am," and I know at this point I need to cut the conversation off. "Well, I have to go, thank you for the offer." Before he can answer I hang up.

"Well, that sounded like a typical conversation with your pops," Dan comments, before taking another sip of his tea, a mirthful look on his face. He knows all about the past issues with my family and has been with me at more than one drunken night to try to forget about it. "What's going on? And don't forget to finish your tea, that stuff's fucking expensive."

I look at the small amount of liquid left in my glass and quickly pick it up, taking the rest like it's a shot of whiskey. Which right now wouldn't be a bad idea.

"My dad just invited Roxanne to spend New Year's Eve with us."

In my mind I think about a long evening with my mother, father and sister all grilling her and it's not the scenario I picture when I think of a celebration. But being out with Dan and whatever bimbos of the month he's hanging out with isn't it either. New Year's Day should signify a new beginning, and that's what I want for myself and Roxanne. I'll have to figure out what to do quickly.

CHAPTER 31

Amsterdam, October 29, 2021
Roxanne

I must say, I was surprised when Andries reached out the following day to invite me out. From my end, I spent the night in my penthouse processing his words. After all, it's the first time someone tells me those three little words in a non-sexual context. *He loves me.* The problem is that I don't even think I'm capable of love, and I know for sure my mother doesn't think I am worthy of it. He's determined to break down my barriers. It's romantic and senseless at the same time. I can tell him that of course, but I don't think he'll listen.

His offer of heading to the book market is exactly what I need. It's only open on Fridays, and with the week I've had, being around old, rare, second hand and out-of-print books is perfect for calming my demeanor.

When he greets me by the Spui Square his eyes are sparkling like they usually do when he sees me. I've tried my best to look far less haggard than I feel. He greets me with a kiss, and his warm lips feel comfortable and taste like home.

"I thought this would be a good way to relax before you see your mother," he offers as we start walking. "After all, a bookstore is the natural place for you to hang out." Part of me feels a surge of trepidation. He still thinks I work at one. He has no idea that it's actually my sister that works there, and my job is a bit more suited to bedrooms than libraries.

Walking toward the place his hand finds mine easily and I can tell he wants to talk about my mother and things in the future, but I manage to keep silent for the most part. I know that later I'll be dealing with more judgement and don't need any from my boyfriend.

I can feel the cobblestones under my feet as we approach, and it's definitely busy. The market is outdoors with rows and rows of long tents set up. Some carry pure white covers, and some have alternating red and white. But the booths mostly look the same, right down to the piles and piles of tomes adorning each one. You can smell the spine glue in the air as you approach and the people who are moving up and down the aisles are all quiet and look serene at the same time.

I'm definitely not looking for anything, but it's always been a benefit to me to be well read in my profession and I truly do love reading. Andries allows me to take the lead and walk around looking at each individual tent. There's a meditation behind it. See a title that looks fascinating, pick it up and check it out. Page through the thin pages and see if the words jump out of the page and tickle your brain right away.

It's impossible not to laugh when I pick up a threadbare copy of Anna Karenina. Andries seems to prefer escape pulp fiction and I see him pick up several science fiction and old fantasy novels, but when I roll my eyes he laughs and puts them away. If he wants my mother's approval, reading old Isaac Azimov novels is definitely not the way to do it.

As if he's reading my mind, he comments quickly. "I liked meeting your mother. She is… different from what I expected." I'm sure he expected her to be a horrible human being because of her treatment of me, but that's not the case. She just doesn't understand my life. In truth, it's my fault, not hers. "I didn't know she used to teach literature."

"She taught for a long time until coming over here." I let the comment hang in the air, hoping that he'd take the hint that I don't want to talk about my mother. But quickly when he looks down I realize it's the wrong thing to say. I should be encouraging him to know my family, not discouraging it. Truly, I want to mend the fences. "She said she really liked you." I conveniently leave out the fact that she wanted to set him up with my sister because her other daughter is a whore. It makes me chuckle to myself just to think about it.

"What's so funny?" he asks, his eyes sparkling, and I quickly grab an old Ray Bradbury book to distract him.

"That you would rather read this."

He laughs and takes the book from my hand. Opening it and riffling through the pages his eyes catch some words.

"A classic." When his eyes meet mine I know he's talking about more than just the book.

As we continue to walk around it feels comfortable. The air is crisp and open and there's many people strolling just like we are, looking at the rows and rows of boxes. He takes my hand and I accept it happily. A real date. It's rare in my world, and I need to learn to appreciate it for what it is, two people who just enjoy spending time with each other.

I decide to offer him a bone. "Thank you for keeping her company. The flowers were really nice of you."

"She's a really great woman. I can see where you get your love of literature." At least she gave me that side of her. "And your sister seems nice as well."

"Well, she's the only reason that I know what's been going on. At least as long as she's happy being the go-between." Andries chuckles for no apparent reason, and I shoot him an arched eyebrow. "What?"

"I have the same situation with my sister Elise. Speaking of which…" He pauses, observing me attentively. "My family wants you to come to my birthday party. And my father has also invited you to New Years' Eve at the estate. So two parties."

We've had this discussion before, and he knows that I feel like I'm not ready to meet his whole family. The pressure feels overwhelming, and I drop his hand under the pretense of poring through another box. "You need to give me time, Andries." For some reason, I'm not used to using my assertion with him like I always do with other men. He's not like other men. Not like the ones who used to pay me for my time. It's a dynamic that I still have to get used to, and the thought of meeting his whole family makes me tense even thinking about it.

"I know." He stops and turns to me, and I can see the affection in his eyes. Taking my hand again, this time I allow him. "You're worth the wait. I just want my family to know the amazing woman that you are." My heart melts slightly. Frosty isn't getting me anywhere with him when he's giving me so much of himself. I accept his hand and we continue along the rows, eventually coming to the end. He's picked up a couple of paperbacks he needs to pay for.

"I should head back to the hospital," I tell him once we leave the market. The responsibility to still be a dutiful daughter is always hovering over my mind. Even though the day is open and warm, family is calling to me.

"Why don't I come with you? Maybe I can be a bit of a buffer."

He's right. Having him there means at the very least Mom can't chastise me for anything. At least I hope.

The hospital still has the smell and sense of illness, but it's much quieter on a Friday with not as many people rushing around. As we approach her floor the dread starts to creep into my chest. I really don't want to be here, but it's…my duty? My place as her daughter to stand by her bedside? I really don't know.

As usual, Andries can sense my unease and I know he's standing beside me like a rock. He's good at that. His hand hasn't left mine. We walk into the room and the collection of flowers has been added to. Mom has lots of friends, and it almost looks like a tulip festival with a myriad of colors brightening up the room. She's awake and has a book in her hands.

"Ah! I'm glad you are back!" Her words go straight toward Andries instead of me and she smiles directly at him. "I thought if you came you could look at this." Her hands hold up an old tome, a first edition by Li Po, who I know is her favorite poet. "Please, take it with you."

Andries accepts it graciously. "Thank you, Yao. I will absolutely look through it."

"Mom." I nod at her and her lips thin as she nods back at me. But then her words come and she's ignoring me again.

"When you're done make sure you go back to the bookstore. I told Lili that you'd come and return it there."

He nods and smiles, glancing over at me.

"You know, Lili is single. And I think the two of you would make an excellent pair. You should ask her on a date." Her words are slightly slurred but still hit me like a knife in the chest.

She must be on a really strong dose of painkillers because she is not realizing what she is saying. Or maybe she actually is. Thankfully Andries looks at me and his look tells me he isn't going to engage with her. "I appreciate the offer."

"It'd give you a chance to spend time with a really educated woman. And she's beautiful too, don't you think?" It's as if I'm not even in the room.

"Mom," I retort, but I can't make a scene in front of Andries.

"Lili is very nice," Andries says diplomatically. "But Roxanne is the woman for me."

"Pah!" Mom laments. "You need better taste in women." I look at her, totally flabbergasted, my mouth wide open in shock at her words. It makes my blood run cold. She's denigrating me right in front of my boyfriend. How she can be so cruel is beyond me!

Finally Andries looks at me. "I think maybe I should go. She needs to rest, right?"

I nod curtly and we walk into the hallway. The noise swells around us but Andries still kisses me on the cheek.

"I'm just a text message away. I hope she starts feeling better."

So many emotions are swirling through me. I want him there, but I want him to go so I can confront my mother's horrible behavior. And the idea that she would try to set him up with Lili right in front of me? What on Earth! I'm so furious that my hands clench and my chest tightens. As Andries walks away I take a deep breath and stalk back into the room where her expression is now one of satisfaction.

"Mother, you need to stop this," I tell her, my tone serious. It's been so many years of anger and despising since the day she found out what my real profession is—or was—she's got to move on for fuck's sake! "Andries has told me that he loves me."

Her mouth presses into a small line, and I know she's resisting the urge to lash out. "He is a good man. Your sister would be much better for him." It almost comes out as a hiss. I can't help but feel a swell of anger rise up in my chest. She's spent over a decade pretending that I don't exist, and now here I am standing right beside her hospital bed, and she doesn't even think I'm worthy.

"After all," she continues. "I'm sure he has no idea what type of… woman you are." The innuendo is that I'm less than human because of my chosen profession. Of course she doesn't agree with what I've been doing but that's nothing unusual. Lili is the good one. Lili is the one who lives with and takes care of her. She wants the best for her favorite daughter.

"What is that supposed to mean? I'm here, Mother. I'm trying to help you."

"I don't need help from you." The words hit me like a slap in the face. It isn't right. She's my blood, my family but she's chosen to turn her back on me and make sure that even the man who has told me he loves me for who I am should be offered to my younger sister like a prize available at a carnival. I have to stand there seething while the machines beep around us and the low hum of nurses on the floor is in the air. She turns her body away, nothing more to be said. As usual.

Breaking the awkward silence, a nurse walks into the room. "Just checking in!" Her bright face smiles at me and then falls quickly. She can see that something is wrong. "Is everything okay?"

"Fine," I say. It's time. To turn around and make sure that I can move on with my life. I'm going to meet Andries' family for his birthday since he's accepted me even though he thinks I'm somebody else. Mama might not think I'm a good person, but I know that I've done the right thing by the man who claims to love me. "I need to go."

My mother doesn't even turn over to see me leave. Walking down the hospital hallway, I wonder if I'm even going to see her again. Lili has been taking care of her for years. She can handle it.

Abandonment isn't the right word to describe the feeling, but it's close. My own blood telling me that I'm not worthy of the man who loves me. When I'm on the verge of meeting his family! There is a future ahead, but the path isn't clear. I just know that Andries is a part of it and that provides me comfort. The air outside the stuffy hospital feels fresh, especially now that I've made my decision to be with him and his family.

CHAPTER 32

Amsterdam, November 3, 2021
Roxanne

According to the doctors, Mom has been recovering well and is ready to be released from the hospital. As we are at less than two months from Christmas, I want to make sure I can buy the bookstore on time to surprise her and Lili. Despite the argument between my mom and I, I still want to gift them the bookstore. And hopefully, that gift would bridge the gap between us.

I can only hope Mr. Beekhof is a reasonable man. After all, my family has worked at his bookstore for so many decades, I'm sure he won't balk at a good offer. And he's getting on in years, probably looking forward to retirement. Hell, Lili basically runs the store now and he just comes in from time to time to check things out.

There's a small coffee shop that is close to the store, so that's a perfect place to meet him. As he walks up, I can see from the straining buttons on his shirt that he's gained some weight in his older age. Part of me always wonders if he hired my mother because he found Asian women attractive, so I make sure I'm dressed in a demure yet revealing outfit. Anything that will help the negotiation. Standing up when he approaches, I see his eyes travel up and down my short dress and he gulps.

I give him a hug and he stiffens. "Thank you so much for meeting me today!" It's a bit schoolgirlish, but that's exactly what I'm trying to act like.

"Happy to see you. I hope your mother is recovering well?" I nod and smile, almost bowing my head in deference. Friendliness and warmth might get me further than assertiveness on this one. "So what did you want to talk about?" He sits down and we quickly order.

"Well, to be honest my sister already runs a fair bit of the shop and my mother worked there for so long, it's almost become like part of our family." Tugging at the heartstrings, my first approach. "You've been so good to our family over the years."

"Your mother was a wonderful worker for so long." He looks almost wistful when he mentions her, and I can tell that he definitely misses her. Maybe they had a thing at one point, but even thinking about that and the fact my younger sister works there now takes my mind down a slightly darker path. Better to just get to the point.

"So what I'd like is to make an offer to buy the store from you. Sort of continue on the family legacy." I slide across a piece of paper with the formal offer. "I think you'll find this generous, and you'll be able to retire in comfort."

He looks down and then back up at me, but his expression isn't surprised. It is slightly confused. Suddenly his body language changes, and he leans back, crossing his arms. "I didn't realize my little store had suddenly become so popular."

"Popular?" I repeat in confusion. "What do you mean?"

"Just the other day, another party decided to call and offer to buy the store." I am genuinely shocked. Who the hell would want a piddly little bookstore to own that barely made any money? Unless they were a developer and wanted to tear the place down or gut it? It's almost the last real bookstore in Amsterdam and had been there for decades. I'm crestfallen all of a sudden and that's not a usual emotion for me.

But I have to compose myself. Like everything else, the easiest way to solve problems is with money. More money. "Can I ask who the party is? And what they offered?"

"I probably shouldn't say. But the man did seem interested in whether or not you were involved with the store for some reason. His name is Karl Townsend." When he says the name my body stiffens.

Karl.

Jesus, I didn't think stopping being his escort would make him so fucking petty. Now the sad feeling becomes anger, but I'll deal with that another time.

Trying not to react, I straighten up and grab the offer from the middle of the table, thinking fast. My instincts sometimes don't exactly catch up with my brain, but nevertheless, I say, "Whatever he's offering you for the store, I'll double it." I know that it won't be as affordable, but to give Lili and my mother their legacy though, it'll be worth it. I've been very good with my money over the years, and nobody knows exactly how wealthy I am, especially my family.

Thankfully his eyes widen, and he leans forward, which is a good sign. "The problem is, Roxanne, that I sort of already accepted. At least verbally. Nothing has been signed though." His eyes are looking down at the paper and I can see him starting to sweat. It never takes much to make that happen. "If you're offering more, I think maybe you two should talk and negotiate. Maybe then it can come down to a final bid?"

Great. Now he wants to basically auction off the place between a person who's had her whole family invested and a guy who's simply out to screw over his former sex worker. And the funny part is, it's the perfect scenario to make him a ton of money he doesn't deserve. I'm surprised he isn't licking his lips. Then he does while staring at my cleavage and I want to put on a coat. "I can give you his contact information?"

"I already have it," I snap quickly. Seeing that he's surprised at my anger, I take a deep breath. "I'll talk with him and then contact you again. I'm sure we can work something out."

He nods. "I hope so. It'd be a shame to see the store go to anyone else, honestly."

Right. So that's why you bite on the first offer and then don't even bother to talk to my sister about it? More words I can't say out loud. "I appreciate that."

Now I need to talk to Karl, and that's going to be a fun conversation. Especially because I know exactly what his motivation is for approaching Mr. Beekhof. Is it revenge?

Does he want me back somehow? One more night with me? I guess I'm going to have to find out.

* * *

Once I'm left alone, I head outside and compose Karl's number to get to the bottom of his little game. I'm trying to relax, but I'm so angry at him that it's hard to keep a friendly demeanor. The ringtone goes on, and I start tapping my heel on the concrete as I wait for him to pick up the call.

"Now that's a surprise," I hear him saying from the other side of the line, his tone already humored.

"I'm not sure what you're trying to do, Karl, but it's best you fucking stop it now!" My voice is loud and aggressive, and I give a long steady breath to calm myself down.

"Me? I was just checking to see if he was interested in selling it."

"Fuck off!" I snap, unable to keep my temper in front of this hypocrite snake. "You know I want to buy that bookshop. You know it and you went ahead anyway!"

"You always want to buy everything, don't you?"

"You're doing it just for the sake of revenge, stop it," I tell him, my tone grave and serious.

"At the beginning, yeah, but then the owner seemed quite interested in selling it and accepted my offer without even negotiating."

"I never thought you'd be such an asshole, I swear, after fifteen years—"

"After fifteen years you dropped me like a dirty sock, Roxie," he growls, cutting me off. "At the very least you could've given me the promotion I wanted as a consolation prize." I can't help but scoff, head shaking at his demand. "But no—you didn't give a shit about me, so why would I?"

"This bookshop is mine," I snarl, my tone insistent. "I'm gonna offer him double and you're gonna back down and go fuck yourself."

"This bookshop is gonna be mine, sweetheart, and your little sister is gonna work for me, unless you want me to tell your boyfriend who you truly are."

I suck in a breath at his statement, and even freeze for a moment in shock.

"It hurts, huh?" Karl seems delighted, reveling in my uneasiness.

"You are not gonna stoop that low, are you?" I manage to force the words out, even though every cell of my body is filled with dread at the idea Karl could talk to Andries.

"I'm just reaching your level, darling," he answers back, his tone amused. "How do you think your lovely Andries, so pure and innocent, will react when he finds out you were a whore for fifteen years, huh?"

Despite his disgusting and beyond disrespectful behavior, my mind starts ruminating for a way out of this. "Can we get to an agreement?"

"I want the bookshop," he demands, and I can't help but scoff at him. "*And* the promotion."

A gush of air rolls out of my mouth, tired of this asshole. "I can get you the promotion, but not the bookshop," I venture.

"Then I'm afraid you're gonna have to pray that your boyfriend loves you enough to forgive you."

"What can I do to have the bookshop and keep Andries out of it?" I ask immediately.

"I want you back." His tone has switched from amused to vulnerable. "I want to go out with you like before."

"That would be betraying him," I pout out. "I can't do that."

"Get me the promotion, we spend the night celebrating, and the next day I'm out of your life forever," he says, sounding like it's no big deal and so easy to do. "You can keep the bookshop and Andries."

"What does spending the night celebrating entail?" I find myself asking.

"You know what it entails." His tone tells everything I need to know.

I heave a long sigh, his words creeping me out.

"I need to think about it." I press two fingers between the bridge of my noise and shut my eyes, trying to fight a headache. "Can I call you back?"

"Don't take too much time, Roxie," he warns. "My patience only goes so far."

I hang up right afterwards, unable to listen to that creep a second more. Then I start roaming around, thinking of a way out. I don't trust Karl at all. If he wants me to cheat on Andries with him, it's because he wants to keep evidence of the betrayal to use against me in the future. The only thing I'm sure of right now is that I need a plan and fast.

***

Sitting on the couch in my office, I've spent the past hour ruminating about Karl and his next move. He's trying to force me to do things I don't want to, and he's going to regret it. I never thought he'd go *that* low, but I guess he felt compelled to threaten me because I broke up with him after fifteen years. A few knocks on my office door pull me back from my thoughts and my attention focus on Poppy who peers in the doorway. "Is everything okay?" She then walks in and shuts the door behind her. "Can I get you anything?"

"Karl is trying to buy the bookshop my sister works at," I disclose, my eyes drifting up at her. "He knows I wanted to buy it for Christmas as a present for my family, which is why he's trying to get it first."

"Are you serious?" Poppy asks, before walking in my direction and sitting on the armchair in front of me. "But why?"

"Because I broke up with him, because I didn't get him the promotion he wanted, because he wants revenge…."

"What a jerk! You guys have known each other for years. You don't owe him a lifetime commitment, for fuck's sake!" She leans back on the chair, heaving a long sigh. "What are you thinking to do?"

"We need to stop him," I tell her. "He's a threat to me, to my relationship with my boyfriend, and to us as an agency."

"Oh, you've got a boyfriend?" She sounds genuinely surprised which makes me smile since I never disclose anything about my private life to anyone. "I just didn't know about that. What if you buy the bookshop first though?"

"He threatened to tell my boyfriend a secret I should have told him a long time ago."

Her eyebrows rise in surprise. "Which is?"

"What I truly do for a living," I fess out.

"He doesn't know about the agency or that you were a sex-worker yourself?" Poppy can't keep the shock out of her face.

"No… It's complicated," I tell her, closing the subject of the conversation "We need to keep Karl under control."

"Roxie." Poppy leans her body forward, sitting on the edge of the armchair. "Don't you think telling the truth to your boyfriend will set you free?" she asks, her expression laced with worry. "Seems like the obvious choice to me."

My eyes drift away for a moment as I ponder her question. I search deep inside me for why I struggle so much with telling Andries the truth. I think my heart has found the answer. "I'm not ready to risk losing him," I say, looking her in the eye. "It's selfish, I know, but I don't want to see the disappointment in his eyes, I don't want the image he has of me replaced by something else." I pause, observing Poppy as she remains quietly listening. "The truth is I've fallen in love with an angel, and I'm a fucking demon."

"You're not a demon, Roxie," Poppy refutes immediately. "You're smart, kind, professional, and above all, you're human, with weaknesses and strengths just as anyone." A smile pulls at my lips as I listen to her. "Now, I do think if your boyfriend truly loves you he'll accept your past, forgive you, and move on."

"That's a very naive outlook," I rebuke. "He's the heir of one of the oldest noble families of this country. He can handle being with a poor woman, but a former prostitute and a current brothel keeper?" I scoff, head shaking at the idea. "The day he knows the truth he'll ditch me like yesterday's news."

"You can't keep this secret to yourself forever though."

"Why not?" I ask her, my words coming off more aggressive than I wanted. "A small price to pay to keep my peace and happiness."

"Then, what are you gonna do about Karl?"

Her question hangs in the air, and I blow out a breath, tired of Karl and his shenanigans against me. "He's a threat and we need to take care of him."

"Ohh-kay," she utters, bringing herself as close as she can to me. "And what do you suggest we do?"

"We need to find something to silence him."

"Like what? Karl is very well connected. Any little rumor would get brushed under the rug immediately."

Poppy is right—even if he was suspected of murder or something along those lines, he'd get the best lawyer in town and the subject will be dropped in the blink of an eye.

I wanted to play clean, but Karl isn't. So why should I? A plan starts taking shape in my mind, and while I didn't want to get to that point, it seems like I have no other choice. It's clear that Poppy is too honest and kind to collaborate, which is fine as I wasn't really expecting her to be any different. No one can know what I'm going to do, though. This plan has to remain a secret. I'm good at keeping secrets so that shouldn't a problem.

Decided, I leap off my seat, soothe my dress and smiling at Poppy, I say, "Thank you for your kind words. It was great talking to you."

THREE WEEKS LATER...

CHAPTER 33

Amsterdam, November 15, 2021
Roxanne

"Mr. Beekhof, rest assured you won't regret this deal," I tell him as we shake hands, the notary and our lawyers sitting beside us as they retrieve the stack of signed papers.

Mr. Beekhof forces himself to smile, but the old man seems to be pretty shaken to have sold his bookshop. While I understand the sentimental value, I'm convinced this is for the better. Mom and Lili were paid terribly, and he never bothered to attract more clients to make his bookshop more profitable, which would have allowed him to pay more decent wages to my family. Put simply, Mr. Beekhof inherited a business but without having an ounce of interest in the business itself.

"I know you'll take good care of it," he says, sounding kind and genuine. "It's just a bit hard for me to let it go after owning it for many years, but truthfully, this isn't an offer I could pass on."

I know that but at least he said it. He's getting far more money than the shop is actually worth, somewhat thanks to that idiot Karl. There's also a massive sense of relief inside me that the deal is signed. I learned long ago, never count a deal done unless there's a signature on paper.

Being with the men I've been with over the years has taught me a lot about business and investing, but also about trust. The ones you think were the most up front were the ones who would stab you in the back without another thought.

My lawyer slides the check across the table and Mr. Beekhof quickly folds it and puts it in his pocket, likely heading straight to the bank after this is all done. He's now able to do basically whatever he wants, and I'm sure that is daunting for any person his age.

I take a moment as he gets up and gathers his things. It's done. My family actually owns the bookshop they've spent their entire lives working in. And the first thought that flies into my mind is whether or not my mother will actually be grateful, or will she let her spite denigrate me for giving this gift to our family?

In any case, Lili will finally be able to put things in place to actually make a living at it and be invested in the success of the store. Heck, I'll even pull a few shifts here and there, and I have lots of resources at my disposal.

Turning to my lawyer and the notary, they both stand up and shake my hand. Formal to the end, of course. "Thank you both. This was relatively seamless. I'll forward your fees in a couple of days if that's okay."

They both nod, smiling at the fact it was so easy. After all, their paychecks are based on time invested, but it also means they can move onto other things.

Then I pick my phone, ready to let Andries know the news, when I find a text message from him:

I hope everything went well. See you at Spectrum, 8 p.m.

Anticipating the closure of the deal, Andries had already booked a table to host the celebration. It's going to be strange celebrating the buying of a store that is literally for my sister without her, but this is a Christmas gift, so I want to keep it as a surprise until then. Andries will be there of course, and then his friend Dan and whatever girl he is hooking up with this week. Plus, if I'm not mistaken, Andries had mentioned his sister might join us. Always funny for me to think that his family might someday become closer to me than my own and how accepting everyone has been of me without even really blinking an eye.

Of course, they don't know everything. It's always like a sword dangling over my head, just waiting to drop. But I'm excited to see them all and there's a massive weight off my shoulders that the deal is finished. Lots of things to think about, but for tonight I have to give myself permission just to enjoy the company and relax.

Spectrum is like a posh cocoon—gray walls, plush chairs, white table clothes—hidden away inside the Waldorf Astoria and overlooking a garden. And despite telling Andries I have only been there once, the truth is my clients used to take me there frequently and it remains one of my favorite establishments in town.

When I arrive at the restaurant, Andries is already there, waiting for me at a table for five. He's sporting a fit white, crips shirt, a few buttons open at the collar and a navy-blue blazer. Upon seeing me, he stands up, his lips forming a slow sexy twist that I love so much, and his eyes pierce right through me. Damn, he looks good.

There's a low hum around the place, but we chose this restaurant specifically so that we can actually hear ourselves. Nothing drives me crazy more than having to shout at the people at my table.

"Hey," I greet as I reach him.

He hugs me and gives me a quick peck on the lips. His eyebrows cock. "So?"

"It's officially mine." Jeez! It's so hard to believe that in just the span of a few months I stopped being an escort and became a bookstore owner.

"Congratulations! That's absolutely incredible!" I know his words are genuine, but like any other practical man he immediately follows it up with money-talk. "I'm so glad the bank accepted the loan; sometimes they can be super unfair on low-wage employees."

I have to take a beat. He has no idea that I didn't have to take out a loan in order to buy it. All cash. Just one of the benefits of making thousands of euros per night for so many years.

"I think the fact the whole family has worked there at some point in their life helped the case." It's an easy explanation.

We sit down and he quickly signals to the waiter. There's a dark glass of bourbon in front of him, and it's exactly what I need. To calm my nerves and get over the nervousness of the day. Once I order he grabs my hand.

"Seriously, such good news," he says, his tone filled with so much enthusiasm that it makes me smile. "I'm so excited for you."

"I'm… excited too. And Lili and my mother will be thrilled." At least I hope so.

"Not to sidetrack, but do you have update about Karl? Sorry to ask, it's just that my dad isn't over the fact one of his best employees decided to use all his paid leave one month before the announcement of the new head of global sales."

His comment about Karl makes me tense up. "Last time I spoke to him, he was dating a new girl and wanted to take some time off," I say, before I notice the waiter filling my glass with water. "We haven't been in touch since then."

"Yeah, I understand, my dad's all over the place," he discloses, chuckling as he thinks something through. "Poor Karl, the guy must have experienced some serious burnout."

"Most likely; he used to work too much," I answer, wanting nothing more but to change the subject to something else. "How's college treating you? Are you enjoying the English program?"

"Yeah, it's pretty chill," Andries replies, sitting back and grabbing his drink.

"College, *chill*?" I always dance around the fact he's so young compared to me. Not that it really makes a difference, but he's definitely in another world where studying and partying are king and queen.

"Yeah, I find it to be alright. I've got time to study, to be with you, to write, and to keep fencing."

When you don't have to work while studying of course it's chill, but I refrain myself from telling him that.

"Do you have a plan to make the bookshop more profitable?"

The truth is I didn't buy the bookshop to make a fortune out of it, but if I can turn it into an asset instead of a financial liability then why not? "Well, um, I'm thinking of hosting literature workshops and tours like I did for you and we'll definitely have a better digital presence than what we have now."

"Maybe you can work out some deal with your friend Josianne," he advises. "She could take her students there for one of the workshops."

He's right of course. One of the things on my agenda, after I talk to Lili, is to give the bookshop more visibility.

"It's a great idea, yeah, I'll give her a ring."

"When are you gonna tell the news to your sister and Mom?" he asks, before taking another sip of his bourbon.

"I'm thinking of doing it at Christmas," I tell him. "I don't want to see Mom before that." He nods with a grim look. After what happened at the hospital between us I know he's aware of the tension. But then he surprises me.

"Does your mom like traveling?"

I blink twice, totally taken aback by his sudden question. "Traveling?"

He nods.

"Um, yes, why?"

"When she'll be fully recovered from her back surgery, maybe we could go somewhere she likes, all of us?"

I chuckle in disbelief. "Andries…"

Andries on the other hand seems dead serious. "What? I'm sure she'll appreciate it. Is there any place she would like to visit?"

I lean back against my chair and ponder his question more seriously. "Hmm, I think she'd love to go back to Paris someday. My dad took her there once and she truly loved it."

"Well, Paris it is. Maybe we could even go there for New Year's Eve."

"We already accepted your dad's invitation," I remind him, right when the waiter puts my glass of bourbon in front of my place setting. "But we can go afterwards."

"Deal. Your mom can't hold a grudge against you forever." He then leans in, gently resting his forearms on the table. "And I'm gonna make sure she can see you the same way I do."

My interest is perked and leaning closer to him, I lower my voice, and ask, "How do you see me?"

His face brightens up with a devilish smile and my heart races as we remain at just inches of each other's lips. "Well, as an incredible woman." He pauses for a beat, reveling in my curiosity. "Talented, passionate, kind, confident, hard-working…."

"That's it?" I ask teasingly, our shoulders touching.

"Oh, there's more." He then leans toward my ear and whispers, "The rest is just more private."

"Tell me," I insist, my voice small.

He takes an opportunity to slide an arm around my chair, coming closer to me and looks into my eyes. His are so striking. "Well, I think you are extremely beautiful, sensual, hot, delicious…."

His lips fall to mine and with a gentle touch he sets my body on fire. I don't know how the hell he does it, but after the stress of today I find myself melting into his kiss and embracing the tongue that slides into my mouth.

Coming too quickly, I know that there's other people about to arrive so when his hand slides up my dress, I have to push him away.

"Andries, behave," I scold under my breath.

He pulls away with a sheepish grin. "I knew we should've had dinner at home."

He pulls away just in time because we can hear Dan coming a mile away as soon as he walks in, always larger than life. Jessica is the girl trailing behind him, or at least I think that's her name. She's young, skinny and looks a bit high, as if she smoked something right before he picked her up. I feel like a mother compared to her.

"Hey!" Dan greets, his tone enthusiastic, as he gets to the table. "Jess, you know Andries and Roxanne."

Andries stands up and gives him a bro hug while I go greet Jessica.

"Finally! I hear we are celebrating tonight!" Dan says, his eyes gleaming with excitement.

I nod and smile as I greet him with a quick hug. It's good to have people who will celebrate your success.

"Congratulations!" Dan tells me, patting me softly in the back. "You're officially a business owner! That's a big accomplishment."

"Thank you." Even though they're young, they know what they are talking about.

"Starting the party without me?" I hear Elise's voice ring out across the restaurant and heads turn. Stalking toward the table, she makes a point of hugging Andries and Dan and nodding at me and Jessica. There's no hug offered.

We all sit down, and everyone wants to talk to me about the bookstore. The only holdout is, of course, Elise who tries to change the subject a few times. I can see her glance at Andries holding my hand and then look away.

There're some snide comments even, but Andries gives her a couple of glares and finally she backs off. Dan and Jessica seem clueless as usual and Dan seems more focused on her minimal amount of cleavage anyway, plus his hand is constantly busy under the table.

"Here's to the future!" Andries looks into my eyes and clinks his glass against mine. He's right. There's nothing on the horizon but the unknown, which is both daunting but also somehow exciting. When he locks eyes with me I know I've made the right decisions.

CHAPTER 34

"I already told you I'm not coming," I say to Lili once more over the phone while I'm on the couch with Andries. It's Saturday afternoon and I want to stay cozy in the living room with my boyfriend, listening to some jazzy beats and reading a good book while he is on his notebook writing. I've got no interest whatsoever to go and pay a visit to her and Mama until Christmas.

"But it's my birthday, for fuck's sake," Lili insists, her tone growing irritated. "You never miss it."

"We can go out and have dinner without Mama if you want." I know she'll never accept leaving Mama on her own.

"Roxie... Don't be like that," she pleads. "You know the impact the betrayal of our dad left on her."

"I know, but that's not my problem," I continue, heaving a long sigh at her insistence. "I'm tired of being a good daughter to an ungrateful mother. I'd rather be on my own than mistreated." The truth is Andries has shown me that I deserve to be loved and treated properly. He's become a bit like my new family and I don't see why I should keep playing the dutiful daughter to a mother who doesn't deserve it.

"Can you please at least pass by just to say hi?" Lili asks with a small voice and it sounds like she's about to cry. "I'm not asking you to stay over for dinner, just have a tea with me and say hi."

"I'm sorry, Lili, I really love you and I know it's not your fault, but Mama crossed the line so many times that I'd rather not see her until Christmas." It's one of those evenings that I can't really forgo.

"Can't you do it for me, please?" At this point, she's almost pleading. "She even asked me why you didn't come to have lunch with the rest of the family."

"And she wonders why?" I ask, scoffing at Mama's reaction. "Is she for real?" I can't help but shake my head in disbelief. "I'm sorry but I'm busy today."

"So you aren't coming to my birthday?" she asks nearly in distress. "Like at all?"

"I'm sorry, Lili, Mama should've thought about it before being such a bitch to me." After seeing how long I've been on the phone, I decide to end this call once and for all. "Well, I've got to go. Happy Birthday, lil sister." And without giving her time to answer back, I hang up.

I know how hurt Lili is for me skipping her birthday, but Mama was just so damn cruel and mean at the hospital that I can't find the will to go and see her again.

"It's your sister's birthday today?" Andries doesn't waste time. I knew he'd be curious about my call with Lili. After all, he's been sitting right next to me through the all thing.

"Yeah, it's her thirtieth birthday and they just got home from the restaurant. Lili can't understand why after the fight I had with Mama at the hospital I didn't show up."

"May I ask you something a bit personal?" Andries asks, a bit apprehensively, his cerulean eyes pinned on me.

Since I know he's so eager to learn more about my family, I mumble a quick, "Sure."

"Why is your mom so mean to you?" His question seems like it's coming out of nowhere and I can't hide the shock on my face. "Like, I know you told me she's very disappointed in your life's choices, but I don't understand why she'd stop talking to you and be mean like that."

"What you don't understand is that children are to honor their parents." Seeing the frown on his face, I realize how different our cultures are and I don't think he'll get it. "It's complicated. Just forget it."

"Try me," he insists.

I take a deep breath in and out, wondering where to even begin. "Mama expected me by now to have a well-paying corporate job, a house of my own, a husband, a family, those things are important to her in a way that is directly linked to the honor of the family." He listens attentively as I speak, but I feel utterly embarrassed talking about something so outdated. "It's a weird concept."

"Go on, I'm listening."

"It's just the way she was brought up. Children are expected to obey their parents and honor their elders. Even to the detriment of their own happiness and individuality. Things are changing now but she was raised like that."

"Well, things didn't change much I can tell you that." I raise a confused eyebrow at his comment, so he explains further. "My dad tried to force me into business school, remember?"

Oh jeez! I try hard to suppress a laugh. "Yes, but if he finds out you aren't doing it, he's not gonna disown you and say you brought dishonor to the family."

"Who knows…." At this point, I know perfectly well he's just teasing me.

"Oh, c'mon, I don't believe it," I tell him, my head shaking. "I'm sure he'll be disappointed and annoyed for a few days, but he'll eventually move on." While I know Andries isn't entirely convinced, I proceed, "For Mama, the fact I didn't follow the path she wanted me to brought great dishonor upon her family and ancestors."

"Damn," he utters, his eyes widening in shock. He remains quiet for a moment as if processing what I just told him. "Um, do you want us to go together?"

"Oh no, please, I'm not going anyway," I answer, shifting under the blanket.

Andries shoots me an arched eyebrow in disbelief. "And are you gonna be okay with that?"

His question makes me pause and I consider it for a moment. "I don't know, I've never missed my sister's birthday before."

Andries takes my hand in his, and my attention returns to his navy blue eyes. "Lili hasn't done anything to you, though, maybe we could just go and stay for an hour and then come back."

Silence settles in as I ponder his offer. Oh gosh, having Andries in that tiny old apartment? No, impossible! Plus, what if Mama decides to show up and tell him who I am for the sake of breaking us up? That woman is vicious and mean. As I keep thinking about whether or not I should pay a visit to my sister, my iPhone pings with a new text message. Speaking of the devil, it's Lili herself:

Please, come at least to say hi. Mama has been in her room since she came back from the restaurant. You can pass by.

I run a hand through my hair, totally undecided. Well, if things go south, I can always skip Christmas.

Fine, I'll be there for 30 mins and that's it, I reply to her text.

Jeez! What I wouldn't do for my sister. I leap off the couch, and stretch my arms as much as I can, trying to find some courage to head to Bijlmer now. "Fine, I'm gonna go quickly, say hi, and come back."

"You sure you don't want me to go with you?"

"I'm sure, I'll be right back." I lean over to him and give him a quick kiss. Then I book an Uber on my phone, and go back inside our bedroom to pick out a pair of boots, my coat and purse.

"So you gonna go there empty-handed?" Andries asks from the living room.

"Oh shit," I utter, reminding myself I didn't buy anything for her. Wait! Of course I did. I take from my coat the key of the store and show it to Andries. "I bought the bookshop."

* * *

"I'm so glad you came," Lili says as she opens the door for me. Then, to my greatest surprise, she even embraces me, and I can hear a few sniffs. I return the gesture, and wrap my arms around her back, squeezing her a bit. "It means a lot to me."

"I did it for you," I whisper in reply.

After she releases me, she invites me in and I step very cautiously inside the apartment, checking right and left if Mama is around.

"She's in her bedroom," Lili discloses as if reading my mind. "Tea or a glass of champagne?"

"Oh," I mouth, looking astonished at my sister's offer. "I didn't know it was such a fancy birthday."

Lili gives me a grin, her eyes sparkling as she trots to the kitchen and opens the fridge to take from there a bottle of Veuve Clicquot. She's sporting a comfortable outfit, simple jeans and sweater, and a high ponytail, and I can't help but wonder if she went to the restaurant to celebrate her birthday like that. Nothing wrong with that, but she could have marked the occasion with something a bit more festive and special.

Noticing that she's focused on opening the bottle, I go and take two flutes from the cabinet and put them on the counter.

There is a small popping noise as the bottle is opened, and I clap my hands while she pours the bubbly with a big smile onto the two flutes.

We take our respective glasses, raise them in the air and then clink them in a toast. "Happy Birthday, Lili," I say, feeling quite guilty to have thought for a moment I should skip her birthday altogether just because of Mama.

"Thank you for coming." She softly squeezes my hand, and the gesture makes me feel even worse.

"I'm sorry to have skipped lunch at the restaurant," I fess out. "I just—"

"It's okay, you are here now," she interposes immediately. And as if she wants to end the discussion, she then walks back to the fridge, and shows me the leftovers of her birthday cake. "Do you want some?"

"Sure, I can give it a try," I answer for the sake of politeness. Cakes and sweets aren't my thing, but today it's her birthday and I'll be the last one to hurt her more than I already did. With a smile on her lips, she cuts a slice for me and puts it on a plate before giving it to me.

The cake is made of chocolate and strawberries and I shut my eyes at the explosion of flavors on my palate.

"You like it?"

"It's delicious actually," I say sincerely. "Thank you." Then looking at my sister, I can't help but feel a pang in my heart. Here's she is at thirty, still living with Mama, no life outside taking care of her needs, no boyfriend, and still struggling financially. Lili is the embodiment of a selfless, dutiful daughter, and ultimately I'd love for her to get out of the nest and fly on her own. "I've got something for you," I announce, taking from my purse an envelope.

"Roxie," Lili chides as I give it to her. "I didn't invite you to give me more money. I've got enough."

I try my best not to scoff at her comment while she's opening the envelope and taking the check from it.

"Ten thousand euros?" she shouts, head shaking. "That's too much, Roxie, I can't accept."

"That's not a gift," I tell her causing her eyes to squint in confusion. "That's your new salary."

Now it's her jaw that hangs open as she looks at me with shock in her eyes. "Are you serious?" She glances again at the check and then back me. "How?"

"I bought the bookshop for us," I announce, reveling in her stunned face. "Now you are officially the manager."

"That's... that's..." Her head tilts down and her fingers go between the bridge of her noise as she tries to contain the tears brimming in her eyes. I pull and tug her into my arms, comforting her. "I'm sorry," she sniffles amid the tears. "I wasn't expecting such good news."

"I understand," I say under my breath as we remain hugging each other. Looking at her in the eye, I wipe some of her tears, but at least I'm wiping tears of joy. "You and Mama worked so hard in that bookshop. It's only fair that it belongs to us now."

"Does Mama know?"

"No, I wanted to tell her on Christmas."

"Speaking of Christmas..." Lili lets her words trail off, clearly undecided whether to say the rest or not.

"What about it?" I press on.

"Um, a Dutch couple that are Mama's friends invited her for a dinner on the twenty-fifth...and I'm her plus one."

I frown in confusion. "What does that mean?"

Lili blows out a breath, staring absently to the floor as if she's struggling to say the truth. Silence settles between us until her attention finally returns on me and she says, "It means we'll have réveillon here, but not Christmas dinner."

My jaw drops at her words and I can't help but look at Lili in total shock. "And I'm not invited to that dinner?"

"Well, after not coming to my birthday lunch..." She pauses for a beat, indecision creeping up again. "Mama said you weren't coming with us."

"She's out of her mind!" I blurt out, ready to storm out of the kitchen and go to her bedroom. "I'm gonna talk to her."

"Roxie, wait!"

But it's too late. I'm already crossing the hallway, and I waste no time to twist the handle of Mama's door and push it wide open. Getting inside, Mama is on her rocking chair, her glasses on, focused on a book.

"Is it true you don't want me to join you and Lili to that Christmas dinner at your friends' place?"

"Oh, look who's here," she says, her tone derisive. "Let me guess, you came over because your sister was begging and crying?" Her eyes travel up to check my face and she then huffs, head shaking. "Pathetic."

My stomach twists into a tighter knot when I see the disdain in her eyes. "I came here for her, yes, and she mentioned I'm not invited to that Christmas dinner," I tell her, unable to keep my defiance at bay. "So is it true or not?"

"It's true, yes." Her words hurt like a knife to the chest. We have never skipped Christmas dinner as a family. It became Mama's favorite time of the year and even when we didn't speak to each other, I never missed it. Never. Like her birthday. "They invited me, I accepted and said I'll bring my youngest with me. They have a son who's single and a doctor so it sounds like a perfect match."

I scoff at her. "I can't believe it. You've always insisted, nagged, and even coerced me emotionally to spend every single Christmas with you and Lili, and now you don't include me in your plans?"

"It's not appropriate to have someone so dishonest like you coming with us." My heart squeezes at her disgusting comment, and despite wanting nothing more but to leave, I stand my ground and keep listening her until the end. "They are a fine family, not having you there will let us save face."

"Oh, wow, save face?" I repeat, unable to hide the shock in my voice. "I can't believe I'm hearing this." I run a hand through my hair, totally stunned at her cruelty. "You still believe I'm a walking shame, don't you?"

Mom heaves a sigh. "In Shenzhen, where we come from, public officers used to handcuff prostitutes and their customers, dress them in bright yellow prison tunics and drag them through the streets for everyone to see. We call it the parade of shame. And that's exactly what you are."

"This isn't Shenzhen, Mama, this is Amsterdam," I remind her just as fast. "A pity you didn't leave your shitty beliefs behind before landing."

Mumbling under my breath, I curse her out in my head, but my attention goes to the door where Lili knocks.

"Hey, um, I wanted to bring you some tea," she informs, stepping very cautiously into the bedroom, her tone ultra-soft and delicate so not to offend Mama.

"Thank you, Lili." Mom bows her head slightly as she accepts the teacup and Lili does the same before making her way out. I can't help but roll my eyes at the whole charade.

Mama takes a sip of her tea in total silence, and I hope there's something in it to clean the bitterness in her heart.

"You want to come to Christmas dinner with us?"

Her question breaks the silence between us and despite wondering what she has in mind, I just nod in response.

I feel like she's going to ask for something in exchange. I'm sure of it.

Mama takes another gulp of her tea like she has all the time in the world, until her eyes fall on me and she says, "Then call your boyfriend right now in front of me and tell him who you are."

I stare at her, totally taken aback. "What?"

"Go on, put it on speaker and tell him the truth."

She can't be real! My chest heaves, blood pumping rapidly through my heart as I process her demand. "How can you be so horrible to your own daughter?"

"My daughter is a fraud," she spits out, before putting the teacup on the table beside her. "Don't you have any shame to be pretending to have your sister's life? She's the one who deserves to be with that young man, not you! She's the one who's a librarian and works every day in that bookshop, not you!" Mom finally pauses, taking a deep breath in and out while I remain totally paralyzed by her vicious words. "Tell him who the true Roxanne is, go on! Tell him!"

I glare at her, head shaking with disdain. "I hate you."

Mama just scoffs in return. "How ironic! You have spent all these years pretending to be proud of who you are, and yet, you can't stomach telling the truth to the only man you've ever loved?" Her question resonates through the walls, but I don't answer. "Maybe it's because you know deep-down there's nothing to be proud of."

My mouth drops open and tears form in the back of my eyes. "I hate you!" I repeat, louder this time. "I truly hate you!"

"You are free to go," she hisses, looking at the open door and then back at me. "No one is retaining you."

"Very well. Goodbye, Mother," I say as I storm out of her bedroom, tears sliding over my flushed cheeks.

Lili walks out of the kitchen, her face laced with concern. "Is everything okay?"

I cross the hallway, then grab my coat and purse, briefly wipe my tears, and try to breathe in and out to regain my composure. "Um, I'm gonna go, it's getting late."

"Roxie, what's going on?" she asks, her eyes observing me attentively as she now stands right in front of me.

"Nothing, just Mama, being her usual self," I say, despite my misty eyes and sniffles. "Well, thank you so much for the champagne." Lili and I start walking in the direction of the door and I take these few seconds to book an Uber. "Let's do some shopping when you have time. For Christmas, you know."

"Yes, I look forward to it." Quietly enough, she opens the front door for me and we stand in the doorway for a moment. "I'm sorry about Mama, but please don't worry about her grudge against you. I'm sure you can come to that dinner anyway."

"That's okay, I don't mind not going," I lie, but it doesn't matter. I wrap my arms around her, embracing my sister tightly against me.

For a split second, I feel tempted to tell her to put Mama in a nursing home and move out of here, but knowing her as I do, I hold my tongue and simply say, "Well, see you soon."

"Thank you so much for coming by," she says as I leave.

CHAPTER 35

The elevator's door dings open and it's a tired and gloomy Roxanne that walks into my place. I watch her taking off her coat and boots, her face laced with a sadness that wasn't there when she left, while I stand in front of her holding a glass of Chateau Pétrus in each hand—a small gesture to lift her up.

"How did it go?" I ask, quite curious to know the outcome of her visit.

Without the heels on, Roxie loses a good five inches and I can't help but smile when she stands on her tiptoes to reach my lips. She discreetly takes one of the glasses out of my hand as she kisses me.

When her lips part from mine she takes a long sip of her wine like she was yearning for it. "Well, let's say it was a bad decision to go and see Mama again."

"Why? Is she okay?"

She seems to be under a wave of stress as she walks past me and heads to the kitchen, her body visibly tense.

"Oh, Mama's doing great, so much so that she and Lili will be attending a Christmas dinner at a friend's house," she announces, before wetting her lips again on the wine.

I take the glass out of her hand before she drinks everything in one go and ask, "And you? Aren't you going?"

She blows out a breath filled with frustration and at this point I know exactly the reason. "Mama made it clear that I'm not welcome there."

"Are you serious?" My question is rather rhetorical, and I can't fathom why a mother would be so vindictive. "What did your sister say?"

Roxie sits in one of the stools on the kitchen and heaves a long sigh. "She said to come over anyway, but if Mama is against it, I'm not insisting." She looks up at me and shrugs. "I'll do something else."

"Fuck, she really hates you." The words just roll off my mouth before I can even process them.

"Yep," she actually agrees without taking offense. "I told you she truly believes I brought shame to her whole family, ancestors included."

Silence settles between us as a solution starts taking shape in the back of my mind. "You know, my birthday is right after Christmas," I begin cautiously, gauging her reaction. "So why don't you come over and have dinner with us?"

"Oh, no, forget it," she snaps immediately, taking her glass back in her hands. "I don't want to be of any inconvenience."

"What are you talking about? I actually should've invited you sooner, I just never thought your mom would treat you this way." If my girlfriend is worried about being an inconvenience at our Christmas dinner, then there's only one thing to do. "Let me call my mom and make it happen."

I pull my phone from the back pocket of my jeans and start typing in it to make the phone call.

"Please, don't." Roxanne tries to reach my phone but I walk around the breakfast counter and standing at a good distance from her I put the call on speaker so that she can hear the ringtone. While I'm mostly teasing her, it seems like her anxiety keeps rising at each passing second.

"Too late, it's calling…."

"Hello?" I hear a female voice saying through the speaker.

"Mom! How are you?"

"Oh, my lil sweetie pie, I haven't heard your voice in so long," Mom laments, while Roxanne is trying hard to suppress a laugh. And I start wondering if putting this call on speaker was such a good idea. "Is everything okay?"

"Sweetie pie?" she whispers in amusement.

I frown, putting a finger on my lips to shush her, before replying to Mom. "Oh, yeah, that's true, I'll call you more often, then. Is it a good time to talk?"

"Yes, I just finished having dinner with your dad," she answers warmly and I can hear her heels clacking on the floor as she takes a few steps, most likely to go somewhere quieter.

"Great, look, um, you remember when Dad invited Roxanne to come over on the twenty-sixth for my birthday?"

"I do, yes." The warmth in her voice that was present just a few seconds ago has now for some reason completely evaporated.

"Well, she doesn't have the best relationship with her mom, and therefore she doesn't have plans for the evening of the twenty-fifth," I begin very cautiously, gauging her reaction, but Mom doesn't say a word and keeps listening without giving me any cue. "So what if I could bring her as a plus one for dinner?"

"You want to bring your girlfriend over for Christmas?" Mom can't hide the shock in her tone, despite her best attempt to stay neutral.

"Just for dinner," I remind her immediately. "Like for the evening."

A gush of air rolls out of her mouth as Mom starts thinking about my request more seriously. "I mean, it's one thing for her to attend your birthday party like any of your friends would, but it's another to come to a family Christmas dinner…"

Shit. I should've never put this call on speaker. I feel horrible for Roxanne to be listening to Mom's comment. After what she went through, I should've been more thoughtful. "I know, but she's family to me."

Her lips twist into a big smile in appreciation and I can tell she wasn't expecting such a response to my mom's concerns.

"But you barely know her, Andries," she ripostes.

"Of course I do," I say, looking at my girlfriend as she leaves the stool and goes to find the bottle of wine. "She's even already living with me. I mean, kind of."

"Isn't she much older, though?" Mom asks.

Roxanne is now refilling our glasses, pretending not to pay attention to the convo, but I know her all too well.

"Yeah, but you and Dad—"

"It's different," she interposes, cutting me off.

I know *exactly* what she means by that, so I take a deep breath in and out, and let my heart take the wheel. "Look, I know she doesn't have the same background as Tatiana, I know she comes from a very different family that won't bring any socio-economical value if a union between us ever takes place, but she just bought her own bookshop and she's very supportive of my writing." Mom remains quiet on the other side of the line, just like Roxanne, who's now standing in front of me, totally stunned by my words. I can even see the gleam in her eyes as I continue. "She inspires me to follow my dreams, I feel alive and thriving when I'm around her, and we enjoy the same kind of books and poetry; and despite her family hating her and treating her like crap, she's constantly there for them." As I say those words, her eyes become misty and her lips twist into a smile I've never seen before. "I—" All of a sudden, she tugs me into her arms and squeezes me tight, so tight that it catches me off guard.

"You what?" Mom says over the phone.

I also embrace her, and then give her a kiss on the head.

"Andries?" Mom says, still waiting for an answer.

Her almond eyes travel up to meet mine again, and as I look deep inside them, I feel like I've never been more certain than saying, "I see a future with her. I really do."

"Do you love her?" Mom asks as Roxie and I remain staring at each other.

I manage to take slow breaths in and out, despite the hammering in my chest.

"I do, yes."

A loud gush of air blows off from the other side of the line. "Well, then I suppose I can ask Claudia to add one more plate at the table."

I can't help but beam with joy and clench a fist in victory. "Thank you so much, Mom," I say, trying to keep my excitement under control. "You've no idea how much it means to me."

"One question though." Mom's tone is now more serious than ever and I swallow dryly at it. "I suppose you also want her to sleepover, don't you?"

Her question catches me by surprise. I mean, it's kind of obvious that I want Roxanne to sleepover but I don't want to tell it so bluntly to her face. "Well, I think it'd be appropriate to host our guest for the night, yes," I say, knowing that Mom pays great value on etiquette and manners.

"Correct, which is what we have guest bedrooms for."

"Mom!" I snap immediately, before tapping the button and switching from speaker to handset. I bring the phone up to my ear and continue. "Are you serious right now? I'm not gonna let my girlfriend sleep alone in another bedroom!"

Roxie is visibly frustrated when I start going a few steps away but I want to keep the convo between Mom and I.

"She's not even your fiancée, damn it!" she grits between her teeth. "What example am I setting up for the rest of the kids if I let her sleep with you under my roof?"

I lower my voice, knowing Roxie isn't too far behind me. "They don't need to know the details, do they?"

"Elise is gonna find out," she presses on. "And—"

"Mom," I say again, bringing her back to focus. "Are you seriously gonna ask my girlfriend to sleep in one of the guest bedrooms like she's too dirty or something to sleep with me?" I stop in my tracks, and a shiver runs down my spine at the humiliation that would be. "It's rude, inconsiderate, and inappropriate."

"Inappropriate is your girlfriend sleeping with you under my roof, *that's* what's inappropriate," she snaps, growing more irritated by each passing second.

"Only for you," I chip back. And knowing exactly her Achilles' heel, I add, "I'm pretty sure Dad wouldn't mind."

I hear nothing but silence from the other side as Mom ponders my statement. After a few more seconds, she finally says, "Let me have a word with him, and I'll let you know."

My lips twist into a smile knowing Dad would be much easier to persuade. "Okay, but in case you send her to sleep in a guest bedroom, I'll be sleeping there with her."

"Andries—"

And before she can add anything else, I cut her off, biding her farewell. "Have a great evening, Mom, talk soon." And with that, I put an end to our phone call.

I sigh in relief, my eyes drifting back to my girlfriend. As I look at her, I can't help but feel terrible for everything she just witnessed. "I'm so sorry. I shouldn't have put our call on speaker," I tell her, my tone deeply apologetic. "I never thought she'd react like that."

We walk toward each other, and, once she stands inches from me, she suddenly leans in, clasps her arms around my neck, and closes the small gap between us for a lingering kiss.

For some stupid reason, my heart does a little somersault at the taste of her lips on mine.

"I love you," she announces in a whisper. "Thank you for all your kind words."

What! Did she really say that? Did she? "Wow," I utter, my eyes never leaving hers. "That's…" I try to find the best words to put on, but I can only find one single thing to say in return, "I love you too, Roxanne."

The way her eyes pierce mine, like she is pleased with my response, makes my heart rush against my chest with satisfaction.

I hold her face between my hands and lean down just enough to press my lips on hers again, but the ringtone of my iPhone breaks through the room, and I find myself sighing in displeasure at it.

"Look who's calling," I say as I pick up the call and put the phone against my ear. Well, looks like Mom didn't waste any time talking to him. "Hi Dad, how are you?" My tone is slightly more enthusiastically than usual.

"So," he begins, sounding playful. "Let me see if I got it right; you wanna have your girlfriend over for Christmas dinner *and* you want her to sleep with you in *your* bedroom?"

"Yep, we're pretty serious so I don't see what the problem is."

Dad keeps quiet for a few seconds as he considers me. "Look, I'll convince your mom, but you owe me one, okay?"

My eyes widen in surprise. That was unusually easy. "Okay, thanks, um, I appreciate it."

"It's all good, I'm glad you met someone." He pauses for a moment and then starts a new subject totally out of the blue. "By the way, Karl should be back in the office Monday. It seems like he was terribly sick or something."

I can't help but look at Roxanne at the mention of her friend Karl. She frowns, most likely wondering what we are talking about.

"Wow, that sounds serious if he needed to take so much time off," I say, mostly to see where he's heading with that.

"Yeah, um, I'm a bit on the fence in giving him that promotion you asked me to after he took an entire month off, but he promised me it won't happen again and I must say this was a first for him. What do you think?"

"I think you can give him a shot, no?" I whisper to my girlfriend who we are talking about now, before I proceed. "If you don't like his performance, then you can appoint someone else."

"True, the other idiot jumped ship for no fucking reason which was a low blow."

"Most likely burnout and exhaustion," I say under my breath. "Anyways, thank you so much for doing this."

"One sec," Dad asks, before I can hang up.

"Yeah?" My heart starts to beat faster over his next set of words and a few scenarios are already crossing my mind.

"How is college going? Are you enjoying business school?" I swallow dryly at his question. What does that even mean? "Elise is always raving about the program, but you never told me if you are enjoying it."

"It's okay, it's just school, Dad." I hope my tone isn't going to raise any suspicion. "You know I've never been too passionate about school."

"I know," he says with a nostalgia I wasn't expecting. A short silence ensues, before he speaks again. "Well, thank you for your honesty. I'm proud of you for sticking around, though."

"Bye, Dad," I say, not wanting to feel even worse than what I'm already feeling for lying to him. "See you soon, and thanks again." I manage to put an end to our phone call, a gush of air rolling off my lips.

"Well, that was close," Roxanne says as she walks back toward me. "I'm surprised he hasn't found out you switched programs yet."

"Me too." I take a deep breath in, thinking how close that was. "Hopefully it'll continue like that."

She wraps her arms around my waist, and looking me in the eyes, she says, "Thank you for everything."

Her voice is soft and warm and it makes my heart race at the sound of it. We're locked on each other but only for a moment. "Mmm," I mumble, trailing my fingers on her body until they reach her cheeks. "It wasn't easy."

"I saw that."

I can't keep the smile from my cheeks as I lean down to her ear, and then whisper, "I hope I'll be well compensated tonight."

CHAPTER 36

Amsterdam, December 10, 2021
Roxanne

Only a few steps from home, the luxurious department store, De Bijenkorf, is a great place to wander around and spend the afternoon—especially when it's pouring outside. Located in the Dam Square, it features high open spaces filled with my favorite brands, spread across multiple floors. It's always been my favorite place to shop at and the fact I'm here with my sister almost feels natural. As soon as we walk in, I'm taken aback by the bright light and the variety of items we can admire just by strolling around.

It's always an expensive hobby coming here, but knowing Lili has a hard time justifying shopping at De Bijenkorf with her salary, I'll have a chance to spoil her. I also need to find something for Andries, since we'll be together for Christmas, he'll most likely give me a present. Plus, knowing him as I do, I bet it's going to be something quite special.

"God, this place is amazing," Lili sighs. She grabs a couple of sweaters and looks at the price tags, almost laughing. "But I think my budget is a bit out of range."

"Don't even think about it. See something you like, and let me know." She glances at me, and I know what's going through her mind; my money comes from a place she's not super happy about. In normal circumstances, she doesn't accept gifts from me—especially in front of our mother, so I add, "You know what I mean. For Christmas."

She nods and we continue walking through the store. Shoppers are everywhere, some with massive piles of bags in their hands and some just drifting and smiling.

"You are coming for the réveillon, aren't you?" she asks cautiously out of nowhere as if she can tell what I'm thinking. "You know despite what happened at my birthday, you are more than welcome to have dinner with us at home on the twenty-fourth."

I heave a long sigh, feeling totally unmasked. "To be honest, I wanted to drag you here to talk to you."

She raises her eyebrows in surprise, and stops scanning through the hangers to focus on me.

"I think I should skip Christmas altogether this year," I announce. Her eyes widen in shock, but I proceed, "What Mama said at your birthday—"

"What! No!" Lili protests immediately, meeting my eyes. "Look, forget her, she's getting old and she's very resentful of what you did."

"I just don't want to see her again," I tell her sincerely. "She's really toxic to my mental health and you can tell her about the bookshop on your own…."

"Roxie," Lili quietly says as she puts her hands on my shoulders, her eyes focused on me. "You can't do that to me, please, let's deliver the news about the bookshop together."

"She might not even like it," I point out, my head tilting down at the memory of everything she told me. "She never wants anything to do with the things I buy for her."

"Hey," Lili gently pulls my chin up forcing me to look her in the eyes. "We might have had our disagreements, but you are my sister and I love you." The warmth in her tone makes me smile. "Please, let's celebrate réveillon together. I'm sure Mama is gonna love the gift."

I huff, pondering for a moment at her words. Even if I'm not entirely on board, it's best to move on for now. "Fine," I say, already tired of standing still in the same place. "Let's go check out some more stuff before I go home."

We start strolling around in silence and I'm glad I managed to distract Lili enough to close the subject about my coming to the réveillon.

Taking in my surroundings, there's a colorful display of lights and decorations representing the season hung between the railings and floors. The place is massive, and after half an hour, we barely make it off the first floor.

That's when I spot him. A familiar haircut and style moving through the store.

Karl.

We didn't exactly end on good terms after everything he tried to do to revenge himself. But now that he's got that promotion at my boyfriend's dad's company, it might be a good opportunity to give him a reminder.

"Keep shopping. I just spotted somebody I want to say hi to," I inform Lili. She nods and wanders off. It's never difficult to find her in the store anyway.

Karl has moved to another floor and he's walking through the men's section looking for who knows what. I don't care. I just want to ensure my future and make sure that if anything is going to get revealed to Andries, it is going to be on my time, not anyone else's.

When I walk in front of him and get his attention, he immediately goes rigid. In another life he'd walk up and hug me, but now he just looks wary.

"Roxanne?"

"Hello Karl. Congratulations on the promotion," I tell him for the sake of politeness.

His eyes narrow. "What are you doing here? You are stalking me now?" It actually makes me laugh that he'd think I'd be following him around.

"I'm just here to talk." I finger a couple of nice shirts. "We didn't exactly end things on good terms, and I wanted to have a chance to close things out."

"I've learned my lesson," Karl sighs. "I'm not gonna say shit to anyone, okay? I just want to live my life in peace."

He's afraid of me. And he should be. It's almost like I can blow his entire life up. His job and reputation would all vanish if I decided to tell people who he really is. It'd also mean telling people who I really am too, so it's not something I'm about to do.

"Great," I say coldly. But there's another part of the whole situation I just can't let go of; the one where he tried to screw me over.

"For future reference, don't try to outsmart me," I say just to confirm it for him.

His eyes narrow and he puffs up. "Or else what?"

"Or else it will cost you much more than a simple month out of the office." He laughs derisively but behind his eyes I can see fear. We both know what I can do to him.

Finally he talks. "You've become a psychopath, let me tell you that. I'm not sure if it's because of your feelings for that boy, but damn you've become totally nuts."

I've always known he has another side. After all, I know him better than anyone, even his own wife and kids. Guys tell me everything. His words sting a bit but then I think about where they are coming from.

"You're seriously going to give up your whole life because of some kid? And confronting me like this? It isn't like you, Roxanne. I…" He drops his voice. "I cared about you."

"It's not because of Andries. I just don't deal well with assholes who try to blackmail me."

"I wasn't trying to blackmail you. I just…" He cuts himself off and I see his hands clenching. "I didn't want to lose you."

"So trying to blackmail me and take my family's store was going to get me back, right? You're a fool." There are other choice words I could use but they aren't needed.

His eyes turn dark. "Your day will come, Roxanne. Karma is a bitch. Believe that. Now leave me alone."

Satisfied, I give him a small smile. Now I can move on and feel confident about the future.

"Take care, Karl. You're gonna need to."

With those words I turn on my heel and walk away. There's a flush of satisfaction. I'm moving on. I have a life. I'm going to change everything into something incredible for myself, and Andries is a big part of that as well.

It doesn't take long to find Lili and she's actually chosen a dress for réveillon that she likes. I happily walk to the counter and get it for her, knowing that one of the best feelings is giving something to other people. I just hope that when I tell Mama about the store that she will feel the same way. Maybe she will.

CHAPTER 37

After the miserable time I had at Lili's birthday, I have no idea why I'm even bothering coming over to spend the holiday with my sister and that old harpy. Actually, I do know why—because Lili insisted. And despite all her flaws, I'll never forget all her help and support. If Mama and I managed to spend all these years without talking to each other when we had to have dinners at the same table, then we could do the same tonight without fail. It's just for two to three hours max and then I'll be right back home. I'm sure Andries must be having the time of his life with his parents and siblings. Despite his mother seeming to be a bit stiff about me, she feels like a breeze compared to mine.

After greeting Lili, I make my way through the hallway, my heartbeat already speeding up in apprehension. I notice the place is just as drab as it has always been despite the Christmas decorations and the discreet tree standing in the living room. The furniture is straight out of an old Sears catalogue and has been there forever.

A wonderful smell of cooking fills the air, causing my stomach to growl in response. Even though she may not be happy I'm coming, I knew Mom and Lili would make a decent meal. It's comforting to smell a turkey. I haven't had anything like it in a long time.

I knock on the entryway to the dining room as I walk in, even though I don't need to. My mother is sitting at the table already moving things around. She still looks so damned frail after being in the hospital. But of course, like the rest of our family, she pushes through the whole thing with a grimace on her face. It's hard to remind myself of a time when she was still healthy and worked at the shop while we were both in school.

"Hi Mama," I force the words out, swallowing all my pride.

She doesn't even turn around. Immediately there's some tension in the air and I wonder quickly if I should have even bothered. Maybe it was a mistake coming here.

"Hey Roxanne?" Lili calls from the kitchen doorway. "Want some wine?"

"Sure," I reply as I take a seat at the dining table. "Everything looks amazing, Lili."

I know that Mama probably had a piece in it, but Lili has always been the decorator. Mama was the cook, and it must be killing her to not be able to march around in the kitchen and tend the stove.

Lili hustles out with the first dish—which is always soup. I'm sure she's rushing the menu because of the tension in the air. Mama still has barely glanced at me and her lips look like a thin red line.

We eat in silence, which is a bit unnerving. My only comment to Lili is about how good the soup is, and I clear the table and offer to help with the other dishes.

It feels like a long time before the main courses emerge due to the awkward tension, and Lili, always the dutiful daughter, carves up the bird and hands a plate to my mother. She keeps her mouth closed but I notice when she moves to pick something up she grimaces with pain on occasion.

There really won't ever be a right time to tell Mama about the bookshop, so when there is another awkward silence and Lili isn't rushing back and forth to the kitchen, I take a deep breath, and, after exchanging a few glances with Lili, who's finally sat down, I turn to Mama and say, "I have something I need to tell you."

Both eyes fall on me, and I can see my mother's wheels turning in her head. What had her stupid older daughter done now? Let's just go ahead and rip the Band-Aid off, shall we?

Blurting it out seems somewhat natural considering nobody is talking. "I bought the bookstore."

Lili sucks in a breath in surprise, feigning to have no idea about it.

Mama on the other hand frowns, looking at me with confusion laced on her face. "You what? What bookstore?"

"The bookstore Lili works at," I explain, barely containing my excitement. "The one you've basically been running for twenty-five years. It's ours. Well, mine technically but I'm gifting it to you both. Merry Christmas."

Only awkward silence follows. Mama still won't say a word, even though she's just been handed a legacy from her daughter. Amazing.

"Oh, my God!" Lili finally gasps. "Roxie! How the hell did you do that?"

The air breaks with the sound of Mother's voice. "You know how she did it. With money she got by being on her back!"

A flash of anger flows through me but I don't bite. It's easier to take a sip of my wine and grind my teeth. "The deal is closed. The place is ours, so in the New Year we can start talking about fleshing out some of the ideas you've had."

Mama just scoffs, and she refocuses on her meal, without an ounce of gratitude. "You think you can bribe your way back into this family, huh?"

I manage somehow to ignore it, instead trying to focus on the fact that my sister seems to be elated. "I thought it would be a nice present for the holidays." Lili smiles at me and nods, quickly glancing at Mama.

There is no further discussion, not that I'm surprised at all. The rest of the meal is eaten in silence. Once we begin clearing the plates, Mama walks away from the table without a word and disappears back into her room.

Now that we are alone it's always easier to talk to Lili. We begin cleaning together which is familiar and the air around us already feels lighter without Mama around.

"Are you gonna join us for dinner tomorrow night?" Lili asks out of nowhere as she puts some plates into the dishwasher. "You know if you just ignore Mama like you did this evening, you can come over."

"I appreciate it, but I won't," I tell her, knowing perfectly well that today was already a stretch. And frankly, it's been too much. I did what I had to do and that's that.

"You have other plans?" she continues, her eyes focused on rinsing the rest of the dishes.

"Yes, with Andries," I admit. "Um, I'm having dinner at his family's estate." Then I dry my hands and take my cup of tea, taking a sip of it.

"His what? Wait." She stops her task mid-way, and turns around to face me. "You are still with him?" She seems totally perplexed and I can't help but wonder why. "I thought you'd stopped seeing him after you spoke to Mama?"

"I never said that," I tell her, quite stunned she even had this idea in mind in the first place. "Of course we are still together."

"How long have you been with him?"

"Since September," I answer.

Lili blinks twice, her mouth wide open. "You've been with him since September? Wow. That's an accomplishment in itself." She then resumes her task and when she asks the next question, my body goes stiff. "And, um, does he know who you are?"

I know exactly what she's talking about, but I pretend otherwise. "Why do you want to know that?"

"Because you are meeting his family tomorrow night and he seems to be serious about you. Don't you think you owe him the truth?"

It's none of her fucking business, really. "I will tell him, *eventually*."

She rolls her eyes at me, head shaking. "Whatever…"

Anger flashes through my body. This whole night has been one big festival of judgement and neither of them will let up even for a holiday. "Okay, be honest. What do you suggest? That I tell him I was a hooker until recently and I'm the owner of an escort agency while eating dinner with his family?"

She turns and glares at me. "Do you really love him, Roxie? Because if you do, you should feel horrible for hiding such a big part of your life from him."

"What I feel is irrelevant." I've said it in my head many times, and it's what is causing the most problems between myself and Andries. The poor guy has no idea what he's gotten himself into and I wonder if he would even care. "I know I should've broken up with him long time ago, but a part of me knows this relationship will eventually end. I just want to enjoy it while it lasts."

Her face becomes a smirk, and I can tell she's horrified at the idea of just using a guy. She's never really dated so she doesn't have a leg to stand on when it comes to relationships, but it's the holier than thou act that is really making me mad.

"And him? Does he love you?" Her words sing with accusation. Like he's too good for me.

"I think so. Look, what is happening here—"

"What is happening here is that you are scared," she interposes, cutting me off. "You're scared because you're in love with a much younger man and a great one with values

459

and morals—something you never had. And you are scared that he won't accept the Roxanne that Mama and I know."

Even though I'd never admit it, Lili is right. I'm scared to death about his rejection. I'm scared to look him in the eye and see nothing but disappointment and betrayal. This should have been a simple fling, nothing consequential. And yet…

"I'm fucked up, I know. He's such a good guy. He deserves so much love and happiness." I suddenly feel a wash of guilt and have to lower my head. The wine doesn't help with the emotions swirling through me.

"I agree, he deserves more than a liar." I can't blame her for her blunt honesty. "Roxie, I know Mama already spoke to you, but please tell him the truth once and for all and leave the poor boy alone. If you really love him, you owe him the truth."

I don't think she realizes it's easier said than done. "And what if he breaks up with me?"

"He deserves to be with someone he can have a future with."

I know she's right. And she has my best interest at heart but also Andries'. He's just a young guy with a whole life ahead of him.

"I know…" I let my words trail off as I ponder hers. "I'm gonna end this. I have to. Should I talk to him face-to-face? Text him? Send him a voice message?"

"I mean, face-to-face would be best, but it's up to you."

"What if I can't do it?" I mean, I've cut men out of my life a hundred times. Why should this one be so difficult?

"This is not about *you*. This is about him. It's better you walk away now before it's too late," Lili advises. She then takes a few steps in my direction and standing right in front of me, she puts on a more serious tone than before. "This boy is becoming seriously committed to you. Don't tarnish your soul with more lies and deceptions at a family dinner."

God, she even had to bring up the religion angle. I guess it is Christmas so maybe that's appropriate.

I'm not entirely sold on the idea of telling him, though. "Do you think he will forgive me? After all, he told me so many times that he loves me."

She almost spits out the words. "What he loves is a lie."

"He loves *me*." She can't possibly understand.

"You? *You* are a fraud!" she snaps at me. "Don't you get it? He thinks you work at a bookshop and that you are a librarian!"

"Just because I'm not working there doesn't mean—"

"Stop! Either you tell him, or I'll do it myself." The threat drips from her mouth like venom. The only problem is that I know she means it.

"You're kidding right? You're my sister!"

"And a human being with a heart," she retorts back. "Something you don't seem to have."

"Fine, I'll tell him tomorrow." It sounds awfully final, but at the end of the day, it might be the right thing to do, especially before the family dinner looming over my head. "I can only hope he'll understand."

"I hope you follow through," she says. "You owe him the truth, Roxie. It's gonna be tough, but so worth it in the end." Her eyes relax and I can see even though she's my younger sister that she really does care. I guess if she didn't, we wouldn't even be having this conversation. Finally I straighten myself and—while it's awkward—we share a goodbye hug. At the end, she squeezes me tightly like she used to.

"Well, I'm gonna go, it's getting late," I announce, before I start gathering my things. "Thank you for the lovely dinner."

Now that Lili told me she's capable to go and tell Andries my secret, I'm completely on the fence. I can't hire someone to take care of her like I did with Karl. Maybe if I tell Andries the truth at his estate, he won't make such a big deal of it in order to keep appearances, or maybe he'll just kick me out like a pariah. Who knows…?

I hit the road en route back to downtown, my mind filled with uncertainty and dread. Maybe our relationship will end, maybe it will survive. *This is not about you. This is about him,* Lili's words replay in my head like a broken record. If the words *I love you* mean anything at all it means at the very least being truthful to them. And while this is hurting me to the point I can't stop the tears from coursing down my cheeks, I know I owe Andries the truth. Truth is love, and I can only hope he'll forgive me.

CHAPTER 38

Amsterdam, December 25, 2021
Roxanne

Andries called after breakfast to inform me that he'd be sending a car to pick me up at five p.m. in Bijlmer to take me to his family estate. I still remember how skeptical I was at first about meeting his whole family, but after seeing how he battled for me over the phone with his mom, I could only accept. At least I've already met his sister, Elise, a couple of times and technically his father once. Even though she's very polite and cordial, she's also the most protective sister I have ever met, kind but very protective. At only seventeen, she's also what most people would describe as down-to-earth, rational, and composed.

I can't say much about the rest of his family, though, but one thing is sure, I imagine his dad, Sebastian, will be fairly surprised—even shocked—to see me back again at his estate but this time as his son's girlfriend. In my defense, though, I had no idea I'd end up dating his son; if I knew, I'd have talked to him much more.

I go through my wardrobe for the umpteenth time, trying to find the perfect dress for tonight that won't scream that I have the means to afford luxury brands—which would force me to admit who I am. My eyes skip through the rows of glamorous and pricey dresses to a more modest black qipao with embroidered red floral print, and a slit from the thigh down. Lili had found it on sale the day we went shopping for Christmas gifts and, as a sucker for more traditional dresses, I had to get it. I remove the qipao from the hanger and put it on the disheveled bed, then take a few mores clothes and dresses for tomorrow, and close the door of my closet.

Lili's words replay in my head as I pack the clothes I picked out into the suitcase, leaving only the qipao I'll wear at dinner tonight on the bed. Everything else I pack mindlessly, including the dress, clutch and heels I'll use tomorrow for his nineteenth birthday.

Nineteen.

Bloody hell!

The guilt grips my insides tightly. I push the suitcase aside and slump on the bed, my arms over my face as I berate myself for not being careful. I should have asked him; I should have known. And now, I'm all in, with a truckload of lies pulling my weight down.

This whole relationship is a faux display of affection. It's not like he committed any crimes though. I'm the fool here, the liar, the woman hiding behind the body of a teenager and a brothel keeper masked with the face of a librarian. So many lies and my head spins from the knowledge of just how bad it is.

Will he be pissed? Will he want me still?

A small part of me is willing to let him go and find a man my age. But the larger part wants to hold onto him, for as long as it will take for the fire that had been ignited between us to burn out. Andries is everything the men I've come across in my line of business are not. My father was the first asshole I encountered. I sigh as the thought of him crosses my mind; thankfully, it evaporated within a nanosecond.

"You owe him the truth, Roxie. It's gonna be tough, but so worth it..." Lili's words echo in my head over and again. It had made sense then, I had even agreed to talk to him, but the feeling of dread spreads throughout my body, clouding my senses. He'll be nineteen soon, and he needs to know the truth before starting a new phase of his life. Yes, he deserves to know.

I heave a long sigh and resume packing. My body lotion goes in next, then my sprays and the red lingerie I ordered from Italy go into the side of the suitcase. It's going to be a surprise. Hopefully, I'll have the last chance to make love to him once more before we part ways.

The what-ifs topple in my head, replacing the feeling of dread. I am a bag of emotions today as the day drags on. With a sudden realization that two hours and a half has passed by while I sit amidst my turmoil, I spring from the bed and go into the bathroom to get my toiletries.

Once everything is packed, I close the suitcase and drop it by the door then walk into my bathroom to take a shower.

I put a finger under the sprays to check the temperature and exhale slowly when the hot water meets my skin. It's been freezing in Amsterdam these last couple of days, so much so that meteorologists are forecasting snow for tonight. This makes the warm water a welcome relief.

I slip under the warm sprays and close my eyes, relishing in the feeling as the water cascades down my back, and slides in between my ass cheeks.

Twenty minutes later, I get out of the shower, dress up, then apply some makeup—not too much but enough to look fresh and natural—and finish by blow-drying my hair.

All of a sudden, the taxi driver who will take me to Bijlmer calls, letting me know he's arrived and is waiting for me downstairs. I don't want to leave my Porsche sitting in their neighborhood for so many nights unattended, so I figured going there by taxi would be my best option. His call sends me scampering around for last-minute stuff I might have forgotten to pack.

I pick up my phone, a long black coat, and my purse then slip into my heels before picking up the suitcase and walking out of my home.

As I'm about to leave, I glance at the open layout of my penthouse one last time, knowing that once I come back here—I'll either still be happy and with a boyfriend, or heartbroken and single.

Well, only time will tell.

* * *

After a twenty-five minute drive, I find myself in front of the high-rise building my family lives in. I glance at my watch and smile; Andries' chauffeur should be here in ten minutes.

The taxi driver helps me with the luggage and since it's way too cold to stay waiting outside, I hurry up, making my way inside the building, and pray for the elevator to work. Fortunately, it seems like it's my lucky day today and I make it to the fourth floor in the blink of an eye. Lili had given me a spare key without Mama's knowledge, so I decide to get inside the flat, knowing they've already left for their Christmas outing.

Thirsty, I head to the kitchen and open the fridge, taking a small bottle of water, which I gulp down in one go. I notice how chilly it's getting inside as the wind spills in through a large crack on the window pane. My phone starts ringing again and this time it's Andries' chauffeur letting me know he's downstairs. *Right on the dot!*

I turn to leave, throwing the empty water bottle in the trash can before closing the kitchen door behind me to at least keep the wind away—and the living room warm for when Lili returns.

The Van den Bosch estate is an hour's drive from here. Not sure if that would be enough time to come up with a speech and get my wits together, but I'll have to figure something out.

"Good afternoon, ma'am," the chauffeur greets as I reach the hallway, before politely taking the suitcase from my grip. He's dressed in a black suit, with a tie that matches his shoes and he's also wearing gloves—the true definition of elegance.

"Good afternoon," I reply back, trailing behind him on the carved-out path. "And Merry Christmas, by the way."

"Thank you, ma'am, you too," he answers, his voice thick and unwavering. The thick coat seems useless as the cold bites into my body and threatens to freeze my blood. Fortunately, the black sedan comes into view, and he doesn't waste time opening the rear door for me.

"Do you work for the family?" I ask, slipping in through the door he's holding open.

"Occasionally," the chauffeur replies.

He seems to be a private person and I'm wary of people like that as I'd have to be choosing my words carefully, so as not to say the wrong thing. I settle into the sleek leather seat and close my eyes for a moment, breathing in and out slowly to calm my nerves.

"Music?" he asks, reversing the car onto the tarred road. My mind boggles for a moment.

Music? Oh!

"Yes, please," I say after I realize what he meant. I've already started building scenarios in my head, and the what-ifs keep piling up.

The car drives at a reasonable pace and the sky has begun to darken, with the clouds closing over the tiny glimpse of sunlight and dragging its curtain unhurriedly over the daylight. As I keep looking out of the window, we cross a few streets baked in Christmas decorations and my breath ceases when my eyes stumble on a couple kissing in the driveway. It looks like the man is dropping the woman off after a day together. Her giggles manage to ring in my head several minutes after we drove past them. The music does nothing to help the dreadful feeling gnawing at my guts.

"Either you tell him, or I'll do it myself."

I promised Lili I'd tell Andries everything, but my heart breaks each time I try to envision his reaction. What I've done isn't fair, especially not to someone I'm sharing such a tight-knit bond with, and I know all too well I've got to tell him the truth.

I still can't believe I'll spend my Christmas beating myself up over and again when I should be basking in the joys of the season.

***

"Few more minutes and we'll be there, ma'am," the driver announces, turning down the radio's volume.

I mumble a short reply, my eyes still shut as I continue to doze in the back seat. Suddenly, though, my iPhone vibrates with a text, prompting me to crack my eyes open. Jeez! And it's Lili herself checking on me: *There yet?*

Well, that's straight to the point.

No, I type, then press *send*.

You're going to tell him, right?

Her reply is rapid. I reread the message, thinking of the best way I can tell her how scared I am.

I have to, right? I reply after a long moment has passed. *Wish me luck!*

The three dotted lines appear on the screen, and then nothing.

Good luck! And Merry Christmas!

I roll my eyes tentatively and send her a sticker with *Merry Christmas* written on it. Perhaps she was typing a long sermon and had decided that this isn't the right time for it. All I need at this moment is someone to tell me that Andries won't kick my ass out of our relationship. That this isn't going to be our last time together and that I'm just exaggerating and making a big deal out of it.

"Here we are, ma'am," he discloses as the car pulls to a stop in the cobblestone driveway. Even with everything bathed in darkness, I can still see how beautiful the property is thanks to the flood lights. Despite being my second time here, it still manages to surprise me. The trees that line the driveway and the large field beside the manor look like something out of a movie but with a modern touch, giving it a breathtaking outlook. The exterior screams elegance and affluence.

The chauffeur opens the door, and with his help, I climb out of the car and straighten my dress. Then, as I run a finger through my hair—hoping it's still in place after having dozed off for a good part of the trip—I cogitate for a second if the dress is appropriate for the occasion.

Oh, stop being paranoid!

Glancing up, I see Andries walking down the stairs toward me. His steps are hurried and the long strides stomping on marble is the only noise to be heard outside. This is no nineteen-year-old; this is a man that has my heart wrapped around his pinky and my soul interwoven with his.

His smile is warm, and the scent of his cologne wafts through the cold hair, filling up my lungs.

"Hey babe," he says with a wide grin, his blue eyes shimmering with delight. "What took you so long to get here?"

My eyebrows furrow quizzically. "It's just six p.m., no?" I say, tugging his head down to kiss him. His lip is cold, but his mouth feels warm as I interlock our tongues, smiling into the kiss.

Andries chuckles as he pulls away, but continues to hold me against his side. "No, it's 6:30. I hope you are ready as everyone is waiting for you."

Oh goodness! My heart tightens at the idea I'm gonna meet his mom. "Yeah, I just need to touch up my makeup and that's it," I say, leaning into him as he tucks my hair behind my ear.

"You look fantastic," he whispers, giving me a quick peck on the cheek. "I can't wait to take this dress off later on," he quips with a small laugh.

I'm about to make a retort when a throat clears behind us. I turn slowly and meet with Elise, who is standing by the top of the stairs. "You guys are gonna freeze out here if you don't bring your asses in!" she shouts, before hurrying herself back inside.

"Come in, let's go meet the rest of the family," Andries lets out, pulling me toward the marble stairs.

The chauffeur has already gone with the luggage, and I didn't even get to know his name to thank him. "Thanks for sending a car over," I say to my boyfriend, rubbing his arm.

"That's nothing, really," he replies.

Once we are about to get in, Andries stops just outside the front door. Standing there, he tugs me into his arms, kissing my hair, then my nose, before trailing his lips to mine.

"Thank you so much for coming over. You have no idea how much this means to me." I smile, reveling in his delicious scent. He looks down for a moment, as if thinking something through, before his gaze locks on mine again. "I don't know about you, but I'm all in and intend to show you how much I love you for the rest of my life."

My lips part and my eyes widen in surprise at his declaration. My goodness! His words are delivered with so much conviction that they ignite a spark at the pit of my belly.

I stare at him; still and speechless. "I, um…" That's the best I can do at this point.

He smiles and pushes open the door. "You don't have to say anything; I know you love me too." Leaning closer to my ear, he then lowers his voice and says, "I see it in the way you moan my name every time my head is between your thighs."

I slap his arm lightly and shush him as I don't want to meet his parents with a flushed face.

We walk in side by side, his fingers still intertwined with mine as if he's offering me moral support.

Breathe, Roxanne.

And yet, I can't, not with the nagging feeling that his parents—especially his mom—can see through my lying tongue and fake life. Mothers have a way of sniffing out lies.

Reaching the entrance, I'm welcomed by a lady that seems to be one of the staff members and she offers her help to take my coat before evaporating through the hallway with it.

"Where's the restroom?" I ask Andries.

"Oh, um, second door on your right," he says, pointing out the direction. He then leans down and gives me a kiss on the hair. "Feel free to join us in the living room whenever you are ready. It's just this way."

I nod and go down the hallway to find a much needed place where I can be alone for a moment to compose myself.

As I get inside the restroom, I close and lock the door behind me, and heave a long sigh in relief, my heartbeat racing in apprehension for the upcoming dinner.

Shit!

This was a bad idea; I shouldn't have agreed to come here. I should have pushed for us to go on a vacation, far away from drama and nerve-wracking family dinners—and especially far away from my sister's logical reasoning—where I wouldn't have had to panic over losing the first man I've ever loved with my whole heart.

I stand in front of the mirror above the sink cabinet, wash my hands, and then start fixing my hair and makeup.

My phone vibrates with a new text as I finish retouching my lipstick. I glance at the screen and seeing that's it from Lili makes my heart beat even faster:

I know you're probably having second thoughts, Roxie, but you have to tell him. X

Boisterous laughter and cheerful chatter filters throughout the house as I make my way toward the room Andries pointed out. It's 6:45, and the property is aglow in Christmas scented candle lights and the colorful light from the huge Christmas tree that stands in the large living room. I take a quick peek and find the room empty. I step inside, glancing at the room decor, and marveling at the way everything matches and there is nothing out of fashion.

Damn it all; I should have been honest with Andries. My Porsche would've been sitting amongst the fleet of luxurious cars outside if I had been.

My eyes dart to the tree. There are cards, and a wish list hanging on the branches. No gifts yet; maybe they'd do it in the morning or had done it already? Whatever… I'm here to spend time with the man I love, get to know his family, and tell him the truth as I can't stand losing him the hard way.

Perhaps I'll summon enough courage to do it tomorrow which is his nineteenth birthday, or before I leave on the twenty-seventh. Just one day more, to bask in the euphoria that comes with being loved by a man that leaves no stone unturned when it concerns matters of the heart.

"Could you help me fix this, please?" a young boy says, pointing at the Santa Claus figure close to the Christmas tree. He has a striking resemblance to Andries, and I could picture a younger Andries holding a Christmas stocking and a hook.

He wants me to help him drape it off the figure's finger. "It won't fit there; we have to hang it where it won't look out of place, and everyone would get to see it without rolling their eyes."

He smiles, giving me a view of his missing front tooth and his brown gum. He then tugs my hand toward the fireplace. "Here, Daddy likes sitting around the fire after dinner on Christmas Day, so he'll get to see it."

I show him how to fix the stocking close to the hearth and save it from the fire.

"You're dragging the lady, Joris," I hear Andries saying as he walks over to where we're standing.

"Oh, not at all," I reply and turning to the little boy who seems be around nine to ten years old, I extend a hand and introduce myself. "I'm Roxanne Feng, by the way."

The little boy shakes my hand and nods. "Joris van den Bosch." The timidity in his voice makes me smile. What a cutie he is!

"Can I take Santa to sit with me at the table?" Another small voice cracks from behind us. Turning around my eyes lay on the most adorable little girl I've ever seen, sporting a red velvet dress with a big bow tied up around her waist. Looks like she's been standing there the whole time and we didn't notice her.

"No, Aleida," Andries replies patiently. "Now, both of you go to the dining room, I need to show the lady the restroom to fix her makeup."

They glance at my face simultaneously and roll their eyes when they notice that my makeup needs no fixing. I had taken the time to do it a few minutes ago, and it's flawless.

"Won't you introduce me to your friend, Andries?" the little girl asks, perking up to look at his brother. Her brown eyes shift between Andries and me.

He groans inwardly. "Go ahead now, you'll meet her at the table and will have the whole evening to talk."

Aleida glances at me. "Promise?"

I chuckle under my breath. "Absolutely."

The moment they turn away, Andries tugs me into his arms and kisses my lips. It's hurried but conveys everything he's feeling and how happy he is to see me. "You look amazing, babe, and you smell like my favorite snack," he breaths against my neck. "Want to get out of here?"

I laugh and push him away gently. "I'm starving, Casanova, and everyone is waiting for us."

He looks behind him at the door that leads to another compartment of the house. "There's no one here," he whispers, trying to drag me inside. "C'mon, don't worry."

But I pull my hand from him just as fast. "Stop it, and tell your dick to calm the fuck down," I scold, eyeing the bulge that is almost visible through his suit pants.

"Just a quickie?" he goes on, giving me a smoldering smile. "I'm so hard, and this dress is a knockout."

He's about to pull up my dress when a female voice calls his name from the hallway.

"Shit!" he mutters under his breath.

"Later, I'll bend over your desk if you want." I peck his jaw, then arrange my dress and put on a poker face.

"Breathe, babe," Andries murmurs beside me, before he puts a hand behind my back and pushes me to walk forward with him.

A blonde woman I don't recognize, followed by Elise and another girl, who's holding a toddler, walk into the living room. My eyes scan their faces until they meet with Elise's. She smiles and touches the older woman's arm. Her face registers surprise, then awe, which mingles with warmth.

"Mom, this is Roxanne Feng, my girlfriend," Andries says as we cross the room to meet them. "Roxie, this is my mom, Julia."

Phew! Her lips turn into a bright smile and her face harbors no ill.

"Roxanne," she says, her voice pleasant and welcoming, and she looks genuinely delighted to see me.

"Good evening, ma'am," I return, matching her tone as we exchange three cheek-kisses. "It's a pleasure meeting you, Andries has spoken highly of you."

"Oh, thank you so much, I can say the same about you." She holds my arms, her face laced with affection. "And please, call me Julia."

Andries then looks at the girl standing beside Elise holding a toddler and proceeds, "Oh, and this is Hannah, the third of the bunch and little Arthur, the youngest."

Like Julia, Hannah is also wearing a carmine gown but her brownish hair is packed in a ponytail, while her mother's blonde hair is set loose.

"Where's Dad?" Andries asks. "Is he hiding or what?"

"I think he's finishing discussing something with the staff regarding your birthday party," Julia tells him before pointing toward the hallway. "Let's go to the dining room, dinner will be served soon."

We leave the living room, and I let them lead the way. I walk gingerly behind Andries, careful to keep my steps even as my heels click on the hard floor.

As we step inside the dining room, I suck in a breath as my eyes stumble on a beautiful medieval tapestry that hangs on the wall. This room feels like traveling back in time, with its big stone fireplace on one side and a long rectangular table for eight in the center topped with white tablecloth, candles, crystal glasses, and silverware. I'm pretty sure this must be the oldest and most preserved part of the estate. It's a formal setting, with top-notch decorations and servers dressed in uniforms lurking in the corners, waiting for everyone to settle before they start serving.

Andries glances at his watch and leaning toward me says, "My dad should be here soon since dinner is at seven."

I give him a cursory glance. "Is my dress okay? I can go change into something more fitting if this is too much for —"

He takes my hand and intertwines our fingers. "I told you this before and I'm gonna keep saying it until you stop fretting," he starts. "My dad is cool, and I bet he's gonna love you." He rubs my knuckles as he proceeds. "There's so much to you, Roxie; I wish you could see yourself through my eyes."

His words calm my racing heart and I let out a sigh in relief. A minute ticks by when we hear heavy footsteps coming down the stairs.

Everyone prances up. Andries mother's face beams. And in this instant, I can see the love she has for her husband spilling through, soaking the room in it. Everything gleams with love and extra attention in this house—from the delicate silverware, the scented candles, the wishes hanging on the tree, to the string lights that hang on the staircase.

"The woman who stole my son's heart," Sebastian exclaims as he walks in my direction. I greet him just as warmly and we exchange three cheek kisses. "Now, I must say, this was really a surprise. But it looks like Andries had his eyes on you since the day you came here. Welcome to the family, Roxanne."

"Thank you, Mr. Van den Bosch," I say, beaming shyly.

"Oh, please, call me Sebastian, I'm not that old, I promise."

A quick chuckle escapes me, but I compose myself right away. "Very well, Sebastian."

Andries squeezes my fingers, while I glance at him from my peripheral and want nothing more than to wipe the smirk off his face.

"I told you he was cool," he mouths with a mischievous grin. "Especially to beautiful ladies like yourself."

Once the initial greetings are over, Andries steers me around to the right-hand side of the table, showing me my seat which has got my name written in front of the place setting. I steal a glance at the name next to mine. Aleida. On my right-hand side is Andries.

"Milady," he says teasingly pulling my chair so I can sit.

He then takes his seat beside me and picks up the napkin embroidered with Christmas trees and Santa Claus.

Julia sits at one of the heads, Andries at her right and Elise at her left, Hannah sits in front of me, and Sebastian in front of his wife.

The head server, a muscular man in his late fifties, comes up with his crew and starts serving everyone.

The smell of roasted turkey, veggies, and Kerststol permeates the air. Dinner rolls are on a silver tray, cranberry sauce, mashed potatoes, gravy, salad, and Brie cheese.

"What's for dessert, Steve?" Joris, who's sitting beside me, asks.

"There's apple pie, chocolate cake, and much more to come," Steve, the server, replies, adding roasted mushrooms with red wine butter to my plate.

"Thank you, Steve." He nods and moves to Andries' plate.

Another server pours the eggnog into my glass, then apple juice for Joris.

"Bon appetite!" Steve says, bowing slightly before exiting the room.

"Steve was a wrestler before he stopped five years ago; now he's running one of the best catering services in the country," Sebastian explains, his eyes on me.

"Merry Christmas, everyone!" Julia blurts.

"Merry Christmas," Andries says, followed by the others.

"Merry Christmas," I utter, looking around the table. Julia nods and smiles.

We dig in and damn, the food is good. The turkey is properly cooked and seasoned, and the mashed potatoes are flavorful and delicious.

"Andries told us you are a librarian," Julia begins, glancing at me albeit briefly.

I chew the turkey slowly, swallow, sip some water, then say, "Yes, I work at one of the oldest bookstores in the country."

"Do you own it?" Hannah asks.

I give a quick nod of my head, and Hannah beams in return. "Now yes, I figured I needed to give myself something befitting after working so hard throughout the years."

Sebastian clears his throat. "That must have cost a small fortune, no? You got a loan I assume?"

Fuck!

I try not to shudder as I utter the next words. "Yes, I took out a loan and it should be paid back in twenty years." I take a long sip of the eggnog, then the water. "You know, it's something I've always wanted, and I didn't want to keep dragging it out any longer," I add with a shy smile. My signature scheming look. "It was so hard, though, and I almost gave up trying to acquire it."

"Wow! That's tremendous," Julia exclaims excitedly.

"Yeah, congratulations, that's a big deal and you deserve it," Hannah replies. She's well spoken, just like her brother.

Congratulations ring throughout, and I can feel my face flushing. I put on a smile and thank them, doing my best to cover the guilt of having to lie yet again. These people had welcomed me genuinely, and here I am, lying through my teeth.

"Congratulations, love," Andries whispers, massaging my knee.

"Thank you."

We resume eating, the only sound from the clatter of cutlery on silverware and Joris chewing a bit noisily. But as a ten-year-old, I don't think I'd have done a better job.

"Is everything okay, Mom?" Andries asks, looking at his mom who seems to be a bit away, lost in her own thoughts.

"Of course," she answers, giving him a polite smile in return.

"You seem to be elsewhere, though," Andries points out. Since his mom doesn't say anything else, he then asks, "Still ruminating about that case, huh?"

Julia frowns at her son, giving a quick glance at me.

"Oh, you have nothing to worry about," I tell her, catching her uneasiness in opening up. "Whatever is said at this table stays at this table."

"What happened?" Andries insists, his interest perked. "Did you speak to the plaintiff?"

Julia heaves a long sigh, and then wipes her mouth on her white napkin as she considers his question. "Well, I'm handling an appeal regarding the alimony for a divorce," she discloses, her eyes focused on me. "Normally, it's pretty straightforward, but this one is quite ugly."

"How so?" I ask, intrigued, leaning forward in my chair to listen more attentively.

"I can't mention names, but the man was married for twenty years and his wife found out he was spending hundreds of thousands of euros on prostitutes over the past ten years. Imagine! Ten years! Assets that belonged to both of them spent on call girls." Julia takes her glass of water and takes a sip, before proceeding. "He even had a property she knew nothing about in Giethoorn where he'd meet with them."

Holy shit! Giethoorn? That's where I used to meet Isaak once a month! Oh my gosh! Maybe it's him! This country is really tiny. I bring my glass of water up to my lips, taking a big gulp to soothe my dry throat.

Julia is still focused on her story and since everyone is looking at her, she continues. "It just breaks my heart, really, those hundreds of thousands of euros should've gone to her and her children, not to a bunch of home-wreckers."

I nearly spit out my water as I hear the last word. How can she say that with such ease in the twenty-first century? While I'm sad for the wife, the onus is on the married man. Nobody is forcing him to pay for sexual services.

"It's a sad reality that I've seen all too well through the hundreds of cases I've worked on," she laments, before resuming her meal.

"It's insane," Andries interjects. "Plus, those prostitutes don't even care if their clients are married or not. As long as they pay—even if half of the money belongs to the wife— they are down for it."

I'm perplexed that he's siding with his mom, but maybe he's just trying to be polite.

"Well, it's none of their business to know if their clients are married or not from what I understand," I tell him, my tone even.

"Which is why Mom is lobbying to change the law," he informs me.

"Andries!" Julia chides instantly.

"Oh, that's okay," I reply with a smile, yet my heartbeat is steadily rising at the idea legal prostitution could be debated in parliament. "Sounds interesting. What kind of changes would you like to see in the law?"

"Well, at the very least, it'd be to hold married buyers liable," she says casually. "Especially if they are using joint-money."

My mouth falls open, and I gasp, both in surprise and shock, at such a radical change.

Before I can even ask another question, Elise jumps in with one herself. "What's your view on sex work, Roxanne?"

"Elise!" Sebastian snaps.

"What?"

"That topic is beyond inappropriate," he scolds.

Elise shrugs, unbothered. "You can't blame me; they were already talking about it," she says, pushing her plate away, and leaning into her chair. Then looking at me, she adds, "Plus, I bet Mom is itching to know what your views are on something she disapproves of."

Fuck!

My palm is sweaty; thank goodness Andries has removed his, else he'd have been curious about me sweating when the room isn't even that warm. I glance at Julia even more surprised and uncomfortable than before. "You do?"

Julia gives the same nonchalant shrug like Elise just did, before forking a bite of her food. "Well, I'd have preferred our country to have adopted the Nordic model, but here we are." She then wipes her mouth with her white napkin, putting it back on her lap. "Sex-work here has become so common and banal that college students would rather be call girls than waitresses."

Elise chuckles. "That's hilarious but so true," she utters, while finishing her meal. "I've come across quite a number of them at school. They call it gigs and go around escorting men twice their age to social functions and sometimes have sex with them afterward." While there's no hate or malice in her tone, I can't help but feel utterly uncomfortable as I listen to her comment.

"Gosh, that's awful," Andries blurts out, joining in the conversation. "Soon enough and they will be teaching sex-work at school."

I feel tempted to share a piece of my mind regarding the advantages of our laws compared to the Nordic model, but little Aleida, who's sitting beside me, pokes my arm over and over again until I pay attention to her instead.

"Have you ever been to China?" she asks, her big brown eyes on me, and her voice so sweet and innocent. "You look like Mulan but with blonde hair."

"Oh, thank you so much, that's really kind of you." I stroke the top of her head, enjoying much more my current chat with this five-year-old. "Yes, I was actually born in Shenzhen and then moved here when I was six."

"Wow," she utters, clearly impressed. "Did you meet the emperor like Mulan did?"

I chuckle, my heart melting at how cute she is. "Not really, no," I admit. "We no longer have an emperor, just a president."

"And the Great Wall? Have you been there?" Joris asks as he joins the conversation.

"No, I haven't. Maybe one day I'll go back and visit it."

"Can we go with you?" Aleida continues as she bounces in excitement in her chair.

And Joris starts doing the same as his sister. "Yes! Yes! Please! Please!"

"We'll all go together," Andries interposes, putting an end to their agitation.

Fortunately, Aleida's intervention has helped to switch the table conversation to countries and places we'd like to visit. A much appreciated change! The atmosphere becomes lighter, and, amid laughter and joy, the table gets cleared. While we speak about our bucket list, Steve brings in a trolley with cakes and speculoos cookies.

"Yummy!" Aleida exclaims, clapping her hands.

Everyone's attention is on the delicious desserts Steve is serving when all of a sudden impish-Elise breaks the silence with a question that freezes me on the spot. "Do you think the government should implement the Nordic model, Roxie?" She looks at me with a smirk on her face, as if she's trying to make me feel tense and nervous by discussing such delicate subjects.

Andries huffs in annoyance at her. "Enough, Elise!"

"It's fine," I tell him with a pat.

Andries mutters something under his breath but I shush him, and my attention returns to his sister. "Everyone needs a chance at survival, a means of livelihood, and if that works for them, why not? I think our current model is okay."

The table has gone silent as soon I finish my sentence. Even Steve has stopped sharing the cake and stands behind Julia to listen.

"Care to expand?" Julia asks, leaning forward in her seat.

Damn it! I take a deep breath in and out, gathering my thoughts as quickly as I can. "To me, the Nordic Model is like saying you can still bake bread, but no one can buy it from you." I go on, fueled by the need to defend something that had put clothes over my back, given me a penthouse and a car some people can only dream of. "If the current model gets replaced by the Nordic one, what will happen is that sex workers will work illegally and they'll more likely become victims of violence, since they won't be able to afford to decline clients due to its scarcity. Plus, clients will want to hide their real identities, meet in remote areas, try to take condoms off, which increases the risk of being exposed to STDs. It happened in France when they started this model."

Oh. My. God.

My head bends over my neck as everyone stares, I can't even bear to look at anyone but my own place setting. What are they thinking? Did I go overboard?

Fuck!

I should have just shrugged and uttered a simple yes. Why did I have to speak like that at a Christmas table?

"Good pitch, but I'm still against it," Elise says, breaking the deafening silence.

Julia gives me a polite smile, and then suddenly stands up. "Steve, can you bring a digestive to the library for Ms. Feng and I, please." My eyes travel up to meet hers as she starts walking. "Come on, let's go check out the books; I'm sure as a librarian you'll love them." She winks at me and nods toward the door.

Oh goodness! What have I done? I swallow dryly at her invitation, but abide.

"Excuse me," I mumble apologetically, and Andries stands up to pull out my chair, helping me to leave the table.

As we stand in front of each other, he lowers his voice and discreetly says, "Stop freaking out; she loves you already, we all do."

Love.

After everything I've done to him, I don't deserve it.

I nod and stalk behind Julia, my body tense all over. Jeez! I can even hear my pulse throbbing in my ears. The library is on the other side of the floor, and candlelight flickers all through the hallway, casting a soft glow in the house.

When we enter the library, I'm instantly taken aback at how beautiful it is—floor-to-ceiling bookshelves cover the walls, and darkly polished mahogany and walnut lend an air of the smoke-filled gentleman's lair. A sitting area occupies the center of the room, while a desk rests against a big window.

"I hope you didn't take offense at Elise's curiosity," Julia begins, walking over to the bookshelves. "She loves to talk about controversial subjects."

"Oh, that's totally okay," I reply, strolling at a safe distance behind her.

"I wanted to show you a little something," she says and pulls out a hardcover book boldly inscribed with Andries' name in gold-colored letters.

"This was the book he started with when he wrote his first poem at the age of twelve," she announces, before making her way to the couch where we sit beside each other. "He's always been a brilliant man, mature, kind, loves wholeheartedly, and introverted but goes out of his way to do things for people even when it makes him a bit uncomfortable."

My heartbeat accelerates and my balled fist digs into my flesh. This wasn't about lecturing me about my views on sex work as I initially thought, but about her son. Julia wants to pick my brain. Maybe she's figured out I'm a liar, and her son definitely deserves better.

"Does he know you keep them?" I ask, taking the book from her grasp and flipping through the pages.

"No. I don't think he does," Julia says with a small smile.

Even for a twelve-year old, the poems are quite good. And, not surprisingly, they all talk about love.

"He's always been a bit different from the rest," she continues.

"I know," I tell her, my voice soft.

"Did he tell you how different?"

"I think so." I swallow dryly, hoping she won't insist any further that I get down to the gritty details. The last thing I want is to talk about Andries' intimate life with his mother.

Julia, on the other hand, looks at me with a smile spreading across her lips. "You see, just like this book that no one knows I've kept here, Andries doesn't know that I'm aware he was a virgin before being with you. He sees love and sex as interlinked things. If he gives himself to you, it's because he trusts you and believes there's a future with you. Which brings me to my next question: have you ever been married?"

What the hell!

She isn't subtle at all. Her face is still friendly, and I perceive no arrogance, but just a mother, looking out for her son.

"Andries is my first serious relationship," I tell her sincerely. "I've always been very wary of men until I met him." I can feel the warmth spreading through my face as I say those words. "He's God sent in my eyes, ma'am."

"Call me Julia, please." She exhales. "What happened? Bad experience?"

I chuckle. "No, just bad observations. Most men are trash and cheaters. The thought of them makes me cringe. I used to think they are all the same until I met Andries."

Julia laughs. "That's fair. Most people learn from experience, but others from observing." She puts a hand on my shoulder. "I'm happy you're free from all of that. I don't have to worry about you taking out your revenge on my son."

"You don't have to worry about anything like that, Julia. Andries is safe with me."

Liar!

"He's just eighteen… sorry, nineteen. I can't help but worry. He's a so kind and wholehearted and I'd hate for him to go through any form of stress in his relationship."

Someone knocks on the door a few times, and after Julia instructs to come in. Steve enters the room with a tray containing two mugs and cakes that he leaves on a low table.

"Thank you, Steve," she says before dismissing him.

We have a bite of our cake in silence, until Julia asks me another blunt question. "What are your intentions with him?"

I nearly jump out of my skin when I hear her speak again. "Well, um, I love him with my whole heart," I say tiptoeing around the subject. My stomach bottoms out with dread as I look into her inquisitive brown eyes. "But I'm scared that he's going to hurt me, scared that this won't work out since he's still so young and has yet to figure his life out."

Julia sighs. "Knowing him as I do, I think he wants you for the long haul."

Andries' words replay in my mind, and I pick up the mug to cover my flushed face. *"I don't know about you, but I'm all in and intend to show you how much I love you for the rest of my life."*

Julia does the same and takes a long sip, then places the mug back on the table in front of us. "Promise me you won't hurt him, Roxanne," she asks imploringly, "and even when you get tired of him, promise me you'll let him down slowly."

I've got no idea if she knows something I don't, but I simply agree with her request. "I will."

She nods but looks unconvinced. "And, please, always be honest with him. He's a sucker for it, and he values it more than anything."

"Sure," I say, before taking another sip of my drink.

"Great." She smiles at me and then adds, "As his girlfriend, I hope you'll always have his best interest at heart."

* * *

Julia had drilled the words into my brain over and again. She's probably scared her son loves me too much and I'm going to mess it up by hurting him. I have no intention of hurting Andries. If anything, my only fear is the lies I've been spinning.

After we bid goodnight to everyone, Andries takes me up the stairs to his room like a kid taking his Christmas gift to unwrap, and I can't help but giggle at his enthusiasm.

Once we get inside and he locks the bedroom door, he observes me as if trying to figure something out. "You okay?" he asks, massaging my shoulders that are rigid with fatigue.

"Yeah, just knackered," I reply, pulling off the heels and then my earrings, and finally my dress. "I'm super excited for tomorrow, though."

"Huh-huh." He cackles. "What did my mom say?"

I shrug nonchalantly, as I go and open my suitcase to get my silk robe. "Nothing. She just showed me a few books and talked about you."

"Pleasant stuff I hope?" he asks, his muscled chest flexing as he pulls his white shirt over his head.

I giggle. "Absolutely."

While Andries is taking off his shoes, I take in my surroundings, and notice how spacious and modern his bedroom is compared to the rest of the manor. However it's the framed picture on his desk not too far from where I'm standing that catches my attention. I take a few steps, and, stopping in front of his desk, I take the frame in my hands, observing the photo more attentively. It's a picture we took together in Ghent and the fact I'm seeing it printed and framed and standing here in his bedroom makes my heart thump in my chest.

I put it back on the desk, and refocus myself. I don't want to let this silly photo leave me emotional.

"Did you have a good time?" I hear him asking as he stands behind me, his arms embracing me.

I nod, turning to face him and I wrap my arms around his neck. "It was perfect. Your family is so comforting, and I didn't feel out of place."

"Even when they were throwing those outrageous questions about sex-workers and so forth?"

I smile. "Even then. It was an interesting conversation."

Andries runs his palm over my face, his eyes staring at my lips.

"I love you, Roxie."

"I love you, Andries."

He bends down just enough to kiss me and then we remain quiet for a long moment, basking in the comfort of being with each other. It feels safe, warm and the silence isn't awkward. I trail my eyes down his face, capturing the way he purses his lips when he's deep in thought. Right now, there's a small smile playing at the corners of his lip as he stares intently at me. My body warms from the knowledge of his eyes undressing me, wanting me.

"I've got something for you, wait here," he announces as he leaves and walks into his ensuite dressing room, then emerges with a box-shaped thingy, sheathed in gift wrap.

"Merry Christmas, babe," he says excitedly as he hands me the gift. "There's another one under the tree for you. My parents got you something."

Damn!

My eyes itch, and I can feel the tears pooling. "That's so thoughtful of them." I sniff. "God, I don't deserve this."

Andries pulls me to him and whispers against my ear incoherent words that sound like poetry and love notes. I let him hold me for a long minute, then disentangle from his arms.

"I also have something for you," I say, putting his present on the desk before I go to my suitcase and pull out the gift I had gotten for him.

"Here." I hand it to him, hoping he'll like it. "Merry Christmas, *sweetie pie*."

Andries' eyes go wide, and I can even see the enthusiasm in his gaze as he starts unwrapping my gift. "Fuck! This is terrific!"

I want to tell him it's just a notebook, but the excitement in his face is so palpable that it'd be awful of me to say something so demeaning.

"Wow, this is incredible," he comments, observing the carmine-colored notebook with his initials engraved on it in gold letters. "A. V. D. B.," he reads out loud with a wide smile that makes him look like the nineteen-year-old that he is. "Jeez, I love this."

"Since you always write on banal notebooks, I figured having a beautiful one would match with the words you put in it."

"I'm gonna pen down every thought, every feeling, every moment, every laugh in here. It's going to be filled with so many memories."

Every moment? Does that mean he'll write down the moment I tell him the truth too?

"Go ahead, open yours," he says, visibly excited.

I peel open the wrap, unveiling a box. I pull it open, and my jaw drops as my eyes behold the necklace with a ruby in the shape of a heart. It's so beautiful that I'm speechless, looking at it with total awe. The gold chain looks exquisite but so pricey that I feel guilty for him having spent so much money on me.

"No, don't say it," Andries interposes as if he could read my thoughts. "I saw it and knew it was meant for you. You'll look stunning tomorrow at the party with it." He tugs me to himself and bends my head backward. "This neck ought to be adorned with the finest gold." He kisses my neck, sucking on the throbbing vein just beneath my jaw. "So beautiful, so pure, and all mine."

"Ah," I whimper as he sucks and bites.

After I put the box on the desk, freeing my hands, his fingers trail down over my robe, and, with my help, he removes the garment, pulling it away, before focusing on my bra and taking it off. He hisses a breath as his eyes take in my breasts with my nipples stiff and erect.

My arousal intensifies, and I let out a whimper at the feel of his teeth and tongue on my nipples, caressing them. Oh gosh... I ache to be lowered over his hardened member and fucked mercilessly as he nips on my skin, sucking and biting while he drags his mouth downwards.

"Tell me how much you want me, Roxie," he growls under his breath as he continues to worship my body with his tongue.

"I want you so bad that my insides feel like they're on fire. Fuck! I'm so wet."

A little huff of breath leaves his mouth as he glances up at my flushed face.

"Take off your panties," he orders in a low tone, closing his eyes as if the sensation is too much for him to bear.

"Babe… Your parents will hear us," I say, trying to be the logical one as the heat of the moment builds up around us.

"We're gonna be quiet, and it's gonna be quick," he says, pulling my panties down my legs. "I want you here, right on this desk."

I give him a bewildered look, heaving a long sigh.

"You promised," he purrs when I refuse to budge, even though my pussy is throbbing, and my clit is tingling at the idea we could fuck now.

"But I didn't mean it," I say, mostly to tease him even more.

"Sure?"

I laugh and try to wriggle free from his grasp. "Yes!"

He kisses me again, slow and filled with fervor. His lips latch on mine as he sucks on them without holding anything back. I moan when his fingers start digging into my flesh, searching, stroking, worshipping.

"I've waited to do this all evening. I wanted to finger you under the table, but Joris kept peeking under it. Fuck! I've been so hard, and my balls ache from wanting you."

I plunge my fingers into his hair and pull. He gasps into my mouth, biting down on my lips as he fights to control himself.

"Fuck," he screeches, pushing me gently toward the table. "You're driving me crazy."

His lips are on the valley between my tits, teasing me before he latches on my nipple.

My hand slides down his chest to his belt and zipper. My fingers deftly push away his pants, tugging them down his legs.

He teases my nipples until they're pointing outwards and aching. I arch my back, pushing my tits forward, unashamed as the sensation ratchets.

Tension rises through his corded muscles, and he lets out a loud moan. His breathing is rapid and ragged, and his rock-hard member presses against my belly.

Damn it! I want to feel him, I want him so bad, and my insides coil as he fingers my pussy hole; sliding in a finger, then another, spreading my juices around to show me what he wants. "Bend over the desk."

The moment I do so, he angles his cock and plunges in with a full force that sends me scampering for something I can hold onto.

Fuck!

My heart pounds and I squeeze my eyes shut then move my hips to meet his thrusts. With his breath hot against my back and his hands wrapped around my waist, we match each other's thrusts, yielding to pleasure so intense and beautiful.

He pushes his right hand under my body and grabs my tits, massaging them roughly as he increases the pace, ramming his body into mine and pulling me to meet his thrusts.

"Yeah… Ahhh," I squeal tightening my pussy muscles, eliciting a groan from him.

He pulls out almost entirely, leaving just the tip. I want to smack his head for teasing me, but his next move has me jamming into the table and forcing its contents onto the floor. I lift my hips, holding the table so tight that my knuckles turn white.

He hit against my G-spot then pulls out.

"Babbbee, I thought you said it's going to be a quickie!" I moan angrily as he keeps teasing me.

"It is!" Then he pushes his dick, hitting my G-spot over and again.

Fuck! My body bounces wildly as he drags me over the edge. "Please... Ahhh... please...!" I whisper.

"Please what?" He breathes against my ear, kissing my earlobe, with his right fingers pinching my nipples repeatedly.

"I'm close! Fuck, right there!" I force my eyes to stay open, breathing hard as Andries pumps into me. Bolts of sensations hit me, and I bite my lips to rein in the moans that are getting louder and louder. I tilt my pelvis forward, silently begging him to fuck me harder. His movement becomes more erratic, and he uses his free hand to push me against him, so I can meet his thrusts and match his pace.

I can feel my orgasm building as my innermost muscles contrast. Blood spills from my lips from biting it so hard.

"Fuck!" he groans, gyrating his hips, as the movement slows.

We both throw back our heads. Each thrust is a burning brand, it's scorching. Unwavering. Mind-blowing.

"Fuck! Oh my God! Yes!" I whimper as we ride out our orgasms, his seed spilling into me, and some dripping down my thighs.

He peppers my lower back with kisses, making his way upwards until he gets to my ear. "You've turned me into a beast, babe. I can't believe I'm hard again."

I chuckle before saying, "At your age I wasn't expecting otherwise." His voice sends a shudder ripping through my exhausted body. I twirl around and smush my face into his sweaty neck.

Then leaning closer to his ear, I whisper, "How about I give you a blow job as a pre-birthday gift?"

CHAPTER 39

V.D.B. estate, December 26, 2021
Roxanne

Soft knocks rouse us at the early hours of the morning. Andries groans and snuggles into my arms, his fist folded under his chin. He's breathing softly and the sound is comforting. The knocking sounds reappear again, this time accompanied by Joris's voice and a failed attempt to crack the door open. "C'mon, Andries, let's play in the snow."

Huh? Did it snow overnight? It must be so damn freezing outside, all I want to do right now is cuddle up and sleep till…wait! Today is Andries' birthday! Oh gosh!

The realization hits and sends me slumping back on the pillows. Andries mumbles in his sleep, the edge of his lips moving in a small smile. I pull closer to him and kiss his lips, running my fingers through his disheveled hair.

"Happy birthday, babe," I whisper against his lips.

"It's morning already?"

I chuckle and tickle his sides. "Yes, and Joris came by, he's asking for you to come and play in the snow with him."

He mutters a curse and swipes his palm over his face. "Did you say today is my birthday?"

I roll my eyes at him. "Yes."

He wraps his arms around me, his eyes slowly opening. "Can I get another blow job, then?"

"Oh, you!" I take my pillow and slap it on him.

"Ouch!"

"Stand up and get dressed; your brother is at the door."

"I'll spank his ass. He should have stayed away. He knows you're here."

I laugh. "He doesn't know you're a sex freak."

He grudgingly leaves the bed and yanks a t-shirt over his head and a pair of boxers. "What do you want, Joris?" he asks, opening the door slightly to peer at his brother.

"Can I come in at least?" Joris asks, making to push the door further.

Andries glances back to check if I'm dressed. I scramble off the bed and pull my nightie over my head, then comb my fingers through my blonde hair.

Andries mutters a clipped yes. The displeasure is evident on his face, but Joris ignores his brother and treads into the room. "Miss Feng, there's a snow battle happening in the gardens," Joris announces in a very serious tone. "Mom and my sisters have paired together, so Dad and I need a team," he explains, folding his hands across his chest.

"Right, but today is my birthday, and I'm supposed to stay in bed and spend time with my girlfriend," Andries interposes.

Joris peers up at me, his young face sporting an adorable pout. "Please, Miss Feng, you have to help me on this one. We can't win if it's two against four."

Andries exhales, most likely knowing I can't resist the cuteness of Joris' plea. He's also on the verge of giving in, but at the same time, I know he's looking forward to being lazy in bed the whole morning with me. He tilts his head toward me, most likely checking what I prefer to do. I smile, telling him to grant his brother's wish.

"I'll stay out of your way throughout the day," Joris says, his voice cracking like he wants to cry. "Please! Please…."

"Come on, Andries, it's gonna be fun," I press on, twitching my lips to rein in the laughter that is bubbling inside.

"Twenty minutes and I'm out. It's freezing out there and I don't get why you all are planning this suicide mission."

Joris looks confused. "What's a *suicide mission*?"

"It's when someone knows how dangerous something is, but still goes ahead to indulge in it," I chirp in when I realize Andries is about to unleash something stupid.

Andries scoffs and raises a brow at me. "Or you could say it's when you no longer give a crap about life, but decide catching pneumonia is the way to die quicker."

Joris smiles, pushing his mane of brown hair back. "I think you're wrong. Playing in the snow is no suicide mission, it's fun. And it's not anyone's fault that your birthday falls on the day we have a snow date."

Snow date?

This boy is cracking me up, but I can't laugh because of how pissed Andries is. He'd find a way to get back at me and I don't want to spend the rest of my day apologizing for siding with his brother.

Andries walks to the door and tugs it open. "We'll meet you downstairs in about twenty minutes," he says, giving his brother who is smirking, a sour look.

"Ten," Joris argues with a pout.

"It's either twenty or you can go find another team, man."

Joris looks like he wants to argue but clamps up and raises his hands in a sign of surrender when Andries gestures at the door. "I'll see you in twenty then, thank you Miss Feng!" he yells over his shoulder.

Andries closes the door with a soft bang. "I should've wrung his neck," he says, puffing out his cheek.

I scowl playfully. "You just want to stay in bed and get dirty." He rolls his eyes. "Let's go get a quick shower."

He grasps my hand, pulling me into him. "A shower with you won't be quick, though."

"You said we'd be outside in twenty minutes."

"I can take as long as I want," he protests, taking me in his embrace, his mouth finding its way to my neck.

But I hold my hand up to his chest and push him back. "You must keep to your word. Little things matter."

He gives me a disgruntled look, then huffs as he removes his t-shirt. "I'll remind you later when you fail to fulfill your promise."

Huh? "What promise are you talking about now?"

Andries glances down at the bulge under his boxers with a smirk.

I mutter something in Chinese. He asks me to translate but I refuse. When his eyes turn dark I leave his side and fly to the bathroom.

***

Twenty minutes later we find ourselves heading outside in order to play in the snow with the kids. I am clad in about three sweaters, a coat, gloves, and thick stockings. Andries has less on, but enough to keep him warm in the cold.

We make our way to the stairs while Andries is still sulking. The expression on his face is hilarious as he grumbles under his breath.

Reaching the outdoors, I can't help but be surprised at how white the gardens are, even the swings hanging on the oak tree not too far from the kids are covered in snow. Joris smiles up to his ears when he sees us approaching and runs in our direction.

The excitement is contagious and soon enough, we join in the happy chatter. The kids play around in the snow, throwing snowballs in the air and laughing excitedly. Julia and Sebastian are not left out. I stand transfixed, watching them throwing snowballs back at the kids and each other like in a true battlefield. Oh, there's also a snowman, uncompleted though.

"Come on, let's go and finish that up."

Andries and I focus on the snowman, trying not to get hit with a snowball on the face.

But it's too late. Soon enough and his sisters are throwing snowballs at us, from every corner. We are surrounded by a snowball attack! But when Andries starts packing snow and makes to haul at them, they stop, running away. We refocus on the snowman, who still needs a head and arms. A few instants later, Hannah comes over to join us, then Elise.

"Happy birthday, brother," Hannah says, followed by the others. Everyone echoes the words and his face beams, until it hits a snowball thrown by Elise.

Everyone erupts in laugher but him. "For fuck's sake, Elise!" he snaps, rubbing his face to remove the remaining snowflakes. "You're gonna see!" He gathers as much snow as possible into his hands and Elise starts running away while Andries runs behind her. The sight of it is hilarious and everyone keeps laughing at them, watching it all unfold. Andries throws a snowball at her, hitting just her coat. When they return, everyone has finally stopped and we can focus on finishing the snowman. I notice the parents have returned inside and there's only his brothers and sisters left with us.

"How many people have you invited for your birthday?" Hannah asks her brother, her gloved hands shaping the head of the snowman.

"Just a few, it's going to be a small party."

Elise chuckles humorlessly. "If you think Dad is gonna let you have a small party you're very mistaken. Every single college student I know is attending."

Everyone agrees except Andries. I guess Elise is right. He's an introvert, but his dad is not going to let him have his way.

Andries looks at me and then asks, "Maybe we should just cancel the party, and go for dinner then?"

Everyone echoes a no. Elise too. She winks at me, before pulling her brother away.

"See it this way—it's your nineteenth birthday, and a chance to introduce your girlfriend to everyone you've ever known," Elise says, looking at me with a conspiratorial grin. "It's only going to be for a few hours anyway; then you can crawl back into your shell."

Andries pinches her jaw playfully, scampering away when she tries to retaliate. "You're just looking for an opportunity to play Cinderella; stop making this about me."

"But it is about you. Oh, happy birthday, by the way, *lil sweetie pie*," she quips. "Does that sound familiar?"

"It does, but it sounds like crap coming from you," he drawls.

After everyone has gone back inside, Andries sits down beside me on the snow, stretching his legs forward. "You hungry?"

"A bit, you?"

He nods, "Yeah. I perceived coffee when we were coming down. Let's go grab a cup and some of Steve's muffins."

"Is Steve the cook?" I ask, stretching my hands for him to help pull me up.

"He used to be, but now he's got his own catering company. He's only here for the Christmas holiday, Dad hired him."

"Oh. He's really good."

Andries chuckles. "Good is an understatement."

We shake the snow off our bodies, before making our way into the house and heading to the kitchen.

Steve perks up when he sees us approaching. He barks orders and before I can blink, breakfast is brought to us on two trays, each one with mugs—one filled with tea—and plates containing muffins, and cinnamon cakes.

"What's your plan for the day?" I ask Andries, accepting a warm cup from one of the staff members.

"Got nothing mapped out except writing," he replies. Then a smirk graces his lips and leaning closer to my ear, he whispers, "Maybe we could go upstairs and spend some time together?"

"Maybe," I say with a grin.

After a few more slices of cake, I carry my tray to the sink and make to rinse them.

"No, Miss Feng, please leave the dishes," one of the housekeepers says pleading with her eyes for me to not insist.

"It's just one," I return.

"We take care of things around here, and you're the Van den Bosch's special guest."

I drop the tray and wash my hands. "Alright, well thank you, then."

Her face flushes. "You're welcome, ma'am."

"Babe, I've got a few phone calls to make," Andries announces, his phone in his hand. "Can we catch up later?"

"Sure," I say as he leans in to kiss my lips.

"If you need more tea or food, you come right here and they'll have it ready for you, or you can ring the maid to bring a cup to the room," he explains.

"Okay, thanks."

"See you later."

After Andries exits the kitchen, I leave too but trail behind one of the men I see carrying stuff around the house. He passes through a back door, then walks down another hallway until he reaches another compartment of the house.

It's a ballroom and sheesh, the decorations are breathtaking. Damn! My breathing ceases and my mouth hangs open as the makeshift water fountain flows; they set it up in a way that no drop touches the floor.

There's a long table with wine glasses and flutes. Flowers are arranged against the wall, with neon lights dancing around in circles.

"What do you think, ma'am?" one of the men asks, coming to stand beside me as I take in my surroundings.

"It's… it's… Gosh, it's breathtaking."

He chuckles. "I think so too. This is one of my best jobs and it keeps getting better."

After a few more minutes perusing the hall and marveling at the decorations, I go back to the kitchen in order to drink some water, but I find it filled with staff running around to get everything ready.

It's going to be a long day. I'm excited and scared about the party. Andries' friends and acquaintances will all be here tonight and I'm yet to tell him the truth about myself. Maybe tonight, I'll tell him after the party.

Maybe.

"You okay, ma'am?" Steve asks, concern lacing his deep baritone voice.

"Yes, I am," I say, taking a glass and filling it with water.

"Okay, I just noticed the gloomy look on your face and —"

"Oh, just dreading the party," I tell him, cutting him off.

"Afraid of the crowd, huh?"

"A bit," I reply, drinking my glass in one gulp.

I'm not dreading the crowd, but the fact that I'll have to tell Andries the truth.

Maybe the crowd too. What if any of my girls are in attendance? After all, Elise mentioned a lot of college students are coming. Gosh, what have I got myself into?

But you're telling him the truth anyway, right, Roxie?

* * *

We spend the rest of the day on the indoor terrace, snuggling on a couch. Andries is already writing in the notebook I offered him while I'm reading a book Julia had recommended to me from her large library.

And yet, I can't concentrate on the words as his face keeps flashing in my mind—especially his reaction when I'll tell him everything.

Andries is humming a song under his breath, engrossed in his writing, and unaware of the anxiety I'm going through. It's crawling up from my toes, seeping into my bones, and rendering me helpless. Jeez! I wish for the umpteenth time that I had been forward from the onset.

"Hi, I'm Roxanne Feng and I'm an escort and agency owner."

The truth would have saved me a lot of trouble. Maybe, it'd have been only a fling, a few weeks, a month or two, then go our separate ways. Not this entanglement with a truckload of expectations and emotions!

I steal a glance at him. His lower lip is in between his teeth and his brows are slightly furrowed in concentration.

"What are you thinking so hard about?" Andries asks, startling me.

I didn't even notice he had looked my way. "You."

That isn't a lie.

His body shifts toward me. "Care to share?"

"Nope."

He huffs in displeasure. "Fine." His attention returns to his notebook, but he then looks at me again and says, "I'm also thinking a lot about you and writing everything down, but I won't share shit with you either."

I snort at his little teasing. "I can always steal your notebook and read it when you aren't around, you know," I tell him.

"Then, I'm gonna make sure you won't find it."

That earns him a kick to his shin.

"Ouch! What did you do that for?" he rebukes, bending down to massage the spot.

I wet my lips moving myself forward to meet him. Then I give him a kiss on the cheek as a form of apology, and say, "I was thinking how much I love you."

"Liar," he retorts. "But I'm gonna pretend I believe you."

As we look at each other, this should be the perfect moment to tell him the truth, but I simply can't bring myself to ruin his birthday with my ugly lies. Maybe tomorrow morning would be better, or maybe never....

* * *

Despite the heaters, the black gown I have on with a slit from the hip bone down offers no help against the cold as we cross the hall that leads to the ballroom. I shiver slightly, and a soft moan slips from my slightly parted lips when Andries tugs me closer to him, breathing on my neck.

A few eyes turn to stare as I stand outside with my boyfriend, waiting for him to be announced. Some girls frown when their eyes notice my arm intertwined with his, but they're civil enough not to stare for too long. They're probably wondering who the heck I am since this is our first time out in the open like this.

"You're gonna steal the show tonight, babe. Your dress is exquisite," he says, nipping on my earlobe.

"It's your party, and I'm just the arm candy."

He sucks in a breath, lifting his shoulder. "You're much more than that, Roxie." His eyes are on my face and for a split second I want to kiss him, but this is not the right time to get all lovey dovey. There are guests to attend to, and a cake that needs to be cut and devoured.

A nagging voice keeps telling me to go in first. I don't know how to tell Andries this as he wants us to go in together upon Dan announcing him. I'm scared. What if it's the universe giving me a chance to spend more time with him before we part ways?

The room is buzzing. It's a good thing I chose the black dress as all the girls are dressed to the nines and their makeup is flawless. The whole place is soaked in so much opulence and intoxicating scents that my head spins. The last time I'd been in a room filled with college students, it was at Dan's party and I wasn't expecting to renew the experience so soon. And to cap it all off, it's my boyfriend's party, not the kind I can just lurk around in the dark and leave anytime I want.

When it's finally our time to head in, the crowd erupts in loud applause and some girls even scream his name. Glancing around the ballroom, I notice Elise with two girls, a glass of champagne in her hand, delighted at the show we are giving ourselves.

I look at my boyfriend instead. My mouth twitches in a small smile as my eyes travel down his body. His chiseled face glows under the yellow bulbs. He looks happy? Angry? Amused? I can't tell as his eyes rove across the faces scampering around him, vying for his attention.

I sulk and pull a glass of champagne off a server's tray, draining its contents in one gulp.

Stay calm, Roxanne, it's just a party.

Andries gives me a quick kiss on the cheek, and I force a smile on my face even when he leaves my side to mingle with some of his guests. I sigh and move to the other side, far from the giggling girls and horny boys. I find a discreet spot, and lean against the wall, observing the crowd, a fresh glass of champagne in my hand.

My gaze shifts to the other guests and a curse escapes my lips when I notice Tatiana standing with Andries, her arms brushing against his, even as he tries to move away from her.

She's been crushing on Andries for forever, but my heart is not thundering because of that—it's rather because of the taunting fact that they fit so perfectly together. She's the same age as him, same background, and she comes from a family that has known his for years.

My iPhone vibrates and rings in my clutch, and a gut feeling tells me exactly who the caller is before even pulling the phone out. Jeez! I knew it! For an instant, I hesitate whether or not I should answer the call, but decide to do so anyway. "Hello?"

"It's so loud in there. Can you go outside?" Lili asks from the other side of the line.

I glance at the entrance door—it's a bit crowded and the side entrance too.

"Is it urgent? I'm really busy right now," I yell back, so she can hear me over the loud music.

"I'm just wondering if you've told him yet."

Shit!

"No, not yet," I answer. "I'll do it tonight. After the party."

"Alright, good luck, then. We'll talk tomorrow when you get back to Amsterdam. Happy birthday to him!" And she just hangs up. I put the phone back in my clutch and move away from the wall. Careful to stay under the shadows.

Elise's friends are around somewhere, and the need to stay under the radar heightens as I'm afraid that maybe one of them would be from my agency. I don't want anyone beating me to my dirty announcement tonight. I want Andries to hear it from me first.

* * *

House music is now echoing throughout the room and the crowd is euphoric. Guests are laughing excitedly and a few are at the buffet table, dishing food into their plates. The fountain I saw earlier isn't water, but cocktails and a small crowd gathers around it as they all scurry for the drink.

"Look who we have here!" Dan exclaims, hugging me tightly. "You look smashing, Roxanne."

"Thank you, Dan. How are you?"

"I'm fine." He turns to the two guys beside him. "Meet Justin and Felix. Roxanne."

I stretch out my hand for a handshake. "Nice to meet you."

"Japanese? Korean?" Justin asks like he's playing a game to figure out my nationality.

"No, half-Chinese, half-Dutch." I cringe internally at his assumptions.

His mouth forms an O. "Wow. That's awesome."

Two ladies walk up to us and pull Felix and Dan away. Dan mouths a sorry, before they follow the ladies away.

"So," Justin proceeds. "Why are you here alone, it's a party and you should be mingling," he says, moving to stand beside me. We are on the other side, close to the food table and the side entrance. Andries is moving around the guests, playing host and smiling brightly. It's his party after all.

"I'm just observing first."

He gives me a disbelieving stare. "You've been alone since you came in an hour ago."

I shoot him a quizzical look. "You've been looking at me for the past hour?"

He shrugs; the movement causes me to notice just how broad his shoulders are. "I had to; I couldn't stop." He gives a humorless chuckle. "And everyone has been whispering about you."

Fuck!

My heartbeat accelerates and my nails bit into my palm. *What are they saying about me?*

My face flushes in panic as I look around the room, searching for a familiar face.

"They're curious too, about the lady in a black dress with a slit so long it leaves the men wondering if you have underwear on?"

The last part sounds like a question, but I ignore it. I'd have smacked his face if it wasn't my boyfriend's party.

"I need a drink," I say, giving him a rueful smile. "Thanks and maybe you should go back to being curious. That would surely save you from getting your lips busted tonight." With that said, I stalk away and into the crowd.

I accept a glass from the server and take a long sip of the champagne. It's chill, just like the temperature outside the room.

"Heyyy, Roxie," Elise shouts, coming over to me. "Are you having fun?" She sounds a bit tipsy.

"Of course, and you?" I drain the glass and drop it on the tray as a server walks by.

"Where's Andries?" she asks excitedly, looking around the room.

"Hmm…" I glance around, trying to help her out. "He's over there on the… makeshift stage?"

What is he doing there?

"Holy shit!" Elise snaps, giggling. "Is he really gonna make a speech and tell everyone you are his girlfriend?" She snorts loud enough to make me wonder how many drinks she already got.

"Are you drunk, Elise?" I put my hand on her shoulder. "You should take it easy."

She keeps giggling, paying no mind to my advice. "They're gonna play the waltz soon, and I need to find a partner!" she screeches, then treads toward the fountain and accepts a glass from a boy. I follow her over and snatch the glass from her hand, giving it back to the guy, before I grab her arm and drag her away. All of a sudden, though, Andries' words echo through the room, stopping me in my tracks.

"Good evening, everyone," he says in the microphone he's holding in one hand, while holding a glass of champagne with the other. "I hope you're all enjoying the party."

The crowd cheers in response. Jeez! I had forgotten about his speech. For a moment, I wish he could forget to talk about me. All eyes are going to be on me and to be honest, I'm not even supposed to be here among this group.

"Tonight isn't just about me celebrating my birthday, it's about reconnecting with friends, old and new. And most importantly, it's about Roxanne Feng, the woman that has proven over and again that life is more beautiful and meaningful when you have someone to share the good and bad moments with. She has been a star, guiding me in my darkest moments and my biggest inspiration. Here's to Roxie, my beautiful girlfriend. Here's to a love that will see the end of time and beyond. Here's to us!"

"Cheers!" Elise squeals.

Everyone raises their glasses and echo "cheers," and the moment they drop their hands, the tears spill. The limelight comes on, and I'm both in bright light and a loud cheering sound from the guests erupt through the room. They're genuinely excited for me. For us.

"A love that will see the end of time."

Andries walks toward me and wraps his muscular arms around me.

"Dance with me?" he asks as a new song comes on.

My eyes mist over, and I smile, trying to stave up tears. His lips twist in amusement as he tilts his head to take in my upper body, then drags his eyes down to the slit.

It's going to be so hard telling him the truth. My heart breaks into a million pieces as he kisses the exposed skin on my chest.

"You're tense. Everything alright?" he asks.

I close my eyes and inhale a deep breath, willing my heart to calm down. Not here, with these people around.

"Talk to me, babe," he says, sounding overly worried.

I reopen my eyes, and smile as I meet his blue eyes on. "Let's just dance."

Just one last moment. Just this last one.

CHAPTER 40

Morning sunlight is piercing through the curtains, chasing the darkness out of my bedroom. My eyes are still heavy from last night, but I feel awake enough to stretch an arm slightly to the other side of the bed until it reaches something. Opening my eyes wide, they lay on Roxanne who seems to be still peacefully asleep. This simple moment right here feels just surreal. I'd have never imagined my parents would be chill enough to let my girlfriend sleep in my room. Jeez, seeing her here in my bedroom feels so great and maybe a bit awkward at the same time. It's like a piece of my private life that I brought from Amsterdam for my entire family to see. Not that I mind, but it feels a bit awkward, nevertheless. Everything about these two days has been perfect, and I couldn't be prouder of her to have fitted in so easily. From the moment she stepped inside the estate, I knew everything would go well. I mean, I hoped so, but she already knew my dad and sister, and she'd already been here before, so it's not like she was a total stranger either.

After checking the clock on the nightstand, I bring myself closer to her and start spooning her, then I lean in just enough to kiss her neck. "Good morning…"

She starts grinding her ass against me in response, making me laugh. "Good morning," she mumbles feebly.

"Did you sleep well?"

"Mmm," she answers, before she takes my arms in hers. "What time is it?"

"Eh, well, it's twenty past ten."

"Oh jeez!" In a brisk move, she releases me and leaps out of bed. "I have to go back to Amsterdam this morning. I promised my sister I'd help her out at the bookshop."

"There's no way I can persuade you to stay, huh?"

"I need to train her." I follow her with my gaze as she opens her suitcase wide and hurries herself to pick her clothes and shoes that are lying on the floor, putting them back inside the luggage. "Once she gets into a routine, it'll be fine."

I sit on my bed, observing her with mild amusement as she wanders naked around the bedroom. "Hey, relax, one of the drivers will take you home after breakfast," I say seeing how stressed she is.

Despite the messy hair and some trace of makeup left under her eyes, she's still the cutest thing I've ever seen.

I leave the warmth of my bed to go meet her, and taking her hand in mine, I lead her to the bathroom. "Let's shower, then I'll help you with the luggage."

* * *

After we are showered, dressed and luggage ready, we go down the stairs and head to the kitchen where Elise is on her own finishing breakfast.

"Hey, where's everyone else?" I ask her.

She just shrugs in return. "Everyone else had breakfast earlier."

Before we can even sit at the table, Claudia walks in, her positive energy filling the air that surrounds us. "Good morning, Mr. Andries and Ms. Feng," she greets, her melodic tone always so inspiring. "What would you like to have for breakfast?"

I notice Roxanne glances at the table, checking what Elise is eating, before saying, "I can have the spinach omelet Elise is having, and, um, what is she drinking?"

"It's a green juice," Elise replies on Claudia's behalf.

"Okay, that's fine too, and a cup of tea, please."

Claudia gives a sharp nod of the head, before her attention switches to me. "Same as usual for you?"

"Same as usual," I reply before we finally take a seat.

Elise is eating with droopy eyes and I can't help but wonder how many hours of sleep she got. "Are you okay?" I ask her, mildly amused.

"Yeah, I stayed up until late," she answers vaguely.

"Really?" My lips twist into a smirk. "Doing what?"

She shoots me a glare in annoyance. "None of your damn business," she chips.

"Oh, c'mon!"

ROXANNE.

"Nope," she snaps while she forks one more bite of her omelet into her mouth.

Feeling humored at her annoyance, I continue teasing. "Wait—did you stay up late with someone in particular?"

"Ha-ha," Elise replies with sarcasm, definitely not as amused as I am. "You're funny, aren't you?"

"Well, then why are you acting so secretive?"

She heaves a long sigh in frustration. "You're so fucking annoying sometimes." And my smile keeps growing. "I just stayed up late chatting with friends, that's it."

"Yeah, right," I mutter, not convinced by her bullshit excuse. "If you have a boyfriend or something, you can tell me, you know."

She rolls her eyes, huffing at me. Then she leaps off her chair, her meal not even finished.

"I'm gonna go," she announces, before wiping her mouth and putting the napkin back on the table. Then looking at Roxanne, she says, "Enjoy your breakfast and, um, have a safe trip back home."

Roxanne nods in response, a beautiful smile gracing her lips. "Thank you," she replies, her tone way more polite than my sister's. When Elise is annoyed she can't fake it and it's just too funny to watch.

Once she walks out of the kitchen, I feel like Roxanne is about to unleash some sort of comment, so I lean forward and lowering my voice, I talk first. "Sorry, I just wanted her to leave so we could have breakfast only the two of us."

"Did you need to be so intrusive and rude?" she rebukes.

"Oh, that's fine, she doesn't mind." And seeing how Roxanne is still staring at me with judgement in her eyes, I add, "She's done way worse, believe me."

"Like what?"

I notice Claudia coming over with a big tray carrying the juices, tea and coffee, and omelets, so I decide to remain vague without telling her any story in particular.

"So many pranks, especially in high school. I swear, she really loved to make fun of me."

"Fair enough," she says, reclining slightly back when Claudia places her omelet in front of her.

Claudia then puts the rest of the breakfast on the table, and I'm already salivating at how delicious everything looks.

I start cutting a bite of my omelet, while Roxanne takes a sip of her juice. The corner of my lips curve up as I observe her. She's sporting a black turtle neck, which perfectly contrasts with the paleness of her skin, the blonde of her hair and her red lips. When she catches me staring, I avert my gaze and focus on my plate.

"And you and your sister?" I decide to ask as we start eating our food. "Did your relationship improve after you bought the bookshop?"

She remains quiet for a moment, focused on her omelet. "More or less," she finally blurts out. "We try to get along."

I want to ask more questions about her family, but I know this subject can weird her out, so instead I focus on something lighter and we simply speak about yesterday's party. The conversation is cheerful and flows effortlessly and about fifteen minutes later, Claudia is back to take our empty plates.

"Oh, by the way, the driver has arrived," she announces.

The driver's already here? I glance at my watch, and, wow! I'm surprised that it's actually time for her to go.

"Do you need help with the luggage?" Claudia asks.

"Just to take it down and put it into the truck, apart from that, all is done," I reply as we leave the table.

Then I take her hand in mine, and in silence, we walk out of the kitchen, cross the hallway, and head to the entrance. My heart's already tightening at the idea I'm going to sleep alone for the next few days. I'm so used to having her around that it feels like a part of me is leaving. Once she retrieves her coat and purse, we stand by the front porch, while the driver is finishing loading the truck.

"Thank you for the wonderful hospitality," she says, plunging me into a hug. I kiss the top of her head, inhaling the rose-scented smell of her hair, my arms wrapped around her. "It was lovely."

We remain in each other's embrace for a moment, and despite knowing she's got to go, releasing her feels harder than I thought. Then I look down and bend just enough to reach her lips for a lingering kiss.

"Call me when you get home, okay?" I ask, my tone barely audible.

"I promise," she whispers. "See you for New Year's Eve."

The driver opens her the rear door and it is with a heavy heart that I watch her getting inside the car.

Despite the freezing weather, I remain standing on the porch as I wave goodbye. She waves back at me from the car window, a big smile on her lips, and even when the car disappears on the horizon, I can't bring myself to move.

The porch now is quiet. Roxanne is gone, and all is left is the memory of her lips on mine and the traces of her perfume on my shirt.

"Mr. Andries?" Jeez! Claudia nearly startles me as she emerges from the front door. "Your mom would like to talk to you. May I escort you to her office?"

"Oh, she's here?" I ask, quite surprised.

As I walk back inside and follow Claudia, I'm actually wondering why Mom didn't bid farewell to my girlfriend. She's usually so polite and well-mannered. That doesn't seem like her.

Claudia opens the door for me, and I step inside, ready to confront her about her behavior.

"Good morning," Mom greets me, as she stands right beside my dad in front of the desk.

Okay, both were here and didn't even bother to say goodbye to my girlfriend? What the heck?

"Ah, Andries, how are you?" Dad says right after.

"Hi Mom, Dad." I glance quickly on my right side and find Elise also here but sitting on an armchair beside the couch. "And… sis."

Now my curiosity is perked. "Claudia said you wanted to talk to me?"

"Yes, please." Mom takes a few steps in my direction, giving me a quick peck on the cheek, and then invites me to take a seat on the couch.

The last time she did this, it was to announce the death of my dog Jojo and I was twelve.

"Is everything alright?" I ask as I sit, a few scenarios already running down my mind. And looking at Elise who's also present, I think I know exactly what this is all about! She most likely told our parents I've switched programs and I'm not doing business school. Yep, that's it! Elise just fussed it out to them. It's obvious.

"Did she leave already?" Elise asks.

"Yeah, she's on her way home." Looking at her and then at my parents, I ask, "Why did nobody go outside to tell her goodbye? I didn't know you were all so rude."

"Darling," Mom begins, taking a seat beside me on the couch and basically ignoring my question. I can't help but find this whole meeting very suspicious, and I even frown as I see Mom struggling to find the best words to begin with. Her silence is weirding me out, but she finally heaves a long sigh, looks me in the eye, and says, "Are you sure this woman is who she pretends to be?"

My jaw nearly drops at her question, and I blink twice, her words replaying in my head. "What do you mean?" My stomach immediately knots.

"Are you sure she works at a bookstore?" Dad interposes, his tone more serious than usual.

"Yeah, I'm sure, she took me there a few times," I reply immediately. "Why are you guys asking?"

No one seems to want to answer me as they all glance at each other.

"Elise?" Dad says to my sister.

"Alright," she utters, blowing out a breath, her expression thoughtful as if she's mentally getting herself ready to share something difficult. She switches in her seat, moving forward, her arms resting on her knees. "Do you remember Patricia and Cassey? The girls I invited from college?"

"Um, barely," I answer.

"Patricia sent me a voice message this morning," she informs, her iPhone already in her hands. "I think you should listen to this." She types something in it and then presses play and the voice message from Patricia begins, *"Hey, girl! Thank you so much for yesterday evening. Cassey and I had such a great time."* I roll my eyes at her overly sweet and bubbly tone. Jeez, so damn fake. *"Look, um, we didn't know if we should share this with you or not, but Cassey has been working as an... well...an escort from time to time. Nothing too crazy, just a side hustle that she does over the weekend, you know. And, um, I'm not sure if your brother knows that or not, but his girlfriend is the owner and manager of the agency she works at. And as far as we know, she used to be an escort herself. Like no shaming here, she's amazing and super professional. We just thought you should know about it. Anyway, thanks again for the party. We had a lot of fun! Talk soon, bye, bye."*

"What?" I scoff, head shaking at the absurdity of the whole thing. "This is a prank, right?"

Elise however doesn't even smile, laugh, or chuckle and remains disturbingly serious—just like my dad and mom.

"I'm so sorry," she says, her tone laced with sadness and even disappointment. "I didn't know what to do when she sent me this voice message so I thought talking to Pops and Mom would—"

"You did well, dear Elise," Dad interposes immediately, his voice reassuring. "You did very well."

"Wait," I say as reality hits me hard in the face. "This isn't a joke you and your friends made up?"

She presses her lips tight, looking at me with eyes filled with something I had never seen before: pity.

"Honey, we are here to help you out, alright?" Mom wraps an arm around me, squeezing me against her in a side hug. "These things can happen to anyone."

Holy shit! Is this for real? I shut my eyes and bury my face between the palms of my hands for a moment as I try to process her betrayal. And yet, as much as try, I can't believe any of it. It can't be true. Roxanne, *my* Roxanne, an escort? The simple thought of it hurts more than words could ever describe. Patricia just admitted it, though. Unless she's trying to sabotage my relationship for some unknown reason, I don't see why she'd be lying. The shock of the news hits me like a hammer, and my heart aches, like it has been snatched out of my chest.

No, something is off. I'm sure something is off. Fuck! It can't be possible! But the more I think about it... Jeez! So does that mean that Karl and Charlie were her clients? And that's why she came with him to my house in the first place? Not as a friend, but as an escort? Fuck! Flashbacks of her with those dudes fill my mind and I just want to punch walls and scream. But everyone's here, watching my every move and reaction, so I have to do my best to keep it together.

"Are you okay, son?" Dad asks, worry dripping in his tone.

One thing is sure, I need to get to the bottom of it and find out if it's true or not. So looking back at Elise, I say, "Can you do me a favor?"

Her brows rise at my question. "Sure."

"Can you get me the name and phone number of the agency?"

"Okay, um, I'll text Patricia and ask her, she should have it." I thought this would be enough to make her stand up and leave the office, but she isn't budging.

Mom, understanding the situation, turns to my sister and makes a more direct request. "Elise, darling, can you give us a moment with your brother, please?"

"Of course." She finally stands up and, to my surprise, stops in front of me and puts a hand on my shoulder to give me some comfort. "I'm with you, okay?"

Despite her question, I've never felt so lost, enraged, and broken inside. Thick tears brim my eyes, but I push them back, and focus on my breathing. But it's fucked up! So damn fucked up that she'd lie to me like that for months! And is she still seeing her clients behind my back even though we are together? Fuck! A gush of air rolls off my mouth, unable to focus on anything but her lies. Well, one thing is sure: she lied like she was used to it, like it was natural to her. Everything she told me felt genuine and real.

Once Elise exits the office, I can't hold it in any longer and despite my parents still being here, I again bury my face between my hands and try to be as silent as possible as I let those tenacious tears fall.

Mom starts rubbing my back in circles in a failed attempt to soothe me. "Hey," she says in a whisper. "It's gonna be okay." Her voice is low and smooth, reminding me of how happy I was just a few hours ago in my bedroom sleeping next to my girlfriend. The same one who I thought loved me and was a librarian who had just bought the bookshop where she'd worked at for years. Memories of my birthday and the toast I did yesterday in her honor starts flashing through me, and I feel like a fucking idiot to have told everyone how proud I was of being her boyfriend and how much I loved her. Fuck! Patricia and Cassey must have had the laugh of their lives when they figured out that this dumbass is dating a hooker.

"I'm sorry," I say as I sniffle the tears back. Then I wipe my wet face with my hand, feeling utterly embarrassed that my parents had to witness this shit show. "I just don't understand," I proceed, letting my heart vent out. "I've been at the bookshop three times, and she knows a lot about literature and—"

"Maybe it's just a set up," Mom interposes, most likely desperate to cheer me up.

"Julia, seriously?" Dad chips as he leaves the desk where he was leaning on and takes a few steps in our direction. "Why would this Patricia lie?" He then sits beside me on the couch and now I find myself squeezed between my mom and dad while I'm completely broken inside. "It's clear she thought about it twice before telling Elise. It's true. It's obvious." His words cut me like a knife, and the fact he's saying those things out loud, make the situation all too real. "Maybe Karl was one of her clients."

"Sebastian," Mom chastises.

"What? I'm just stating the truth."

"Look, those things happen," Mom repeats like a broken record. She wipes a tear from my face, before pressing her lips on my head. "If you need our help to confront her—"

"I can handle this," I reply, a smile of appreciation curving the corners of my lips. "Thanks." And I also give her a kiss in return, but on her cheek. "I should've figured this out myself, though. She went to a cabaret with Karl and then to the opera with another guy a few months ago." I swallow the lump in my throat, the thought of any of those guys fucking her being so disgusting that I can't even breathe. "But I thought they were just friends like she said. I trusted her."

"It's hard to detect those things," Dad answers and I must say, I'm positively surprised he's just as concerned about me as Mom is. "Don't blame yourself." He puts a hand on my shoulder and then gives me a side hug. What is he doing? Is he trying to get the years we were off back? How come he's being so affectionate with me all of a sudden? The gesture is unexpected, odd, but, truthfully, also much appreciated. At least, they aren't judging me, and their support is quite helpful to digest the news.

"Can I ask you a very personal question?" Mom takes over.

"Yeah, sure."

"Did you…" She lets her words trail off, considering me for an instant. "…have unprotected sex with her?"

My eyes widen in surprise as I process what she just said. "Seriously?"

"What? If she had sex with strangers, then it's worth checking for STDs, don't you think?"

"Mom, she's clean, okay?"

"How do you know that?" she presses on.

"Sex workers get tested frequently, don't they?" I reply back. Fuck! A call girl servicing men is the last thing I thought my girlfriend would be.

"Maybe it's worth checking?" Dad steps in, his tone matching Mom's. "Better to be on the safe side with those things."

"Fine, I'll take a test," I say, standing up. "I'm gonna go, um, I need some time alone."

"Are you sure you're gonna be okay?" Mom's face and tone are laced with concern and she leaves the couch at the same time as Dad, walking toward me.

"Yeah, I just need some fresh air." She stands in front of me, and gives me another hug but this time a tight one. I wrap my arms around her as a dozen different emotions flood through me at once. I wish I could take something that would end the pain once and for all, but alas, there isn't yet any remedy for broken hearts. "Thanks for telling me about her and for being so supportive."

"Oh, honey, that's what parents are for," she says, her hand stroking my cheek.

Thinking about Roxanne's dad who abandoned her and her mom who doesn't speak to her, I can't help but say, "Well, I guess not everyone is as lucky."

And without further ado, I walk out of the office.

* * *

Outside, the air is freezing and the sky is of a bright gray, nearly blending with the white of the snow that covers the lawn. Walking through the gardens, I find our snowman still standing there, and simply looking at it is enough to remind me of her. I go and remove the snow on the swing chair before sitting on it. There, I start bouncing myself slowly back and forth, my mind far away as I try to process everything that just happened.

"Hey," I hear Elise saying as she walks toward me. "Mom told me I'd find you here."

"Hey," I mutter, unable to give her the time of day.

Elise sits beside me on the wooden swing chair, and without saying anything further, we just stay there, reveling in the silence that fills the space between us.

She then looks at me, and decides to break our quiet moment. "I'm so sorry to have involved Mom and Pops, but I know this isn't something to take lightly."

Her words are calm and soft—so different from the usual Elise. Looking at her, I can see the worry in her eyes, and I find myself smiling at her. "They want me to get tested for STDs," I confess. "This is insane...."

"They are just worried."

As I keep observing the blanket of snow surrounding us, I can't help thinking about yesterday morning when I was sitting on the ground with my girlfriend, still totally unaware of what was yet to come. "You know," I begin, turning my attention to her. "I should've seen this coming—I saw her several times out with men much older than me," I admit. "I always thought they were friends or clients from the bookshop." I scoff at my own naïveté. "I'm so fucking dumb."

"You aren't dumb," Elise protests in return, draping an arm around me for a quick squeeze. "You are just..." She pauses, searching for the best word to describe me. "You are just in love."

"Yeah, well, that was still a stupid move." I take a deep breath, let it go, and watch big, foggy billows come out of my mouth and float away. "Lesson learned." Looking at my sister, I notice she's still staring at me, a frown on her face. "You were right, I should have dated a girl like Tatiana. At least I know she isn't into selling her body for a few bucks."

"I always told you; you should be with someone from our inner-circle. Someone from a good family that we know well." I can't help but roll my eyes at her words. For some reason, I've got the feeling this is what Mom and Pops have always thought of my relationship with Roxanne. They just didn't feel comfortable enough to tell it to me. "There's a reason why I always thought Tatiana was the right woman for you."

"This is something Dad would say," I point out.

"He's right, though." Oh, here we go again. I knew Elise would say it out loud. "She'd have been a great girlfriend."

"Who else knows about this?" I ask, forcing her to change the subject of the conversation.

"Well, let's be honest, when we go back to campus in January, *everyone* will know by then."

"Shit," I utter under my breath, already dreading the idea of being the center of attention. Images of my peers passing by me and snickering in my face are haunting me down. "I hope it'll be all forgotten within the week," I find myself saying.

Elise doesn't comment anything further about it, she just keeps quiet, her eyes a mix of sadness and pity for what I'm going through.

"Well, I'm gonna go back inside, it's just too cold for me out here," she announces, standing up, her hands plunged inside her coat pocket. "By the way, I sent you the contact details for the agency."

"Oh, thanks."

"What do you intend to do?" she asks.

I remain quiet for a moment as I ponder her question. Then looking her in the eye, I say, "Meet my girlfriend in her natural habitat."

CHAPTER 41

V.D.B. estate, December 29, 2021
Roxanne

Andries has barely spoken to me since I left his family estate. His answers have been cold and short, and I can't help but wonder what the heck is going on with him. Despite his insistence that he's just busy or tired, something feels really off. We're supposed to meet in two days though, so I hope we'll be able to clear everything up by then. With New Year's Eve approaching, the work at the agency has been non-stop. Meetings, negotiations, and more meetings... The ringtone of my iPhone nearly startles me as I return to my office after lunch with a prospective client for the agency. Looking at the screen, I can't help but roll my eyes seeing my sister calling me again. I know exactly what she wants to hear from me and I'm pretty sure she's not going to like the answer. *"Either you tell him or I'll do it myself."* Her words replay in my head and, for a split second, I wonder if she went ahead and talked to Andries behind my back. Curious if she has done some serious damage, I pick the call to speak to her briefly.

"Hey, sis," I greet, settling on my desk chair. "How have you been?"

"Don't play with me," she retorts back, already annoyed.

"Uh-oh," I utter, unable to comply with her request. "Did someone bite you or what?"

"Have you spoken to him yet?"

I heave a long sigh, tired of her constant pressure of how to handle my life and relationship. "No," I say, and, for some reason, a pang of shame squeezes my heart. "And you?"

"I haven't, but you have until the end of the year to do that."

"What!" I snap in shock at her demand. "Stay out of my relationship!"

"You told me you'd be honest with him," she continues. "I thought you'd quit being a liar."

"But why do you even care about it?" I press on. "It's my relationship, not yours."

"Because this is betrayal!"

I hear a few knocks on my office door, and before I can even instruct to come in, the door cracks open and Poppy sneaks in, standing by the doorway. "Roxie?"

I put my phone down, my attention focused on my assistant.

"Your two o'clock is here," she informs me.

"Ah, yes, please let him in." Another prospective client to meet with. Seems like everyone needs a last minute plus one for New Year's Eve.

I stand up, ready to end this call and start my meeting. "Lili, I'm gonna have to go, I—" My heart is in my throat and everything fades away when I see a familiar young man walking into my office. "Andries?" I hang up immediately, my mind blank, and my blood freezes at the sight of him.

Poppy has already shut the door behind him, and I can't for the life of me believe this is real, and yet, there's a pair of blue eyes standing on the other side of my office watching me.

"Roxanne." His voice echoes across the four walls of the room as he paces slowly in my direction, taking in his surroundings. "Nice office."

I'm so stunned that I can barely find the words to speak. "How…" It's all my fault and no matter who told him, I know I deserve whatever the outcome of this encounter, but I need to know one thing. "How did you find out?"

"A girl on campus that went to the party said to my sister she works for you," he discloses, his tone even, and he stops right across my desk. "I just wanted to make sure it was true."

I need to find a way to explain myself, so without further ado, I say, "Look, whatever you think about—"

"Are you also an escort?" He forces the words out, and I can tell by his face how much he's hurt. "Answer me," he demands, the pain palpable. "Are you one of them?" Despite him repeating the question, I feel so ashamed of what I have done than I'm totally paralyzed, unable to speak. "Karl and Charlie were your clients, right?"

I avert my gaze, looking absently downward, and nod. "I stopped seeing them once we got together," I manage to say.

He scoffs, head shaking, and runs a hand on his hair, visibly disturbed at my words. "And yet, you couldn't bother telling me the truth, huh?"

"I'm sorry, I didn't know what to do, I knew you wouldn't approve of it," I blurt out in defense, then I walk around my desk to go and meet him. "It belongs to the past now."

I try to touch his arm, but Andries pushes my hand away, looking at me totally appalled. "So you kept lying like it was the right thing to do?"

"I'm no longer doing it," I repeat since it seems like he doesn't understand. "I stopped."

"You stopped?" he repeats in outrage, scoffing at my answer, before glancing at my office. "For fuck's sake, you're still selling pussy to men! You just stopped selling yours!" The prejudice in him shocks me to the core.

"No one is forcing those girls to do it!" My voice breaks through the room and I realize in that instant how loud I am. "They are well-paid and protected."

Andries averts his gaze, as if too creeped out by my reaction to keep looking me in the eye. We keep quiet for a moment, a frigid silence settling between us as we digest everything we said to each other.

"How come an educated woman with an English degree like yourself ended up in such an industry?"

"You know why," I find myself answering, growing tired of explaining myself to a rich brat who has no idea what poverty is.

"No, I don't."

"Because the money is better than any job I could land with my fucking degree," I tell him, feeling more and more drained of this fight at every passing second. "That's why! I work less and make more. It's not rocket science."

"So you have no intention of stopping this?" he asks, pointing a finger around my office.

I press two fingers between the bridge of my nose, trying to calm myself down as I ponder his question. "If by 'stopping' you mean closing shop, then no, I don't."

He considers me, then his gaze travels down for a moment. "Very well." All of a sudden, though, he takes something from his coat's inner-pocket and asks, "How much do you charge?" His tone is serious and devoid of any emotion. When I realize it's a checkbook he's holding, I frown immediately. "Is it by hour or by service?"

"Andries…."

"Tell me! I wanna pay you for the time we spent together. Really, I insist." He picks a pen from my desk, opens his checkbook, and starts filling in the details. "How much do you charge?"

"Andries, stop!"

I try to reach him, but he puts an arm in front of him, barring the way.

"There's no reason for me to get a free pass on this."

"You're crossing the line here," I warn him, but he pays no mind and continues writing the rest down.

"Three-hundred-thousand euros for the time we spent together and fucked. Good enough?"

My mouth drops open and tears form in the back of my eyes. His attitude is way more off than I thought it would be. "You're an asshole," I say as he tries to hand me the check.

"Take the fucking money."

"I won't!" I say, thick tears brimming in my eyes, but I push them back and cross my arms over my chest to make my point.

"Why not? That's what this is all about for you, isn't it?"

I remain standing there, looking away, without saying anything further. There's no point in throwing more gas into the fire.

Since I'm not taking his check, he leaves it on the desk, and puts his checkbook back inside his coat's inner-pocket.

"Now we are all settled," he announces, his voice grave. And I've got the feeling this also means our relationship is over. Even if he doesn't say it directly. "If you think it's not enough, feel free to send me an invoice, you know my address." My heart aches as I witness our relationship falling totally apart. I tried to get myself mentally ready for this. I knew it'd come, but no matter how much pep talk, we are never ready for a separation we don't want. "I wish you all the best with your brothel. Looks like you're doing just fine for yourself."

"So it's over, huh?" Tears slide over my flushed cheeks, but I can't help it. I'm a fool for behaving this way in my office. My heart is taking a reel and I feel powerless in front of this deadlock. "All those declarations of love and now you're out?"

"I didn't know I was in love with a manipulative liar," he retorts, his features deepening. "And I don't want to have anything to do with this industry, *nothing*."

"It's just a fucking business," I protest, shocked how he can be so blind and obtuse. "What's your problem?"

"I think we have irreconcilable differences when it comes to your 'business.'"

He's about to pass by me, heading outside, when I grab his arm, forcing him to stop.

"Are you seriously breaking up with me?" I ask as I try to find the answer in his gaze.

"You'll be fine," he says, releasing himself from my grasp, his tone emotionless, despite seeing the pain he's fighting so hard on his face. "You're in control of your life and feelings, remember?"

My head tilts down and my eyes are on the floor as I recall this comment of mine. And yet, despite what I told him at the bookshop, I refuse to watch my boyfriend leave this office with the intent to end our relationship. I refuse to believe this is how our story ends. When I hear the door click open, tears burst out of me, and I can't help but cry at the sound of his last two words before he shuts the door behind him. "Goodbye, Roxanne."

THEIR STORY CONTINUES

IN *ANDRIES.*

Don't have the sequel yet?

Enjoy 10% off on your next purchase using the code FLYER10 at melaniemartins.com (code has to be manually entered at checkout).